DEATHLESS

The Vein Chronicles
Book Two

ANNE MALCOM

Deathless
The Vein Chronicles #2
Anne Malcom
Copyright 2017

ISBN-13: 978-1545489178
ISBN-10: 1545489173

Cover Design: Simply Defined Art
Edited by: Hot Tree Editing
Cover image Copyright 2017
Interior design and formatting: Champagne Formats

DEDICATION

To all the vampires out there in the 'real' world, whose blood of choice is black in color and caffeinated in nature.
To the insomniacs who both suffer and thrive on the monsters that come in the dark.
Sometimes words need darkness to be born.
Sometimes minds need darkness to survive.

GLOSSARY

Awakening: In the first two hundred and fifty, then five hundred years of undeath, a female vampire's heart begins to beat once more, for one year. In which time the body is more vulnerable to attack and the unyielding and cold body becomes accommodating to life. Accommodating enough to conceive and carry a child to term.

Apollo: Olympian deity, recognized to be the god of sun and light, among author things. Also responsible for the curse of the vampire. Immortal.

Ambrogio: The first vampire. A human man turned immortal by the wrath and the gifts of the gods themselves. Mortal. And then immortal.

Artemis: Apollo's twin sister, goddess of the hunt. Immortal.

Extermuis: Supernatural bar which caters to the most depraved of immortals and invites all sadistic pleasures.

Eleos: One of the lesser known and lesser seen of the gods. Often seen wandering the woods in human form. Goddess of mercy and compassion with the ability to see the future of mortals and god alike.

Hybrids: A weapon created by dark magic. Humans turned into animalistic form of vampire, with all the strength of a traditional vampire but little to no mental capacity, expect loyalty to their 'parent' vampire.

Hades: God of the Underworld, where every dead soul is banished to upon leaving the earth. Owner of every dead, and undead soul. Immortal.

Ichor: The blood of the gods which was bestowed, or cursed, upon the first vampire to enable immortality.

Mortimeus: Vampire version of school, whereupon vampires learn the history of their race and are schooled in murder, torture and sadism. Only vampires of the highest Vein Lines are able to attend.

Praestes: Literal Latin translation of 'protector'. A generation of humans designed to fight vampires and supernatural creatures. Their blood one of the only things fatal to vampires. Mortal.

Selene: Human destined to be sacrificed to Apollo and instead falls in love with a human man. The love is the death of her and the birth of all vampires on this earth. Mortal.

"The curse. The deathless night. The blood will run.
From the Ichor of the gods to the veins of a mortal.
The blood will run.
In the moon the sunshine will die, yet in the sunshine the moon
shall endure, watching over the light with a shadow that is not
menacing nor comforting,
merely the deathless night that will swallow mankind with its
wrath,
or save it with its harmony.
Fatal to the destined.
Harmony in death."

THE BEGINNING.

Stories of gods always start with humans. Because without mortals, immortals would not exist. Gods would not be great, for they would have no lesser beings to lord their powers over.

For supernatural creatures to exist, their natural, weaker counterparts must endure, for without them the world would perish.

It is on the bones of the weak that the flesh of the strong is created.

But then even the powers of the gods sometimes couldn't rival those of humans. Because it is in weakness where the strongest of things is born.

Ambrogio wasn't extraordinary. He was a traveler, a human who was more aware of his mortality than most, so he sought adventure to fill his short life.

He found it in a woman, as men often do.

She was a great beauty, though that was not the reason for the adventure to be found within her. Sometimes it was as simple as a soul recognizing itself in another.

Such a concept may be considered supernatural or fantastical in a society forward in time where simplicity of love was complicated by the wretchedness of humans. But back in the days where life was more than fleeting, and humans still believed in gods and monsters, such things were commonplace.

For monsters to exist, love like theirs had to as well. They were one in the same, after all.

Selene and Ambrogio walked together in the sunlight, basking in the rays, the gentle warmth on their skin nothing compared to the inferno flowing through their veins from their intertwined hands.

On their walk through the woods in the shadow of the temple to which the residents of Selene's town offered gods their worship—which, unbeknownst to Selene, would be her, for she was the loveliest of all, with the purest of souls—they encountered a goddess who was closer to mortal than god.

Eloes's compassion for those who were weaker in mind, body and spirit distanced her from the gods who found humans of little consequence, though it was in the sacrifice of humans that gods derived their divinity.

Destined to walk between the two worlds, she often wandered in those same woods. Upon seeing the couple, a powerful premonition swept through her, one she knew would be the beginning of something bigger than either gods or mortals could imagine.

Her ability to empathize with the humans gave way for her to see the future of those destined for both greatness and depravity in the human race.

She saw both such things in the lovers.

Light and darkness.

> "*The curse. The deathless night. The blood will run.*
> *From the Ichor of the gods to the veins of a mortal.*
> *The blood will run.*
> *In the moon the sunshine will die, yet in the sunshine the moon*
> *shall endure, watching over the light with a shadow that is not*
> *menacing nor comforting, merely the deathless night that will*
> *swallow mankind with its wrath,*
> *or save it with its harmony.*
> *Fatal to two.*
> *Harmony in death.*"

Her musical words filtered through the twilight of the woods and into the ears of the young lovers, too blind to see the god but not too deaf to hear the words of their future.

Of their demise.

The words shivered them, despite their inferno, but didn't scare them, for if there ever were mortals so fearless it was those under the enchantment of love.

A love so strong and powerful the gods themselves, for all their powers, could not reproduce it.

Apollo, the god of sunlight, watched with a much simpler and more poisonous emotion. Jealousy coursed through the veins of the god who coveted the mortal woman with hair the color of fire and eyes carved from emeralds themselves. She was, after all, destined to be his, forever in her death. The sacrifice written in the sun that shined down upon the humans, the sacrifice they planned so that warmth would continue without the wrath from the god with whom their fickle mortality was poised.

Apollo watched his destined walk the woods with another, the prophecy not silent to his ears either.

The human man had no powers of a god, no immortality. He simply walked in the sunshine with his love and took what Apollo so craved. Walked in the light of what Apollo himself had gifted the humans.

With the power of jealousy—the closest human emotion the god possessed—and the immortal powers no human could aspire to, he cursed sunlight to reside in Selene's skin, and then made it so Ambrogio could no longer wander in daylight. Nor could he touch the skin of his lover, as the sunlight resided within her. It was Nyx, the god born of chaos with dominion over the darkness, who was too happy to help Apollo banish the mortal man to the shadows of the night.

Unwilling to banish his own love to the darkness too, Ambrogio left the town in which he found his greatest adventure, his love and his destruction.

Selene still fostered the love for a man she could not touch, or see in the sunlight. She followed his journey away from those woods, across oceans, and therefore from the temple that would bring her to Apollo.

Though Selene followed her love, the sunlight still held Ambrogio's demise and the sunlight still resided in her skin. So the lovers were sentenced to be separated, for mere mortals couldn't change the actions of gods.

Ambrogio knew this, and sought out the only god who could take him from the darkness. The god who resided in darkness. Hades took his soul so Ambrogio could be reunited with his sweetheart once more.

Hades was not a being to bestow a gift without a curse.

Ambrogio's was to feed on the blood of others to keep his heart beating, which it did only for her.

It was this deal with Hades that angered Apollo's sister, Artemis, the goddess of the hunt. Such a creature, neither human nor mortal, hunting on the flesh that was hers angered the goddess. Artemis cursed Ambrogio with immortality, for immortality was a curse when the heart of an immortal lived within a mortal human.

She snuck into the darkness where Selene slept and fed Ambrogio the Ichor of the gods, turning him from the creature of the night that fed on flesh into the deathless one. The first human to be cursed with immortality.

The first human to become a vampire.

Eleos had watched the lovers with interest after her first premonition and hated the wrath of her brothers and sisters, for it was bitterness and anger that the gods bestowed on the purest and most innocent of emotions. Though it was only from the purest and innocent of emotions that evil could be birthed.

She appeared after Artemis, giving Ambrogio the opportunity to make Selene an immortal of sorts. It was not in her power to take death away from a mortal, but she could give life in death and make Selene the goddess of the moonlight, so Ambrogio could walk with her in the darkness that would always reside in his soul.

It was only under the bequest of his love that Ambrogio agreed, with the knowledge that his soul would never meet with Selene's as it was in the possession of Hades for eternity.

So he drained the blood from his one true love, sending her to the heavens to give her somewhat of an eternal life. Not quite living, not quite dead.

Deathless.

It was through Selene's watchful but cold embrace in the moonlight that Ambrogio grew dark and twisted from the lives he took with the loneliness of a being without a heart or a soul.

And as the years passed and his mind turned sour and unrecognizable to the one who watched over his darkness, Ambrogio yearned for something darker than him. Some*one* darker than him.

For even an immoral being was created from a human. Even the twisted murderous ones needed a companion to wade through the pools of blood they created. So he craved one, one without the heart that had caused him the eternity of pain.

Hades, with a greedy heart of his own, gifted the first vampire with Lilith, so they would create more creatures whose souls would belong to the king of the underworld also.

The children of the Vein Line created from love, hate, and blood.

Ambrogio's heart stopped beating the moment his love was drained dry. The truest vampire, in its final form, was created.

The gods witnessed their creation, their vampire. Apollo, satisfied since he had won in the end. Artemis was melancholy because the goddess of the hunt now had new predators to contend with, deadlier than she intended and stronger and more heartless than once thought.

Hades was as happy as the Devil could have been, because with the soul he owned—and the ones to come—it meant he would always win.

The Devil always did, in the end.

But then it wasn't the end, was it?

Eleos had been watching the events of the years, the interference of gods in mortal matters for such things as worship, jealousy and the price of a soul. She knew the prophecy of such a love and knew that one day, the world would be at the precipice, fed with the evil lust for power. It would need something more than humanity but less than godliness.

Another mix of Selene and Ambrogio.

> *"And so it shall be that the one with hair like fire*
> *and the one with the love to frighten even a god*
> *will once more walk this earth in the sunlight.*
> *And it will be in the blood that her survival is written.*
> *That earth's survival will be written.*
> *And it is in the deathless soul of Ambrogio and Selene*
> *that the fates will be decided.*
> *The blood will run."*

ISLA

The end.

Endings always wrap up everything so neatly, don't they? All of life's and death's complications and disasters seem to rectify themselves with supernatural speed and efficiency as we hurtle past the big heroic climax to chase those two words to the end of forever.

Or at least that was how it worked in fictional narratives.

Real life, or real undeath, was a lot different.

The end came and went, endings weaving through reality without any of the theatrical finality we've come to expect. Mostly it was a sizzle. A quiet snuffing of the candle. Nothing was normally wrapped up, healed, satisfied at an ending. No, things were usually messier than they3 would ever be.

Harmony was a long way away from this ending.

Chaos, on the other hand, well it tangled up in this end like a snake around its prey.

This end, of undeath as I knew it, came first with the ecstasy of warm blood filling my mouth. Filling my black, twisted, and warped soul.

The one that had, until moments before, been dying a rather unfortunate and painful death.

It was the last image I properly saw—the vision of another soul dying inside those eyes that had become something half of me resided in. I thought that would be the last image on my mind before the Devil himself came to clutch me and drag me downstairs for an eternity of torment.

Boy, was he in for a surprise.

Not just over the fact that I'd shake shit up and show him what real torment was.

No, over the fact that his hot, clawed hands sank into me, grazed my flesh but didn't find purchase.

Because my fangs sank into something else.

Something I was so sure would be the end of me.

And maybe it still was.

But what an exquisite way to go.

Thorne lifted his lips from mine as if he could sense the cold creeping up my throat.

"I love you, Isla," he rasped, eyes wet. "I'll find you," he promised. "Wherever you are."

I blinked away the redness in my vision. "I love you," I whispered back. Then I leaned forward as he exposed his neck to me. I sank my fangs into his skin and welcomed the grave.

He had been the last anchor that kept me attached to this earth. Then there was nothing but the crimson in my mouth, in my mind, in every part of me. In that crimson, he disappeared.

And as I continued my feast, *I* disappeared too.

Maybe that was the trick the Devil pulled. The greatest. Not convincing the world he didn't exist, but convincing the souls he came for that they were safe.

So he could feast on that hope.

Stupid me for hoping, really.

Hope combined with love, after all, was fatal.

Oh, and a thousand-year-old witch's curse. Think that also factored in.

But whatever it was, the details, they didn't matter.

The crimson, the sweet nectar of life on my tongue, was the only thing that did.

And then it was the death that chased it away.

All of it.

Clear me a drawer, Lucifer. I'm moving in.

SOPHIE

D EATH WAS A PART OF LIFE.
Sophie knew that.
More than most.

Even more than the vampires who seemed to think they had monopoly over it.

Letting them think that was probably wise.

Sophie wasn't wise. Even though she was a couple of centuries old, wisdom did not come with age.

One needed only to look at a four-hundred-year-old vampire named Isla to know that.

A stab of pain twisted in her stomach, so strong, so intense she almost doubled over.

Almost.

She wouldn't look at Isla. Couldn't. Because then her

friend, the only true one she had in immortality, would present her with what she'd seen all too much of in her life.

Death.

And the final kind. Not the kind Sophie experienced in order to make sure she lived longer than her less magical human counterparts.

The kind you didn't come back from.

She could have given in to that pain, but that would've made her weak. Isla didn't approve of weak, almost as much as she didn't approve of sweater sets.

So she chose the emotion that Isla would approve of.

Rage.

Her hands sparked with blue in preparation for such an action. The power in the recesses of her body stirred, shaking at the chains she'd put there in order to hide the entirety of the magic that may just kill her.

She wasn't afraid of that power now. Or death.

She and death were old friends, after all.

"Sophie." The harsh voice gave her pause, just as she was about to unlock those chains.

She blinked away the haze that the magic had started to bring over her vision, the wooded area of Thorne's backyard coming back into view and the slayer standing in front of her in clear color.

The slayer who had no place being in front of her. No place looking at her the way he did.

"Silver, step away if you don't want to be a pile of limbs that Thorne will have to use as firewood," she instructed, her voice morphed slightly with the power she was forcing herself to swallow.

She had to.

It wasn't an empty threat. Unleashing the power from her

depths would mean casualties if anyone was standing too close. She knew that. She knew it because even the small taste was shaking her, making her feel like her skin might just split because it was too much for her body to accommodate.

You couldn't just do that, welcome immense power into the world without first learning how to control it.

Sophie knew that. But then logic had no place when death was around.

And death had been around far too much. Therefore, logic was a long-forgotten friend.

If it ever was a friend at all.

"I'm not goin' anywhere," Silver said firmly.

Her hands crackled once more, the power in her body recognizing the challenge.

It took all her willpower to not unleash it on the attractive yet obviously suicidal slayer.

He watched, rapt, as the sparks illuminated the very molecules of the air and then petered out, retreating into the cage she kept them in.

"You want to became a charred version of a slayer?" she asked, her voice husky with the exertion. It may not have been a marathon, but working with power required energy, both mental and physical. Her mental energy was waning, stricken and ruined considering she'd just watched her best friend die. "You don't, right? So get the fuck out of my way," she hissed.

He folded his arms in the gesture that these males seemed to think was a soundless form of communication of their strength and general badassery.

Little did this baby slayer know that Sophie had more strength in her little finger than he did in his entire body—literally. And she and the corpse of a vampire inside held the throne on badassery that all the slayers in their little gang couldn't even aspire to.

But one must stroke male egos; that was how she'd survived in Salem, after all. That and she spelled all the preachers to go after every single witch who pissed her off—after she bound their powers, of course.

Another story for another day when she wasn't mourning the loss of the only creature on the planet who might approve of such things as mass murdering women who slept with her boyfriend.

As she sucked in air to mutter a small spell to put Silver in his place, and make sure he stayed there so she could leave, a rush of air whipped her hair around and Scott appeared in front of her.

Blood stained his cheeks, trailing out of the one eye he had left. Vampires survived on blood, and it also leaked out of them when surviving got to be a little too much.

She reasoned that, on better days than this, the patch covering his empty socket and the scar peeking out from underneath it actually improved Scott's general look. Made him look less like a college frat boy who date-raped girls on the regular.

But now she didn't think much of it, apart from hiding the flinch at the etching of despair on his features.

Her own were carefully schooled.

Scott was young, hadn't yet learned the importance of not wearing feelings on your sleeve and how deadly such a thing could be to your life and sanity.

He'd learn or he'd die.

Sophie had done both.

But Scott's death would likely be far more final than hers.

Half vampire or not.

"It's not true," he stated, his voice somehow firm and weak at the same time. Like if he said it, it might make it so, make it reality. But also in a way that he knew reality, fate and the universe herself did not listen to the words of anyone, even immortals.

Especially immortals, because they cheated death, for a time anyway. No one was truly deathless, not even Sophie, despite the many deaths she'd experienced and lived through.

Sophie regarded him coldly. "The corpse in the room not ten feet away would beg to differ," she said, ignoring his flinch. "And not the corpse that's still walking, talking, insulting ninety-nine-point-nine percent of the population. As in *dead*. Bury, burn, bronze in the middle of Barneys kind of dead."

Scott's grief came on her in waves but she shrugged it off. She'd turned most of that off, the taste of emotions that had become stronger and more palpable since her powers had become so.

It was necessary, since even the small bite of Thorne's sorrow she'd experienced nearly brought her to her knees.

And, interestingly, Rick's.

She narrowed her eyes at the flicker of the vampire king in her peripheral, pacing at the edge of the woods.

It was his fault.

That was it. Finding someone to blame, settling the entirety of such an event on someone else's shoulders made everything clearer. Starker.

For it was the king of all vampires who had inflicted those injuries in the form of a public execution that had Isla's death on the agenda, when it was merely meant to be torture of some demons and a cocktail after.

He had brought her in front of the vampires of the court, her own family, and tried her for treason—love for a slayer was of course one of the worst crimes a vampire could commit.

It didn't matter that he hadn't intended to execute her,

merely making it seem so.

Nor did his ignorance of the spell rendering her nearly mortal serve as an excuse.

It might to a logical mind.

Without a second glance at either of the men—or one man and one vampire man-child in front of her—she rushed towards him.

Silver's emotions followed her. Which meant his body did too, as she had lost purchase on her spell while she was calling up the powers she'd bound tight.

"It's not worth it, Sophie," he growled.

She didn't slow, nor did she tamp down the sparks at her fingers.

"Revenge is *always* worth it," she hissed, her voice morphing with the power she unleashed.

The king, for once, did not take notice of his surroundings. Grief made people weak. It was the best time to strike.

Plus, he had no right to feel such an emotion. He was the entire reason she was gone, as it were.

The hot sense of satisfaction that came with hitting the vampire with the full voltage of her power momentarily chased away her own sorrow.

She welcomed it, the bloodlust she had tasted only through proximity to vampires; now that very same need coursed through her veins. That need to suck the life from the one who took someone from her.

She would become a bloodsucker, except instead of sucking the blood from Emrick, the king of all vampires, she'd use her power to drain him of everything. His immortality first.

He had slammed into a tree with the force of her power, cracking the trunk so it looked half cut by an axe that was Rick's body.

It worked well enough.

He had been caught unaware, but he was a warrior and a thousand-year-old immortal. He was immediately ready to strike back, jumping from the remains of the bark, ripping away the pieces of trunk that had impaled him.

He was quick, darting halfway over the distance that separated them in less than a second.

Sophie was quicker.

With a flick of her fingers, he was frozen in the middle of the clearing that seemed far too calm with the chaos swirling around the day.

She sensed Silver's approach. And his intention. So with another flick of her pinky finger, using it with a little grim satisfaction, she froze him in place. She didn't rightly need to use her pinky finger, or any finger at that. She wasn't Sabrina; magic didn't need hand gestures. But it was the theatrics of it all. And Isla was ever the drama queen, as well as a vengeful bitch when she wanted to be, so what better way to honor her memory than with vengeance splashed with a touch of theater.

"Sophie," Silver gritted out.

Another flip of her hand had his mouth snapping shut.

The power pulsed through her at such a rate that those spells, small as they were, didn't take an ounce of her energy as they should. No, as she focused her attention on the king of all vampires, her energy increased, as did the power she'd locked down.

Now that it was unleashed, there was no control. It was a living thing inside her. Something separate than her. Something ancient. Something terrifying. And at this moment, apt.

Because when presented with death, what else was left to fear?

What do you have left when you no longer fear death?

She stepped forward, dried leaves crunching underfoot, not noticing that the very leaves on all the living things she passed died and withered merely from her proximity.

If she had noticed, she would've been disappointed, not at the magic in her creating dead things but that it didn't work on undead things.

Yet.

But it would.

She circled him, her power morphing, changing her in such a way that she knew she approached a cliff, a precipice. In which the Sophie she was for two hundred years would die for good this time, replaced by whatever this power would birth.

Not good.

Not evil.

Just pure power.

Perhaps a god.

She only noted the approaching cliff distractedly, not worrying about the freefall and that final death.

Her eyes were on Rick's granite jaw and the way his eyes were hard with the stare of a creature that had looked death in the eye many a time. After all, he was a creature that credited its existence to Hades himself. And Hades lurked behind her eyes.

"You'll meet him properly this time, not just acknowledge him and then escape," she hissed, leaning into his face. "No, he will grasp you in his claws and drag you down to the underworld. But not before I'm done with you."

She didn't use a hand gesture that time, merely flared her eyes slightly as the Ichor of his immortality drained from him.

His body jerked despite the spell that kept it still. She imagined having the Ichor of the gods ripped from your being would be painful.

Then she remembered the pure hot agony just with the small taste of Thorne's thoughts. The half-remembered pain of her own grief that was no longer familiar to her. The cliff was nearing, after all, and as she sped towards it, the layers of her being seemed to melt off.

"I will take away your immortality," she promised, her voice thick and not really her own. Another voice, the voice of whatever it was she had unleashed, spoke at the same time as her, echoing beyond the words, so much so that the molecules of the air twisted in discomfort at the power filtering through it. "And then I will let you taste mortality. Taste it, experience the brutal claim of it."

She paused, sucking deeper—his Ichor, his life, his im-mortality—watching in delight as his fangs sank into his lips as he fought against the pain.

"Then, and only then, once I have mangled your soul as much as I can, that's when I will pass it off to Hades to do with what he will," she promised, circling him. "It will be ruined but he will find new ways to torture it. If he uses his imagination."

It was close, the end of his immortality. The air shimmered with the power of the connection between the two of them. She could see the glints, like icicles sparkling in sunlight trailing from him to her.

Though there was no sunlight. Light had no place here.

She had almost absorbed it all when something hit her side. Hard. The power in her recoiled as it momentarily stopped the exchange, cutting the connection abruptly.

Despite the power of the impact, she hadn't moved. The power inside her didn't will it to be so.

But the cliff was still in the distance, very close but far enough away that the old her was distracted by the impact and the scent, and the vampire who had toppled to the dead ground after trying to tackle her.

She could've bound him in place too, the weak young one with only one eye, fear and grief spiraling off him.

But she didn't.

For no other reason than she wasn't off the cliff yet.

The sparks in her hands flared in impatience with their thirst for it.

More power.

Blood.

But she watched the vampire struggle, its arm hanging from its shoulder limply, the power of the impact having dislocated the bone from the socket. It must have been painful but he ignored it, meeting her eyes, his body flinching with the pain caused by the power there.

Excruciating pain, she imagined.

Even for an immortal.

Especially for half of one.

But he didn't look away. "Sophie, this isn't what she would have wanted," he gritted out, his voice thick with the effort it took to manipulate the sound waves she now owned.

"This isn't about what anyone wants," she hissed. "This is about me. About us," she corrected, acknowledging the being inside her on an afterthought.

She was growing impatient and the cliff was growing closer, which was rather comforting even when, at the corner of her mind, the piece of her that remained panicked at the proximity.

Became aware of the true death should she tumble from the cliff.

He snatched her hand as she tried to turn again, the power itself almost obliterating him while barely giving her pause.

Although it did give her pause. Enough to watch him crumble lifelessly to the ground and stay there, which was good. Happily she turned to finish what she started—death.

But as her eyes locked on the vampire king's—which were hardened without fear, only resignation of the underworld—something gave her pause.

Another presence in the clearing, a taste to the air which cut through the bitter stench of death.

It wasn't life,

but something sweet and sour and the same time. With an edge of an emotion that had no place there. Or in this wretched world at all.

Hope.

"Really? Dude, going on a weird witchy killing spree is the way you were going to play it after my timely death? I don't hate it, but I thought you'd try to be a little more original."

The sarcastic voice cut through the power and brought the tumultuous ride to the cliff to a screeching halt.

The being inside her hissed in protest, but she turned despite it, though the effort was tearing her in two.

Isla's bloodstained couture greeted her first. Then she met her friend's emerald eyes, sparkling with life and sarcasm, like always. Her hair glinted off the sun like blood spilling from her skull, tangled in places. Yet it was possibly the only place she didn't have blood.

Her stained red lips stretched into a grin, revealing fangs.

The power was not ready to leave even as Sophie clawed at it to go back to its cage, fighting to find her own voice and silence the other.

"How?" she gritted out, her voice thick but her own.

Isla shrugged. "Apparently slayer blood isn't fatal to this vampire. It's like the immortal version of those green juices humans think cures cancer. Apart from Thorne's blood obviously chasing off witchy curses, it doesn't kill me as promised. And it tastes delightful." She kissed the tips of her fingers like an old Italian woman, then tilted her head at the scene around her Sophie was just noticing.

Dead plant life in a ring like a nuclear bomb had been set off; the lifeless form of Scott; the frozen king of vampires, hovering between immortality and the grave; the equally frozen and mute slayer.

Emerald eyes flickered back to her. "Now I do like the fact that girl power is well in play here. The Spice Girls would be so proud. 'If you wanna be my lover, you gotta let my friends almost kill you with weird power.'" She frowned. "Doesn't roll off the tongue quite as easy. So how about we stop killing Rick, defibrillate Scott, let Silver go and talk about this over cocktails?"

Her voice and words may have been easy but Sophie didn't miss the undertone, or the slight way her body was poised, ready for attack. The power inside recognized the threat, jumping from the cage she was struggling to close and encouraging her to strike. To end them all, and specifically the vampire in front of her.

Her best friend.

The one who should have been dead, as the gods willed it.

But they didn't seem to.

She sent the lock home on the cage.

But not before that otherworldly voice whispered to her a premonition so sure that she knew it was future reality better than she knew that classic rock could only be heard on vinyl.

"*The blood will run. The earth will burn. The three shall fall.*"

ISLA

I wasn't dead.

I was still undead, in fact.

Firstly, because even Hades himself couldn't have designed a punishment as cruel as having the sweet ambrosia like nothing I'd ever tasted in almost five centuries ripped from my tongue.

Yet it was. The heavenly substance that wasn't simply blood but life itself stopped coating my tongue as my mouth was ripped from the taut skin of a muscled neck.

And it was me who did so.

Detached myself from Thorne's neck.

I didn't know how I did it. Or what part of me recognized the slowing of his heart and the twang to the blood that made it sweeter than anything.

Death.

Had anything ever tasted sweeter on my tongue than death? My own was mixed with Thorne's, and it was as delicious as it was repulsive.

But it was *Thorne's* death. And that echoing heartbeat that had become my soundtrack to everything was slowing, taunting me with the longer silence between beats.

So I wrenched myself from his neck.

And that's how I knew I wasn't dead.

Because it sucked, the loss of his blood on me. Inside me.

And not in the right way.

It took a few snatches of time, in whatever vortex I'd been lost in, to understand what was going on. Namely that I wasn't dead—a feat in itself, considering I had not one but two certainties on that score.

The first a curse put on me by some ancient witch to drain my immortality before killing me as a mortal.

Then there was the poison that was the blood of the slayer, who just happened to be the man I loved. The man I had pleaded to let be my end because dying with him as my executioner was the only way for me to go.

Wasn't the best executioner the man who held your heart?

Wasn't the person who held your heart—even if it was broken, mangled, blackened, and charred—the only person who held the keys to your demise?

Although I did glimpse the silhouette of Hades and hear the screams of all the souls he held within him—not a sound I would ever forget—the slowing of Thorne's heartbeat, the taunting silence of what would be the world without that in it? It was even worse than Paris Hilton without auto-tune.

Haunting.

It was stark color, the removal of the crimson from my vision decidedly uncomfortable considering I was willing to live, and die, in the bloodlust. Yet the body that had been welcoming death for all these months was no longer its friend. Or acquaintance. We weren't on speaking terms, death and me.

My body felt recharged in a way draining an entire football team couldn't.

And I'd done that.

Once.

Or twice.

Before I got my conscience, obviously.

Okay, the second time was technically after, but they deserved it.

But the glaring reality brought with it the disturbing sound of a faltering heartbeat. Thorne's eyes gaped at me in surprise, then joy, and then they went weirdly vacant.

In a way that chilled my bones which had moments before been flaming from the inferno of his lifeblood.

"Thorne," I demanded. "This is not a *Romeo and Juliet* situation. You do not die in my place. No one dies here. Not me, it seems. So you're not allowed," I ordered. My voice shook, not from the proximity of my own death but from his.

I'd been close enough many a time to chirp happily in its face. Never had I let fear seep into my voice. Or even my soul.

I got it now. The Romeo and Juliet thing. The prospect of death was endearing, enticing, and preferable to the reality of a world in which Thorne didn't exist.

The silence, save for the faltering heartbeat, was something much scarier than the impending doom I'd just been faced with. Than the vision of Hades and the underworld full of tortured and depraved souls.

The reality of another death much more terrifying than mine.

Thorne's.

The clock swayed and I was still, glued to the spot despite my panic; I worried if I moved, it would tear the fragile fabric of the moment in which we were stuck.

The moment between life and death.

The moment tore itself anyway. As such moments did.

With the improved, louder and not so much ringing in the sound of both of our deaths.

Because in the moment between moments, it was a cool sort of certainty that told me life, or even undeath, without him would not be preferable. And it would be short.

He had been as still as I had, but not out of fear. His stillness was out of severe and life-threatening blood loss.

Because he wasn't a mere mortal, he healed. Fast. Not completely, but completely enough to move quickly, clutching me by the neck even as his own was stained with blood and the two puncture marks from my fangs.

"Isla," he demanded roughly, his voice dry.

I blinked at him.

His lips crashed down on mine before any other words could be said. As our tongues clashed together, so did the marriage between life and death, both of which we'd tasted and somehow merged together. It was all of it, life and death and blood and love, embroiled into one furious kiss.

Then it wasn't, his mouth hovering over mine as his eyes burned into me.

"You're still here," he rasped.

"Yeah," I whispered back. "Lucifer will have to wait a little longer to get his most coveted soul."

His eyes blazed. "No, that soul doesn't belong to the Devil. It belongs to me."

I stared at him. "You want that twisted, tarnished, depraved, and ugly thing?"

"I don't want it," he said. "I *need* that twisted, tarnished, depraved and exquisitely beautiful thing in order to keep my heart beating. I know that because it almost slipped out of my hands."

"Yeah, and then your heart nearly stopped beating because I almost drained you dry," I said, laughing nervously.

He stared at me as if etching every inch of me into his memory. Then he blinked, his face clearing with cold realization. "You survived it. My blood."

I nodded.

Yes, that was a pesky little detail that had gotten lost with the fear that I was watching the man I loved more than Jimmy Choo die before my eyes.

For the second time.

I technically shouldn't have been undead to watch the death of the second man I'd ever loved in my immortality—well, the first in my immortality, considering the very first was when I wasn't a vampire, merely a stupid girl who fell for a human.

Apparently that stupid girl may not have died the day my

sarcastic woman with fangs emerged. The day of Jonathan's death. Maybe I'd only thought she'd died.

Because that same girl fell in love with the one mortal on the planet who could kill her.

Slayer blood was, after all, one of the main things nature had done to create some form of even footing.

Fatal.

To all vampires.

Except me.

Thorne's blood wasn't fatal to me.

I wondered if his love would be.

"It saved you," he rasped, his voice rough with not just the aftermath of death but the close brush with the definite destruction that lurked behind his tortured eyes. The ones drenched with a love so deep I was certain it would kill me.

No one could survive that.

Not even an immortal.

"Let's not go wild," I corrected. "Nobody can save me. That's a job for me, if I so wish, which I don't. I'm rather enjoying being damned. Plus, it's the twenty-first century. Women can save themselves from ancient witch curses and slayer blood that was meant to be fatal but somehow wasn't," I snapped.

He grinned, but it was the darkly comic grin of someone who did so only to stave off the worst of the demons—or perhaps welcome them in for tea. Or a steaming hot cup of O Neg.

"You're still Isla. Still *my* Isla," he murmured, almost to himself. His eyes were looking at me, really looking at me, but at the same time they weren't actually seeing me. They were entertaining—or possible fighting—those same demons he'd obviously invited in for tea.

His arms tightened around me to the point of pain, despite the fact that he wasn't even back to full strength.

I reminded myself that I needed to get the skinny, or perhaps the fat on that little nugget. How such an apparently human man healed almost as fast as a vampire, and alluded to the fact that he was able to live for about as long as one.

But now wasn't the time. You know, since I'd almost died in front of him, then almost killed him after deciding to commit suicide via slayer—whom I loved—and then in turn almost killed that slayer.

That slayer who had shaken off the worst of the demons or was at least ignoring them for now in order to focus sharp eyes on me. "You aren't allowed to do that again," he growled.

"What?" I asked, trying to snap myself from my own demons. It was easier to do, since mine were BFFs and we had sleepovers and braided each other's horns.

"Almost fuckin' die in my arms," he clarified in a voice so rough it actually hurt more than the brutal grip of his hands. "No curse worse than that invented on the planet."

I held up my hand. "Belladonna's sisters might take that as a challenge. Let's deal with the current one we seem to have beaten and find ourselves a witch-type person to bippity boppity boo and tell me what I want to hear," I said, thinking about the fact that I was, until mere moments before, supposed to be dead. I wasn't complaining; in fact, I was pretty glad about it. But half a millennium on this earth meant I knew this wasn't a gift.

Life was never a gift freely given.

Death, more often than not, was the cost.

I reluctantly moved from my spot in Thorne's arms—or rather *tried* to.

His biceps flexed with exertion as he held me in place. Though they didn't need to. His demon filled gaze did that all on its own.

"Isla. You almost died. In front of me. You think I'm gonna let you go now? Or ever? I need to keep holdin' you to make sure this shit isn't something my broken mind didn't make up in order to escape the world without you in it."

Again those demons surfaced, acknowledging my own that came with the pain in his voice, in his very soul. Only because my own soul, if I had such a thing, felt that agony too, at the prospect of a world without the thundering heartbeat that was more like a roar in my ears.

Never had I welcomed that roar more. Never had I wished that I would never be haunted by that terrible silence again.

I blinked at him. "Well, I need to think of something that your mind wouldn't conjure me up doing that will make you sure of that fact," I said. "I could tell you about the Great Fire of London. Yeah, it didn't start on Pudding Lane." I paused. "Well, it did, just not by a baker. It was by a demon. Well, if you want to get technical, it was me goading the demon by telling him that he couldn't even light a pipe on fire, let alone a city. It got away on me, but boy were the flames pretty to look at." My eyes flared with the memory of the inferno, although it had been nothing but a flickering candle compared to the heat from Thorne's arms around me, from his blood pouring through my veins.

His eyes cleared like the sudden loss of storm on troubled seas, the illusion of calm settling them—for a time, at least. He choked out a harsh chuckle. "That's my Isla," he muttered, kissing my head. "And you're not goin' anywhere. I need to know the why of this too, but not now. I need to sink into you. I need to fucking drown in you to remind myself that I wasn't just staring at the dry wasteland of a world without you," he growled. "Surest way I can be is if I come home to the place where I belong." His eyes turned to an inky abyss. "Inside you."

I flinched at the same time my lady bits did. They were doing a good flinch but my body wasn't; it was reacting to what my ears were only now picking up.

And when I concentrated, I noticed the unnatural scent to the air. The musty smell to it and the way it thickened unnaturally in a way that was both too familiar and an omen in one.

Magic.

Ancient magic.

And not the good stuff that would get me out of the situation I was currently in.

No, the bad stuff that might just swallow the situation and then the rest of the fucking wretched world.

"Oh fuck," I hissed, detaching myself from Thorne and darting out the door in a swift movement that even he, as some sort of updated version of a slayer, couldn't catch up with. Nor properly see with his more than human eyes.

I was very regretfully out of Thorne's arms and then staring into the eyes of my best friend.

And then the eyes of the other creature that had been lurking inside her, waiting for death to come to the party before it turned up fashionably late.

TWO

S OPHIE BANISHED IT. THE POWER THAT HAD BEEN stirring within her, the kind I had recognized and not in a good way, like you recognized Chris Hemsworth on the street checking you out. Yes, that happened. The man wasn't blind. Of course he checked me out. And asked me out.

And a girl doesn't kiss and tell.

Okay, she does, but it was Chris fucking Hemsworth— Thor, for God's sake. I hadn't had better, since... well, Thor himself. Oh, and afterwards, Thorne.

Even a god had nothing on my slayer.

But no, it wasn't that good kind of recognition.

No, it was like when you recognized the one-night stand that was a result of draining too many drunken frat boys and imbibing enchanted drinks. Sophie only banished it for a while, though; the remainder of the magic still lurked around her, as did the creature inside her. Whatever those irises had been, they weren't Sophie's.

The pulse in the air around her, even now, wasn't comfortable. Or normal.

Or it was more abnormal than it usually was. Much more.

The thought worried me.

A lot.

But then so had the seemingly dead Scott—who Sophie had to resurrect. Luckily he hadn't probably been dead; even she didn't have that power.

Well *Sophie* didn't. This new power that lurked behind her eyes most likely did.

And a power that could snatch souls back from Hades himself was a good kind of power to have on our side. Especially when we were in the middle of fighting a supernatural war.

Problem was, a power like that, one older than perhaps time itself—ancient in a way that scared even me, and I got bangs in the eighties—it didn't have anyone's side. It only had one purpose.

Destruction.

And it was that very power that got us—read: me—into the situation we were in, cursed by thousand-year-old witches and fighting humans turned into gross versions of vampires.

So the death magic was likely something we needed to treat like orange-tinted lipstick—steer clear of it at all costs.

After the resurrection of Scott and his subsequent freak-out, clutching me and jumping all over me so hard I had to shake him back to the ground to which he had been slumped, I was distracted.

And then there was the issue of a stony-faced and weirdly not-homicidal King Rick, whom Sophie had given back his immortality.

Hades would have been angry about the loss of not only my soul but that of a royal vampire. Angry enough to do everything to make sure those who cheated him would not stay on this earth for long.

Rick had stayed frozen, even after Sophie said she released both him and Silver. I'd known Silver had been released since he'd darted over to Sophie the second he'd found purchase over his limbs, clutching her shoulders and shaking her, asking, "What the fuck possessed you to pull that fucking shit?"

What the fuck indeed.

Instead of pondering that, I had to deal with Thorne's heartbeat rapidly approaching, coupled with Rick's frozen stare centered right on my face. Thorne's burned into my back. I didn't need to look back to know that; some sort of invisible string connected his consciousness to mine. I couldn't read his thoughts exactly, but his emotions were clearer and starker than they had ever been. Almost like they were my own.

I idly wiped the stray blood from the corner of my lip, sucking it on my finger and having to suppress the moan that came with the smallest taste of Thorne's blood.

Despite the fact that I'd gotten my fill, I craved more. His approaching heartbeat enraptured me with the circulation of that sweetness in his body. And then I remembered the quiet between those heartbeats.

It lessened my cravings slightly.

Through all of it, Rick continued to stare.

I shifted uncomfortably on the dead ground.

"I know I don't exactly look crash hot, but you don't have to stare at me like a circus freak. A girl is entitled to look a little ragged after, you know, being cursed by a witch and then almost dying. Technically a process sped up by you," I told him. "I'm not pointing fingers, but if I was…." I lifted my bloodred pointer finger to the level of his chest. Then I frowned at the chip in the varnish.

"Can someone not design a nail polish that doesn't chip, even in death?" I muttered to myself. "I've even got the perfect name for it: Deathless."

Somehow the word hung longer in the air than I'd meant it to, but I didn't inspect the meaning of this, or the mutterings of Silver and Sophie, who were still exchanging curse words.

Unfortunately, due to the sheer amount of weird fucking shit happening in this day, I had to prioritize.

I glanced to Scott, who was sitting against a tree trunk, dazed but okay. I guessed I was partly to blame with him looking dazed, considering I was the one who had pushed him when he was recovering from almost dying. He should have known better, trying to *hug* me of all things. I'd only *almost* died.

There were only so many intense emotions I could take from men over my lack of being dead.

I was pretty glad too, but I kept my shit together.

And the fact that *I* was the one with her shit together at that moment should have worried someone.

"Go find yourself a hiker, perk up," I suggested to Scott.

He frowned at me.

I held my hands up in surrender to the glare that was a little more menacing than it used to be thanks to the eye patch and scar. Instead of looking like a puppy, he looked like a slightly more grown-up, one-eyed puppy who might nibble at your finger. And it might even smart just a little.

"Just trying to help," I muttered.

I glanced back to Rick, who still hadn't moved. The stillness in itself was unnerving. Vampires were still creatures, to a point, but after he'd been frozen in place and almost killed by a weird witchy version of my favorite witch, I reasoned he'd want to do some calf stretches at the least.

"Um, Sophie, I think you put this one back together wrong," I informed her, stepping forward so I could wave my unfortunately chipped nails in front of his glassy stare. "All the king's horses and all the king's witch—who wasn't technically his—couldn't put Humpty together again," I muttered, still waving my hand.

The motion did something, shocked him into movement so he was no longer dong his best 'Rick statue' impression. No, he was doing his best 'crush Isla's ribcage and spleen' impression by yanking me into his brutal embrace. The scent of death still lingered on him, the hug imprinting it on my clothes, though my soul was already tattooed with the stuff.

Death itself didn't have a singular scent. Those who feasted on it knew it always had the same base notes, but the flavors were vastly different. Mostly it was somewhat natural, even when taken by supernatural beings. Because that order had been designed by nature. Nature had created vampires—as long as you didn't believe in the Greek god version—to suck on and kill humans for their lifeblood. So even in their death, it was part of the food chain.

Death brought on by black magic did not have the natural taste. It barely even boasted those base notes. Because of the way in which nature was manipulated to create and foster this death magic, the scent of the death itself was rancid and twisted.

Which had been on my soul since the moment Belladonna had cursed me. Now it was staining Rick's very soul.

And Scott's.

It was the worst I'd tasted, and I'd seen some black magic from some dark bitches.

Powerful ones too.

But nothing like this.

Which brought with it that glimmer of fear at those eyes that hadn't been Sophie's.

Again, no time to analyze, considering the male fury amped itself up oh, about *a hundred thousand* percent.

"Hands off her. Now, Emrick," Thorne commanded in a velvet tone that promised death if it wasn't heeded.

Of course it wasn't heeded.

Rick was king, after all, and kings didn't seem to like to be ordered around, on account of that being *their* job.

In addition to shackling people, and vampires, and torturing them in front of a room full of aristocratic assholes who also happened to be vampires.

"You beg now? For this human? This slayer? You didn't beg for your own life that night in your apartment, yet you're willing to do so for his."

The glaring memory of that did something to me, but I didn't have a physical reaction like someone else did.

Rick's arms flexed around me painfully at Thorne's command, and then they were gone.

Mainly because they were ripped off me by the forceful, strong hands of a man who ordinarily shouldn't have been able to achieve such a feat as forcibly removing the king of vampires from… well, anywhere. Especially considering the version of death he'd just flirted with.

And struck out with, fortunately.

He had his knife at Rick's throat in a blur of motion that was impressive but only possible because I was half-distracted.

At the thought of him really, *really* not striking out with me.

Death made me horny, apparently.

"You think you get to touch her, ever?" Thorne hissed at Rick. "When the last time you were doing so, you were drawing blood, drawing the fuckin' *life* from her?" Anger morphed his voice into something unrecognizable.

Though my downstairs area definitely recognized it.

Rick, interestingly, didn't move or attempt to fight back. Though I knew he was capable. Against a run-of-the-mill slayer, I'd say it would've taken all of the effort of a strong exhale to get one off him, but with Thorne? I had a strange and irrational feeling that he might have met his match.

Because I had strange and irrational feelings all of the time, I rolled with it.

"How is she alive?" Rick demanded, eyes on Thorne. Not me, the woman who was actually the topic of conversation. It was a nasty character trait of these men, to talk about women with each other, a residual stick from the patriarchal era when women had no voice.

Of course, even in the patriarchal era, I had a voice. A loud one. I wasn't just a woman, after all.

I was a vampire. And a badass one at that, if I did say so myself.

"Not alive. Undead," I offered.

I glanced to Sophie, who was standing next to a stone-faced Silver, watching the exchange with a flicker of interest, her face otherwise blank. She was unnervingly still too. Which meant a lot more than a vampire being still. She was human, for one. And the little witch had some form of ADHD; she couldn't go a hot minute without moving or exploding a demon or two.

"Ten grand on Rick," she offered, breaking her Sophie statue impression with her mouth, at least.

I grinned at her. "Oh, I'll not easily bet against my man."

I glanced at his strong body, the radiating fury within it

and around it and the small puncture marks decorating his corded neck that were almost healed. Those marks sent shivers down my body, heated up my blood—Thorne's blood flowing through me.

Mine.

He was mine, and now he had my mark. It was a carnal and raw instinct that I didn't quite recognize. One that felt very ancient. Had the same taste as the air in the clearing.

But at the same time as being older than even me—which didn't make sense at all—it was also fresh and new, some jigsaw piece that I didn't realize I needed until it slotted into the jagged place I thought would be empty forever.

Completed me.

Ugh, did I really just think the phrase 'completed me'? I might have to get the witch to curse me again if I kept thinking like that. I didn't deserve to be undead if I got soft.

With love.

"You gonna kill me, Thorne?" Rick challenged.

The challenging spark in Thorne's gaze gave way to more rational, and therefore unwelcome thoughts.

I didn't do 'rational' thoughts.

But here they were.

The kind of thoughts that again reminded me not just of the scene in the throne room that Rick was *so* getting punished for, but for the familiar way they spoke to each other afterwards. Granted, I had been drifting out of consciousness and on my deathbed and all that, but my memory of it was still clear enough.

"She's a vampire. She'll make it through," the cold voice snapped. *"You're here and you're human."*

"Not quite, Emrick. And maybe before you pulled this fuckin' stunt you might have tried to think of anyone but yourself."

There was history. With Rick, I understood; you lived on this earth long enough, you'd be hard-pressed to find someone you didn't have history with.

Weirdly, for me, it always seemed to be bad blood.

Like the stuff boiling between these two.

But Thorne was human, and a slayer. Two things that should have denoted a distinct *lack* of history with the vampire king, who was approximately one thousand years old.

Yes, Thorne had hinted at the fact that he was older than his thirty-five-year-old body, but we hadn't gotten to the specifics.

It hit me that we hadn't gotten to the specifics on much.

How could you know so little about a creature yet know it all at the same time?

Though this wasn't the time for such thoughts, considering the creature in question—my boyfriend, for lack of a better word—was looking very much like he might take on a vampire king in a death match. Not ten minutes after I'd almost drained him dry.

Almost, but still.

"I should. This should be the nail in your coffin," Thorne seethed, fists clenched at his side while his arm rested on his belt, and the enchanted blade that was perched on it.

The blade that was spelled specifically to kill vampires. Among other creatures.

I didn't want him to kill this particular one until I got answers.

"Um, just me again," I said, waving my fingers and crunching my heels on dead leaves as I made it to the death match. "I'm mighty curious about how the slayer, who seems to have a lot more pizazz than his other counterparts, and the king of all vampires, AKA the one who most likely has all the reasons in the world to kill that slayer, are talking to each other like old enemies. But not the kind you kill."

I narrowed my eyes at them.

Thorne's eyes fastened on Rick, something passing between them. "You touch her again and I'll forget it all to cut you up with this. Slowly." He gestured to the knife at his belt. "Because history doesn't mean shit when I've got the future in my hands dyin'," he said, his glance on me.

Then he lowered the gaze, stepped back and yanked me into his side, his entire body relaxing as I molded into the hard flesh.

To be fair, my body had the same natural response.

My mind wasn't as easily swayed. I darted my eyes between the two. "Someone has to spill as to who copied whose outfit to create this history that seems so much more than biology," I demanded.

Rick's eyes met mine. "Oh, it's not more than just biology," he said. "In fact, that's all it is. Biology."

The way he said it unnerved me, as did the low growl in Thorne's throat at the words. The warning. "We don't have time to talk about this shit," he declared, his attention moving to Sophie. "We gotta figure out what the fuck happened with Isla. And you need to tell us how she's still alive—"

"Undead," I interrupted happily.

I got a sideways glare. "And how we can make sure she stays that way."

Sophie's brow furrowed as she thought it over but she didn't speak, namely because she knew me and knew I wasn't likely to let it go. She'd been there when I'd been publically chastised by a certain monarch who was mad at me for getting caught in the butler's closet with her husband.

I could hold a grudge.

To be fair, I did organize to get her head chopped off.

I was still pissed, though.

Immortals were the best at holding grudges. Hence me needing to know how this one had started and been nurtured in such a way that neither of them had killed each other yet.

And why Rick had risked everything in order to save us. We had been renounced in front of the Sector and the Vein Lines, my own included. He should have, by all the laws of our kind, killed us.

But there we were.

One alive, one undead.

"Nope. We don't change the subject. In fact, you've got a lot to answer to. Both of you." I squinted at Thorne's face. "Considering this was looking like mincemeat not three hours ago, yet now you seem to have healed miraculously. And survived me almost draining you to death with enough pep in your step to go around threatening vampire kings, who you seem to be on a first-name basis with," I snapped. "So the witches will wait."

Thorne stared at me. "That, my Isla, is history," he declared. "And history can wait. I'm holding the future in my arms this very second. My sarcastic, infuriating, and beautiful future. That's shit that can't wait. And that's the shit I'm going to ensure stays constant before we go traveling into the past."

I pouted at him. Then glared, then considered breaking his arm. For two reasons. Firstly because I was pissed off, and when I wasn't pissed off at someone enough to kill them, I'd at least break a bone. The second reason being research to figure out how long it took to heal.

I opened my mouth to argue again, because I was getting my way despite the flowers in his words and the vague amount of logic in them.

Sophie beat me to it.

"As much as I want the *E! True Hollywood Story* on this"—she waved her hand up and down in Thorne and Rick's area—"situation, Thorne is right. The black magic spells cast by thousand-year-old witches not only bent on killing you but starting a war between every supernatural creature and human in existence is a little more pressing. Right now, we can't focus on a bromance gone wrong."

I scowled at her.

When she put it like that, I sounded like an asshole for arguing. I didn't mind sounding like an asshole—preferred it, in fact. But only when I felt like I was going to win.

I didn't think I was going to win here, so I conceded.

But not before thinking about the way the skeletons in this closet, the ones I suspected were there and Thorne thought belonged in the past, might be the very thing that turned the history into a future problem. History, after all, was always the bloodiest.

"Fine," I huffed.

And then before anyone could do anything, I darted forward with a renewed strength that felt familiar and welcome at the same time as it was strange and new, snapping Rick's arm off at the socket.

The rippling crunch of it echoed through the clearing delightfully. I held up the severed arm, inspecting it with satisfaction, the muscle still impressively strong when not connected to a shoulder. I looked up at his grimace of pain, which was a relatively mild reaction, considering the extent of the injury.

Yes, immortals could grow back limbs—and quickly if one was strong and old enough, which Rick was—but it was still somewhat of a painful inconvenience that was not met without some following violence.

I waited for it. Welcomed it. The blood sang in my body,

rolling through my limbs and giving them a strength that was beautiful. And a bloodlust that went beyond the need for Thorne's blood. It was a need to yank off more limbs and try out my new moves that I knew I'd have.

Rick didn't make any move to attack, which was curious since the king of all vampires was notorious for punishing those who slighted him. And ripping his arm off and waving it at him—which I was doing—could have been considered more than a slight.

Thorne must have known that too, as his heat was suddenly at my back, poised to protect me. As was Sophie, a flicker of blue sparks at the corner of my eye alerting me to the fact that she'd edged forward slightly.

I rolled my eyes, putting my hand on my hip, still holding the arm. "Seriously, guys. It takes one little brush with death and you're treating me like a helpless human who can't dish out her own revenge." I waved the arm. "I'm quite capable." I turned to a blank-faced Rick. "Which is what I'm doing. Well, considering what I dreamed of doing to you while you had me and the man I love strung up and beaten like pigs in front of your court of snakes, this"—I waved the arm—"is pretty much a day at the spa. But you're lucky. I'm feeling warm and fuzzy about the scent of death in the air and the dead crunch of wildlife under my feet." I smiled at him. "So you get this. For now. I'll not make any promises, mostly since I never make promises because I don't like present Isla making future Isla's decisions for her. I find it rude. But also because I reserve the right to continue with the torture if your explanation as to why you almost killed me is not sufficient," I spat.

He blinked up at me, a clear and regal look on his face despite bleeding from a socket where an arm used to be. "A member of a prominent Vein Line called you out in front of the court," he informed me tightly. "You know I had no choice. I didn't plan on executing either of you, but because I didn't know about the fucking curse on you, I didn't realize I had to be... *gentle* with the fragility that was your immortality."

Though his tone was Rick's signature cold and emotionless special, I couldn't help but read the small teasing taunt at the 'g' word. Almost like he *wanted* me to rip off his other arm.

I stepped forward, my fury flickering around me like a cape. "Try and be *gentle* with little fragile me right now. I dare you. Because you try to insinuate that I'm weak, even with a thousand-year-old witch's curse inside me, and that'll be the last thing that head thinks before it wears a crown *much* closer to the ground," I threatened.

Promised, actually. Death promises were the one little loophole I gave myself. I figured future Isla would never be mad at killing someone because of a promise past Isla made.

His mouth twitched. "I'll carry on," he muttered. "Because of our... relationship, I wasn't likely to let your death be at my hands. Or at anyone's." The way he said that, the inflection of his even and flat tone, gave me pause.

And gave Thorne's fury the much unneeded kick-start. His body tensed even more behind me.

I knew he was itching to yank me into his arms once more; I could practically taste his need, and my own, which pissed me right off. I didn't need to be in my man's arms while he declared me his property to other interested parties.

I needed that like I needed a tweed suit. Being not at all. Unless I wanted to look like a twat.

Thorne knew that too. So he didn't yank me to him.

"Well it was almost at your hands, my friend. Your Highness. Or Your Douchebaggerness—a personal favorite of mine." I winked at him.

His jaw hardened. "As previously mentioned, I had *no fucking clue* about the curse. I would not have touched a single hair on your head had I known it wouldn't be replaced to its original glory."

Cue another palpable wave of fury from Thorne. "Watch your fuckin' step, Emrick," he warned.

We both ignored him.

"And if you'd told me about a curse, not only would I have gone about that particular event in another way, but I might have been able to help, saving you and myself from almost fading away to nothing."

The intensity behind his words was in direct conflict with the blankness of his face.

"We had it covered," Thorne clipped, reverting back to the male 'talk for the woman' mentality he was so eager to slip back into like an old sweater or something.

Rick raised his brow. "You had it sorted?" he repeated, his cultured inflection over the words as opposed to Thorne's rough grumble making it sound like an insult. "You held her in your arms while Hades prepared a fucking bunk for her. It seems dumb luck that she's here, standing and spouting her usual nonsense at all."

"Not dumb luck," Sophie cut in, her voice empty and full at the same time.

She stepped forward, her power once more pulsing around her.

Hers.

Maybe a little stronger, or a lot than it had been. But the appearance of whatever had been in the clearing before was gone. Or at least cloaked.

I'd have to pencil in an exorcism instead of mani-pedis this week.

"Thorne's blood curing Isla was not dumb luck," she continued, eyes on Rick, then me, then Thorne. The gaze was not familiar; it was probing, empty, and working some sort of spell considering I felt the touch of magic rippling over skin.

Instinctively I flinched away from it, despite the familiarity of Sophie's aura. Though it wasn't completely familiar. It was changed.

I could sense the power. I knew hers had been building, just not this much.

"Homegirl got *powers* now," I muttered to her.

She gave me a jaunty grin before flipping the bird, making me feel slightly better.

If she was still doing that, she was my Sophie. Maybe we could take the powers for a test drive before returning them back to the lot.

"Thorne's blood is not a *cure*," Rick snapped, his controlled tone slipping. "Considering slayer blood is toxic to any vampire who drinks it."

"Well, *almost* any vampire," I corrected. "Seems I'm special. We already knew that, of course, but now they don't need to look for reasons to put me in the history books. They actually have one." I paused, not noting or caring about the shock on Rick's face. "Though, I'm interested to see how you're going to handle my almost execution and the Vein Lines asking for blood. It was Selene's family, wasn't it? Asking for revenge after how I technically damned their daughter to be imprisoned for eternity. Gosh, you'd think they'd have let that go by now. I think I did them a favor. Besides, they've got a spare."

I thought of Selene's sister, the quiet and weak little vampire who wouldn't do well in a fight, compared to Selene, who was a lot of things but not weak since she tried to overthrow an entire monarchy. Though she did fail. And failure was a defining mark of weakness in my book. I'd failed at nothing in my undeath to date.

"Or was it the Carlisles? They've got a bit of a grudge over me too. But I think they started it." I paused, screwing up my nose in thought. "In fact, I *know* they did. They couldn't really expect anything less than me blowing up their estate in Turkey as revenge for bidding on that painting I explicitly said I wanted. I didn't care how many conservation societies it pissed off. It was so worth it."

"It wasn't either of them," he returned.

He regarded me evenly, waiting for my words to sink in and his to process, calmly, as was his way. Even though he had half an arm growing out of his shoulder.

I shrugged. "I piss a lot of people off. Throw a stone, even in this clearing, you'll find someone. Like the king whose arm I just ripped off," I offered helpfully.

He didn't grin, though such things were rare, so I wasn't offended. I was comfortable in my hilarity. I made myself laugh, which was the main thing.

"It was a Vein Line. Yours," he said flatly, not unkindly.

The air charged in the clearing as Sophie's palms crackled with more blue sparks. "We really need to kill your mother, Isla," she commented casually.

"I don't disagree," I muttered.

Yes, my parents and I didn't exactly enjoy the warmest and fuzziest of relationships, and they may have tried to have me assassinated a handful of times, but it wasn't as big a deal as outing me for a capital crime to the king of our race.

"Well it seems they've gotten serious on getting me killed," I muttered.

"Your mother didn't want you killed," Rick offered. "She wanted you sequestered until the time of your Awakening.

Then she would have the power to ensure a proper vampire was chosen in order to make sure the deed was done."

I didn't show surprise because I didn't feel any. My mother was nothing if not sadistically predictable. "Well of course."

Thorne didn't exactly have the same mild reaction. He was no longer behind me but beside me, his hand snatching mine. Well, snatching Rick's, which he didn't like if his jerked reaction and the force with which he threw the arm across the clearing was anything to go by.

"Hey! He might have wanted to keep that," I protested.

Thorne glowered at me.

"Fine. I'm sure he's got a whole closetful," I muttered.

He glared at me. "Your Awakening?" he seethed.

"I don't think it's the time or place to speak about it," I said.

"It's the exact time and place, considering it set in place a course of events that almost took you away from me," he hissed.

I gave him a look. "Well, that course had already been set, considering the evil witchy curse upon me." My eyes found Sophie's. "Speaking of which, did your little magical colonoscopy tell you if I'm still sporting it or if Thorne and his blood fixed me right up?"

She was about to answer, but Thorne beat her to it.

"Isla, explain," he demanded.

I blew the air through my fangs in frustration. "Honey, talking about my vampire time of the quarter millennium isn't really appropriate to chat about in front of company, especially my family's plan to imprison me, rape me, impregnate me, and then kill me once I bore them an evil bundle of joy." I threw my hands up. "There. Happy? Now I've said it and you've made everyone here very uncomfortable," I accused.

"I'm not uncomfortable," Sophie volunteered. Bitch.

I glared at her. "You will be when I burn you at the stake while you're wearing polyester. Works better than firewood."

She rolled her eyes. "Find a new threat, dude. Burning at the stake is a little tired."

"But it's memorable, at least," I shot back.

She poked out her tongue, another comforting reminder that the juvenile and inappropriate witch I'd come to know and cause big amounts of trouble with was still driving the crazy train that was her brain. It was when someone else took the wheel that we had to worry.

The furious human in front of me was demanding attention, unfortunately.

"You knew this for how long?" Thorne asked quietly.

I didn't mistake his quiet for calm. I knew the biggest of fury was usually cloaked under the stillest of waters.

Sophie tightened the muscles in her neck in an 'oh shit' gesture.

A small grin tickled the corner of Silver's mouth. Scott was staring blankly at the entire situation like the little idiot he was. Rick was, of course, impassive. Or perhaps just focusing on growing his arm back.

And Thorne was raging, for lack of a better word. His inky black hair framed his chiseled features like a dark crown, emphasizing the sharpness of his harsh jawline which held tight when he was pissed. Then again, he was always pissed at me for one reason or another.

His steely gray eyes were solid silver, glistening and focused on me.

"Knew what?" I tried to go for dense.

His grip tightened on my upper arms in warning.

"Oh, the whole Awakening plan? Don't worry, it was

before I met you." I waved my hand.

That was the wrong thing to say.

"And you've been keeping it from me this entire fucking time?" he hissed in accusation.

"No, I haven't. It just slipped my mind," I said, not completely dishonestly. "And I knew you'd overreact."

That was also the wrong thing to say, considering the physical wave of fire that had me concerned about my eyebrows thanks to the sheer weight of Thorne's fury.

"Slipped your fuckin' mind that your family, one of the most powerful in vampire society, has been planning on kidnapping you and fuckin' raping you in order to get a child out of you before killing you? And you thought I'd overreact about that? Because that's something that happens every day in your world, right?"

I tilted my head. "No, not every day, just once every two hundred and fifty years. And we've got more pressing matters to attend to."

His eyes held mine hostage. "We're killing your family. Every last member. And their deaths will last decades," he declared.

I grinned. "Oh I do love your sweet nothings. And yes, we are. But in order to do so, we've got to fight the war, which is kind of why I agreed in the first place."

I glanced to Rick, who had been silently watching the entire exchange, as had everyone else in the clearing, which I didn't exactly mind. They'd all seen me die; it wasn't like there were many secrets left.

"We need to fight the war in order to gather evidence on my family so I can get the sanction from our almighty doucheness to kill them," I said happily. "Though Mother obviously has some of my brilliance with her having the same idea." I waved my hand. "No matter. She failed. That in itself is just great. But we've got to keep on keeping on should we go with my original plan and kill them all."

I smiled at the group in general.

"Let's start the killing now that I'm not dead, shall we?"

THREE

Three Days Later

"I'M NOT COMFORTABLE WITH THIS." THORNE'S VOICE matched his emotions. Pissed off was the flavor of the evening.

I wished his alluring blood was the flavor of the evening. Not that I hadn't already had a little nip, as the fading mark on his neck indicated.

It turned out the slayer, who abhorred vampires and the fact that they feasted on human's lifeblood to survive, got totally turned on when the vampire he was fucking did just that.

I discovered that in the midst of what was basically a three-day reunion. Of the sexual kind. Because when you see the person you love almost die right in front of you, it kind of works as an aphrodisiac.

We had gone from Thorne's place to my apartment after a

very uneasy exit with Rick. Like things were uneasy between Russia and America in the Cold War.

Each party held back their nukes.

For now.

That was most likely because Rick had promised to make some sort of announcement about the vampire community not coming after us with their pitchforks. It was something big. Condoning a slayer and a vampire and not killing them both?

Yeah. Big.

Apparently there was a big summit with all factions about this upcoming war, and treaties needed to be signed.

Treaties between vampires and slayers.

Yeah, I had to take my jaw off the floor too.

So there was that.

We parted ways, with me making Sophie promise not to get all *Exorcist* until I could find myself a Father Merrin type to be on standby while I watched her head spin around.

I worried about that witch. Especially since she damn near sprinted from that clearing when things had been sorted.

Scratch that. Nothing had really been sorted.

She still had power inside her that could level the world and destroy her. Thorne and Rick still had history that remained a mystery; despite my not-so-gentle cajoling, Thorne had kept murmuring "later." I'm not a girl who accepts "later" as an answer. I don't accept anything but the answer I wanted. Then again, I don't usually ask people many questions. When I really wanted to know something, I'd torture it out of them. But Thorne had his own idea of torture in mind.

Of the sexual variety.

So I'd accepted "later."

There were more important things to do once we'd finally gotten back to my apartment building. The drive back into the city was silent but for the gentle thump of Thorne's heartbeat. For someone who loved the sound of her own voice almost as much as red-soled shoes, that silence was a big thing.

I'd let it continue. So had Thorne, though he'd made sure his hand was firmly on my thigh for the entirety of the drive.

We'd stood in my elevator in silence, our hands intertwined, each of our demons doing the talking.

And then the moment the door opened, Thorne pounced.

Or maybe I did.

It was hard to tell.

But it had been violent.

We broke the sofa.

And the bed.

And the coffee table.

But not each other.

Because maybe we were already broken.

Wasn't that what love did? Broke you into as many pieces as humanly, and inhumanely, possible so you couldn't put yourself back together?

Not without the other person, at least.

That's what I felt—scattered yet whole at the same time.

And everything made sense when Thorne slipped into me, his eyes flaring, blood on his lip from... I couldn't remember what.

"Isla," he murmured. "This is us. Home. You're not to ever go anywhere a-fuckin'-gain. Not even Hades himself can take you from me. Not now, not ever."

Then he'd kissed me. With the blood on his lips and him inside me. I'd gone a little wild.

Just a little.

That's how I'd discovered that Thorne had enjoyed me biting him.

Because after the bed was broken, we were still struggling amongst the shattered headboard, small splinters of wood stabbing into us, and his eyes had gone to my extended fangs.

"Do it," he growled as he pounded into me.

He had been on top of me, his muscles taut from the exertion of the struggle it had taken him to get there. And then he wasn't. I was on top, my hair cascading downwards and spilling over his sculpted and scarred chest, the two of us still connected in a brutal coupling that was better than heaven and hell combined.

"Do what?" I asked, my voice little more than a throaty snarl.

His eyes never left mine as he moved his head upwards, stretching the skin of his neck, which pulsed in invitation.

I flinched with the meaning of the gesture, my fangs aching with need that mirrored that of the need between my legs. My entire body willed me to latch on, every instinct of a vampire going to the blood that was both the sweetest and bitterest on this earth.

But one instinct stopped me.

One that wasn't a vampire one.

It seemed like a human one, no matter how much I rejected that.

"Thorne," I hissed. "This goes against everything you are." The words left my mouth slightly muffled as I'd spoken around my extended fangs.

His arms brutally snatched my neck, crashing our foreheads together. "Everything I am is *this*."

He moved so he slammed into me at a new angle that speared through me with a delicious mix of pleasure and pain.

I let out an unintelligible sound as I saw stars for a moment.

Then all I saw was quicksilver in his irises.

"All I am is what you are," he growled. "Nothing more and nothin' fuckin' less. And I want to be inside you in every way possible. Despite whatever I was, whoever I was before, you drinking from me, me givin' your fuckin' *life*? That's everything. You give it to me, babe. I'm givin' that shit back to you."

The words were spoken with so much intensity they seemed to vibrate the air. They sure as shit vibrated the empty and dead organ in my chest. Made it almost beat with the power of them.

Almost.

But my own chest cavity stayed silent.

I was undead, after all.

And as I'd explained to him between sessions eight and nine, my Awakening was at least a decade away, so the beating inside my chest and the fertility that came with it was nothing to worry about.

So after he'd claimed my mouth in a brutal kiss, allowing my fangs to puncture his lips so the warmth of his blood flooded my mouth and dripped down my throat, electrifying my body, he leaned back to his previous position.

That time there was no hesitation.

From my human self or vampire self.

Because he wasn't just offering the blood my vampire self craved as a natural necessity.

He was offering *life*, which was what my human self chased with a desperation that bordered on insanity.

Insanity was, after all, what I was known for.

So I sank my fangs into the taut skin of his neck.

And drowned.

For better or worse.

Reality had to come back in eventually.

Even for insane people.

Maybe especially for insane people. And vampires.

Reality came in the form of Duncan bursting through the door while we were having a rare moment of not being horizontal, or vertical, or fucking hexagonal in the kitchen.

Thorne had been cradling a cup of coffee in his hands, eyes on mine as he sipped from it.

I'd been doing the same, but mine was laced with blood from the healing marks on his wrist.

"We should probably talk," I said.

His eyes flared. "Probably."

I raised a brow at him. "Seriously, Thorne," I told him as he stalked around the breakfast bar of my kitchen.

Naked.

Obviously.

One did not have a six-foot-something, muscled demigod in her apartment and her bed with clothes on if there was an option of nudity.

I was functionally insane, but even someone in a straitjacket and on horse tranquilizers would've agreed with me there.

I was naked too.

Because duh. He might have been hot but I was too. Besides, being naked was not only necessary but preferred for all of the sex.

And we'd been having it *all*.

The sex, that was.

The words? Not so much. And even as someone who preferred violence, blood, and sex to words—of which I'd had all three in those three days—it was time for the words.

"Since when are you serious, baby?" he asked, voice thick as he headed over to me, hand resting on my hip.

Not lightly.

He hadn't been gentle or soulful these past three days.

Which was good. Gentle and soulful was for One Direction fans and idiots.

I sipped my cup, not breaking eye contact. The mix of coffee and his blood was something rather delightful. It gave me pause.

It was his blood.

It was doing something to me. Changing me. As a connoisseur of the plasma, I knew it well. I knew the good, the bad, and everything in between. Though blood was like pizza and sex—it couldn't really be bad.

But it couldn't be *that* good.

I knew that. Because not only were we cheating nature by the fact that I was still here, unbeating heart and all, after drinking it, but the more I drank the more our connection tightened, like there were invisible ropes of steel connecting us. The overwhelming need I felt for him at that moment was for all of the obvious reasons: his dark eyes swimming with the promise of sex, love, and eternity; his sculpted body; his growing stubble that had scratched between my legs like razors; the feelings he'd stirred within me. Yes, all of that contributed to the overwhelming need I had for him.

But there was also more.

I also felt his need. The first suck of his blood that time, it had almost knocked the breath out of me. You know, if I'd had breath in me.

But it had done something.

The wave, the tsunami and hurricane of feelings he had for me came hurtling from his body at the same rate as the ambrosia of his blood and the intensity of his climax.

It wasn't mind reading exactly because I couldn't get the

details of his thoughts.

Just the flavor of them.

But the flavor was enough. More than enough, as I could barely handle my feelings towards the human man who was meant to be designed to kill me.

But then again, maybe he still was.

Maybe this was natural evolution for the slayers, a new weapon in their arsenal.

"I'm serious since a witch cursed me, almost killed me, then you," I replied. "Oh, and I guess I was kind of serious before that when I almost died a couple more times, got in the middle of a supernatural war and fell for a slayer who embodies everything I should run from." I paused as a fresh wave of his emotion bowled through me. "Oh, and since my fucking tailor butchered a custom Alexander McQueen. Yeah, I was pretty serious then too. Probably more serious than the rest of the stuff. A war?" I waved my hand dismissively. "Pfft, we have those all the time, and there'll always be more. A custom McQueen made for me by the man himself? No, I can't get that again, unless I figure out how Sophie can practice necromancy magic," I mused, my mind going to the friend I hadn't heard from in three days.

Though, to be fair, the only things I'd heard for the past three days were the thundering of Thorne's heart and the soundtrack to crazy sex.

"Maybe it might be a *little* far to break the laws of nature for a dress," I muttered. My eyes went to the faint marks on his neck. "Especially since we've broken more than a few already."

His eyes went dark with the reminder of it. "Or maybe we're just figuring out what nature had designed for us all along."

My brow rose. "Nature designed bloodsucking monsters

and humans with toxic blood designed to fight them just so one of each could become the exception and have a lot of sex and drink that blood?" I asked dryly.

"Essentially," he murmured. "But there's a fuck of a lot more to us than sex and blood."

"Really? I was under the impression there wasn't more to life than sex and blood," I returned.

"Yeah, but you're not living just a life. Neither am I. We're living a death too. And in our death we've got a fuck of a lot more than even nature intended."

I swallowed his words at the same time I did my coffee. "Yeah," I whispered. "Which is why we need the words. Death, mainly. And a lot of other things. Like the war we're still fighting. Like the specifics of your not being dead. And being way stronger than your average human. And your eternity." I tasted the word on my tongue. It seemed so much heavier now that it wasn't my future alone. With another at my side, it seemed like less of a wasteland. More of a minefield, maybe.

Eternity was a long time to spend with Thorne. I reasoned even that would fall short. But it was a long time for one of us to find that eternity cut short. And then facing it alone, the dark wasteland that I had once happily skipped through wearing my favorite pumps? That emptiness was practically the scariest thing, even scarier than kitten heels. Not facing it alone but the memory of the moment, right now, of the other half of my soul being alive.

I swallowed the pure terror that came with that thought to move on.

"And your relationship with Rick." I frowned. "I feel like that explanation needs to be a frontrunner."

Something about their interaction had been nagging at the back of my mind. Something unpleasant about it all. Something that didn't taste right and gave me a sense of foreboding.

I had been acting like a responsible vampire for the past three days and ignoring it.

Foreboding was the quickest way to kill a buzz.

But death was inevitable.

And why did I feel like death wasn't finished with us?

The change in Thorne's demeanor was palpable through our new connection, a wash of icy water and a steel wall battering down over his bones.

"There is no relationship," he clipped, eyes hard. "We've had encounters over the centuries."

I raised my brows. "The *centuries*? And these encounters haven't left either of you dead."

A statement not a question, since he was breathing, heart beating in front of me.

Thank Hades.

Despite the confusion of it all, I was thankful.

"No," he answered stiffly, sipping from his mug. "Although not for lack of trying on both our parts."

I gave him a look. "Honey, I know you. Which means you've likely tried to kill *a lot* of vampires in your time. And until I'd witnessed the exchange between you and Rick, I thought I'd been the only one who survived. Through my womanly wiles and superior fighting skills, obviously, but also because you kind of like having sex with me."

The desire returned, and he yanked me to his body so his lips fastened against my neck. "It's not just havin' sex with you, Isla," he growled. "And it's more than kind of like. I kind of like breathing 'cause it keeps my heart beating. Without it I couldn't be here." His eyes found mine. "Similar to how I feel about what I'm holdin' in my arms. My fuckin' soul."

The emotions rolling through him, and in turn me,

confirmed his sincerity.

"You don't get to alpha male your way out of this with heartfelt declarations. I've been around the block. I know the manly devices you use as evasion tactics. You're not evading this with sex, the thing that makes me the only vampire you've not killed." I paused. "Among other things." Another pause. "You're not fucking Rick too, are you?" I asked seriously. "I don't approve of cheating," I continued. "In fact, I'd likely rip your beating heart from your chest and make you eat it if you cheated on me," I informed him happily and seriously. "But you and Rick would be an interesting and erotic form of foreplay to watch before the main event, the heart ripping."

I wasn't strictly into man-on-man; I was all about people screwing and loving who they wanted, gender, species, whatever. But I didn't think it'd turn me on quite as much as the thought of those two.

Thorne obviously didn't share my feelings, since his body went still and rage flickered through him. "Isla," he growled in warning.

I waved my hand. "I kid, I kid," I muttered. "So if you're not a jilted lover, what are you?"

He stared at me, something in the air, something unpleasant that was new to everything sweet and pleasing that had been there for the past three days.

Or maybe it had always been there and I'd just been ignoring it.

He sighed and ran his hand through his hair in frustration, or nervousness if I wasn't mistaken.

Thorne didn't get nervous.

Ever.

Not even when he'd literally been strung up for execution in front of a roomful of vampires.

There had been rage then. Fear too. Not for himself, for me. Even without the heightened senses that his blood gave me, I could taste it on that horrible day.

But not nerves.

So it had me nervous.

I never got nervous either.

And I had also been strung up for execution once or twice. Or twelve times.

So no nerves.

Until now.

Because his nerves meant something. And the nerves that came with the realization that a witch wielding a curse may have the power to destroy me yet so did the man in front of me.

No magic needed.

Just a mass weapon of destruction.

Some people called it love, I guessed.

"You want to know how I'm here, how I've been here on this earth for longer than you? How I'm considerably harder to kill than any normal human? How I can scar, how I can bleed and my heart can beat but I'm as strong as a vampire with iron skin and a lifeless organ in their chest? How I can have a heart that beats for only one fuckin' woman since I laid eyes on her?"

I blinked. "You're older than me?"

He stared at me. "*That's* what you're focusing on?"

I shrugged. "The other stuff is important too, I guess. It's just I didn't really count on you being the older one in this relationship. I kind of liked being a cougar. I think I pulled it off well. I even bought some leopard skin pumps to go with the entire persona." I waved my hand around my face. "And I was going to audition for *Real Housewives of the Underworld.*"

His mouth twitched slightly, but the seriousness that cloaked an apartment not used to such emotions remained.

"Sorry to burst that bubble, baby, but I've got some centuries on you."

I crossed my arms, unworried about my nakedness. Thorne wasn't worried about his either, but his eyes did move down to my chest area with the movement.

Then lower.

I ignored the pang that came with that hungry gaze and snapped my fingers at him.

"Buddy, eyes on me when talking about your immortality and the centuries you have on me. This look could be considered pedophilia. How many centuries?" I demanded.

His eyes snapped up. "Enough."

I glared. "'Enough' is not something that satisfies me. 'Enough' doesn't exist in my world. No such thing as enough shoes, or bags, or dead bodies of people that piss me off. And you're pissing me right off with this 'enough' crap. Specifics, Thorne. Are we talking about you being around when humans were still in caves and rubbing rocks together to make fire?"

His jaw tightened. "I've been around long enough to watch the Norman Conquest of England. William was a stubborn bastard to work with," he said.

I pursed my lips. "And this isn't something you'd decided to share with me?"

"We've had a lot going on," he commented.

I nodded. "Yeah, we have. But there's been time for you to be like, 'Oh hey, Isla, you know how it's been fucking haunting you, my humanity and mortality? Now you can go back to worrying about jeans becoming accepted as formal wear because it's not a problem since I'm almost a *fucking millennium old!*'" My voice rose to a yell at the end, and I slammed my cup down on the counter with enough force to smash the porcelain and scatter it across the marble countertop.

I frowned at it.

"Great," I hissed. "That was part of a pack of ten they only sell in a small town outside of Florence. I despise odd numbers, so now I either have to smash more, or travel there to convince those fucking monks to make me some more." Stomping over to my cupboards, I snatched one off the shelf. "I do need a trip, but since there's *so much going on*, I'll go with the other option."

Thorne had good enough reflexes to duck when I hurled the mug at him. It smashed on my window instead. The force with which I threw it made the panes vibrate slightly but not break. I'd designed them to withstand some shit since I'd thrown Viktor out the window once and he'd hurtled thirty-eight stories. Paying off the police had been a total bitch, and so had getting the window replaced.

"Jesus, Isla," Thorne muttered, straightening.

I put my hand on my hip, glaring at him. "Nope. Not him. But you should know, since I'm sure you fucking met him and got some of your self-righteousness from the bearded messiah!" I yelled.

He crossed his arms. "You gonna let me explain the rest or you gonna throw more dishware?"

I glared at him. "Oh I'm done with the dishes," I told him calmly. "It's knives next, since I know you're less breakable. I'll just test how much instead of listening." I grabbed one of my sharpest and fondest from the knife block. It cut flanks of steak and demon flesh like a charm.

He gave me a look. "I was going to tell you."

"When? Before or after I died from a curse which you knew was fatal to me?"

His fury was a cloud over the room. "You can't bring that shit up, Isla," he ordered. "Throw all the fuckin' knives you want, but you do not use the image of you lifeless in my arms as a weapon."

I pursed my lips, hating that his words hit me and that I actually regretted what I said, considering the same pain I'd feel if he reminded me of that silence between his heartbeats.

Because I did apologies even less than I did turtlenecks, I stayed silent.

He took my silence as what I meant it for, because apparently he knew me even without this crazy fucking connection.

"Right," he said. "Praseates—a majority of us, at least—are human. Humans who are born and who die. Who are slightly stronger than regular humans, of course, but they can still die with a lot more ease than it takes to kill a vampire. And their lifespans may be a little more than normal, give or take a handful of decades. But just as vampires have bloodlines that are more powerful than others, Praseates have it too. We are a species that is human yet was designed to fight that which is not human. You've got your creation myths that gave you life and an afterlife, right?"

I nodded once. The story of Ambrogio and the gods who made him what he became was learned at Mortimeus, I didn't have fond memories of it mostly because of all the fucking papers I had to write on the asshole and the punishments I got when I wrote "It's a load of bullshit" at the end of each one. It was, in my opinion, a load of bullshit.

Obviously I'd seen a lot since I was alive. And undead. I knew witches existed, magic too, and werewolves and demons.

So I didn't doubt that gods existed.

Not the one those humans in churches worshipped but many who lived on different planes, ones who weren't concerned with humans much more than humans were concerned with the lives of ants.

I found it hard to believe.

Then again, we were immortal bloodsuckers who had superior strength and saw centuries pass like weeks.

I was more of a Darwinist myself. I'm sure old Charlie wasn't thinking of bloodsucking vampires when he made his findings, but they still held up to inspection. Evolution was what we had to thank. Nature, not some jealous god.

But it was only my opinion. Which was almost always right.

But Thorne wasn't finished with story time, his eyes on me yet faraway at the same time.

"We've got our own myth. Our own origin story that we take with a grain of salt. Or a lot of it." His tone said he wasn't as convinced as I was.

Still holding the knife, I wandered to the small bar I had fitted in the kitchen. I had one in almost every room; I didn't want to have to walk all around the apartment when I felt like a drink.

"I'll do you one better than a grain of salt. I'll do a bottle of tequila," I informed him, grabbing the bottle and forgoing the glass to drink straight from it.

Maybe not as couth as a crystal tumbler, but something in the air told me it was not a time to be couth.

This was a time for tequila. And couthness and tequila were never mutually exclusive.

Not for the fun people, anyway.

Thorne watched with that same blankness to his face, but his mouth twitched slightly before he refocused.

"Apollo—or more accurately, his jealousy of a mortal man—was the catalyst for the change that made vampires," he began, surprising me with his knowledge of our origin.

Then again, he'd probably read *Art of War* and knew the whole 'know thy enemy' thing. It made sense. I didn't know shit about slayers. Merely because, until now, I hadn't considered them more than a cardio workout and bags of skin that slowed down my day. I researched the latest trends in heeled shoes and that was about it.

Nor did they teach us anything in Mortimeus about slayers. Apart from that they were something to be killed, sought out for sport. There was even an actual event where our teachers gathered slayers and set them loose for vampires to hunt and kill.

Like softball.

But no, apart from talking about how they were inferior to humans and their blood was toxic, we knew nothing.

Or at least I did.

"His love for a human woman and subsequent wrath at a human man were what possessed him," Thorne continued.

I nodded. "Yeah, he was a jealous asshole who didn't take no for an answer. So instead of sleeping with one of her friends to get back at her, or even killing Ambrogio, which would have been my recommendation, he'd done something that apparently set in motion the events that created the perfection you're currently staring at right now." I gestured down my body with the knife I was still holding. "So I guess I would thank him for being a jealous and wrathful asshole if, you know, he was the actual reason I was here."

Thorne raised a brow. "You don't believe?"

"In Santa Claus?" I asked. "Sure. A fat jolly man who creeps into children's beds at night and empties his sack. Completely believable." I paused, taking a swig. "Not one but *two* gods concerned enough with human matters to create a supernatural being strong enough to fight the gods themselves, counting Artemis?" I shook my head.

Thorne regarded me. "Well, whatever the truth to it, it's

what the basis of my species' creation story exists on. Because this wrathful asshole of a god created vampires, even by accident, out of love for one human and hate for another. Eloes created us out of love for them all. She saw the ravaging of the human race from creatures that could cut them down and drain them with little conflict. Werewolves were concerned with themselves and only fought vampires when the human they drained belonged to them. Witches didn't have enough love for humans to protect them. So it was down to humans themselves. Eloes witnessed a valiant warrior named Caius fight for his village against the vampires, sacrificing his life willingly when he understood the fight was lost and if he did so he might just save his family.

"As he lay dying amongst the ruins of his village, she visited him. His injuries were fatal, and the god did not wish to practice death magic. Instead of offering him life, she offered him safe passage to the underworld and the protection of his sons if they became Praseates. They would have powers that mirrored the courage of their father and life to span across the centuries like the vampires themselves. He agreed."

He paused.

"And so began the line of our race. Rules governing the league were not as sophisticated as any supernatural being because we were not supernatural. Only those with not just the purest of blood but with the same heart of Caius. Humans who wanted to exist within the human life they wished to protect. Somewhat stuck between the two. Some bloodlines were muddied from that very need. Breeding with a 'human' still made Praseates, but the powers waned through the centuries. A few families remained who kept their lines pure."

I tasted everything he said, thought it over carefully. Though I kept the magnitude of my shock to myself considering how much the little story had blown my mind.

"Aristocracy still exists," I muttered. "Within any race or society, the purest bloodlines, the ones with the strength, will always rule. I'm guessing your family must have been some-what of a counterpart to mine?" I asked.

His gaze flickered with the memory of his loss. They'd been slaughtered, his parents. If they were as strong as he said they were, I guessed it was likely an assassination.

He nodded once. "They were," he agreed. "Leaders of each faction are decided by blood."

"And you're the leader of yours," I stated. "Interesting. For a society that abhors creatures that consider blood the basis for everything, your same society structures it around every-thing." My thoughts swam, the room flickering for a minute as a strangeness washed over me. "Blood is life and blood is death," I murmured in a voice that sounded like me yet didn't.

Thorne stilled. "What did you say?"

I blinked. "I don't know, I say a lot of things. Once I even said that I didn't mind a collection from Versace," I babbled, uncomfortable with the words I'd just uttered, at the grim sort of heaviness in the air they'd created. Plus the wave of intensity that came from Thorne as I uttered them made me shiver. I didn't need whatever that was on top of everything else.

So I continued. "That's a great story, really informative. And it explains a little, I guess. But a little is not a lot. I'm all about a lot. So I get you're an aristocrat of your race and likely not set to die soon thanks to the blood and your courage of heart or whatever, but how does Rick enter all of this?"

His eyes hardened and he mused over his answer for a while. I didn't like the pause. I'd experienced the pause. It was something humans did when they were looking for a way to structure words to do the least possible damage, even when the information itself was destruction.

I'd witnessed it but never used it. Me? I was the opposite. I tried to do the most possible damage with the least amount of words possible. Usually following it up with a broken bone or two.

But his pause had me bracing for something akin to a broken bone.

But the break had to wait, as a Scotsman chose that moment to hurtle into the kitchen.

Thorne jumped to attack and I threw my knife on instinct.

Duncan caught it, blade first, grinning. He glanced down to the knife and his bleeding hand that was already healing. Then he looked to Thorne before spending a lot more time gazing at my nakedness. "Now this seems more than a little fun, and I'd hate to be the one to break it up. In fact, I'd like to join."

He ignored Thorne's growl.

"But you two can't hide in here and fuck. We've got a war to win. And if I can't fuck my way through it, neither can you."

And then there was reality.

And reality had this nasty habit of getting in the way of destruction that I'd just dodged.

But destruction would come eventually.

It always did.

FOUR

S O THAT'S HOW WE ENDED UP AT EXTERMIUS, DODGING whatever information would cause the break in order to break something else.

Duncan had apparently been sent by Rick, who was in some location discussing treaties and had ordered Duncan to find intel on the rebellion.

Duncan "got fucking bored as shit doing it alone and reasoned Isla could stop getting orgasms and start killing some fuckers," so he came to retrieve us for the mission.

And, interestingly, Scott.

Who, once again, jumped on me the moment he saw me.

I was so getting a spray bottle and filling it with something that burned the skin off a vampire. I was sure Sophie could fashion something like that for me.

It wasn't like Scott wouldn't heal eventually, and it would

teach him a lesson on how much I didn't approve of his excited displays of affection.

"Yes, I'm glad I'm alive too," I'd hissed, pushing him off. "But don't forget things like the fact that I'm a vampire and so are you, not a teenage girl meeting Justin Bieber for the first time. I will rip those arms off if they keep attaching themselves to me."

I didn't even know why I used that reference. Scott would probably have the same reaction to Justin Bieber himself.

Thorne came because... well, he was Thorne and apparently came with the package.

"Don't you have slayer duties?" I asked.

"Slayer duties involve not letting a rebellion gain traction and murder humans en masse," he replied dryly. "And my specific duties include making sure you don't do anything stupid."

Duncan had barked out a laugh at that. "That's a duty that is impossible. Or will kill you." He paused, still not Thorne's biggest fan by a long shot, so he smiled at the prospect of his death. "But God loves a trier."

Thorne returned the smile with a glower. He wouldn't be sharing beers with Duncan anytime soon.

But to be fair, sharing beers with Duncan meant you first had to watch him drain the bartender. After, of course, he'd poured the drink, because "I'm not pouring my own fuckin' beer."

"What about your annoying little sister?" I'd continued, deciding to make sure they didn't murder each other.

Bringing up the brat might have meant he would remember he had to look out for her and go make sure she wasn't dead or anything.

I liked being with Thorne. Too much, really. But he did try too hard to keep me out of trouble, so I needed the distance, precisely because I didn't want it. Like Scott, I needed to remember I was a vampire. And vampires didn't go around holding hands with their slayer boyfriends while on missions to stop a war between supernatural factions.

And I wanted trouble. Trouble had missed me. "She's surely out there hunting werewolves while wearing bunny slippers or something. Shouldn't you make sure she's still in her cage?" I continued.

I didn't think Thorne had taken my suggestion and put the little cretin behind bars, but one could only hope. She'd managed to escape his compound outside the city, steal an enchanted knife, and then come to the Upper East Side and try to hunt vampires.

I didn't know how old she was, but she hadn't even grown the second set of teeth humans had.

Too young to hunt vampires, but not too young to get killed by them. Not that I cared about her getting killed, but Thorne would, and then it would affect my life.

I'd expected him to react negatively to my attitude about his sister—he was weird like that—but the corner of his mouth tipped up slightly.

"You worried about her?" he asked evenly.

I rolled my eyes. "Well, considering she's almost died like three different times, I'm pretty sure *you* should be concerned that *I'm* the one who saved her those times. Worried about the fact that a vampire, who couldn't care less if she lived or died, just happened to be in the wrong place at the wrong time and is the entire reason she's still breathing, annoying people and shedding teeth like an old person sheds hair."

His mouth twitch turned into a grin. "Yeah, you're worried."

I scowled. "I am not. The only thing I worry about on a

daily basis is if my lipstick is on my fangs. The rest doesn't affect me at all," I lied.

He tilted his chin down and looked at me through the top of his lids. "No, because admitting that you care about a being other than the one you stare at every day in the mirror is a fate worse than death."

I nodded. "Exactly," I agreed.

He'd just shaken his head, yanked me to his chest and kissed my head in a vaguely patronizing gesture that annoyed me.

What annoyed me more was that I let him.

The little cretin was at some slayer safe house with the rest of the small, vulnerable humans.

I'd learned they were much like young vampires in that respect. At their weakest, not likely to survive any full-scale attacks before they came of age.

I got the impression that there was some ceremony to do that, but Thorne had been tight-lipped.

I wasn't exactly curious, unless they sacrificed some virgins or something. They didn't. Thorne had been weirdly horrified when I'd asked and he realized I was serious.

Humans.

Even the improved version like Thorne still had pesky humanity that ruined them from getting to their full potential. Probably why they died more often than vampires.

Then it worried me that humanity might be rubbing off on me.

And just like I'd let Thorne wrap me in his arms and kiss my hair, maybe I'd let that happen too.

I'd sacrifice a virgin to stop that happening.

Or the old Isla would.

Who knew what this Isla would do.

This new Isla was unpredictable. That's why I was glad we were standing outside a bar in which the worst of the worst hung out.

My people.

Which was why Thorne was obviously uneasy. I may have considered murderous sociopathic supernaturals my brethren but he considered them enemies.

I glanced at him. "Babe, you're wearing leather pants and a tee that resembles fishnet stockings. I'd be worried if you *were* comfortable with it. It would mean that someone has replaced my boyfriend with a very realistic doppelgänger, one still very pretty to look at but not one I'd keep around after the dirty deed was done," I told him as my heels clicked along the empty parking lot.

The night was unusually warm for an autumnal New York evening, not that it mattered to me. The sliver of skin showing between my skintight leather skirt and thigh-high PVC boots didn't feel the chill.

Thorne snatched my bare arm. I wasn't wearing a fishnet top like his, merely a bandeau bralet covered in chains and drapery. Though it was part of the costume, I was considering keeping it.

For bedroom purposes, at least.

Or when I felt like eliciting some stares on Wall Street.

Thorne yanked me to his body, the thick ridges of his muscles barely hiding from the world. I rather liked that part of his costume and was definitely contemplating having him keep it.

His eyes seemed to glow in the gritty air of the parking lot, attached to mine with the fevered intensity that had become the norm ever since Sophie uttered the words of my perhaps timely demise.

He had argued tooth and nail about coming here. But I

always got what I wanted.

"Isla," Thorne murmured. He cupped my cheek without the brutal ferocity that had become characteristic of his touch. But something worked behind his eyes, something that told me he was back to when Sophie had met up with us with some new intel not long after Duncan had brought reality back in with him.

Some disturbing intel.

She also brought coffee, which was kickass.

"What do you mean you don't know whether the spell is broken?" Thorne had hissed from beside me.

"I mean that we can't be truly sure until we find the witches and kill them," Sophie replied.

"She had my blood. You said that's the fuckin' cure," he'd thundered.

"Yes but—"

Sophie stopped talking and two sets of eyes settled on me, or rather the cup that had elicited the rough sucking sound interrupting their very serious conversation.

Thorne's murderous glare had transferred to me.

I'd given him an innocent look. "What?" I asked. "That was an iced frap with extra cream, an extra shot, caramel and cinnamon. I had to get the most out of it. It's my duty for women who can't enjoy these and have to substitute with almond milk and sugar-free, happiness-free bullshit. I can't put on weight, so I'm doing it for them, really." I paused. "No, I can't even keep a straight face while saying that. I'm doing it for me, obviously. Fuck those little nitwits."

"Jesus, Isla," he'd seethed. "Can't you be a little more serious about the prospect that the spell that could kill you might not be broken?"

I'd rolled my eyes. "Can't you be a little *less* serious? Come on, this whole 'Isla's life is in danger from some witch bitches with PMS on steroids' is getting old, even to me. *Isla*." I clarified the last part for kicks, like I did for most things.

Thorne's fury had intensified at that point, the taste of it permeating the air. I liked it much better than my iced frap with extra cream, an extra shot, caramel and cinnamon.

His gaze darted to Sophie. "Talk to her," he'd demanded.

She gave me a serious stare. "Yes, Isla, you must under-stand the weight of this situation." She paused. "It's not cara-mel. *Vanilla* is where it's at."

I gaped at her. "Vanilla? Seriously? Could you be any more cliché?"

She'd grinned. "I like vanilla. *Outside* the bedroom, of course." She winked.

Thorne had looked like he might just have steam coming from his ears.

I'd patted his thigh. "Don't explode from rage, honey. I just got this sofa reupholstered."

He'd gaped at me. Then Sophie.

"Oh go find yourself a valium," I muttered. "It's fine. Sophie will find the witches and kill them. Then the only thing we have to worry about is the faction of supernatural elitists who want to enslave the human race and kill both of us before they do so." I paused. "Oh, and my mother. She needs to go above those murderous fanatics. And above Hades himself, if we're getting specific." I waved my hands. "We'll burn that bridge when we come to it. For now, Sabrina, your new awesome and totally fucking terrifying powers will help us out with that, won't they? We need to get some mileage out of them before we figure out how to drain them out so they don't become our biggest problem."

My voice was easy, playful even, but I was as serious as

Birkenstocks on a lesbian. Just because our plates were a little full with wars, spells, and otherworldly sex didn't mean Sophie's problem wasn't at the table. It should've been at the top, but getting hold of the pesky little witch had been like stapling Jell-O to the wall.

She gave me an easy look, much like my voice—normal, sarcastic even to the naked eye. But my eye was not naked. I saw the trouble brewing beneath the surface. "Of course," she said happily. "New mojo makes such a feat pretty easy. I'm just waiting for a specific ingredient for the spell."

"Ingredient?" I asked, screwing my nose. "Can't you just snap your fingers and enchant it into existence?"

"It doesn't really work that way."

I pouted. "Well that's lame. That's how it works in the movies."

She stood, yanking down her black jersey skirt, which had ridden up and exposed the tattoos on her pale and shapely upper thighs.

Thorne's survival skills were on point since he didn't even break his concrete façade or blink in that direction.

Maybe his fury was the reason he wasn't checking out her pins, or he was too focused on glaring at me, or because he saw no woman but me. The last was likely bullshit, or almost certainly bullshit, but it was comforting for my blackened heart.

And meant good things for his to remain in his chest.

"Okay, you go source your eye of newt," I told her. "Or wolfsbane or, even better, wolf heart. We'll wait patiently."

Her eyes, which had flickered weirdly with the mention of wolf heart, changed to disbelief. "Patient? You once almost killed a bartender for taking too long to make a cocktail."

I rolled my eyes. "Once."

"Six times," she countered.

"Who's counting?" I snapped. "Plus it's not exactly patiently. I'm going to a bar tonight to hopefully kill something, or a lot of somethings," I informed her cheerfully.

She grinned. "Make it extra bloody for me."

I grinned back. "Always. Find those witches so I can pencil in a burning at the stake for tomorrow night," I requested. "No offense."

"None taken. I'll bring the marshmallows."

And on that, she was gone.

Thorne's fury was not. He'd been broody since the whole announcement.

Well, *broodier*.

I'd chosen to ignore him and went shopping for the night ahead of us instead. He had to make sure the slayers hadn't burned the place down or tripped over a twig and stabbed themselves with their knives and such. Of course, he didn't specifically say that; he said he had to "check on some shit. Don't get into any fucking trouble while I'm gone." Then he'd kissed me roughly on the mouth and given me a weirdly intense look.

"I can promise I won't go looking for trouble," I told him, though I couldn't keep a straight face. Nor could I lie to him, even about something as simple as that. Which troubled me, since I basically existed on blood, sarcasm, lies, great taste, violence, and sex appeal.

And now Thorne, it seemed.

"No, I can't actually promise that. It would be a boring day otherwise. But I promise I'll limit the trouble to nothing bloody." I paused, screwing up my nose and thinking of how annoying the human race was in general. "Wait, I can't promise that either."

"For fuck's sake, Isla," he muttered.

I smiled at him. "Love you too, honey." I finger-waved at him.

I'd shopped and not killed anyone, which made me kind of broody, but it helped that I came home laden down with bags.

I frowned when I opened the door to Duncan drinking my whisky, lounging on the couch.

Scott was cradling a tumbler of clear liquid, his eyes—well, *eye*—lighting up as I entered the room.

I pointed at him. "I swear to fucking Karl Lagerfeld, if you come near me and try to hug me or even smile, I'll carve out your other eye and I won't even feel bad." It was true at that point. Maybe I'd feel bad later.

Luckily, he didn't make me test that theory.

"And if that's water, I'm throwing you out the window," I informed him, nodding to his glass and dropping my bags at my feet.

"It's vodka," he said quickly.

I nodded once. "That's lucky for you."

I glared at Duncan. "How did you get in?" I asked. "I told the doorman not to let anyone in."

He grinned, showing fang. "I know. He was the entrée."

I groaned. "You killed him? I really hope you cleaned up after yourself."

"I was going to but this one stopped me," he grunted, glaring at Scott.

I gaped at Scott's courage to do such a thing to a Scotsman who had a history of killing someone who even looked at him wrong.

Then again, so did I.

"And Scott's still here, grinning like an idiot?" I asked in amazement.

Duncan rolled his eyes. "Couldn't be arsed killing the little fuck."

I hid my smile. If I didn't know better, Duncan actually liked Scott. He had the knack for making you not want to kill him, only maim him every now and then.

Thorne had stormed in not long after as we began speaking about the night ahead, even broodier than when he'd left.

He'd given me a once-over, not acknowledging Duncan or Scott. "You're not covered in blood," he remarked while crossing the room to snatch me in his arms.

I gave him a look. "I know, I'm upset too," I replied.

Then he'd kissed the utter shit out of me, made me go all weird and girly for a hot second, then poured himself a whisky.

Then we'd planned.

Now we were here.

Actually, he'd taken one look at my outfit and fucked me against the front door of my apartment, made me drink deeply from him and gave me one of the best orgasms ever.

Now we were here.

And my post-orgasm glow was getting seriously dampened by his stupid broodiness. You'd think he'd be more cheerful, considering he had an orgasm too.

I glared at him. "I'm not going to break," I snapped. "I'm still rather durable."

I moved quickly, pushing Thorne backwards so he slammed against a car, my hand circling his neck before he could blink. The dull thump of his pulse under my hand became hypnotic for a second, trying to seduce me as if I hadn't just indulged less than an hour before. Using the willpower that hopefully was going to be enough to keep me alive, I kept my eyes on his and my teeth off his jugular.

"I'm more than capable of handling myself," I murmured.

"Don't you worry your pretty little head over me after some witch put a silly curse on me."

His anger glittered in the air. "Silly?" he gritted out, fingers biting into my hip. "This spell could fuckin' *kill* you," he hissed.

I rolled my eyes. "They tried that once, remember? It's not likely to happen a second time."

His eyes blackened. "No, it's fuckin' not. Not that I'm gonna let that happen. But you're actin' like you're still invincible. You're not. And you want to go in there"—he nodded to the nondescript building across the parking lot—"and risk a life that is the most precious thing I've ever held in my hands. So I'm asking you politely, for once, to go about this without daring death to come and fuckin' snatch you from me."

I regarded him. "Well, if using that many curse words is you asking politely, then I'll comply. But you're going to have to promise me some depraved things later on if I can't do it here," I murmured.

The warmth of his desire replaced the inferno of his fury. "Oh, I can promise that," he rasped then quickly pressed his mouth against mine and firmly took hold of my hand.

"Remember, you can't do the whole alpha male routine in there." I nodded to the building looming in the distance, looking all but dead.

Which it was, if you wanted to get all technical.

I focused on Thorne.

"After Sophie worked her magic, they'll think you're merely a lowly human. One I own. You'll have to do what I say or you might be responsible for blowing our cover and turning the night a lot bloodier." I grinned at the prospect despite my promise, the one I'd only made moments before. But promises were the most fun when you broke them. "Think you can do that?" I asked sweetly.

He glared at me. "Let's go," he growled in response.

I grinned and kept hold of his hand, leading us across the parking lot. The night was still and had an air of foreboding to it. Then again, what night didn't these days?

That's what I loved about this whole war thing. Never a boring night with Netflix and a run-of-the-mill murder.

No, it was always some sort of mass killing spree that would end in blood, explosions, and a lot of death.

Just hopefully not ours.

FIVE

EXTERMIUS WAS A BAR THAT DIDN'T HAVE ANY RULES, regulations or species limit. Anyone and everyone was allowed. Apart from slayers, of course. Humans went in but rarely came out. Parts of them came out, surely, just not alive parts.

The purpose of the bar was for depraved creatures to catch a drink and try to outdo each other's sadistic pleasures.

To see and be seen.

Kill and be killed. Murder of humans was encouraged. Murder of patrons was accepted.

The worst of all of the supernatural creatures, in other words.

Which was why it was the one bar I steered clear of.

"You've been here before?" Thorne asked under his breath as we crossed the parking lot.

"Not lately," I admitted.

Because he was Thorne and seemed to have some sort of Isla radar as to when my story had more to it—granted, almost all of my stories had more to them—he slowed his gait to give me more time to explain.

I knew he wouldn't let it go.

"Okay, I might have been banned for a few hundred years," I said sheepishly. "It's been lifted now."

"You said the most depraved and sadistic of all creatures patronized this place," he remarked.

I nodded.

"And that anything and everything was allowed, that there were no rules."

I nodded again. "Like fight club."

His eyes saw through me. "How the fuck does one get banned from a place with no rules? Isn't such a thing impossible?"

I gave him a look. "Nothing's impossible, just extremely difficult. You do have to work pretty hard at it, but you will achieve it. I'm nothing if not an overachiever."

"Should I even ask how?"

I grinned. "Not if you don't want to get nightmares."

He hardened his jaw and nodded once.

I didn't have time to discuss the semantics of how many demons it actually took for me to blow up the original establishment.

The building showed me that they hadn't gone to huge amounts of effort to improve it, even though a hundred years before it was little more than a shack in a dirty plain outside a growing city.

"Remember," I whispered to Thorne as we approached the steel door, "we can't save the humans in here. Most will likely already be dead. We're here to look at the bigger picture. Few for the many and all that."

Thorne nodded once, but I could taste the way his entire body recoiled against the plan.

The new pesky piece of humanity that was growing inside me did the same thing. It pissed me off, so I banished it do the depths where bad fashion choices and questionable choices in bedmates resided.

The door opened before we could get two feet from it.

A tall and muscled werewolf towered over us, his golden eyes searching us. "Vampire and a human," he mused, his voice thick. "Business?" he barked.

I yanked Thorne to my side, jerking his head back and licking the side of his neck. "Oh you know, just to show my pet here a party." I winked at the wolf. "Maybe if you're a good boy, I'll save you his heart for later on. If there's anything left." I gave him a smile with full fang, my voice devoid of anything resembling humanity. I welcomed it, that twang of sadism that had been nothing more than nature to me during my heyday.

It was much easier to welcome the mindset of a sociopath than that of anything with a conscience.

The wolf grinned, showing a mouth full of sharp, pointed teeth. He stood back, letting us through the door.

I gave him an easy smile and Thorne did his best to look submissive and weak, though his stature and general aura were in direct conflict with that. Luckily I wore sadism as convincingly as I did faux fur, so it counteracted him. It was even convincing me; I didn't feel anything at the slight repulsion that came from Thorne at my demeanor.

I led him through the narrow and dimly lit hallway, the lingering stench of blood, death and cheap whisky.

The cheap whisky offended me the most. We were

immortals, for fuck's sake; we could afford and had access to the good stuff.

We emerged into a wide and cavernous room, and Thorne sucked in a savage breath before steeling himself. I didn't have an outward reaction, though I was simmering with fury and disgust.

My mask of sadism stayed in place, but it obviously didn't go as deep as I first thought.

The room wasn't dark and dimly lit like the hallway. It was bathed in artificial and fluorescent, illuminating the evil in the room.

It was a bar, by the conventional sense of the word. A long silver steel bartop ran down the right-hand edge of the room. Bottles of liquor peppered the wall behind it, but by the smell of the room, it wasn't what the patrons were imbibing in.

Blood was on the night's special.

With a side of death, pain and suffering, naturally.

The edges of the room were framed with booths, though that was where the illusion of civility left. If it was ever there. Cages dangled from the ceiling, scantily clad human women clinging to the bars, emaciated bodies displaying protruding bones and decorated with bruises. Blood trickled from cuts on their wrists and vampires lingered underneath, glasses extended to catch the crimson drips.

Long wooden tables ran down the middle of the room. An obese human male was splayed naked on one, a vampire feasting at his neck while a demon leaned over his mouth, opened in a wordless scream as he sucked out his soul. Werewolves were served hearts on a silver platter in the booth closest to me. A table of vampires lazily refilled their goblets from a woman who was hanging upside down, her throat slit so a pool of blood formed a puddle on the table. Though it veered inwards at the middle so the blood didn't drip off the sides, as if it was designed for that purpose alone.

Wouldn't want to make a mess.

I squared my shoulders and stalked confidently towards the bar, meeting every pair of eyes that turned to face me. I blew a kiss at the demon sucking the soul. He grinned back at me.

I dragged Thorne along with me, not blinking at any of the emotions coursing through him, which luckily didn't show on his face.

A quick scan of the room told me we didn't have an empathy demon in the house, which was good. They'd obviously expect such feelings from Thorne, a human in the snake pit, but the lack of fear would raise some serious red flags. A human without fear was either insane, which the empath would have been able to rule out or trouble.

Small favors and all that.

"Gin and tonic, please," I asked the bartender, flipping my hair. "Hold the tonic."

The young vampire wasn't clad in the trappings of tasteless BDSM castoffs like the waitresses, low-level vampires showing more than they hid in cheaper versions of my outfit.

The young vampire didn't actually look anything resembling a vampire. It wasn't just his slicked-back hair and the simple button-down, fastened around his thin neck. It was something about his aura, which didn't exactly exude low-level.

I shelved that as he nodded. He waited, eyes touching Thorne.

I laughed, realizing he was waiting for me to order Thorne something. "Oh honey, he's not getting a beverage. He *is* the beverage." I winked at him.

A glimmer of something that looked like anger flickered in

the young vampire's eyes before he turned to make my drink.

Interesting.

I leaned my back against the bar, scanning the room for the vampire I was looking for. This was where Earnshaw had met his intermediary. Obviously before I'd killed Earnshaw.

Dante had called me earlier in the day and told me he'd heard whispers about a couple of heavy hitters in the game meeting that night.

He was becoming useful.

Maybe he just wanted to get laid. He'd be in for a cruel surprise when he found out about me and Thorne. Then again, so would I.

My death.

Just because King Rick was strangely now on our side, it didn't mean the rest of the supernatural community would like our renewed relationship status.

I would not get all of the likes if I changed the status on Facebook, nor would they come up with a great nickname for us to rival Bennifer.

Pity. Thisla had a nice ring to it.

But even a rule from the king wouldn't save me from even half of the vampires in the community, and the rest of the supernaturals—who didn't exactly love me in the first place—wouldn't be sending congratulatory blood baskets.

My eyes rested on Duncan's large form, bent over a human woman. He lifted his bloodstained mouth to meet my gaze and gave me a brutal smile.

He lived for this shit.

Then I found Scott, almost unrecognizable. He'd shed his master geek image and transformed so almost I believed he was the vampire who wore seven-thousand-dollar suits with three-hundred-dollar haircuts and brutalized teenage girls like he was currently doing before I locked eyes with him. Well, eye, considering his empty socket was covered with a sleek leather patch that matched his outfit. He actually looked menacing and… almost attractive.

That was until he gave me a decidedly inconspicuous thumbs-up.

I shook my head. "Idiot," I muttered under my breath.

He'd demanded to be part of this 'mission' the moment he'd found out about it.

So there he was, for better or worse, a rabbit in the wolf's den. Though the way he throat-punched a much larger full-blood vampire who tried to cut in on his date for the night had me slightly optimistic at his chances of survival.

They went from nil to about thirty seventy.

As good as he'd ever get in this place.

Hopefully the universe was feeling generous.

But the universe was always a selfish bitch and only idiots relied on selfish bitches—this coming from a selfish bitch herself.

I snatched the drink from the strangely sassy bartender, sipping it as I turned around to inspect the bar, trying to figure out what to do next.

The men had tried to plan further than this but I'd informed them any actual plans they made would be shot to shit by me. I was a 'fly by the seat of my pants' type of girl. Or 'fly by the seat of my leather skirt,' as it were.

Then again, it was that attitude that had me banned and neck-deep in corpses the last time I was here.

"Come, pet," I hissed, dragging Thorne by the belt buckle and sauntering over to a table of vampires, the corpse of a young girl serving as some kind of souvenir.

"Heya, fellas, got room for one more?" I asked sweetly.

I hoped they didn't recognize me. Most vampires who came to these establishments weren't of the higher Vein Lines; classy vampires liked to commit their depravity in much more upmarket establishments with better whisky and silverware.

But then again, I got around—in both senses of the term. I was as infamous in the uncouth circles as I was in the aristocratic ones.

Though if I was honest, I was more comfortable here than I was at any kingly ball. Sure, the sadistic murder did put a damper on the mood, but these monsters walked around without their masks, which was as refreshing as it was disturbing. But their skeletons weren't in their closets amongst thousand-dollar gowns and shoes. No, their skeletons and dead bodies were out for the world to see, scattered at their cheaply shod feet.

You had to admire them for that, at least. And I would. After I killed them.

The main one had decided to fondle the young girl's body in a way that legitimately made my skin crawl and Thorne's body to literally vibrate with disgust and fury to such an extent I thought he might break his cover. I didn't break my glare at that one, with a bald head and unfortunate skull shape. He was watching me with eyes too small for his weird-shaped head, angular cheekbones making him look like a skeleton. Outside a closet. He wasn't a dumb skeleton nor sadist, though. Not many of these psychopaths were. It was ironic, really, that the ones who committed the most inhuman acts were probably those most in touch with human, and inhuman, nature.

Hence why I didn't spare Thorne a glance. Such an action, no matter how small, would give them an inkling that I thought of him as anything more than a blood bag.

Which was why I didn't blink at what he was doing to the body.

He was doing it because there was a sick sort of enjoy-ment, obviously. It wasn't a candy bar in his pocket—but it was a test. Likely used before to weed out any weaker vampire. Or expose a spy.

I was a lot of things, a lot of wonderful things and depraved things. A weaker *anything*, I was not.

So I kept his eyes and kept my humanity, however small it was, buried in my own skeleton-filled closet.

Thorne did the same.

Lucky for both of us.

"Sure," the vampire said finally, his voice curling with a thick Boston accent. "We've always got room for a specimen so... delicious."

I grinned initially because I thought they were talking about me—I *was* a delicious specimen. But I hid my frown well when I realized they were talking about Thorne.

That pissed me off, though not for the sake of vanity—I didn't need a corpse-fondling, weird-skull-shaped psychopath to tell me I was delicious. I only needed one man with a human heartbeat who was currently getting eyed up by the aforemen-tioned psychopath to tell me that.

I slid smoothly into the booth anyway, yanking Thorne down first so I sat on his knee.

I made the gesture look derogatory instead of like he was the one in control. I smiled at the vampires.

"I like to multipurpose my meals," I stated. "I'm not a fan of nylon booths. They're sticky." I screwed up my nose.

The bald-headed vampire crossed his leg, inspecting me.

"What's your name, sweetness?"

Again, he wasn't talking to me.

Thorne stiffened, but thankfully they took the gesture as fear and not the fury it was. Not as perceptive of the human condition as they could've been. That and Thorne was exceptional at hiding his emotions.

I patted his cheek with what someone might call a slap, or a punch, but that someone wasn't a pissed-off female vampire so it was fine. "Oh, he doesn't speak," I said airily. "I cut his tongue out. You know, those humans with the big muscles and broody stares, always trying to alpha their way out and into things." I gave the men around the table a pointed stare. "And I needed to make sure he knew who was boss."

My words were carefully chosen. The vampires around the table, save for Weird Skull, were all younger and weaker than me. Which was the reason for the particularly brutal actions this girl obviously had to endure before her death. The weakest of us all always tried to hide that by committing atrocities disguised as strength.

They needed to know I was stronger, and that I wasn't afraid to let them know that.

In the form of ripping some heads off if need be. I decided it would be the sandy-haired vampire across from me wearing a cheap suit and too much aftershave.

There was no excuse for poor tailoring.

The silence was heavy at the table before Weird Skull nodded once.

"Admirable. These humans are prone to too much chatter. And begging. I prefer to crush the windpipe," he remarked.

I nodded in approval. "Works too. But sometimes they can't breathe and then they die too quickly. I'm all about delayed gratification." I grinned, hoping no one wanted to see the tongueless wonder.

No matter how much alpha bullshit Thorne uttered, I'd never cut out his tongue. He was far too good with it when he was using it for evil and not for good.

And I kind of loved him, I guessed.

Weird Skull grinned, abandoning his fondling to sip from the glass of blood in front of him.

"Indeed," he muttered. He nodded to his friends, dressed in cheaper and more ill-fitting suits. One actually had on a red polyester shirt underneath, which made me even more excited to kill him later. "This is Lukas, Stefan, and Jakob."

He returned his gaze to me, though not before it flickered hungrily over Thorne once more.

I gripped my now-empty glass tightly.

"And I'm Orpheus," he said smoothly.

Totally fake name, considering the Greek origin of such a name and his accent. Then again, his accent was likely fake too.

"Weird Skull is so much better," I murmured.

His brows narrowed. "What?"

I grinned at him. "Isla, cursed to make your acquaintance," I said instead.

He perused me, eyes going over the red hair that was piled messily at my head.

I could have lied and made up a name. But I'd worked hard at dragging my reputation through the gutter for four hundred years, so I'd totally risk a bloodbath at having him recognize it. A bloodbath was coming either way, anyway.

"Isla," he repeated, tasting the name on his lips and deciding whether it was going to be instant or delayed gratification.

I leaned forward to snatch the glass from his grip, casually bringing it to my lips and preparing to drink. That was before the waves of Thorne's revulsion made my stomach turn and rile so violently it was almost as if the reaction was my own.

I didn't outwardly react, or even pause. I continued to bring the glass upwards and pretended to drink, even though the blood that stained my lips repulsed me. Which was strange,

even considering I'd had a healthy snack on Thorne's blood earlier that night.

A vampire with blood was rather like a Labrador with,
well, anything. You couldn't really get enough or get 'full.'

But I reasoned the connection I'd mostly enjoyed as a side
effect from the blood was the reason. And some of that pesky
humanity escaping from my skeleton-filled closet. I guessed it
wasn't hard; the thing was a walk-in and it was still overflowing.

The vampires luckily didn't notice me faking it—men
never did—as I demurely wiped the blood off my lips with the
back of my thumb, idly smearing it on Thorne's chest.

I hated myself a little at that moment, using every ounce of
my mental strength to block Thorne's reaction.

"Happy to have you at our table, Isla and alpha," Orpheus
said finally.

I smiled back, showing fang. "Oh, we're happy to be here."

Delayed gratification it was.

The blood would come.

It always did.

The evening passed completely and utterly unpleasantly for the
next hour. I had to play evil and go with the conversation, all
the while demeaning Thorne enough to play my part and yet
making sure no one drew his blood.

That's where Sophie's little spell would fail. The vampires
would smell the truth in the blood immediately.

Wasn't that always the case?

It was likely in the blood that we'd find the truth tonight,
but I first had to find the right one to keep and torture before I
killed the rest.

That was Scott's and Duncan's jobs too, to idly and subtly ask questions about the revolution without sounding like spies.

"Anyone got any fuckin' idea where I can join this rebellion that's brewing? I always like to be on the bloodiest side of the fight, and that king sounds like a right tosser," Duncan's voice boomed over the crowd, though it wasn't hard since he was yelling. "And lording it over these measly ants is preferable too," he continued, squeezing his human so she elicited a painful squeak.

Duncan's version of subtle was brazen crassness, which worked exactly as it should—who would believe a spy would be dense and bold enough to walk into a bar full of enemies and shout so?

A single moment of silence followed Duncan's question, and then the steady hum of conversations from supernaturals and whimpers of pain by their human counterparts returned. I watched a couple demons size Duncan up before sauntering up to him.

Success.

Scott had disappeared at some point. I really hoped the little idiot hadn't gone and got himself killed, or in need of saving.

Damsels didn't get saved here. They got drained.

Orpheus's eyes had been on Duncan. "Idiotic," he muttered.

I followed his eyes. "Oh yes, the way he's draining her, hardly effective," I commented on the human tucked roughly into Duncan's arm, deliberately misconstruing his meaning.

I knew Duncan had less problems than me with killing innocents—he was a hitman for hire, after all—but I also knew that he would most likely try to get the human out unscathed if he could.

He'd likely drain her himself if he couldn't, but the thought was there.

"No," Orpheus scoffed, glancing back to the table. "Declaring so publically his allegiance. Even here, there are those who sympathize with the monarchy, who would wish to remain in the shadows."

"Well, the lighting is much more favorable on unfortunate skulls in the shadows," I returned, grinning.

He gave me a quizzical look at the insult, but I continued before he could figure it out. "Yes, I do agree. For such a revolution to be successful it must remain where we've been undutifully banished—the shadows. Until the last moment, at least, and then emerging as a force that will overwhelm the enemy so no chance can be given to the traitors."

I leaned back, circling Thorne's neck and licking down the side of his jaw, brushing it with my fangs but being careful not to puncture the skin. I glanced back up to the rapt and hungry eyes on me. "But that's just my two cents. It's not like I'm sitting at the naughty table to give war advice. Just wishful thinking."

He gave me a long probing look. "You have interest in overthrowing the monarchy?"

I shrugged. "Crowns are made as accessories, not weapons to sit on the heads of weak vampires governing our race. And humans don't deserve to even *think* they rule the world, even though we know they do not. That's not good enough. They need to *know* they don't." I smiled. "They need to know their place, which is beneath us."

I gave Thorne a pointed look. "Before we drain them, of course."

Orpheus continued to gaze at me.

The look told me I had the right man.

I just had to play it right.

"And it's between fashion weeks, so I've got some free time," I added. I stood, dragging Thorne with me. "I'm going to hit the little girls' room, and hit him hard." I trailed my finger-nail along Thorne's taut bicep. "I'm into sharing my meals, but not into sharing my orgasms." I winked. "But you're welcome to play after he's done and drained. We can talk about this more when I'm less… pent-up."

A fresh wave of Thorne's fury washed through me at the sickening gazes I got from the less well-dressed vampires at the table. Interestingly, the fury at my talking of orgasms and the leers I got with that was on par with watching the brutality of the human race before us.

So he didn't like that. I'd store that for later.

Orpheus nodded once. "Oh yes, I'll take you up on both of your offers once you return." His eyes hungrily roved over Thorne in a way that I did not like.

At all.

My own fury found its head. Only I could look at Thorne like that. Yet another reason to make his death slow.

I winked at him. "Sounds like a plan."

Then I dragged Thorne along with me, not even glancing at the death and despair being dealt around me.

I registered it, though. The total number of humans in the place: seven alive and able to leave that way, three too far gone. And six already dead.

Six demons. Ten werewolves. Fourteen vampires. Eight witches.

And a partridge in a pear tree.

Not really a challenge, especially with me feeling more than on top of my game and with Thorne, plus Duncan. Scott would likely trip over a corpse and stab out his other eye.

Hopefully he'd kill a demon or two while he did so.

The bathrooms were separated individually for purposes exactly like I'd explained, moans of pleasure and screams of pain coming from behind the closed doors.

I didn't slow my gait. Nor risk even a glance at Thorne.

One door at the end of the dimly lit and red carpeted hall was open.

I closed it firmly behind us, locking it and registering the room. It had a cubicle for the facilities, a small rickshaw bed with bloodied handcuffs attached and a very cheerful piece of artwork on the wall depicting the Devil rising from the underworld and feasting on children.

I took out the small crystal Sophie had given me before she left and crushed it in my hands. The blood that came from the shards mixed with the magic she'd encased inside to enshroud the room in a slight fog that would work like magical soundproofing for the next ten minutes or so.

"Okay, we're good," I said to Thorne, deciding not to meet his eyes and see myself, three hundred years before, reflected in them. Not wanting to see his reaction to my truest self in his eyes.

We had a job to do.

Killing came first.

The rest could come later.

Or leave later.

"We've got the right guy in Weird Skull. Though I think there're a few lowlifes to pick from if we feel the urge. I think it's best to get someone who's the highest up we can find. They'll know more and I won't have to get the blood of insignificant lackeys under my nails. It's so hard to get—"

I was cut off by Thorne advancing, then pouncing on me. It was the first time he'd well and truly caught me by surprise, mainly because I'd been studiously intent on the children-killing painting. His mouth met mine and hands tore into my hair with ferocity that I hadn't even imagined.

And I was pretty good at imagining ferocity.

The kiss sent all the emotions, his and mine, that I'd been shielding myself from rushing back in. Like a waterfall, they showered over me.

I couldn't even distinguish Thorne's from mine, nor properly catalogue them. There was only one that mattered, anyway.

Need.

He lifted me easily and my legs wrapped around his waist without hesitation, never breaking the kiss. He didn't go for the bed, slamming me brutally against the wall instead, so hard the plaster cracked and the painting beside me went crumbling to the ground.

I barely noticed.

My attention was on Thorne's hand supporting my ass while the other ripped my panties off.

I let him take all the control, the control I'd snatched from him all night. Or pretended to, at least.

My nails scratched at his back, catching myself at the last moment from drawing blood. Though that was all I ached to do.

That was all every single one of my instincts screamed at me to do.

But they were silenced when Thorne slammed into me so hard my head smacked against the plastering, cracking it further.

The plaster or my head, I wasn't sure. I didn't care.

Thorne filled me with his warmth and his love, combined with his disgust and anger, all accumulating to the most angry, violent and delicious sex I'd had in… ever.

That was a mean feat considering I'd had a lot of good angry, violent sex over the centuries.

The great stuff was only in the past few months, and exclusively with Thorne.

But this topped them all. I screamed my climax into his kiss as his body tightened around me before he gave me all of his release.

His forehead rested against mine while he was still inside me, eyes on me. And it was another one of those moments, ones I shared exclusively with Thorne, where the world fell away, as did time itself, and we slipped into one of those crevices reserved for secret lovers.

And then we climbed out.

Or more like clawed our way out.

Thorne's mouth pressed to mine for a closed-mouth kiss before he slipped out of me and set me on unsteady feet.

I blinked rapidly as he fixed himself and then me, pulling my skirt down with incredible tenderness, which had been absent before.

"Not that that wasn't…."

Thorne's eyes darkened, telling me it was exactly the same for him. Thankfully, so I didn't have to find the words.

"We were meant to use this time, and that spell, for planning on what we were going to do next. Not that I ever like doing what I'm meant to do. I despise it, actually. And plans. And kitten heels," I added as an afterthought. "But we might need one. A plan, not a kitten heel. No situation calls for that. A plan, maybe, in this one."

Thorne clenched his fist, fingering the blade at his waist that was hidden by a glamour that would likely fade in the next hour or so.

His eyes glowed with something, an emptiness that impressed me. "Oh I've got a plan. We kill them all."

It was such a reverent promise that I was silent for a moment.

Then I grinned. "Sounds like the perfect date to me."

SIX

WE RETURNED TO THE TABLE, ME SANS PANTIES BUT thoroughly satisfied. The scent of sex had cut through the blood and destruction in the room, so we had caught more than a few eyes on the return walk.

Not that sex hadn't already permeated the air, but even I recognized now that whatever we had was more. It was a lot more.

And it was noticed.

Luckily not for what it was.

But for something.

"Not-so-gentlemen," I greeted the vampires at the table.

That time I slid into the seat, leaving Thorne standing.

I grinned at Orpheus. "I don't think he can physically sit after what I just did. But we don't need him for that at the moment anyway. He'll just stand there like a good little pet until we need him. Promises, after all. And I always keep them," I lied. "And he's all yours once we discuss... other matters," I purred.

His hungry eyes flickered over Thorne with a warm malice that sparked a fire of rage within me.

I knew Thorne could, and would, defend himself, but I felt a visceral need to do that too. Protect him. Us. Anything that threatened to bring back that silence that wasn't the thundering of his heartbeat.

"Oh I think that arrangement is more than satisfactory," Orpheus said, focusing on me.

I leaned back in the uncomfortable chair. "Of course, that only stands if I'm talking to someone who is more than a lapdog." My eyes flickered over the cheap suits. "I've already got one of those, plus a pet werewolf chained up at home. My taste in associates is like my taste in shoes—expensive. Meaning I want someone who is going to give me more bang for my buck. You know, get me in with the right people so I can kill some things that actually *matter*. I'm a classy girl, no mediocre blood bar bombing for me."

Orpheus monitored my words and the easy confidence I said them with. "Well, you're in luck. Some race traitor Rominskitoff bitch is rumored to have taken out one of our top corporals, and fathers. I've been promoted, which means you're talking to someone expensive," he said proudly.

Oh I loved how arrogance and pride always overrode intelligence and basic survival instincts.

I trailed my fingers around a forgotten glass of blood. "Father?" I asked with faux confusion. "I thought this was a war, not a breeding ground. Children are mighty breakable in their first twenty years. I may like delayed gratification in my meals, but I don't like it in my vengeance."

I needed to push him enough to make sure he knew about

the hybrids. That would mean he likely knew enough to take me to the next player of the game, which would hopefully be a member of my family.

I was almost certain that they were in on this, and I had more than a little renewed bloodlust for my Satanic mother after she'd organized my execution last week.

Turnabout was fair play. Though Rick may have saved me from direct execution by an angry mob with his new ruling, their pitchforks would be flaming if I killed any member of my family without proof. Even the king couldn't save me then.

Not that I wanted anyone, king or slayer lover, to save me. I was responsible for that particular job. I'd saved them a lot more than they'd saved me.

Plus, my parents were already expecting an attack from me considering that before my mother ordered my execution, they'd promised to imprison and rape me on the occasion of my second Awakening to ensure there was another Rominskitoff heir that they could rip from my—most likely *really*—dead arms and raise to be like any of these people in this room.

My family was what one would call 'dysfunctional.'

I planned on killing them all when the time came. I just had to put in the legwork first.

Orpheus's laugh brought me into the present. "No, we're not talking about children. We're talking about a new weapon we're building in order to give us everything we need to win this war," he stated.

I waited for more, but he merely stared at me.

"I'm not growing old here, but I am growing bored," I said with impatience. "You going to fill me in on this new and great weapon? Because if I have to guess, I'd start by telling you that I'm a *Star Wars* geek, and then my guess would be the Death Star, which would most likely be inappropriate in this context. Plus, not exactly the greatest of all weapons because it had a nifty little flaw that stopped all that delicious death and destruction."

Orpheus's mouth twitched. I was pissing him off. Good. People tended to be more chatty right before they planned on murdering someone. It's like they learned nothing from the movies.

"It's not something I'm going to utter in a crowded bar to a vampire I've only just met. You must be vetted by our witch, who is more powerful than you can imagine. She can see your true intentions and potential. Then John will decide whether you're worthy to be in the cause. If not, he'll kill you for being too weak and knowing too much or being a spy."

I grinned. "Sounds perfect. When do we see the witch?"

A spark of excitement had me giving some real pep to the smile. The witch could be one of the *Hocus Pocus* bitches, and then I'd get to kill some birds with the same dagger. Spell and helping to quell a war. Score one for Isla.

"You see her when I can contact her. After you give your part of the agreement."

His eyes left mine and went to the edge of the table where my slayer had been standing silent and sentinel.

"Of course." I nodded, yanking Thorne's wrist so he slammed into the table. "But just to be clear, you have a direct line to the witch herself? As in a way of contacting her?"

His eyes were on Thorne. "Yes, of course. Like I said, I'm expensive."

I shook my head. "Stupid male fucking arrogance," I muttered.

Then the killing began.

We didn't have an organized signal with Duncan and Scott—who had just appeared, looking still undead as he had been before—but Thorne plunging his dagger into the throat of red shirt guy was signal enough.

I pouted at him. "I wanted to be the one to kill someone wearing polyester, and not as part of a costume." I sulked as I quickly broke Orpheus's neck so we could save him for later.

I made it so only a couple of vertebrae kept his head attached.

"Stay," I ordered the twitching corpse.

Duncan had let out a yelp and said, "Let's make this a fuckin' *party*!" Then he threw his human bodily at the bartender, who surprisingly caught her and put her out of harm's way, before he started ripping off the heads of demons.

Thorne had already killed the other one at the table. He jerked up at the same time as me.

He threw his blade into the skull of a vampire about to rip into Scott, who was too busy fighting a demon to notice.

I glared at him. "You're all about saving damsels," I muttered.

Then, out of frustration more than necessity, I ripped the heart out from a passing werewolf.

The fight was bloody enough, but like most cowards, the clientele that weren't part of the revolution didn't stay for a fight.

They scattered quickly and I let most escape, mostly because I couldn't be bothered running in this skirt. I did want to be able to wear it again if I could. The ones I did kill were the ones trying to drag half-dead humans with them.

Duncan was fighting two demons off while Thorne yanked his blade out of a vampire, grinning with a fire in his eyes that reveled the warrior inside him. Or the monster.

My own monster responded to his.

He took a hit and the crunch of bone at his collarbone

straightened my spine, my monster roaring in protest. I was about to delimb the demon responsible, but Thorne used his good arm to block another blow and slam a blade into its temple.

The battle was still going but I sensed the two men had it covered.

As much as I would've liked to stay and show them how I could out-kill both of them, we were on a time crunch.

Weird Skull's bones were knitting back together. We had to get him down to the dungeon before he woke and I had to repeat the process all over again.

I snapped the neck of a vampire trying to go for Thorne's throat, slowing him. Thorne glanced down at the corpse after killing the demon that had distracted him in the first place. Then up to me, his eyes wild.

"I'll let you take care of that one, ensure your masculinity stays in place." I yanked Weird Skull out of the booth and hoisted him over my shoulder. "I'll be downstairs torturing him for information. Have fun with the rest of the killing, honey," I said sweetly, blowing him a kiss.

He shook his head with a twitching mouth as his fist came into contact with a warlock attempting to utter a spell. A broken jaw was the quickest way to shut him up.

"Only torture," he ordered. "Don't get fancy or reckless."

"Sure," I muttered over my shoulder, snatching Scott by the collar so he missed a deathblow from a morphed werewolf.

"Fancy and reckless are kind of my best character traits, so it's technically his fault for not registering that," I said while dragging Scott along. "You can help with the torture, maybe learn a few things," I told him while I kicked down the door leading to the dungeon.

It wasn't locked, but I thought the whole kicking it in thing seemed more suited to the situation… and my outfit.

We made it down to the dungeon to see it was already occupied. The vampire who was feasting on the graying man in chains was as surprised to see us as we were to see him.

"You should have put a sock on the door or something, dude," I informed him.

I had thought anyone down in the dank room would've heard the battle above but, although their soundproofing may have sucked upstairs, here you could only hear the screams if you really craned your ears, even with vampire hearing.

I nodded to the vampire, who'd jumped from its almost drained corpse.

"Take care of that, will you?" I asked Scott, my package starting to twitch with telltale signs of waking up.

I turned to the other wall where two sets of manacles lay empty.

I didn't watch to see if Scott failed in subduing the vampire, concentrating on my own task and letting the other people around me either die or succeed.

Scott appeared beside me, stained with blood but undead enough to help me chain Orpheus to the wall. I added my very own accessory, a copper dagger I plunged through his heart, almost fatally.

It was just enough to act as somewhat of a wake-up call as he snapped his abnormally shaped head up and screamed in pain.

I stepped back, crossing my arms and smiling at the grimacing vampire.

"Well, good morning, sunshine," I greeted.

He blinked once, twice. Then his glance went down to his chest. He was smart enough to register the copper blade that stopped him from struggling. The white-hot pain he'd likely be feeling would've been an indicator too.

His eyes met mine, swimming with such pure hatred and rage it tickled me more than a little pink that I hadn't lost my touch at creating such glares. "You race traitor whore," he spat.

I grinned. "So many people keep saying that to me. I think I'll put it on a T-shirt. Or my number plate."

I yanked out the blade that I'd snatched off Thorne at the last minute, reasoning he'd be able to handle himself without it.

He and Duncan were having a much too easy time up there. I wanted to keep him on his toes.

And I'd wanted the blade for selfish reasons.

The pain that radiated through my palm while holding it wasn't a picnic, but I handled it.

Much better than the little bitch in front of me.

I scowled. "You're whimpering over a little copper to the heart? Come on, dude, that's just embarrassing," I said, stepping forward.

His eyes followed my movements before settling on the blade, the low hum it was emanating causing him to register what exactly it was.

Pure fear decorated his unpleasant face before he masked it with false bravado. "I'm not telling you a fucking thing," he lied as the blade trailed closer to his cheekbone.

I grinned. "Oh you will, but I hope you let me have some fun first. It's been a while since I tortured an asshole, and I'd really like to get my hand back in."

Then there wasn't much talking, only screaming.

After the screaming came the talking.

His breath came in long strangled pants, blood dripping from between his lips.

The fact that he was using the mouth to breathe when he didn't rightly have to meant I was doing my job correctly.

"Please," he choked through his grimace of pain. "That's all I know, I swear."

I tilted my head, regarding his broken body that, thanks to my little dagger, hadn't healed. Wounds that would kill a human, certainly. Agony would be a pitiful word to describe what kind of pain he was in. You couldn't lie through that.

"I believe you," I said.

He had given me more than I'd hoped for, which arguably wasn't much. But now I knew the location of the witch in question and how to contact her. Plus some more info on whoever headed this operation and some of his recruiters who had been responsible for what's-his-name's promotion, and unwittingly, his death. They should have been thanking me, really. You don't want someone working for you who holds up so poorly under torture.

He blinked, hope glimmering through those pain-drenched irises that usually watched others suffer. "You do?"

I nodded, checking my nails and frowning at the small chip on my ring finger. All these bloodbaths were wreaking havoc on my manicures. It was upsetting.

"So y-you'll let me go?" he asked hopefully.

I smiled at him, forgetting my manicure for the time being and making a mental note to invest in a beauty company when I got back to the office so I could go about creating that Deathless polish that would never chip. 'Holds well even under the most trying of tortures' was the working slogan. "Of course."

The glimmer turned into something close enough to grasp. "Really?" he whispered.

I rolled my eyes, moving forward in a lithe blur of movement, making short work of detaching his head and laying it at my well-heeled feet. "No," I said to his corpse. "Of course not."

I glanced to Scott, who had been watching the entire thing with an impassive gaze. Interesting, really, since I honestly thought he'd go all… Scott-like and respond to the torture even worse than the dude I was torturing and faint or something equally ridiculous. But he was calm, like he was watching *Real Housewives* or something. It was great.

Maybe he wasn't a lost cause.

"Really? Fuck. I'm losing my touch. Who do these vampires think I am? Mother fucking Teresa?" I shook my head. "I blame movies. Too much mercy and not enough blood." I paused. "And that stupid emotion that seems to translate between species."

Scott looked down with his one working eye. "What? Fear?"

I rolled my eyes. "Vampires don't feel fear," I contradicted him. "At least not the really awesome ones, present company included." I paused. "I'm meaning me as present company, not you. You'd likely be scared of a human with PMS." I thought on it. "Though, Sophie on the rag is homicidal. And not figuratively either." I smiled at the reminder that her time of the month was coming up. More killing. Great.

I strolled around the dank dungeon. "No, not fear. I'm talking about hope. That's what killed him. And that's what'll kill us all if we're not careful. If we hope idiotic things about creatures who will never change, that nature will ever change. Because it won't. What's set in stone is that I'm eternally beautiful and that nature will always conquer all. Not love. Not hope. Not friendship or rainbows or unicorns. Just the bitch they call Mother Nature. And her form of PMS makes Sophie's look like a toddler tantrum."

"So you're saying there's no hope?" Scott asked, that naivety back in his voice.

I rolled my eyes. "That Lindsay Lohan might get her shit together and win an Oscar? No, likely not. There's no hope in our world, Scotty. Only death. And blood. And that idiot should have known exactly that." I eyed him. "Promise me if you're getting tortured you won't turn as quickly as he did." I nodded to the headless corpse.

He nodded once. "I'll do you proud."

"I do doubt that, but I appreciate the sentiment."

I noted a thundering heartbeat and turned to see Thorne descend the last stair.

"Great timing," I said, clapping my bloodstained hands and ignoring the lance of pain that came with the motion considering I was still holding Thorne's blade. "I'm all done here. How was the battle? Did you do anything I wouldn't do? That's leave survivors, if anyone's wondering. Because I wouldn't do that."

I watched Thorne approach in much the same way he watched me, searching his body for injury. He was covered in a fair amount of blood, only a miniscule amount of which was his. The crunch of bone I'd heard earlier, signifying a dislocated collarbone, seemed to have healed, as he was holding his muscled arms in a rather normal way.

The sweet ambrosia coming from the shallow cut on his cheek called to me like a pair of Manolos at Barneys.

Other than that, he was unharmed, which had my psyche relaxing slightly.

His own jaw slackened only slightly as he came to stop in front of me, glaring down at my hands before snatching the blade from it.

"Fuck, Isla," he growled, sheathing it in his belt and grabbing my hands to turn them palm up.

I frowned as he did so, eyeing the slightly singed and blackened skin that was a result of holding the knife.

"What have I done now? Apart from all the work while you two were up there having all the fun. So I stole your little knife. I knew you'd be fine without it, and honestly you don't deserve to have it if you can't hold onto it."

Thorne covered my hands with his own, glaring at me. "I don't give a fuck about the fuckin' knife, Isla," he clipped. "I give a fuck that you are literally singeing your fuckin' palms and hurting yourself in order to use it."

I rolled my eyes. "It's a little pain and it's totally worth it. I've lived through worse." I paused. "And died through it too."

I tried to take back my hands but Thorne's grip was firm.

"You're not to use it again for reasons like this shit. I'm not having you hurt yourself unnecessarily."

"I'll hurt myself whenever I like. That's my prerogative as a cold-blooded female. And a feminist. Now give me back my hands," I demanded.

His gaze was unwavering, as if there weren't two other vampires—three if you counted the headless corpse—witnessing this exchange. "No, babe, you said I don't deserve having something if I can't hold onto it. So I'm holdin' on. Forever."

I blinked at him. Once, twice.

Only he could say things that made me feel all blossomy on the inside after torturing a vampire and him killing a nightclub full of creatures. Evil ones, to be sure, but still.

"Jesus, are we in a fuckin' Rachel McAdams movie?" Duncan groaned.

I didn't miss a beat, nor did I lose eye contact with Thorne as I yanked one of my hands from his grip, drew the knife from his belt and threw it in Duncan's direction.

The mutter of curses in Gaelic told me it'd found its home.

"I consider that necessary," I said.

"I'll allow that one, babe."

SEVEN

"I DON'T LIKE THIS."

I rolled my eyes. "You are aware that you sound like a total broken record. You uttered much the same thing tonight. Approximately three hours ago. And in that same raspy tone," I replied to Thorne, shrugging on my bright red dress and abandoning the S&M chic I'd been donning.

I glanced down at the pile on my closet floor regretfully. It had been ruined with the fight and couldn't be used for the bedroom activities I had planned for it.

I got to have sex in it, look amazing and kill some things in it, though. An outfit well worn, I thought.

Thorne's eyes followed me with a dark desire that had me craving him and a repeat performance of the bathroom act as I shrugged it on.

"You shouldn't be going," he clipped.

"And people over the age of fifty shouldn't be wearing skinny jeans, but it happens. We just have to deal," I snapped, slipping into my Jimmy Choo mules.

"You shouldn't be going alone," he continued.

I rolled my eyes. "I don't need a babysitter. I've gotten on fine enough for the past five hundred years."

He raised his brow. "You didn't have a fuckin' curse on you for those five hundred years, and from what I've heard, 'fine' is not enough of a description to how you got along. You started at least one civil war."

I frowned at him. "Did Sophie tell you that? Bitch. She was partly to blame for that too." He didn't answer, so I moved to the mirror to wipe an errant splatter of blood from my chest. "I may or *may not* still have the curse on me, and I like the odds. They're at least fifty percent in my favor," I corrected.

His eyes narrowed. "And fifty percent too fuckin' much towards your demise," he growled.

I snapped on a gold choker so the thin chain hanging from it skimmed down my breasts, a tiny small golden and diamond dagger finishing between my cleavage.

"You're such a 'blood bag half empty' kind of guy, Thorne," I sighed. "Look on the dark side: we killed a lot of assholes in the rebellion tonight, got some info which Duncan is relaying back to our almightily ruler and I get to wear my new mules." I grinned. "Not bad for a Tuesday."

He didn't. "Except for the small matter of the curse."

I rolled my eyes. "Broken record," I muttered. "So concerned with curses and death and other such boring things."

I ignored his glare, snatching a clutch from a cubby in the wall where each bag enjoyed a little home of its own. I may have been questionably cruel to humans, and vampires and werewolves, but I made sure to treat my bags with kindness. It was only fair.

"Witchy wasn't clear on the deets of this curse you're still so concerned with. Which is why I'm getting them. And a much-needed drink. You should be glad. We'll likely be rid of this witch shit before the week is out. Then we can focus on fighting a war and making sure no errant vampires who are trying to assassinate one or both of us are hiding in the shadows," I informed him cheerfully.

Thorne's face appeared in the mirror behind me, his gaze fastening on me in the reflective surface. His hands settled at my hips, yanking me into his unfortunately clothed body.

His outfit had fared even worse than mine, though I guessed he did considerably more of the fighting than me. That's why I preferred simple old torture; it ripped less wardrobe items and once you'd perfected it, there were hardly any bloodstains.

"I should be there," he rumbled.

I kept eye contact. "No, you shouldn't, considering the bar where I'm meeting Sophie is full of supernatural creatures who would flay you as soon as look at you. And not in the good way."

He eyed me. "There's a good way to be flayed?"

I grinned. "Of course."

It mixed through us, the sexual promise of the shared look in the reflective surface. His hands tightened at my hips, the sweet musky scent of desire floating in the air as he yanked me back to nuzzle on my neck.

I rolled my head back and allowed myself the small waves of exquisite pleasure that came with that motion before I lifted it off his shoulder.

I met his dark eyes, filled with that same monster I'd glimpsed in the battle, the one who was becoming more and more common when I was around.

"Hold that thought," I murmured, chasing away the

weird pang of guilt I felt from turning the human to a monster. I should've been proud of such a thing. "It's girls' night. Afterwards," I promised.

My words chased away the film of desire over Thorne's eyes. He went back to serious.

"Could she not have picked a better fuckin' bar?" he hissed. "One I could come to that doesn't have every creature that may or may not be after your head there as clientele?"

I rolled my eyes. "Well, Sophie picked the place, and since she hung up on me when she called to arrange the meeting, I kind of have to go to where she wants. Who knows, she might even curse me more if I don't do what she says. She's got scary new powers and I don't want her using them against me. Plus, Dante makes the best cocktails this side of the overworld. I think he puts ground-up human souls in there or something to make them extra tasty." I licked my lips at the thought.

"You just fuckin' took down an entire bar, Isla. You really think you're going to be able to go in for a drink without incident? Considering you just said there're multiple vampires out for your head," Thorne snapped, eyes flickering with anger.

I was coming to the conclusion that it was either fury or desire that was his default when looking at me.

I either pissed him off or turned him on.

Although I could probably say the same about him. Except for all of those vapid lovey female feelings that made me actually want to smile at him, and not sarcastically or murderously either.

It was dangerous.

"Well, they're at least as many vampires out for my ass too, so it's either I'll get hit on or hitmen on." I shrugged. "I can handle either."

He spun me around quickly, clutching my face. "This isn't a

joke, Isla," he growled. "This war. This spell. Any of it. I've been on this earth long enough to know the calm before the storm flattens everything in its path. I know it. And I'm quite willing to fight in this war. To get bloody. Covered in the blood of my enemies is only seconded to being inside you," he growled—or more accurately his monster growled, making my stomach dip. What man talked about bathing in the blood of enemies so sweetly?

Not many, I tell you.

His eyes flickered with something akin to fear. "But losing you? That's a storm I won't weather. A war I won't win." His eyes danced with demons that were too fresh to be banished. "You're so intent on making sure you look death in the face at least once a week."

I laughed, though mostly to shrug off that nasty little blossom of insanity that some people called humanity. The only insane character trait I was likely to fight harder than the velvet trend that didn't seem to want to go away. "Honey, I'm not the one looking. Death is always staring at us. You're just intent on looking away."

Though it wasn't death staring at me through those quicksilver eyes. Or maybe it was.

"I ain't gonna look away from shit again. And even death can't take this from us. I won't let it."

He kissed the ever-loving Satan out of me before I could reply.

Before I could tell him that death took everyone.

You didn't have to stop breathing to die.

As we soon found out.

I've been known to light up a room. With my beauty and style, of course. But also with enough matches and some gasoline.

A good fire is something to make people take notice. And realize you're serious about your crazy.

But I wasn't standing on a burning anything when I walked into Dante's bar. And I knew I looked good—great, in fact—but that, or even a teeny fire, would not have warranted the stares I got as I waltzed into the crowded establishment.

It was after 3 a.m., the lonely time of night when most humans dealt with the monsters in their minds. And the time when the real monsters dealt with the humans unlucky enough to encounter them. Or more likely the time when those monsters wet their whistles.

And obviously gave me a variety of death glares, a couple of disbelieving looks, impartial glances, and even a couple—biggest surprise of all—almost respectful glances.

I could've been hallucinating. That would be a better explanation as to why someone, anyone, looked at me with respect.

It made my skin crawl. I preferred hatred and murder than respect. I didn't want the responsibility of having people respect me. Or monsters respecting me.

No respect was the best thing. The ideal was feared.

"Yeah, I know, I'm back from the dead, like for the second time. I'm amazing," I declared to the room. I didn't need to raise my voice, handy when everyone in the bustling bar had superhuman hearing. My eyes flickered around the room. "*And* I'm boinking a slayer. He's a great lay, if y'all were wondering." I winked at the demon closest to me. "Anyone got a problem with that and is actually brave enough to tell that to the chick who's already burned down an entire bar tonight? With the corpses of those who challenged her heading down to Hades extra crispy?"

I held my arms above my head, doing a little circle of the room.

There was a murmur of conversation, mostly whispers of "fucking insane" and "not worth the trouble."

I grinned when a demon decided to charge forward. The very one I'd winked at, in fact.

"I really hoped at least *one* person would be stupid enough to take me up on my invitation," I said cheerfully, landing a solid punch to the center of his face so all the bones crushed in a delightful crunch. When he crumpled to the floor, I impaled him with the heel of my new shoes. At least they were red and patent leather and unlikely to stain.

He made a strange gurgling sound as the blood bubbled inside his mouth while his bones knitted together.

My eyes went to Sophie, who was twirling a fucking umbrella, of all things, around in her drink, looking a little bored and a lot chic.

Her black hair was mussed to the point between unshowered and homeless and fabulous and trendy. Her eyes were bordered with enough kohl to serve an entire high school of emos, and her dress was plain back, skintight and showed off every inch of her tattooed skin. Her ripped fishnets and thigh-high boots covered the tattoos she had on her legs.

"Cute boots," I remarked casually.

She glanced down, extending her leg outwards from her stool to inspect them. "Thanks. They're new. I was wondering if they went with this outfit."

"They work in a big way," I informed her.

"Not too much?"

"Definitely, but too much of a good thing is precisely better."

She grinned.

I grinned back. "Oh, can you do some mojo to make sure his healing is at the speed of a human? Or even a... I don't know, what heals slower than a human?" I mused, twisting my heel so a delicious crack of ribs filled the air.

She scrunched her nose. "Not much. Weak race. Human it is."

The air rattled slightly, tasting musky and bitter with the spell that Sophie silently cast.

Sophie.

Just Sophie. Not some creepy yellow-eyed version of Jack Torrance or any other character Stephen King could dream up.

A win for now.

I yanked my heel out, shaking the worst of the blood off. "Thanks."

She lifted her glass. "Anytime."

I looked around the room. Most of the creatures watched with idle curiosity. Others, regulars, had returned to their conversations at the first crack of bone. I'd done this before.

Once or twice.

Or ten times.

I was thinking of demanding an entertainment fee.

"Anyone else?" I asked. There was a pause. I grinned, showing fang. "Didn't think so."

I strutted over to kiss Sophie on both cheeks. "Where the fuck did you get an umbrella in your drink in here?" I asked, sitting. "Is Dante losing it? I really hope so. Watching people break from reality is almost as good as binging *Scandal* on Netflix," I said, rubbing my hands together.

The man himself appeared in front of me in a plume of smoke, looking upsettingly hinged.

I jumped. "Asshole," I hissed. "Doing that is a great way to get yourself killed. I don't like surprises, unless they come in

Tiffany boxes or coffins."

He grinned, leaning on the bar in a way I knew he did precisely so his biceps and tattooed arms flexed just right.

It was impressive. And he knew how to use those biceps and other appendages that were just as impressive, but alas, I was ruined for man, demon and vampire alike.

Not werewolf.

I'd never gotten that desperate.

Or had I?

The nineteenth century was a dark time for me.

"Are you sure it was surprised?" he asked. "I'm certain it was scared," he teased, obviously with a death wish.

I glared at him. "The only thing that scares me is Donald Trump's hairdresser. Now get me a drink without an umbrella." I paused, glancing at Sophie's. "No, wait, *with* the umbrella. The pointed end looks perfect for spearing demons' eyes," I added, pleasantly.

He rolled the eye I'd just been imagining spearing and using as a garnish in my cocktail. "You've spilled enough blood in here tonight." He nodded to the demon writhing on the floor, whom everyone was just ignoring now.

I glanced at him once, then back to Dante. "Like there is such a thing as too much blood. That's like saying there's such a thing as too many reality shows on wife swapping—not possible, in other words. Now, drink."

He gave me a look. "Is what I'm hearing true?"

I gave him a look of my own. "That bartenders who don't tend to sassy and beautiful vampires shoot their mortality rates up by one hundred percent? Yes, I do believe it's true."

He leaned forward, his eyes dancing with flames. "No, that in addition to tangling yourself up in this fuckin' war, you've got yourself in bed with a slayer. And are going public with it."

I snatched Sophie's drink, sipping. "Of course I'm going public. My life is far too boring otherwise. An assassination attempt only every other day, and the war seemed like it needed some spice. And what am I here for if not to add spice. And sugar. And everything nasty. Like a Powerpuff Girl, but one with better clothes, a filthier mouth and more fangs."

"Jesus," he muttered.

"I don't think he's here. He came and went a couple of times, I know, but he's been MIA for a few thousand years. I can ask Lucifer if he's seen him when we next have brunch, if you like?"

"Isla, are you ever serious?"

"Bleh. No. Wait, yes. About headbands on babies, I'm serious. They're wrong and evil and should be outlawed."

Dante shook his head. "You're going to get in over your head. Quickly."

I grinned. "Over my head is where my legs feel most at home."

The air turned hot once more, but at least some of that wretched sincerity left Dante's eyes. "That slayer, he there to stay? I assume since you're riskin' everything you have for him? Even you aren't that crazy to break so many rules and risk your own life for anything less."

Hearing it said aloud jarred me a little, but of course I didn't outwardly react. "Well, I guess. I'm a risk taker in general, but it seems like he might last longer than most. Also, I don't like your doubting of my insanity. I'm totally insane," I argued.

Dante gave me a look. "Just checkin'. Don't approve, but I get it. Lovin' the wrong person at the wrong time is the only right thing you can do."

Demons, or maybe angels, flickered in his eyes. Because wasn't that what haunted demons themselves? The most wicked haunted the most good, and therefore the most good must haunt the most wicked.

I didn't get to inspect the melancholy in his look, fortunately, because he turned to get my drink.

"Okay, thankfully we didn't have to Dr. Phil that shit," I said to Sophie. "Now we can chat."

"About the curse?" she asked, sipping her drink.

"I was going to say about where you got those boots, but I guess the curse," I said, resigned to the fact that fashion and general debauchery might have to take a back seat to fatal curses and wars.

Adulting.

Yuck.

I guess after four hundred years I had to at least entertain the thought.

"Hit me with it," I sighed. "Not another curse, please. Unless I don't have one on me. Then hit me with a new one, just to keep it interesting. As long as you don't damage the outer perfection." I gestured down. "I challenge you to do your worst to the basket of crazy that perfection is cloaking."

Sophie shook her head. "I doubt even I have the power for that."

I raised my brow at her in question, not daring to mention her new powers in such a place with all the eyes and ears and empaths.

Perhaps why she chose this exact establishment.

Smart, my witch.

"I'll keep the curse in the chamber for when this one is lifted," she said.

"Ugh," I moaned, snatching the drink from Dante's hands and downing it in one gulp. "Another," I demanded.

He muttered something under his breath that sounded

deceptively like a death threat before turning way.

"Seriously? Still? But I feel right as rain. Fit as a fiddle. Healthy as a horse. Sprite as—"

"Yes, the curse is still somewhat active," she snapped, breaking my cliché roll and ignoring my glare that came with it.

"Somewhat?" I asked.

"The witches still live and so does the curse. It's death magic, so it can only be killed with the deaths of all of witches."

"I thought slayer blood was the cure?"

"It is. It was." She screwed up her nose. "It stopped you from dying the original way, as a mortal. But it doesn't stop the curse from killing you."

"That doesn't make any sense," I pointed out.

"I fucking know," she hissed. "All I know is I sense death and magic and that's the only conclusion."

"We kill them, then," I said happily.

She nodded once.

"Well, turns out I've got some information acquired by a great friend of mine to help."

She raised her brow. "And by that you mean tortured out of something before you killed it."

"Precisely. So I did my job and your job for you, considering you were meant to be finding the witches. I got digits for one of them. I doubt the ones we're looking for, since those haven't likely gotten a cell phone number just yet, so soon after being let out of a cave. But I'm sure I'll persuade this one just like I did a certain weirdly shaped vampire," I said.

She looked at me. "I found them. Well, one of the two. She's the one released from her prison. I'm guessing the other isn't strong enough yet."

I glared at her. "Why didn't you tell me?"

She sipped her drink. "I just did."

I rolled my eyes. "Earlier."

"Because this was more fun."

"So where are they?"

Her demeanor stopped being as playful. "Russia."

I cursed under my breath. "Of course the one we can find is in the fucking motherland. It's where all things that try to kill me seem to hang out. Witches. My mother."

That reminded me. My mother was responsible for my almost execution, and requested the front row. I needed to send her a selfie to taunt her with my very undeadness.

But then the selfie wasn't necessary.

"They're staying at—"

"Please say Castle Dracula," I said.

Count didn't live in Transylvania, though he did vacation there. Russia was his true home. Less tourists.

"In your parents' compound," Sophie said.

"Drat," I murmured. "Castle Dracula would've been *so* much better. And when I'm preferring that vain asshole's company you know it's bad." I paused. "But then again, the presence of the witches is great proof to denounce and assassinate my entire family. Silver lining," I said happily. "When do we leave?"

She raised her brow. "We can't just hop on a plane to battle one of the darkest and most powerful witches to live and fight your family as well," she said.

"Why not?"

"Because it's suicide."

"Only if we lose," I argued.

"We need a plan."

"Plans are for sissies."

Our argument was cut short by the sharp gaze that had been on us all night, and I'd been trying my hardest to ignore.

"You've attracted a stray," I observed, my eyes touching the werewolf who seemed vaguely familiar.

And attractive, if you preferred the scarily unwashed and broody men. And that they turned into dogs.

Which I didn't.

Then again, all men were dogs, one way or another.

Sophie didn't turn. "I'm aware."

My eyes narrowed to something much more interesting than witches or wars, and more bloodstained: Sophie's love life.

But that conversation was cut short before it all began.

On account of the blood.

Always the blood.

"How is this the second bar death match I've found myself in tonight?" I asked when I slammed a werewolf down on the bar.

"Because you're Isla?" Dante questioned, ripping the head off.

I grinned, showing fang. "Oh yes, that's right."

Then I throat-punched a vampire going for Sophie's, well, throat. Not that she strictly needed my protection, or the wolf's who'd damn near jumped over his own corpse to snap at anyone who got past her spells. Which wasn't many.

Shame there was a good many murderous vampires and werewolves and the odd demon killing everything in their paths.

And they seemed to have one goal.

Yep, you guessed it—moi.

I ducked a knife that hurtled towards me, going after the demon who threw it. "Now that wasn't very nice," I gritted out.

There were a lot of supernaturals still here fighting. More

than I expected. Maybe because they didn't have a choice.

Fight or die, the choice was usually made for you.

Running was a third option, but that didn't work well when this place had one entrance and one exit.

The fire marshals really fucked up on that one.

"Get the vampire!" a large demon roared from the outskirts of the fight.

It wasn't in human form and it was red all over with bulging muscles, kind of like a red version of the Hulk without the ripped clothes and sporting horns on the top of his head.

I grinned over my shoulder at Dante while snapping the jaw of a wayward wolf. "Looks like I know who I'm dancing with tonight."

"Isla," he warned.

I, of course, didn't stay for a warning. It was like staying for the credits at the end of the movie.

Yawn.

So I waded through the battle, getting a scratch or two from a werewolf who was very sorry for that. And a broken rib from a vampire who should've known better.

But I made it to my date relatively unscathed.

I grinned up at him, standing a good enough distance away so he would have to lean forward and warn me of movement if he did choose to lunge at me.

"You called?" I asked. "Or rather sent in a small army to do the dialing. But I assume you're the one I answer to."

His eyes glowed with flames. "You come without a fight and I'll try to make sure you're not bleeding from the inside out when I deliver you to him," he growled, throaty and strange, not used to forming words. From the depths of the pit, then.

"As charming as that little promise is, I think I'd like to meet The King—you know, Elvis—on my terms. So pass."

The flames extended to his hooved hands. "So be it. He said you'd put up a fight."

I didn't get to ask about the mysterious 'he,' not that I was overly curious, because he chose that moment to lunge.

The big bastard was quicker than I intended so the blow to my chest landed hard enough to cave it in, despite me dodging the worst of it. I went flying above the battling bodies and crashed into a snapping werewolf, landing teeth first.

Luckily, it was the werewolf who was Sophie's pet so it yanked me to my feet. Its eyes darted to Sophie, whose own were starting to glow all freaky-deaky as she was surrounded, and then to me, a big hulking demon with a steroid problem stomping forward at that moment.

Wolfy growled in the demon's direction, seeming conflicted.

I straightened, despite the awareness and pain that came with the movement on account of my crushed chest. "Chill, Cujo. I've got this one. Go make sure the magic inside Sophie doesn't have her head twisting all types of ways, won't you? We've got enough excitement for tonight."

On that, I stepped forward as the wolf didn't hesitate to heed my command. Though it was likely because it was of the Sophie reason, not my commanding tone, it was still pretty darned good, if you asked me.

I made a mental note to inspect that little love story when I wasn't in a death match with the horned wonder.

I glanced down to my chest, noticing my missing necklace. A crunch under my boot told me the fate of it.

I glared at the charging demon. "That was custom Cartier," I hissed. Then I lunged. It was a good lunge too, considering I landed on his shoulders and managed to wrap my legs around his neck in order to rip off one of his horns.

The bellow of agony that erupted was glorious. The spurting of inky black liquid smelling like charcoal and dead fish was not.

"Ew." I cringed away on instinct, for my dress more than anything else. The demon took advantage and crushed my shoulder under its grip to fling me to the floor.

My survival instinct for my dress and the body inside it was much more on the ball as I rolled away from the large foot aimed at crushing my skull. That would have taken much longer to recover from.

Read: never.

"I hate it when Thorne's right," I muttered to myself, wrenching myself off the floor. I was a little hunched, standing half-bent over on account of my cracked spine and my arm dangling unnaturally in front of me as the bones tried to knit shattered pieces together. "There's no such thing as 'just a drink' for me. I'll never hear the end of this."

Well, that was if this wasn't the end of me.

Though I refused to let a red-bodied, one-horned demon be the end of me.

No way, no how.

If any demon was going to end me, it was going to be the king himself, and not Elvis.

So I dodged his next attack, not as gracefully or as badassly as I would've liked, but it served its purpose—namely not getting me dead.

I played dirty by ducking between his legs and hitting him where it hurt.

I wasn't above taking cheap shots. Death wasn't that expensive, after all.

The groan of pain helped to tell me that I was working the cheap shots like a pro. I capitalized on the pain by darting out with my good hand and crushing his kneecap so he came down on one knee.

I met black eyes. "Hello. You've reached the end of the road. Please give the devil my regards," I told him easily, planning on breaking his neck—a feat the same as felling a large tree trunk, but I was confident I was up for the challenge. When the snap of his bone signaled my victory, the snapping of mine signaled his final victory in death.

It was cheap, after all. Maybe it was two for one.

At least it wasn't painful, the short fall into nothingness.

Though nothing never was painful.

That's what made it so dangerous.

EIGHT

"**L**EWIS, IT'S SCOTT. WE NEED A MARK, STAT," A SLIGHTLY unnerved voice demanded.

"We don't have time for this," Sophie snapped.

"Well if you healed her, like a good witch should," Dante's annoyed and maybe slightly worried voice cut in.

"I can't heal her. Not when she needs blood. No witch can reproduce what the blood gives. It's kind of the point. Magic cannot reproduce life, nor can it change death."

"Well, why the fuck are you here if you can't do that?" Dante challenged.

A low growl came from what sounded like the back seat.

Did we run over a dog on the way to get me some blood?

"Just pull over and snatch that human," Sophie suggested impatiently.

"Isla wouldn't do that. They could be innocent," Scott cut in.

"Did you see his outfit and his beard? No way that dude was innocent. I'll bet a hundred he's got some woman locked in his basement," Sophie said. "Dante, pull over. We're getting Isla a snack."

"No, we've got something," Scott said, the muffled voice at the end of the phone he was on not as clear as it should've been.

Then again, nothing was as clear as it should've been.

"It better be close. She needs it." Sophie's voice was grim and had an edge of worry that I didn't rightly like. Not at all.

"It is. Did you call Thorne?"

"Yes, I called him. He's out in Slayerville, and even the power of his rage and shouted curses isn't going to get him here any faster. I'd really like it if I didn't present him with the sight of Isla's corpse for the second time in a week."

Her voice was blasé and sassy, but even in whatever static coma vampire state I was in, I could hear it.

The fear.

Because my voice sounded like that too when I talked about someone I loved dying.

I didn't feel like I was dying, though. Sophie was right; I'd already done that once this week.

This wasn't that.

I would admit I wasn't in a good way, and the absence of pain usually meant absence of life. I was numb in a way that told me my broken bones weren't knitting themselves back together as they had been all night.

Not good.

"She's not going to die, and we've got a drug dealer in two blocks," Scott said, his voice sounding different. Stronger.

I was vaguely proud of the little punk.

They grew up so fast.

Or not, in Scott's case. Unless you considered a few decades 'fast.'

Which I did.

It was all relative.

As was the time it took to get those few blocks and weather the nothingness.

On first thought, it was preferable to the immense amounts of pain my broken and shattered body had given me before. But the nothingness wasn't preferable for extended amounts of time. Not when the mind was trapped in what it knew was still its head, though with nothing to anchor it but the sounds around it.

The nothingness taunted me with the reality that I could just float away.

And it wasn't darkness at the edges of my vision that people liked to describe the welcoming of nothing. No, it was stark white where nothing could hide, where there was no depth or tangibility to anything. White everywhere.

And worse than feeling the nothingness was the grating sound of everything around me that wasn't quite there to touch but was close enough that I heard the screech of tires, the opening of a door, the frenzied protests of a human.

"Hey, dude, what the fuck do you think—"

Snap followed by silence.

Death.

Silence like that had a sound of its very own.

The wetness that trickled from the dead body splashed onto my face. I heard the droplets on my granite skin instead of feeling them.

"Drink," Scott demanded.

Then there was a small twitch. A warmth, a drop of crimson against the stark white that was starting to make me hate the color in general. Which was annoying since my new Prada was a beautiful shade of snow.

Then another droplet, followed by a warmth trickling down the area that I knew was my throat. That I could feel was my throat. Feeling came with pain, the screaming protest of my spine as I fastened my one working arm on the still-warm corpse and sucked deeper.

More warmth filled my throat and then my stomach, hurtling down the nerve endings raw from agony.

The interior of the SUV's cab flickered quickly into existence before I banished it again once I closed my eyes. The blackness welcomed me back like an old friend as I continued my meal.

But then the warmth did something unexpected.

Something that blood hadn't given me.

When I drank from someone, I tasted their life. The warmth of it, sure, but it was a pleasing type of warmth, what I imagined to be like the sun catching the damp skin after a swim in a lake on a summer's day.

Kind of like the warmth that came with Thorne's touch, though Thorne's touch was an inferno, and then it beat even that.

Because the blood was no longer pleasant and life.

The blood was unpleasant and decidedly deadly. Like an alcoholic so desperate for the drink that they don't realize it's drain cleaner until the buzz they'd chased was in fact their demise.

I dropped the body abruptly, frantic to get the blood, the poison, the fire from my veins and my mouth.

The first logical thing to do was spit out my latest mouthful of blood. Scott was sitting closest, so he bore the brunt of that.

"What—"

His words were cut off by more blood.

That time I didn't consciously spit it out; it expelled itself from my body quite literally in a disturbing amount, like that puke scene in *Pitch Perfect*. The amount was disturbing because it was coming out at all, and because I surely didn't take in that much blood in a few measly swallows. I could barely think through the ocean of shudders that vibrated my body as my stomach roiled and writhed and basically just rebelled against me to rid itself of the poison.

The problem was, much like chemotherapy worked on cancer patients, it was a poison to kill everything in the body: the bad stuff—the cancer, of course—but whatever remained that the body needed to survive too. It was merely a question of what would win first, the cure or the poison. That's what it felt like my body was doing, poisoning itself to cure itself. Ridding itself of every inch of blood I contained through the entirely gross process of puking it all over the place.

"What the fuck is happening?" Scott yelled over the sounds of blood leaving my body.

"It's the curse," Sophie yelled back. "Fuck, her body is rejecting all blood but his."

His.

Mine.

My slayer.

"Where the fuck is Thorne?"

My vomiting stopped, as did the fire, which was good; it meant the poison was all gone. But the lack of heat gave way to an icy chill that was too cold for even a vampire. A dryness to it that seemed to make my skin suck in on itself.

My vision was tinted with crimson from where capillaries had burst under the pressure of the vomiting saga. But I saw the thinness to my skin that was seeming to wrinkle before my very eyes.

That's what happened to vampires under severe blood deprivation. They crumpled like paper and didn't die. Not immediately. Or ever. But there was a point in the process that the body, even the immortal one, couldn't come back from. The terrible space between undeath and Hades himself. Unless someone took pity on the vampire and sent its soul to the underworld, a vampire could conceivably live forever in that state, undead yet not living either.

And my crimson eyes watched the skin deteriorate at a disturbing rate, the iciness getting worse. I felt like those idiots who climbed mountains for nothing other than 'because it's there,' the ones who got the severe frostbite that literally froze their limbs off. Handy if they ever had to eat the weaker ones for substance, but not so much when you were trying to not die.

I'd never felt that, because as a vampire, one of the many perks was not getting frostbite and losing extremities.

My smugness to a lack of frostbite seemed to be an omen for the very moment of my cells themselves freezing.

"You need to meet us at Seventy-Third and Park. Now," Sophie demanded into a phone, eyes locking with mine.

I managed a weak wink that felt like sandpaper was trapped behind my eyes.

"Isla's...." She kept staring at me. "She's in need in some serious Botox in the form of your blood. So be ready to open a vein in approximately two minutes because if you take any longer...." I could practically feel the anguish across the phone. "You're going to get to experience the wrinkled version of your beloved that you'd planned on avoiding considering the whole immortal thing. And trust me, this is not a pretty picture." She was trying to inject some blasé sarcasm into her tone, but it wasn't even convincing the wrinkled and severely dehydrated being she was talking about.

I felt kind of bad, presenting Thorne with my life in the balance not once but twice.

But then again, I felt worse about the death comment. It did seem to have its eye on me. I imagined death to be like that menacing eye in Mordor in *Lord of The Rings*, atop a sleek, polished tower, its eye seeing all and snatching them when need be.

The eye was focused on me fully now. And I didn't like that.

At all.

I thought I was fading away into the nothingness once more when the clearness of his command filtered through even death itself so it was palpable—corporeal, even.

"Hold the fuck on, Isla. Don't you dare fucking leave me again." The rough command was yelled through the phone.

So I held the fuck on.

For a moment.

Or longer. It was difficult to tell because I used the warmth that came with that voice and the memory of the heat of his skin to keep the unrelenting chill of death at bay.

And then the heat wasn't an imagining; it was there, real. A fiery furnace but in a good way. Like I remembered in my human days in Russia, how the cold would seep into my bones in such a way that I was certain my fingers would fall off. And then one of the maids who was thoughtful enough to remember I was a human when my parents forgot, or ignored that fact, would light a fire in my chambers, bringing me a hot mug of wine. I'd cradle the drink in one hand while using the fire to warm me.

That was what it felt like, the cradle of an open flame

around me and then the hot sweetness of that drink pouring down my throat.

"Drink, Isla," Thorne commanded, his voice an echo in my head that had somehow been full of centuries of memories yet empty at the same time.

At first I thought it was too late, that my body would regret the sweet nectar of the blood, that the dryness of my throat would make it impossible to drink.

A hand pushed my hair from my face. "Baby, remember you're not leaving this world," he murmured. "Not without me."

And that was something to make me drink, as was the gentle vibration of his heartbeat that had filled the silence of the roars of memories.

And there was nothing but the heartbeat.

And blood.

And life.

"Cool, so now we know that drug dealers are not a good choice for a post battle snack," I said, breaking the long and uncomfortable silence.

I grinned at my grim-faced boyfriend, who looked slightly more on the iridescent side than usual. But he still looked hot all anemic. Under fluorescent lights, no less. How did it take me so long to understand he was immortal?

No human looked good under fluorescent lights.

Only few vampires could. Luckily I was one of the few.

Even after a brush with death.

But brushing with death did wonders for the complexion. It kept one young.

I was still tucked in Thorne's warm embrace. And though I

no longer felt the cold from inside my body, it didn't mean the heat on the outside wasn't rather nice and I was loath to leave it.

So I didn't. I spoke from the position in the embrace.

His arms tightened around me as he glared at Sophie, whose brows were furrowed between us in a look that I did not like. It looked far too serious and far-reaching for me. I much preferred the not-so-serious and not-so-far-reaching looks she normally sported.

"How did this happen?" he hissed.

The echo of his voice was filled with emotions that almost felt like my own from the freshness of his blood that was pouring through me.

I felt his fear that was receding, giving way to something more functional, and hotter.

Fury.

In its purest form.

I thought I'd gotten angry, furious. There were more than a few winners of *The Bachelor* that I *so* thought shouldn't have been there, and then there was the family that killed my husband and tortured me over the centuries.

So I had experience with anger.

But nothing was quite like this.

Nothing like the fury of the world, trying to take something away that should be immortal. Not just me. What he felt for me that, because of this connection, seemed almost separate to me. To us. It couldn't even be contained in two bodies. Two supernatural bodies.

It was within the both of us and somehow residing within the connection that was invisible to anyone but me.

And it scared me.

My own fear that time. Because having his feelings laid out

so raw and exposed was somewhat like a mirror, presenting me with the cold reality of my own.

Which was what I had been afraid of.

I loved him. He knew that. I knew that. But even I had been holding back from realizing how much, because it wasn't the love of those cheesy movies that made your life better for being in it.

It was complete and utter destruction.

It was an ugly kind of love that, in its beauty, coiled around every part of you with a connection to another person that made everything you were dependent on everything that they were.

And that reality, the insanity of it all, scared me more than death itself. Because in the face of love, death was simple.

But then simple wasn't exactly on the night's menu after Thorne's contribution.

Sophie's face told me that.

And the whole almost dying at the hands of a rebel faction out for my blood, then not being able to do the simplest thing that I had done in the world—kill.

"The witches," she whispered. It sounded strange. Too throaty for her.

I tried to reason that she might just have a tickle in her throat, considering even the proximity to death left one rather suffering the flulike symptoms that came with exposure.

"They need to die. Now," Thorne growled.

"I agree. We need to go with my plan," I said from beside him, the contrast of my even voice and his animalistic growl showing the differences in our sanity. Or insanity. His was only controlled if he let go of the fury into his voice. Mine was never under control, so it gave me free reign to play with the crescendo of my voice. There was nothing like acting out of my tree when I spoke in the same tone of someone working at the DMV.

"And what's your plan?" a cultured voice asked smoothly. It was smooth in a way that shimmered with the fury beneath the surface of the promise of death.

All eyes darted up to the entrance to Sophie's office, where Rick and Duncan stood. We'd decided to regroup there after me having the almost dying episode yet again—it was closest and had booze.

We were in dire need of booze, and we didn't seem to have the best track record with bars.

Dante had made off after it became apparent I wasn't going to die, and after a rather volatile stare-down with Thorne.

"I've got to go check on the bar," he'd said, glancing at me. "Or what's left of it."

"It needed some new décor, and corpses and blood are always an improvement." I grinned. "You know my details. Send my people the bill."

He gave another look to Thorne. "Yeah, I will, but the price of the wrong choice at the right time is death," he warned, then was gone in a puff of black smoke.

"That was Dante," I told Thorne. "He likes to show off. Trust me, it's all for show. I've done the legwork in finding that out the hard way." I waggled my eyebrows as I spoke.

Thorne hadn't been entirely impressed, although I didn't know if it was because Dante was a demon who feasted on human souls or because I'd unwisely admitted we had bumped uglies. Most likely a combination of the two.

I blamed the blood loss.

And because I liked stirring up trouble.

But trouble liked stirring me right back, considering the king of all vampires was standing in the doorway not one hour after I'd almost died—again—and then I'd decided to tell my boyfriend I'd banged a demon right after he saved my life.

The boyfriend, not the demon. Though I guessed Dante had helped a little, considering apparently he was the one who fought the rest of the vampires off my lifeless corpse and threw me into the van that Scott somehow had waiting at the mouth of the alley.

Rick's cold eyes flickered over me, the sheer amount of blood covering what I guessed was every inch of my body, then at Thorne and the healing puncture marks at his neck.

If he was surprised or concerned or any of the above, he surely didn't show it. His façade was hard as ever, but a small muscle in his jaw ticked, almost imperceptibly.

"My plan is no plan at all," I told him happily, deciding not to show my surprise at his appearance or the fury lurking beneath his kingly exterior.

Duncan frowned at me. "I like it, lassie. But I don't like that you seem to be having all the fun without me." His own fury was different than Thorne's, plainly exposed in animalistic beauty, and Rick's, a cultured mask with a depraved monster lurking underneath. His was cloaked in humor and a flippancy that only came out when he was really mad. I knew at least some of it was from being left out. He didn't wear concern well, or at all. When you lived forever, you became acquainted with the fact that you couldn't form attachments too easily, for death would inevitably sever them and you'd be left with a huge gaping hole.

Duncan already had that hole. He'd perfected a persona and a life where it wouldn't get bigger.

I poked my tongue out at him. "You were the one who wanted to play messenger boy for the king. Is lapdog your new official title? Because the kennel is a little full right now."

I nodded to the silent werewolf in the corner who hadn't seemed to need to go off and howl at the moon or anything.

In fact, there had been no howling. And no words. Just staring at Sophie in a weird, intense way that reminded me of the way Thorne was looking at me.

One that got my hackles up in a way that, had we not had a lot going on, I'd totally be investigating that situation.

"How did you know we were here?" I asked, focusing on the task at hand, giving the werewolf the back seat until later. Scott had already explained his presence, as he'd been on the phones at the Sector and heard the reports of a huge battle in a bar, coming immediately since he knew it had to be me.

I reasoned he was just stalking me.

Duncan held up his phone. "Text. Great invention. Saves a lot of pigeons."

"Okay, well I hope you're not here on my account. I'm fine, nothing a little slayer blood—of the right flavor, of course—can't heal." I gave Thorne a grin, which he did not return.

Rick's eyes flickered to me, then Thorne, then Sophie. "What is the explanation for this?" he demanded, unbuttoning his suit jacket in order to sit on the sofa across from us.

It was such an inherently human gesture that it was almost jarring, but I was exceptional at going with the flow. And also being pissed off. I was great at that.

"We were getting to that bit before we were so rudely interrupted," I snapped.

He eyed me evenly. "You are aware I'm still your king?" he said blandly.

"You must have forgotten your crown. I need shiny things to remind me, considering I'm a little forgetful on account of all the near-death experiences," I replied just as blandly.

At that, Thorne's façade cracked slightly.

Of course it did. I was insulting his nemesis—who was his nemesis for reasons still unknown, which I would find out when people stopped trying to kill me.

I was hoping for a free week next week.

"By all means, continue your explanation as to how Isla is not only able to survive on blood that should kill her but also almost die when she drinks blood that is designed to sustain her," Rick invited, tone somehow implying it was all Sophie's fault.

Monarchs had the niftiest way of shifting the blame.

My hackles went up for my best friend. "Yes, because *Sophie* was the one who started this war, dragged me into it with blackmail, then got me cursed by a bitchy witch and *then* almost killed me in order to keep his crown from tumbling from his oh-so-kingly head," I snapped.

Thorne's hands flexed around me. "Easy," he murmured.

My death glare went to him. "I thought you'd be applauding my next plan, which would be to rip his throat out since you two don't do sleepovers and movie nights," I snapped.

It wasn't an empty threat. I was feeling testy, and when I got testy, people died. It was somewhat of a habit.

He met my eyes. "I just need an explanation, and it looks like Sophie has one. So how about we save the throat-ripping plan? Until later, at least," he asked with a twinkle in his eye.

"I guess," I huffed like a child denied chocolate after a meal. Denying a vampire murder after a meal was basically the same thing.

He kissed the top of my head and then focused on Sophie. I did too, but not before glaring at Rick one last time and bringing my finger along my throat slowly in a cutting motion. Obviously this little event made me more childish and murderous than usual.

"You were saying, Sophie?" Rick prompted, as if I didn't make the gesture or talk at all. Almost as if he didn't care. But I noticed the slight edge to his voice, the way his jaw was held tight and his stillness on the sofa was too still. Even for a vampire.

Sophie glanced between Thorne and Rick, grinning. Then she focused on me and her gaze sobered. "I'm not an expert on this by any means, but a little reading and a lot of guesswork has me thinking that whatever happened with this curse, it has a caveat that even if you beat it you're still cursed." She glanced at the almost-healed cut on Thorne's neck. "His blood saved you and so it shall sustain you. And only you and only him, for no other blood shall pass through the lips or the veins lest you perish from the lack of the Ichor in your veins."

I blinked. "Wow, that's good. Did you just make that up on the fly?" I asked, impressed.

Sophie held up a very old and very boring-looking book.

"Not enough pictures," I said, squinting at the words squashed together on a page so it was almost unreadable.

"This is a grimoire from almost the first of us. Since records began, as legend goes," she explained. "Since the four."

I knew witchy lore had something about four sisters and the four elements, the connection with nature bestowing the powers of the earth within each of them and then birthing the first four witches.

Yawn.

"Looks the part," I said, deciphering the language to be that of a long-forgotten dialect that even I couldn't read properly. And I was old enough to be fluent in dozens of languages, both out of necessity and boredom. Plus, I liked being able to insult as many people from different cultures as inhumanly possible.

"It specifically mentions the Herodias sisters," Sophie continued.

I frowned. "Herodias, as the witch queen, or the princess of the Herodian Dynasty, depending on which history you want to adhere to?"

All eyes went to me. Even Thorne raised his brow.

"What? I read sometimes," I defended.

Sophie grinned and went back to her little speech. "The Herodias sisters were some of the most powerful witches in ancient times. They were also known for creating havoc."

I inspected my nails. "Well, I'm sure we would've gotten along with them great in other circumstances."

Everyone ignored me.

Sophie sucked in a breath. "Witches are born of the earth, from the soul of nature itself. No god bestowed power over the first mortal women to gain the powers of the elements. Not like the vampires or werewolves."

Her eyes went to me and then the werewolf in the corner. Their eyes lingered just that smidge too long, the sign of something more.

But then she glanced back to the group at large. "No, it was the benevolent power of nature herself that gifted the first of our kind with gifts.

Not the powers of gods but the powers of mortals unrealized. Or maybe forgotten powers the gods had left strewn about the leaves which had settled into the soil when they wandered the earth." She trailed her finger over the book, not reciting from it, saying it from memory.

Impressive, I couldn't even remember what *Vogue* said the ten essential closet items were for winter, nor the amount of people I was meant to have killed for Lewis this week.

Sophie continued.

"It was neither good nor evil, what the four were blessed with, just power itself. But it is dangerous, that neutrality, especially when put into human spirits. Which is why the most ancient of us created the rules that bind every witch, that forbid the use of natural powers for unnatural acts. Because it's there. The power."

Something flickered behind her eyes at that moment, something that would've given me chills if I weren't tucked nice and close to my own personal heat source.

"But that unnatural power, it must be taken using the gift we were bestowed, and it tarnishes it, warps it to something ugly. Malena was not born wicked, as is the way with most of the wicked people. She was the head of the family. In witch covens, it is the oldest girl who is given that place in the family." Her eyes narrowed at the men in the room. "Witches had the monopoly over feminism before anyone. Warlocks knew that females were the most dangerous. Just a side note, that works in this situation too." She gave me a wink.

I flashed fang.

"Malena wasn't happy with rules. She believed that power was a living organism and should be allowed to grow. As did her sisters, Belladonna and Ucillia."

"Horrific names," I muttered.

More ignoring me.

I'd have to rip off a limb soon, if only to get someone to pay attention to me.

"Malena, she pushed the boundaries of the powers given to her by nature and was given leniency because of her power, as the council was mindful of the fact that she could become the greatest asset to the coven." She paused. "But then they couldn't put off punishment when she created the abominations. The humans of the village that she turned into the vampires that had walked the earth since before even The Four, yet they had none of the human characteristics of those Strigoi encountered by the coven in the past. This creature had strength not given by gods or nature but from a deal with the king of the underworld, greedy for more rotten souls."

Another pause.

"There was a trial. But the love Malena's sisters had for her, and the prospect of her being hung from the neck, was too much for them to bear, so they admitted to Malena's crimes as their own. The council were only too happy for such admissions, for the sisters were weaker and they were still loath to lose Malena's power. Hence their quick execution."

I rose my brows. "Ruthless."

Sophie nodded once. "The council has not changed, for their pursuit of power and the witches who wield it stains the blood of these books, even if one can't see it," she murmured.

I knew she was thinking of a time closer than a few thousand years. The time being now and the council trying to put the tattooed and sarcastic witch in their trophy cage. Or weapons bunker.

They'd have an interesting time if they tried that, considering this vampire needed a drinking buddy and wouldn't let her friend get taken away lightly.

My gaze met the wolf's intense stare.

Neither would he.

But I focused on Sophie again, that otherworldly twinkle to her eyes and the slight hum to the air, originating from the witch herself.

I didn't think she needed a werewolf or an exceptionally strong and beautiful vampire to save her.

I think she could do that job quite well herself.

And the one of destroying her.

Yeah, she could do that too.

Or whatever was inside her could.

But apparently history wasn't done with the present.

"Her sisters were dead and Malena was released. And the council naively thought that such a punishment would remind Malena of rules and consequences. Put her in her place, so to speak."

I shook my head. "They need a crazy advisor on the council. You know, someone who's the token insane one to be able to tell them exactly how that wouldn't work. Because when dealing with the most powerful, you're almost always dealing with the craziest, and you need someone to fight crazy with crazy." I gave Rick a look. "You need one of those. Might help when dealing with certain beautifully insane vampires." I grinned.

Thorne's arms flexed around me.

Sophie smiled. "Indeed, they did need that, for the wrath brought forward by Malena leveled the village. And she used the power stolen from dead witches to warp the laws of nature and bring forth her sisters from the grave. Their souls, darkened with death and the blackness that was needed to arise from the grave, brought forth the darkness that had always lived somewhere inside them. Malena was forever marked and warped with the ugly stench of such magic.

"The story goes that they wreaked havoc over most of Eastern Europe before an army of the strongest supernaturals on the planet formed an allegiance to bind them."

I looked at her. "Not just witches?"

She shook her head. "That's apparently it." She glanced down to the page. "And the Herodias sisters were banished to the cave, which was neither in the space of living nor dead, since their crimes to both life and death meant they would never embrace the reaper for the stillness of death, nor ever taste the beautiful chaos of life. Forever bound, or shall the earth be tainted and ruined should the chains of their prison be broken."

I chewed my lip. "Well, hello, ruined world. Someone let the dogs out. It's not a party until some uninvited guests come to fuck shit up."

Sophie grinned. "Yeah, worldwide destruction could be described at that."

"Or a great party," I countered.

Rick nodded to the book. "So this text, it explains not only the witches but also the curse? And I'm assuming how to defeat them?" he asked, obviously getting impatient.

Sophie glanced at him. "Most of the writings in here are given as much credence as the words in the Bible. They can't be read as prophecy and are open to interpretation. But this passage"—she pointed at the page—"talks almost specifically about this curse and the ramifications of it."

Thorne had been little more than a statue since she'd uttered the earlier verse. As had Rick.

Even Scott and Duncan.

Drat, I was the last to catch on. Again.

"So you're telling me that Thorne's is the only blood I can drink?" I asked. "Until we kill the witches?"

There was a long pause I didn't like the sound of. At all.

"Right?" I probed. "Then I can go back to my usual diet of psychopaths and rapists?"

Even saying it, thinking of the taste of the blood earlier, the wrongness of it all, my stomach roiled in protest and an unintended shiver rippled through me before I could stop it.

Of course, Thorne noticed and his worried gaze immediately darted to me. "I'm fine," I snapped. "Someone just walked over my grave. Or wrote a date on it."

My response merely added to the cocktail of his fury.

"Sophie," I demanded. "Please help to make sure that Thorne does not pop a wisdom tooth with all that jaw clenching," I requested. "And tell him this will be over as soon as 'Ding Dong, the Witch is Dead.'"

Sophie looked at me. I didn't like the look. It was the one she gave me right before she told me that I didn't suit the shoes I'd been salivating over for months. Said they made my calves look weird.

I still hadn't forgiven her for not giving me the magical version of a plastic surgery 'calf job.'

It existed. I knew it did.

I glanced down at my calves for a moment before locking eyes with her once more.

"Death magic was practiced on you, and you combatted it with death blood that turned into life blood. It cannot be undone," she said, her voice shifting with a strange fluid quality. Something moved in the air, like a breeze, yet there were no windows open. Sophie's eyes started to glaze over but not fully.

"It is because the two have returned that the blood shall not be sullied with anything but the design of the gods should the world hope to flourish in the new age of peace."

"Nope," I said immediately, not liking the direction this was going and abruptly bursting from Thorne's arms. The loss of his heat was regrettable, but I needed to get the hell out of Dodge.

Fast.

I knew the sound of her voice and the taste to the air, and I did not need to be anywhere near this fucking train wreck.

Thorne was too quick, taking hold of my elbow before I made my escape.

"What the fuck are you doing, Isla?" he demanded.

I eyed Sophie, the disappearing Sophie. The blank-faced stranger with her features remained, watching me with sightless eyes that birthed a deep disquiet inside of me.

"Nostradamus over here is about to spout some sort of future premonition much like she's done before. Freaked me the fuck out the first time, and now I've got a tricky feeling it's about me and I'd like to be as surprised about my future as I am with what comes out of my mouth. So I'm going to leave before she ruins it all without so much as a spoiler alert. I'll still not forget what she did to me with *Lost*," I informed him. "And I don't need to know this is all a concoction of an insane mind while I'm shaking back and forth in some mental institution in Sunnydale. I saw the *Buffy* episode."

His hand on my arm stayed firm, firm enough that I knew I'd have to hurt him to break the grasp.

He knew it too, his eyes twinkling as they searched mine. "We need to know, Isla," he said quietly.

I tried to blink away the stare and everything that came with it, including the waves of his emotions. "Not the future," I argued. "No good has ever come from such prophecies. Watch a fucking movie, dude. Any movie. Chosen one, end of the world, death. CliffsNotes version, but that's usually the gist of it. So I don't need to read the book or watch the creepy play in front of me. I've seen *all* the movies."

"*Our* future. And I'd like a blueprint so I can avoid any more incidents where I hold your lifeless body in my arms," he hissed.

I glared at him and was about to do something I'd most likely regret—what else was new?—in order to get out of the room when the voice started speaking.

The voice that was flat and old and young and everything and nothing at the same time. That was certainly not Sophie.

"She will be deathless, this *chosen one*."

I gave Thorne a pointed look, mouthing "Told you so" at him, but his gaze went from me to Sophie as she continued.

As much as I didn't want to, and I *really* didn't want to, it was somewhat of a siren song, that voice. Music dragging the ear and the attention so I couldn't move, even if I wanted to.

Sophie stood in the middle of the room, sightless and seeing everything at the same time, her eyes taking on that glassy quality of someone who was dead and saw all the secrets of life.

"The one like the one who came first before her. First before her, but was the one who submitted to the mortality she was plagued with. Her head of fire in the sky for all to see, the emerald of her eyes in the oceans which glint from the sunlight that banished her mate to the darkness until it was no longer the place where monsters lurked. For the light was their home more than shadows.

"In the shadows and in the light, they come back. Come back with the chosen one. Deathless until the blood of her mate is drained or ash if the heart of stops beating. Then her death shall come swift and fast and on the heels of this, the end of the world."

I stared at the empty-eyed Seer Sophie who was creepily like a wax version of my friend. That was bad enough I'd seen the movie. It sucked.

I was still thinking about the Paris Hilton death scene when I should've been more focused on her words. For they were said by wax Sophie in that strange empty and ancient voice that sent shivers up my spine.

Not that I'd tell anyone that.

I was a fucking *vampire*, for Lucifer's sake.

I didn't get shivers.

So I kept my face in its natural state—resting bitch face.

And beautiful. Obviously.

"Chosen one? Me?" I repeated, feeling very uncomfortable with the sheer number of eyes on me that had settled there after everyone had stopped gaping at Sophie. Don't get me wrong, I loved having all the eyes on me, but only for the right reasons, like my beauty, my style, or I was killing something in a really epic way. Or pissing off a large group of my vampire brethren.

Not like this.

"Your connection to the creepo witch of the future must be hinky," I declared, giving the now blinking, not-wax Sophie a gentle tap on the side of the head like they did with those TVs that were on the fritz.

She glared at me in pain.

Well, I thought it had been soft.

"*I'm* no chosen one," I continued. "Beautiful one? Yes. Intelligent, witty ,and hilarious at the same time? Also yes. An icon of the vampire world? I'll take it, if that's what my fans would like to call me." I paused. "But not chosen, and not with my death causing the world to end. Too much pressure. I don't even like voting on *American Idol*. The power goes to my head."

"Yeah, because your head is *so* small otherwise," Sophie muttered, still rubbing her head.

Wolf man in the corner was shaking from his exertion to stay there. He had been poised for the change since the air turned thick like the dampness before a storm, and then it had gotten worse when I'd given Sophie the little love tap.

I gave him a sympathetic smile. "Nobody put Wolfy in the corner before?" I asked sweetly.

I got an annoyed growl at that, plus a glare from Sophie.

Curious. As was the way her gaze darted to his and she didn't glare or back me up with a fiery insult.

Yes, very curious.

But we had bigger fish to fry, apparently.

"You remember that? The whole 'chosen one' shit you just spouted? That sounded like the script of a bad movie?" I asked Sophie, realizing that she wasn't as blank-faced and confused as she had been the day at the bar.

She blinked at me. "Yeah, I do, but it wasn't me." Her words were slow and slurred, as if she had to wade through a swamp in her mind to say them. To fight someone else for the control of her motor functions.

It was creepy as all hell.

"No shit, it wasn't you. Since when do you talk like Shakespeare went all vague and believed in vampires? The question remains that, if it wasn't you, then who the fuck was it?"

"I think there are a lot of questions that have arisen with this prophecy. That's the least pertinent," Rick cut in smoothly.

I glared at him, finding it rather comforting to move my attention away from the friend who was only half there and becoming someone who spoke in prophecies instead of profanities. "I disagree. The fact that she didn't black out like a sorority girl in Cabo is worrying. I mean, we need to talk about that and all the powers that are like the sparkling elephant in the room. *That's* what we need to focus on, not the gobbledygook she just spouted," I informed the room, desperate to get out of a situation where I was chosen for anything but the most depraved in high school. Or prom queen. I felt like I wore a crown daily, but that would've been a nice title to add to the résumé.

Thorne's hand was still on my arm, most likely because he sensed my need for escape.

"Isla," he warned.

"Thorne," I mimicked his tone.

Another glare from him and a warning flex on my arm.

He looked to Sophie. "You know what the fuck what you just spouted is about? Specifics in real people talk?"

I raised my brow at him. "I don't think the man who speaks in grunts, growls and 'babes' gets to define 'real people talk.'"

Duncan barked out a laugh, but the rest of the little group ignored me.

Sophie looked too serious for my liking. Although she just had someone using her vocal cords like puppet strings, so she did have the merit to look more than a little freaked. "I don't know," she said, rubbing her bare and bloodstained arms as if to ward off the chill or the foreboding of the future that was getting a little more complicated than 'kill witch,' 'fight war,' 'be awesome.'

A lot more complicated, in fact.

"These powers are getting a little beyond my knowledge of magic itself."

I snorted. "Understatement of the century. I'm telling you, we need to focus more on Sophie's puppet master problem than the whole "chosen one" thing. It's the plot of every lame movie. I'm thinking it's a distraction from the real conflict."

"Puppet master?" Sophie repeated.

I nodded, making the motion of controlling an invisible puppet with my own bloodstained arms. "You know, whatever it is inside your brain that's making your eyes go weird and ramping up your PMS by about a thousand percent."

She blinked. "I've got it under control," she clipped.

"I really disagree there," I said. "Considering you just had an out-of-body experience and uttered things like 'mate.'" I shuddered. "You would never use that in a serious context unless you were making fun of, oh, I don't know…." I looked at the brooding man. "A wolf. Actually, I feel like there's a sparkling elephant in the room, and a big old wolf who needs a haircut and an explanation. Are you doing some sort of doggy daycare for extra cash, Soph? If the PI business is really that bad, you could always sell your spells for money. It's better than having to pick dog hair off your newly upholstered armchair. Or prostitution. That's the oldest profession in the world, and there's nothing wrong with getting laid and getting paid for it."

I grinned at the wolf, who showed teeth but said nothing. I wondered if he was a mute.

Thorne had eyes on him too, as did the rest of the males, but they didn't seem as overly concerned as I did.

Sophie's eyes flickered to the wolf, and the brief contact of their gazes was something even I felt.

"He's here because I owe someone a favor."

"What, you lost a bet?" I asked.

She glared at me. "He's not important right now."

I glared back. "I disagree. The wolfman who is two seconds away from humping your leg or urinating around your desk is important at this juncture. We're kind of at a sensitive moment in this whole situation, and we can't be risking that the dog will yap his snout about town."

The room of males was strangely silent, each set of eyes whipping between us like spectators at a tennis game.

"He can be trusted," she said tightly.

I crossed my arms. "I'm going to need more than that."

"You're not getting more. Not when we've got bigger fish to fry. Namely finding out this chosen one crap," Sophie said.

"Ugh. End of the world, yes, yadda yadda yadda," I sighed. "I'm sure it's nothing. Let's just kill the witches and go from there."

"We're going to have to do some research on this," Thorne cut in.

Sophie nodded.

I gaped at them. "You're talking about reading books instead of fighting? What have I walked into, Oprah's book club?"

"She just talked about the end of the fuckin' world and you being the catalyst for that, Isla," Thorne growled. "I think that warrants a bit of pause."

"Last week she talked about how she thought we should stop cursing every woman in Ugg boots we encountered. We need a grain of salt, a slice of lemon, and a shot of tequila to go with everything she says. Especially with this whole *possession* thing she's got going on," I told him.

"She's right," a voice cut in.

All eyes went to Scott, who'd been leaning on the doorframe.

"Scott, I totally forgot you were here. I thought you had a roller derby or something to go to," I said.

He glared at me. "It's Ultimate Frisbee, and it got canceled," he corrected.

I swallowed a chuckle, only because he looked so serious.

"You know about this?" Rick asked him. His voice was serious, like he was actually considering Scott as someone who didn't live in his mom's basement.

Well, his mom was dead, so that was out of the question, but that was the spirit of his entire persona.

Scott nodded. "The Deathless Prophecy."

I gaped at him. "How in the fuck do you know anything about a prophecy? You're a half breed who works in the Sector. I don't think a book on prophecy comes with the induction booklet. And with things like Ultimate Frisbee and Jonas brothers concerts on the agenda in addition to annoying me, I thought your pocketbook would be mighty full."

He focused his one eye on me, deceptively serious. That unnerved me more than the rest of it. "I read. A lot. As you say, I'm a half breed, and that fact means I'm in this world at somewhat of a disadvantage. But it also means I'm more likely to make friends with people on the fringe. And the fringe is where the knowledge is."

I continued to gape. "You're serious? And not talking about people who play Ultimate Frisbee and collect My Little Pony?" I asked.

"Isla," Thorne warned.

I gave him a look. "What? I'm just making sure. You never know with him."

"It's a book of the origin of all things. A friend of mine said it's passed down from generation to generation and was considered little more than bedtime stories. But the Deathless one is the one who is neither undead nor alive, who has the blood of the one who will kill her in her veins and on the heels of eternity they will ride, with the Great War determining the fate of the planet." He recited it in that same kind of empty voice Sophie had before but it was from memory, like he was looking at the page in his mind.

"Well this is becoming more and more like a daytime movie special," I muttered. "Two people with the fate of the world in their hands? Yeah, it's never *that* easy. The world is a big place. Two people can't save it, nor can they ruin it."

No one was listening to me anymore.

Which was pissing me right off. They were listening to the one-eyed half breed who actually said once that he thought *Dracula* was a great representation of society's version of the vampire in the modern world. I would've felt better if he'd spoken of Eric Northman—at least he was hot.

Rick was looking rattled. Which rattled me a little, if I was honest. The king had looked rattled exactly twice since I'd met him, both when I was on Death's door. Luckily I had scampered away before he answered.

But I bet he was getting frustrated now. Death, not Rick. Well, maybe Rick too.

"I recall this legend," Rick said slowly, focused on Scott and not me. "And at the summit we just held, a witch of one of the covens was mentioning it, saying that the events of the past decade brought about the prophecy of the Deathless, though we took little stock in prophecy considering the problems of the present."

I pointed at him. "Yes, that sounds like what we should do. Focus on the present. Not the future. Yolo. Wait, it should be Yodo. You only die once. Except for me, of course. And all vampires, if we want to get technical. Shit, Yodt doesn't work. Whatever. All the more reason to live in the now, dudes."

Rick stared at me. "The present and the future seem very mixed right now. And it would be unwise to discredit such things that give us warning. It could be fatal, in fact. We have an alliance that is unprecedented with the attacks of hybrids increasing throughout the globe. This problem is not going away, not with the power behind it that is more than the world has seen in ages."

His eyes flickered to Thorne, something passing between them before it was gone.

"Well, a fight's a fight. We'll not complicate it with this shit. Tell me where to be and who to kill and I'll be there. For now, I need to get laid," Duncan cut in.

He winked at me, saluted Rick and then was gone.

I watched his back fondly, wishing I was able to exit this fucking mess with the same ease and simplicity of the Scottish hitman.

But no, I had to be the fucking *chosen one.*

"I think he's got the right idea," I put in, frowning and wanting to call out "Take me with you."

But I didn't think Thorne would've appreciated it at that moment.

No one listened to me anyway.

"I'll contact the coven to see what I can find out," Sophie said. "Though I think my involvement in prophecy needs to be understated, considering I *really* don't want to be sequestered."

It was at that point that the mute werewolf decided to speak. "That's not fuckin' happening."

"Of course it's not happening," I snapped at him. "If you hadn't noticed, Sophie has these nifty new powers that would likely blow that place to the ground if she so wished."

Sophie grinned at me. "Don't tempt me."

"That's what I'm here for. To tempt you to make all the bad decisions. They're usually the most fun."

For once she didn't take me up on it. She was still serious. "I'll do what I can to see what I can get from this, but Isla, prophecy is what our race is built on. You've just been too busy ignoring the society that you so badly want to be separate from to notice."

I threw my hands up. "Well who wouldn't want to be part of a society that builds itself on the ramblings of a crazy and borderline-possessed witch?" I asked the room, then eyed Sophie. "No offense."

She shrugged. "Can't beat the truth."

No. We couldn't.

And it seemed that the truth was staring us in the face.

And the truth just happened to look a fuck of a lot like death.

NINE

"I'M BORED," I DECLARED, SNAPPING THE DUSTY BOOK shut and throwing it on the oak desk.

Thorne looked up from his own. "You've been reading that for approximately twelve minutes."

I pushed up and paced the dusty library. "Twelve minutes too long. I haven't got eternity, you know. Well, technically I do, but still I wouldn't want to waste it *reading*." I paused. "Unless it was something that wasn't a prophecy about me having the fate of the world on my shoulders. I don't look good with anything on my shoulders. The shoulder pads in the eighties showed me that. I don't have the frame for it."

It had been three days since the little prophecy announcement, and it was the most boring three days *ever*. We had the location of the witches, and we had a witch of our own in the chamber, yet we were fucking *reading*. Because wars were won in libraries, apparently.

Thorne seemed happy about the turn of events, and not just because it meant we got to take sex breaks on the desk. I had been doing my best to stay away from all reading portions of our little activity. I had a company to run and minions to order around; therefore, this was the only day I actually had to be in the library.

Apparently what they'd found meant Sophie's words weren't just hot air.

And it also meant that Rick was attending all sorts of councils that seemed duller than beige sweaters about stopping the 'kill on sight' orders for slayers, since the whole 'slayer tied to the fate of the world' thing was gaining traction.

Two vampires from the Sector were coming for tea. Or blood. I'd had to call Lewis to find myself a nice juicy mafia boss who'd escaped prosecution a couple of times and had a body count to rival my own.

"You haven't been around lately," Lewis commented on the phone.

"Oh yeah, I've been busy. Dying. Coming back to life. Fighting a sect of vampires intent on ending the human race as you know it. Oh, and *Scandal* just came out on Netflix."

There was a long sigh on the other end of the phone. "You better not do anything stupid like get yourself killed, Isla," he ordered roughly.

I smiled on the other end of the phone. "Awww, does that mean you care about me?" I cooed.

I got dead air as my answer.

Then the location of the latest sucker to get drained for my little tea party.

He was in the kitchen—the mafia boss, not Lewis. Hopefully he wouldn't get too cold before they arrived, considering Theonexia and the sharing of his blood would be the only thing keeping the vampires from trying to kill Thorne and me.

Self-righteous vampires from the Sector wouldn't likely break one of the race's oldest rules.

As I paced, I thought. Which wasn't good. Because idle hands were the Devil's work, after all.

That motherfucker already seemed to be working overtime to mess up my day.

Scott had come in with his book and we'd read the passage the day before. Not as entertaining as *Fifty*, and it didn't turn me on near as much.

Or at all.

It will start with two and come in threes.

The curse will be cast.

And with the three of two shall the history be made—the future, already written with the spilling of the blood, being the first of the three.

The blood which is designed to be fatal will cause death to abandon her. Yet it will make death her constant companion. Deathless in all ways except the blood.

It is in which the beginning began that the new ending shall be written for the future or for the present.

The three will determine.

There will be a Deathless one.

There will be one who takes Death's embrace like a lover's caress, and the animal within the two will roar at the moon, for its agony will blanket the earth.

And there will be one as mortal as the weakest of humanity to bring down the strongest of immortality.

Eternally they will walk the earth, or the earth will perish without them. With the Great War to be fought and the prophecy to be filled, it will end. Or it will begin.

As it was and always has been.

In blood.

The blood will run.

The Deathless night.

The curse.

The blood will run.

"That's cheerful," I commented after reading and then banishing the light that came with the words. I needed the shadows. That's where monsters resided, after all.

"It's not even necessarily about me and Thorne," I continued. "It could conceivably be anyone. Brad and Jen. Or Brad and Ange. Or Brad and the fucking nanny," I listed on my fingers. "Besides, there're three other people involved in this. Well four, it seems. Three couples. And I don't have any couple friends. I *hate* couple friends. So there we go, I don't brunch or do quiz nights with anyone in a relationship and the world is safe," I declared.

Thorne hadn't thought so.

Rick had agreed, even despite the steady stream of hate between them that I was still curious about.

But whatever, I had arguments to win.

Which I wasn't. Winning, that is.

No one agreed when I suggested we "ignore Scott's creepy bedtime storybook and start cracking heads and taking names."

Not even Duncan.

Duncan.

"Sorry, lassie. I'll go into any fight without blinking. But war? War's different. We need to know thy enemy."

I scowled at him. "Did you just quote *Art of War*?" I hissed.

He shrugged.

And then I'd stabbed him with a letter opener.

Even that hadn't helped. So he was away having all the fun and fighting a coven of hybrids on the other side of the state while I was stuck in a library.

Reading.

Well *I* wasn't.

But Thorne was.

I focused on his dark head, bent over some ancient text that Sophie had carted over with her wolfy shadow before leaving as quick as her combat boots could take her.

"The animal within the two will roar at the moon, for its agony will blanket the earth."

That light shined in again, illuminating the dark places and showing me with a cool certainty that the universe seemed to have plans for us. And not just me. My friend.

And a werewolf.

If she was destined to be with anyone, I would've been a lot happier had it been a demon of high caliber. Then he'd be able to talk to the man downstairs about wiping the slate clean of all this prophecy stuff.

I didn't like words in a book telling me how I'd live my life.

Or how it would become my death.

It pissed me right the fuck off.

And since the universe was rather hard to stab with a letter opener, I focused on something more corporeal. And bled more.

My heels echoed on the floor of my study like a warm drum as I stormed over to Thorne. His eyes met mine and he settled his solid gaze on me.

It was tinged with what had settled there since… well, I'd come back from the grave with a very particular taste in blood and a pesky title of *chosen one* that I despised more than being known as the chick who accidentally saved a country from nuclear winter that one time.

I stared at him. "They were wrong," I hissed.

He was no longer surprised by my spouting things that didn't rightly seem like they went with the conversion, so he simply said, "Who?"

"Everyone!" I threw up my hands, gesturing around the library. Immortality gave one a lot of free time—in between wars, of course. And before there was TV and online shopping, there were books. So I had a lot. Not all that were ever written, but a nice collection. One I had the irrational urge to set aflame and throw off my balcony.

"Every twit who wrote sagas, epics and fucking poems about this great thing called love. Because it's not great. I'm a vampire, for Lucifer's sake. I kind of have the monopoly of pain and suffering. Granted, I'm usually the one delivering it, but it's merely details." I narrowed my eyes at him. "You know what's ruined me more than lost limbs, burning flesh, and daggers to the fucking heart? You. This love. It's the most suffering I have ever experienced. And the worst fucking thing? Like some masochist, I don't ever want to stop suffering because that means I'll stop loving you. So yes, these idiots with their tales of love are liars in the ninth fucking degree, and if a good portion of them weren't dead I'd kill them all myself."

Thorne had weathered my rant with a blank face, maybe because he'd weathered many a rant and also because he was maybe trying to tread carefully around the bomb he'd only just defused that could, at any moment, start the ticking clock to explosion.

"No, babe," he said finally, looking from me to the aged books full of bullshit. "You're wrong."

I raised my brow at him. "And you're brave, saying that to an emotional female who just happens to be a vampire and has the power to rip your fucking heart out," I said blandly.

His face stayed impassive. "Yeah, Isla, you have that power," he agreed. "But it's not about you being a vampire. It's you being you."

"They're one and the same," I snapped.

"No, they're not. What you are doesn't define you."

"I disagree—it is all that defines me. That and my excellent taste in shoes."

"You know what defines you? The fact that you kill as easy as blink but risk immortality to save a race that wants you dead. That you will break someone's arm for looking at you the wrong way but you'll break someone's neck for hurting someone you love. That list of people may be small, but that's all the more important. Because you give everything you are to the people you love, and that shows you something. And it shows you that these epics, poems, fucking tragedies were specifically right. Because the good ones, the great ones, they are full to the brim with pain and suffering and blood. But they've withstood in their own right. Become immortal because of that ugly, powerful, beautiful, heartrending kind of love. And that's what we have. There'll be blood, of that I have no doubt. Mine. Yours, though I'll do anything in my power to prevent that. But there'll be blood. And suffering. Death, but not yours. Or mine. Because what we got, baby, it's immortal. And it ain't got shit to do with the fact that you're a vampire or I'm a Praseates."

I paused at the words. At the truth to them. But then the truth was a tricky thing. Much like a great pair of shoes. Looked and felt great, but for you to look good and feel better about your outfit you also had to welcome the pain that came with six-inch stilettos.

I didn't know, of course, but I'd heard enough whiny hu‑mans bitch about the pain.

I'd almost snapped their ankles to show them real pain and then educate them on the importance of sacrifice.

And sacrifice for fashion was the biggest of all.

Or so I'd thought.

Until I met a man I'd sacrificed it all for.

But then it turned out someone had already decided that sacrifice. And if there was one thing I didn't like, it was being told what to do. I'd tell people what to do until the demons came home because I knew better than most people.

All people, in fact.

Which was why I didn't need such a thing as prophecy to tell me what I'd die for.

Who I'd die for.

I was quite capable of doing that for myself.

And it pissed me off that the universe and I had come to the same conclusion.

The man standing in front of me professing his undying love.

The undying love that just happened to be written in a book older than either of us.

So I didn't blink in the face of his words.

Outwardly, at least.

"I'm a rule breaker," I informed him. "It's like strength training for me. The heavier, more taboo said rule, the more fun it is to snap and work my biceps. That's why I had so much fun doing it with you. Oh, and I guess the whole love thing too," I added when his eyes flickered with fury. "But I thought I was breaking the biggest rule of our kind when really I was going along with some god's plan." I narrowed my eyes. "I don't like plans. Or being told what to do. I like to surprise everyone, myself included, with the fucked-up shit I do. Now it seems that this entire existence has been written in the stars. For young romantics, it may be all very soulful, but I'm not young, nor romantic. And the very thought of anyone, even a god—*especially* a god—telling me who to love before I figure it out for myself makes me *itchy*," I declared. "And not in a good way."

"No one decided how you felt about me," he declared. "You're too stubborn to let anything influence your emotions. I knew you loved me from the moment you didn't kill me."

I smiled at him. "So sweet. That's how I knew you loved me too."

He stared at me long and hard in a way that told me I was to also stay stoic and silent.

"I can't deal when you look like that," I snapped, obviously not doing what his glare told me to.

So he stepped forward, snatching my face roughly.

"It is not by design, or blueprint," he murmured. "Though it feels divine—*you* feel divine—it wasn't gods or even the Devil who created this. It was a prophecy created to be broken. We are not loving each other *because* of a plan but despite one. Because it's written in the stars that death will take me from you, and I won't let that happen. Not for gods, not for the Devil himself and sure as fuck not for the universe."

I stared at him. "You can't do that. Guarantee a forever. Decide you own me."

His eyes flickered. "Think I just did, babe. Eternity. I'll accept nothing less."

I wanted to be mad. I really did.

But even I wasn't so irrational as to try and carve up something so good in the midst of everything that was turning to complete and utter shit.

"So apparently being owned by someone isn't a death

sentence. It turns out to be a life sentence. Of eternity."

"And is that a bad thing?"

"I haven't decided yet. Because if you ever decide to create a joint Facebook account, I'll end it right there."

His soulful intensity rippled with my words and he shook his head, yanking me into his chest, which was vibrating not just with his heartbeat but with his slight chuckle.

Then he pulled me back to meet his eyes. "How about we take a break from the reading portion of the afternoon and prove to the gods and the Devil himself just how much someone couldn't have designed what we have? How about I show you that nothing could've imagined what I'm going to do with you, *to* you, for eternity?" he rasped, his hand brushing the corner of my breast and then roughly tweaking my nipple.

My stomach dipped at the delightful promise and I leaned in. "Only if you agree that once this starts, I'll be showing you just how no god, nor even the Devil himself, will be able to rival the depraved things I can do," I whispered.

His eyes darkened as he took hold of my ponytail, yanking my neck back roughly so his teeth could run along the flesh that was both icy cold from my nature and in a fiery inferno from his touch.

The promise of engulfing flames was enough to make me welcome any kind of destruction as long as it came at Thorne's hands.

Of course, that's when a short rap sounded at the door.

We froze and I cursed myself for not hearing the two vampires from the Sector ascend the elevator.

"Fucking fuckers," I hissed.

The knock at the door echoed through the apartment that already was full of all sorts of words left unsaid, and maybe too many left said.

After all, there was only so many times you could open your heart to someone without it bleeding all over the place.

Without it dying.

It was just science, really. Undead or alive, love was fatal.

I didn't need a prophecy thousands of years old to tell me that. No, I just listened to that little voice inside that most of the time I ignored because it was so utterly dull. Its whispers turned to roars when Thorne's heartbeat wasn't close enough to drown them out. When Thorne wasn't close enough to drown it out.

The voice of survival. That ingrained instinct that everyone had. And it was telling me something that I didn't rightly need to hear.

Something that seemed to ring in with that knock.

Thorne pulled back from my face at the same time I screwed up my nose in distaste.

"Company's here, dear," I said. "And although I wouldn't really care much, or at all, if they had to wait or even watch you ravage me, they might learn a thing or two." I winked at him. "And these stiffs might do something idiotic like try to kill us if we keep them waiting too long." I paused, knowing the vampires at the door could very well hear me. That was what made it fun. "So let's get this over with. I'll be prepared for murder or tea. In fact, we can offer both. Be a doll and heat up the pot of blood on the stove, won't you?" I asked as we walked into the kitchen.

His hardened eyes focused on the pot that was indeed full of inky red liquid that I'd drained from the mobster Lewis offered me.

Thorne didn't like it, considering protecting humankind was meant to kind of be his 'thing,' but he was getting rid of some of that humanity and self-righteousness, thankfully. What worried me was where some of it was going.

He knew Theonexia and the sharing of human blood was required in order to stop us from having to ruin another sofa with the blood of two representatives from the Sector.

He gave me a long look before kissing me on the head and storming to the stove, turning it on. I stood and waited because I knew the alpha male in him would not let me walk to answer a door for the two vampires who may or may not try to kill me and him.

He was strange like that.

Not that I minded. I liked that we were keeping them waiting.

And his butt looked fucking brilliant in those jeans.

"Ready?" he growled, eyes on mine when he returned, grasping my hand.

"Not really," I admitted as we walked towards the door. "I'm much more comfortable with fighting and murder. These peace talks really freak me out."

The corner of Thorne's mouth turned up. "Well, sometimes peace talks are required in war."

I rolled my eyes. "I know. So annoying."

Opening the door, I was presented with three vampires, two of whom I was expecting. The third, I was not.

Neither was Thorne. His body went stiffer at the third vampire, fury radiating off him. The bones in my hands protested as he squeezed too hard, obviously restraining from doing anything like lunging at him.

I scowled. "What are you doing here?"

The woman gaped at me, her ordered facade cracking.

"You *dare* greet your king like that?" she asked in horror. "The correct term in addressing him is Your Highness. Treat the ruler of your race with the respect he deserves."

It was Thorne's turn to have the hands in his bones cracked with the amount of restraint it took for me not to rip her hair from its tight chignon and bring her head with it.

Thorne didn't heal as fast as I did, so it was perhaps unfair that I broke the bones. But he was tough and barely even reacted, if but a little stiffening of his jaw.

I smiled a tight smile. "I am treating him with the respect he deserves," I told her. "He's still here, and he hasn't got anything pointy sticking out of him, like, I don't know, *this*."

My hand was out of Thorne's in a flash and at his belt, where the enchanted blade was tucked more often than not these days. It was, after all, a war.

Both vampires reacted rather dramatically as I casually waved it in front of me. Sweater Set nearly crawled up the wall, and her male counterpart actually hid behind the king I was pretty sure he was meant to protect with his undeath.

I raised my brows at them as I easily twirled the blade around before fastening it back in a smiling Thorne's belt.

"Chill, dude and dudette. If I were going to use that, you wouldn't even have the time to reconsider your frankly criminal choices of outfits for the last day of your deaths. You'd just be dead." I gave them both a look as they hurried to right themselves. "But that did not go well for either of you."

I fastened my gaze on Rick, who had, of course, been smooth and calm during the whole exchange, despite the initial hardening of his jaw at Thorne, then our intertwined hands. That seemed to cause him more trouble than the knife with which I'd kind of threatened his life.

The moment his eyes locked with mine, they softened

slightly, something moving in them. Something that had been a small glimmer that night of the explosion at his compound and had been there a lot more after me almost dying.

Then it was gone.

And I was able to gather myself enough to move my attention from the attractive vampire king in the exquisitely cut suit to the mousy woman in an ill-fitting, gray polyester skirt suit with kitten heels.

Fucking *kitten heels.*

"See, Sweater Set, you're on my turf right now. And my turf means my rules." I paused. "No, wait, whosever turf I'm on, it's my fucking rules because that's just how I play it. I hate being told what to do. I guess I'm Peter Pan in more ways than one. I don't want to grow up, nor do I want any authority-type figures thinking they can tell me anything. Though I can't fly and that kind of sucks. And I don't have a little fairy in a kickass but kind of slutty outfit as a best buddy. But I do have a witch and she's pretty badass. She even cast this spell that means as soon as you came out of the elevator your immortal asses are going to be rendered mortal should you decide to do something untoward."

I smiled.

Sophie had done no such thing because no such spell existed except for the one I was currently dealing with. Black magic was required to play with life and death. And that was a little cliff she wouldn't be able to hop on her broomstick and fly up from anytime soon.

But they didn't know that.

Sweater Set scowled. "In addition to your—" She moved down to the intertwined hands that had once more found each other despite the broken bones and death threats. "—*fraternization* with the enemy, you are admitting to having connections with a witch not only practicing forbidden magic but performing it in your place of residence on two members of the Sector and your own king?"

"Yes, that's exactly what I'm admitting. Thank you so much for laying it out like that. Your little friend there does seem like he needs someone to paint him a rather vibrant picture. Doesn't get social cues," I explained, looking at the slack-jawed and reasonably vacant-looking male vampire. "And the king in question did try to have me executed not that long ago. That's something a girl doesn't forget in a hot minute, so I'm more than a little testy." I paused. "Oh, how rude of me to exchange death threats on a doorstep like some kind of heathen, or werewolf."

I screwed up my nose as I stepped back to let the three vampires in. It didn't escape my notice the way Thorne positioned himself in front of me very purposefully when the vampires passed, nor the way he did it when Rick moved smoothly inside, meeting his fury-filled eyes with a cold indifference he'd practiced in the face of naked rage.

Again, I put that on my to-do list, along with Thorne—he was hot when he was homicidal—killing witches, winning a war, and making sure my best friend didn't tumble off a cliff and turn into some kind of witch bitch. And also not tumble into bed with a werewolf, of all things.

"I'll just go get some blood for our guests," I said, gesturing to the sofa. "Why don't you sit?"

There was a long pause as the invitation hung in the air, and it was Rick who moved to accept it. And even though the Sector was a governance separate to the crown, they still answered to it, so they sat as well.

I winked at Thorne. "Honey, could you give me a hand with the glasses? They're ever so heavy," I asked sweetly, fluttering my lashes.

I was very satisfied with the incredulous gape from Sweater Set, which I'd decided to shorten to SS. Rolled off the tongue much easier.

Thorne and I disappeared into the kitchen, where, as organized, we used the blood of the mobster to distract from the fact that I gently put my fangs to his wrist, eyes on his the entire time. The way his eyes darkened with blatant desire had me wanting to ravage him here and now.

But there were responsibilities of making sure the Sector didn't organize our execution and such.

So boring.

So after letting my lips linger on his wrist for a beat longer than I needed to, I removed them and turned his bleeding wrist over the small glass I'd saved for myself.

Obviously I couldn't let the Sector know the little gem that was me drinking from Thorne and only Thorne.

Something to be kept on the down low, considering making public enemy numbers one and two more vulnerable by knowing that number one—me, of course—needed number two and only number two; otherwise, she was fucked.

Putting a target on his back and/or advertising my vulnerability were not on my to-do list for the night.

Hence me giving my glass to Thorne while I cradled the three meant for our guests. They weren't likely to take a glass of blood offered to them by a slayer, so I was the waitress for the evening.

Thorne and I exchanged a look that I knew meant no words were necessary. Not that we could speak them; vampire hearing meant that the stare of lovers was the only thing we could share. Oh, and a quick kiss.

The air in the living room when we came back was more

than a little chilly.

Just how I liked it.

The three vampires silently took the glasses offered with obvious distaste and reservation. Despite Theonexia forbidding hosts from presenting tainted blood to guests, at Apollo's wrath, they paused.

I grinned at them. "I'm so touched that you consider me brave or crazy enough to go to battle with a god. Fills me with so many warm fuzzies."

They ignored me.

Why was everyone doing that?

Rick bringing the glass to his mouth and tipping it down his throat in a smooth swallow signaled the other two to do the same.

I rolled my eyes, sipping from my own glass, giving Thorne a heated look as I did so.

His eyes glowed.

The silence that bathed the room after the sipping of the blood was uncomfortably brilliant.

Unfortunately, or fortunately, I had things to do—namely Thorne—so I decided to move the party along.

"So, what? You're going to kill me now?" I asked conversationally after I'd drained my glass.

It was addressed to the room in general, but SS took it upon herself to answer, lifting her brow. "We will not break the most sacred law that helps keep us from the animalistic humanity that lets wars and battles ravage mankind," she snapped. "Despite your obvious distaste for any law that governs our kind. Taking up with a *slayer*."

I tilted my head. "I thought it was more frowned upon than actually *law* which will show the wrath of the gods or whatever. You know, like murdering someone at a wedding. People don't like it, but they deal." I paused. "No? Okay, then."

She put the glass on my coffee table, without a coaster, which made me stabby—it was new. I'd just had to replace everything thanks to Thorne and me destroying all the furniture.

This was one of my best coffee tables yet, and she was ruining it with her fucking rings.

I squeezed the stem of my glass as she brushed her palms on the cheap fabric of her skirt.

Her eyes met mine. "Once this mess has been cleaned up and the rebels have been taken care of, you know the Sector will recommend the extermination of the problem you've decided to give us. I will personally make sure that this problem is rectified, and the slayer alliance that our king is proposing will end with the execution of the one who doesn't seem to know its place."

The silence that came after the less-than-masked threat—a Vegas bride had more veiling on her shit—was heavy.

I made it so it lasted a lot longer than was comfortable. Though Thorne, taut and furious beside me, was anything but comfortable. In fact, due to my heightened emotions and the connection we now had, I would've been damn near homicidal off his emotions alone.

You know, if I wasn't already homicidal as shit. Side effect of being a vampire.

And of being a woman when some asshole said something like that about your man.

I smiled sweetly at the vampire in front of me. "Now I know you didn't just threaten Thorne, my…." I searched for the word. 'Fated one' and 'mate' sounded so douchey. "Man companion." Equally as bad, but I said it with enough confidence and venom that the term rolled off the tongue sharp enough to cut a bitch.

Not sharp enough to take the head of this vampire, unfortunately.

"I *know* you didn't just do that," I continued. "Not in my own home, in front of me, the vampire very well known for, shall we say, overacting. Slicing off that demon's arm for spilling a drink on my dress?" I waited for dramatic pause. "Yeah, that really happened. But to be fair, she was a total bitch and it was fucking *couture*," I seethed. It may have been a decade ago, but vampires never forget. I did smile over the fact that the blade I used was enchanted and now she still didn't have an arm.

It was the little things.

I kept my smile as I regarded them but added a little more insanity to it, just to freak them the fuck out even more. "I know you're not stupid, or suicidal enough to do such a thing," I said. "But if you were stupid enough to threaten him right in front of my *fucking face* in my *fucking house*, I'd rip your throat out," I promised. "Then chop off your head, burn you, and sprinkle your ashes on the steak I planned on having for dinner." I grinned. "If you don't do it again, I'll just stick with regular peppercorns. Aren't as zesty, but I can go without."

I let my own silence descend as Thorne's fury remained, an invisible pulse in the air. But the corner of his mouth twitched only slightly, communicating his amusement.

I smiled, that time slightly less insane. Just my usual crazy.

"Okay, great. Now that the pleasantries are out of the way, we can get down to it. Can I get anyone a scone? Fresh baked this evening."

If I wasn't mistaken, I might've seen a little twitch at the corner of Rick's mouth, even though he sipped from his glass to hide it.

The king, amused?

Well this was turning into a fun night.

I really hoped I got to kill SS at the end of it, but I didn't think that particular wish would be granted, unfortunately.

Her mousy male vampire companion fumbled with an iPad—interesting to see the Sector had gone paperless—and pressed some buttons with a pudgy hand. "You were denounced by your own Vein Line," he began.

I crossed my arms. "Yeah, my family's sweet like that. Plus they didn't get me a birthday present this year. Almost five hundred. A big one."

He glanced up at me, then back down to the screen, obviously deciding to act like I hadn't spoken.

I was going to have to start killing more people to show I was serious about getting the attention I deserved.

I'd start with SS.

"You have been accused of treason in the highest degree, the betrayal of the crown, monarchy and Ambrogio himself for taking up with one who is fated to destroy us all."

I grinned at Thorne. "Did you hear that, honey? My mom knows we're together and is happy enough to tell the entire vampire society."

Thorne grunted out a harsh chuckle. "I'm sure she's browsing for wedding china as we speak," he muttered.

I grinned even wider at his ill-timed joke.

Ill-timed jokes were the best kind, and the most hilarious.

"I'll register us at Slayers r Us," I continued.

The disproval in the room was heavy enough to bottle and sell as perfume to humans.

SS chose that time to speak once more, her pinched face darting between me and Thorne. "You're not going to renounce your crimes to the Sector?"

I rolled my eyes. "Love is not a crime. Have you even

listened to Bob Dylan or John Lennon?" I asked defensively. "Also, I don't deny anything. Because mostly I've done all the outrageous and depraved things people accuse me of. And the things I haven't done give me inspiration for future acts, so it means even if I haven't done it, I probably will do it at some point in the future."

"You refuse to take anything concerning our race seriously, but your blatant disregard for rules that have been in place for centuries is less than pleasing. In fact, it's reason for immediate imprisonment," she said.

The moment the words left her mouth, Thorne lurched forward, his fury blanketing me. "You try to imprison her. See what the fuck happens," he dared her.

I patted his hand and grinned at the way she blanched with his motion. "Now, now, honey, SS isn't going to lock me up, just like I'm not going to put her in fashion jail for her horrific choices, no matter how much I want to. There's just no simplicity in this life or even in death. It's this pesky war. They need us," I observed.

The ensuing silence made me smile wider at the fact that I was so very right. Of course I was.

Rick cleared his throat and leaned forward slightly. "The Sector recognizes the sacrifices and valiancy in battle you've offered to the crown in the face of this rebellion, as well as the need for an alliance to fight it since our enemies are doing the same with creatures throughout the community. In times of war is when rules held for centuries are broken and reevaluated for the sake of survival. We need to be able to adapt in order to keep ourselves separate from animals. And humans."

The way his cold voice spoke the words told me—and, more importantly, Thorne—exactly what he thought of humans and the fact that they were classed lower than animals.

He let that sink in while keeping my eyes. "Both the Sector and the crown are offering you a full pardon for your crimes."

I smiled at him, clapping my hands. "A full pardon! That's even better than that pony I was wishing for. Now I can sleep at night without fearing the monsters in the night will come and snatch me away from the warm body I'm lying next to." I paused. "Oh no, wait. I didn't want a pardon. In fact, I'll sleep even less with that little thing. It means I've done nothing wrong, or at the very least, something right, and that's so not acceptable. What will that do to my carefully frowned-on reputation?"

Something in Rick's eyes moved with rage while the corner of Thorne's mouth tipped up. That was becoming the thing with these two, moving around each other like a seesaw. One was enraged and the other was ecstatic, either because of the other's rage or with whatever lay between them, dictating it.

And I wasn't dense enough not to know that one of the things laying between them was a red-haired and magnificent vampire who the king didn't have rightly platonic feelings for.

But even I wasn't self-centered enough to think that I caused this much animosity between them. It stank of something aged, hatred fermented through the years, through history that was much more than just nature dictating them as enemies.

"Take the pardon, Isla," Rick said smoothly, standing. The puppets from the sector followed suit.

"No," I pouted.

"You're going to take it because it also comes with the guarantee that attacking you, or the human belonging to you, is a crime of treason tantamount to death. And once the treaty with the slayers is signed, it will likely be necessary for your survival."

I rolled my eyes. "Oh yes, a little pardon is going to save me from the race of vampire-human hybrids employed by rebels who are intent on overthrowing your power and everything you represent. They'll totally bring down your whole regime, but they'll keep all the pardons granted to wayward vampires for nostalgia's sake."

"Isla," Rick said once more.

I glared at him. Then at SS and her mentally challenged colleague.

Then at Thorne, the one who would give me the horror of silence and the gaping hole that would come with it if he did die.

"Fine," I bit out. "I'll take the fucking pardon."

TEN

"**Y**ou're joking. This is a hilarious, classic Thorne joke, right?" I asked as I paced the living room in his house in the woods.

I hadn't wanted to come for a sleepover in Slayerville, but he'd insisted since he had the brat for the night.

It was taxing, having to work around the human.

I hadn't wanted to come in the first place.

He'd insisted.

I'd argued.

He'd used sex as a tool against me and I somehow found myself agreeing.

I almost ruined it all when the little human attached itself to my midsection upon my arrival.

"Isla! I'm so happy you've arrived," she shrieked.

I flinched, taking her arms as gently as I could so I didn't snap them, as was my natural instinct.

"We talked about this," I reminded her once I'd detached her from me.

Her grin remained and I was disgusted to see the front tooth which she had lost was now only half there, in the midst of a growth cycle. It was rather disturbing.

"Stop smiling," I demanded. "I want to keep my dinner in my stomach, and your little toothy grin is making me sick."

She immediately complied. Well, the smile remained, but the teeth were cloaked by her lips and her eyes sparkled with excitement.

Her hair was piled messily on her head, fastened with butterfly clips, of all things. The same creatures decorated her tee shirt but were somehow juxtaposed with black jeans and boots.

I decided to ignore that, for I might just commit murder for fashion crimes alone. It didn't matter how old you were; there was no excuse for that.

None.

"What did we say?" I continued, thinking back to our last conversation.

"That I must not hug, touch or come within five feet of you. And I'd get exactly one warning before any limb in your vicinity will be broken." She parroted my exact words from months before rather dutifully.

Impressive. I didn't think small human brains had the capacity for such a repertoire.

I nodded. "How many warnings have you had?" I asked her.

She pouted. "One."

I clapped my hands. "Great. You're all out. So keep those sticky fingers off my person and my clothing and you might get to keep them."

I had hoped she'd cry, or at the very least scamper off in fear and never talk to me again, but she did none of the above.

"Can we negotiate that rule when you teach me how to fight?"

I gaped at her. "What on earth gave you the idea that I'd teach you how to fight?"

She glanced to Thorne, who was talking on the phone as he had been all night, speaking to someone called Alexus about some meeting the next day that I hadn't cared enough about to fully eavesdrop on.

I was too busy staring at his biceps flexing as he held the phone.

And trying not to snap his little sister's neck.

It was rather hard.

Or that's what I was telling myself.

I certainly wouldn't admit that I *liked* the little cretin.

"Well, Thorne told me that you'd been training some of the others—"

"The *fully grown* humans," I interrupted. "You are not that." I frowned down at her miniature stature.

She folded her arms. "I'm grown enough to fight," she protested.

"No, you're grown enough to die," I countered.

Her little eye twitched. "Same thing."

"Being grown enough to die isn't the same as being grown enough to fight."

She gave me a long look that was suddenly devoid of the childlike innocence that her distance from the ground and stupid hair pins communicated. It was something that reminded me that she'd seen death. Been in the middle of a warzone. Not that she garnered any sort of special sympathy for that alone. A lot of children did that.

I'd done that.

And look at me. I'd grown up to be gloriously unhinged.

"No. It's the same thing," she repeated firmly. "If I'm going to be grown enough to see death, I'm going to be grown enough to know how to meet it with a fire in my belly and fight in my heart," she said.

I stared at her.

She stared back.

And I relented.

Like an idiot.

So the evening was spent training with her and trying my best not to accidentally snap her neck.

I wanted to get laid, after all, and killing Thorne's sister would likely have put a damper on the mood. Even if it was by accident.

Then I'd had to 'put her to bed.'

"You're old enough to handle a dagger, fight a vampire, and grow adult teeth. Put your damn self to bed," I instructed her.

Thorne, who was finally off the phone, gave me a small smile.

Her eyes had widened. "Please."

I rolled mine. "No fucking way."

I put the little asshole to bed.

Well, she put herself in there in her pink pajamas with owls all over them. I merely watched the process with a scowl while perusing the room that alternated between pink dolls and taffeta and weapon paraphernalia. Her books were lore on vampires and the supernatural community in general.

I frowned at them. "Can you even read?" I asked out of curiosity.

She looked at the books, yanking the covers of her pink

comforter to her chest. "Yes, I can read." Her eyes did that same thing they had done earlier which had me in this taffeta, weapon-filled nightmare of a room. "But Thorne usually reads to me," she said.

I stared at her. "Fuck right off. Thorne does not read to you." It was a statement, not a question.

She screwed her nose up. "He does too. And he also says those words are bad."

I screwed my nose up. "What words?"

"The cuss ones."

I rolled my eyes. "Yes, well I think he should worry more about subjecting you to a battle in which your little limbs could get ripped from your body than swearing. Which is fucking awesome, by the way."

I winked at her.

She grinned. "Okay. *Well....*" She drew out the word in question.

"Well, don't die in your sleep," I told her, intending on leaving the room.

"Will you read to me?" she asked shyly. "Just for a little while. There's a book I've been reading that I found at a bookstore. Thorne hasn't been reading this one. He doesn't even know. He'd probably be mad." The words tumbled out quickly, almost running into each other with the speed in which she blurted them.

I raised my brow. "Thorne, mad? I'm intrigued."

She pushed up from her position half-hidden under the covers to reach under her bed, unearthing a large book with a battered spine and an old smell.

She extended it to me. I took it out of curiosity. "I thought it'd be a Mills and Boon or something," I muttered, thumbing through the pages that smelled of something almost ancient and somewhat familiar.

I frowned at the title. "*Strigoi.*" I glanced at her. "This isn't from Barnes and Noble."

She shook her head.

"And where did you get it when you're meant to be on some sort of slayer lockdown?" I asked.

She bit her lip. "Can you keep a secret?" she asked.

"Of course," I lied.

"Well, Stacy is meant to watch me, but sometimes she doesn't because she drinks a lot of wine and then her boyfriend comes over and then they make a lot of kissing before going into her room and... doing stuff."

"Having sex, you mean."

She gaped at me.

I rolled my eyes. "I'm not giving you the birds and the bees talk, and frankly you're too old to be ignorant to it. You know death, so you better be sure you read up on what sex is."

Her cheeks stayed flamed. "I know what it is," she mumbled.

"Okay, well don't get all weird. It's natural. Just don't have it too soon, and promise me if someone tries to make you do it, you either kill them or text me and I'll do it for you."

She grinned. "That means I can have your phone number," she said excitedly.

Fuck.

Why did I get myself tangled up in this shit?

"Yes," I relented. "But only if you've got someone for me to kill. No other reasons like braiding your hair. Despite it being a total disaster, that's not my job."

Her hair was indeed a mess, namely because she didn't have a mother to do it. Thorne wasn't going to do so, and that slut Stacy was obviously a wino whore so neither was she.

I made a mental note to deal with Stacy.

"No, only killing," she agreed solemnly.

Why did I feel like she was going to go out and try to find things for me to kill that might just kill her in order to kill me?

Oh well, not my problem.

"Right." The book felt heavy in my hands. Vampire strength meant it should have been little more than a feather. Color me intrigued.

I ran my hand over the aged cover, the faded script of the text and the swirling designs of the pattern on the front barely visible, even to vampire eyes.

"So what made you want to read this?"

She stared at me. "They tell us to hate vampires since... well, forever. And I know I should hate them because they killed Momma and Poppa, but I know good vampires and bad vampires, just like good people and bad people. So I wanted to learn about them so I can decide for myself."

I gaped at her for a second before schooling my expression. It wouldn't do well to let the little creature know I was borderline impressed with that explanation.

Instead, I opened the book and started reading aloud.

"Ambrogio wasn't extraordinary. He was a traveler, a human who was more aware of his mortality than most, so he sought adventure to fill his short life.

He found it in a woman, as men often do...."

I got so lost in the story I seemed to be there at the same time as being in that ridiculous bedroom at the same time of being nowhere at all.

"...Deathless.

The children of the Vein Line created from love, hate and blood."

I stopped talking but the words repeated themselves in my head, taunting me with their very proximity on the page. And in my life.

It wasn't lightly that I had believed any of this prophecy crap. And there it was, staring me in the face.

Origin stories that told of where we began when the prophecy fairies kept saying things about history repeating itself.

"Is that how it happened?" a small voice asked.

I snapped the book shut with an echo that sounded throughout the room, as if such a gesture would make all of this go away. Like it was somehow that easy.

"Aren't you meant to be sleeping?" I snapped.

She yawned, despite the murder in my tone. "Yes, but I like listening. You have a nice voice."

"Of course I do."

She smiled. "I like you, Isla. Thorne does too. You make him happy. I like that too. He's not normally happy. He's actually never happy. Not since I've known him. So yeah, it's cool."

I stared at her, still holding the book, its weight more palpable in my grip as the truth of her little words piled on top of it.

I didn't know what to say.

"Well, time to go to sleep before I knock you out myself, if only just to shut you up," I said, turning to switch off the light.

There was another strange little light in the corner of the room, bathing it in a bluish glow. I walked over to turn it off too.

"Don't."

I turned around.

"I'm afraid of the dark," she murmured, small and child-like, the first time she'd actually sounded like the little human she was.

I followed her eyes to the small flickering of light the stupid little lamp was exuding. I ripped it from the wall, engulfing the room in shadows.

I walked through them easily.

"The dark is probably the stupidest thing you could ever be afraid of," I informed her once it had blanketed us in its embrace. I could see perfectly well, but human eyes couldn't see a thing. Which was the point. She was a slayer, or meant to be one in training. "Actually, it's the thing you should be the least afraid of. Monsters rarely hide in the dark. It's the light you should worry about." I started to walk out the door, crushing the lamp in my hands. "You wanted me to train you, kid. This comes with the territory. You've got to learn about the right things to be afraid of. And in order to do that, you've got to hang out in the darkness and make friends with whatever monsters you find there before you can fight any others. Because the monsters you find in the darkness are only your own anyway."

And then I'd walked out. Before I too had to face my own monsters in the dark.

I went back into the light in Thorne's living room, faced his attractive eyes and saw the monster anyway.

Then he distracted me with a suggestion that made me accuse him of making a joke, despite it being impossible.

"I'm not joking," he said with a grim face.

I rolled my eyes. "Yes, I know that, Thorne," I hissed. "Because you don't joke about shit, even the serious shit which this is. Which makes it worse. Because I'm totally partial to any inappropriate, borderline-sick jokes, and I would encourage their use in any situation. But I know you have a weird thing about mentioning killing babies, even in jest, so I know you're serious. Which means I'll have to very seriously say I'd rather hack my arm off with rusty garden shears. And I'm not joking. I will literally hack off my own arm rather than do what you're suggesting. Which is, just in case you've had some kind of break from reality, us going for a little visit to your big old slayer compound and having a chat with the head of the faction here in the continental US. You know, the one who will most likely want to kill me." I waved my hand. "All of that sounds fine, fun even. You know how much I like going to a party where everyone wants to kill me. Small talk is incredibly dull."

He raised his brow. "You're okay with that entire part of the plan?"

I gave him a look. "Um, of course. Fighting? Check. Potential to kill people who piss me off? Check. Risking my undeath in new and exciting ways? Check. All of the things I want in a romantic getaway with my man."

"Well then, what are you fucking mad about?" he asked in exasperation.

I raised my brow at him. "Um, that it's in fucking Oklahoma. I *hate* Oklahoma. Can't we schedule it in Vegas instead? The City of Sin hasn't seen a real sinner until they've met me."

His jaw ticked. "Fuck," he muttered.

And apparently that was him resigning himself to the fact that me going to Slayerville headquarters was not going to end well.

A girl could only hope.

ELEVEN

"SORRY, WE HAVE TO... UM... AH," THE YOUNG MAN stuttered as he blocked my entrance through the slatted gate, the only entrance to the facility which was fenced at least seven feet high with electric wire by the sounds of the gentle hum emanating from it.

It was topped with barbed wire. Overkill, if you asked me. And a total waste. If some supernatural creature did want to punish themselves by coming to fucking Oklahoma, they wouldn't let a little thing like three thousand volts and a little pointy metal stop them. In fact, that would most likely be the only fun part of the entire trip.

Well, the most fun part would undoubtedly be killing the slayers who resided behind the fence. The low hum was easy. The fifty or so thundering heartbeats?

A pre-turned vampire would be able to pick that shit up.

I smirked at the quivering mess in front of me. Had Thorne not been standing beside me, his heartbeat would've been near deafening with its frantic and loud palpitations.

As it was, no human's, werewolf's, or witch's heartbeat could rival the gentle thump of Thorne's. I'd grown used to it; like his presence, I didn't likely know what I'd be able to do without it.

I didn't like that thought.

Nor did I like the near-paralyzing fear at even thinking about going without Thorne's heartbeat.

Onwards.

"Sorry you have to what?" I asked. "Be *more* of a sniveling human? Give it a try but I think you're already there, sweetheart."

He swallowed visibly, and I noted the way the veins in his throat did so. Despite the gentle burn in my own throat, thanks to the fact that I was yet to give myself a little respite in the form of laevisomnus the vein didn't look appealing to me. In fact, it was almost... unappealing. Not that I'd tell anyone that; it would give more credence to the whole prophecy thing that everyone was stuck on.

Though me violently evacuating the blood from the human in the back of the van hadn't exactly helped.

The ambrosia of Thorne's blood was right beside me, highlighting the difference between the finest wine in the world and water from the gutters.

I gave his neck a glance and the dull ache in my throat quickly turned into an inferno that rivaled the first thirst after turning. I could hear the blood and its journey around his body, which I followed up the column of his neck to his eyes, hard and expressionless and looking at me with confusion, worry and a little desire at my hunger-filled gaze.

I snapped myself out of it. Quickly breaking from Thorne's gaze, I moved back to the human, glaring at him expectantly.

"We can't let you through," he said, eyes more than a little unsteady as he glanced to me, then Thorne, then the other slayer and vampire behind us.

I glared at him. "And why the fuck not? We traveled here, to *Oklahoma*. We sure as hell didn't come for the scenery and food. We came here to sing 'Kumbaya' with the slayer bigwigs. Maybe you didn't get the memo as to who I am. I'm Isla, the vampire. You know, the fabulous, attractive one who saved a fuck ton of your brethren from becoming worm food? Yeah, that one." I smiled sweetly at him. "I'm going to put that ignorance on your ancestry, which you can't really be blamed for. Now move, Skippy. I've got a plane to get on when this is over with. And a chemical bath to get all this *nature* filth off me."

I screwed my nose up at the expanses of grassed area and rolling hills full of more fucking grass.

The kid looked like he might step aside, or have an asthma attack. I was hoping for the latter, just for some entertainment. Then he was pushed brutally to the side so he smacked into the tin guard house with a resounding *whack*.

I glanced at the hulking man who did so with interest. Even I wasn't planning on being that brutal with him, and he was technically my not-immortal enemy.

This one gave me serious No Neck vibes. Although he did have a neck, and a head of hair that looked like John Stamos and Rob Schneider had a drunken night together and this was their unfortunate love child. The hair, not the man. He was bulky, so the obviously slayer-issue GI Joe outfit he was wearing almost burst at the seams.

Not natural, the muscles. The slightly sweet twang to his blood told me that.

I decided to christen him Roid.

"You're not going within five more feet of that facility until we search you for weapons," Roid declared, crossing his meaty arms on top of his chest, which boasted boobs bigger than mine. He glared at me in disdain. In hatred, in fact.

I didn't know why; I wasn't the one who gave him the D cup.

"And it's going to be a thorough fucking search, since it's a vampire bitch walking through my door. You ain't going anywhere until I'm satisfied you're no threat."

Thorne stepped forward, his fury coursing through his veins. And mine. "You better—"

I put my hand up. "I'm gonna cut off your no doubt *very* masculine and threatening statement, honey," I said sweetly, giving him a smile. "Given the fact that I'm very capable of taking care of myself, you know, because I'm a vampire. And a strong, independent, and bloodthirsty one at that." I blew him a kiss. "I totally appreciate the gesture, though. I'll thank you for it. Later. For now…." I moved my eyes back to Roid, who was now glaring at Thorne.

"You should be ashamed of yourself, Thorne. Betraying not just the entire line but your fuckin' species, going to bed with a dead thing," he spat.

Again Thorne seethed, making to charge forward. Silver helpfully held him back.

Roid was a writhing mess on the ground before he could heave his considerable bosom in my direction again. Thankfully too, since it was gross.

His screams were, as expected, high-pitched and girlier than Scott's.

I put my heeled foot on his throat for dramatic effect more than anything. His broken femur was more than ample enough to make sure he was no trouble to me.

"Isla," Thorne warned, though there was a reasonable amount of satisfaction in his tone.

I glanced at him. "Yes?"

"Don't kill him," he ordered.

I pouted. "But I want to."

He gave me another look.

I rolled my eyes. "Fine," I sighed. "You never let me have any fun."

"Cock-whipped," Duncan muttered under his breath.

My head snapped back to the Scotsman who was leisurely leaning against the electric fence, his body only vibrating slightly with the volts going through it. His eyes danced with challenge.

"You can kill him," Thorne conceded, eyes following mine.

I stretched my lips into a smile, my fangs protruding at the motion. "You promise?"

Duncan grinned. "You can fuckin' try."

"Thousand bucks on Isla," Silver shot at Thorne, whom he was still loosely restraining.

Thorne shrugged out of his hold with an ease that told me he could have done so even when his friend had actually been trying. Though he probably would've dislocated Silver's shoulder, which wouldn't have given me any pause, but I knew Thorne was weird about stuff like that.

"No fuckin' way I'm takin' that bet," Thorne told him, crossing his arms at me. "I like my money."

"No, you like rogering this one, that's what." Duncan nodded to me. "Which you wouldn't be doing on account of the fact that she'd chop ye cock off if you did take that bet, for which you'd win that thousand bucks, by the way," Duncan continued with a grin.

"Can I kill him now?" I gritted out.

Thorne laughed, glancing down to the idiot who was still screaming like a five-year-old, then pointedly to the men still holding guns, though they seemed a little perturbed at our conversation.

I followed his gaze. "Oh right," I muttered. I put some more pressure on Roid's neck, just for fun, then fastened my erratic attention on him. "So, where was I?" I asked him.

He let out a mew of protest as my heel drew blood. I glanced at the crimson dot with disinterest.

"Oh right, we were at the part where you insulted my boy-friend, and me and my entire race. But not before you tried to exert whatever little authority you've been given in order to compensate for the shrinkage situation given to you by narcot-ics that give you muscles and yet no strength." I paused, pre-tending to think. "Yeah, I think that's where we were. I'll tell you something now, for free." I glanced at his leg. "Well maybe not for free, but a snapped femur is still a bargain price for this little gem." I moved my gaze around to the men holding the weapons. "Oh, and you better listen up too, toy soldiers," I add-ed on an afterthought, just in case one of the dimwits actually decided to pull a trigger. "I don't need those weapons created for weak men to have power without strength. Or destruction upon a world that's already been ravaged enough by human-ity's greed and treachery. No, I don't need any of those fancy weapons."

I paused, opening my mouth slightly so my fangs ran se-ductively—or at least I liked to think so—along my bottom lip. "I *am* the weapon, gentlemen. Because since before your fuckin' grandfathers were having wet dreams about lifting your grand-mothers' petticoats, I was here. Well, not here in Oklahoma, because I'm not fucking insane, but here on this ruined planet.

You know what I was doing? Wreaking fucking havoc. And I can do that with my little finger. You know what I can do with my entire body?" I waited for them to feast their eyes on such a body. One did not prepare a monologue like that and not go for dramatic pauses. It wasn't my first rodeo. Or even my hundred and first. "Total fucking destruction," I said on a whisper that even meager human ears could pick up.

I took my foot off Roid's neck, who had finally gone quiet and was just rolling around moaning. Not great, but preferable to screaming. I scowled down at him.

"This did not go well for you," I informed him happily. "Like not at all. At least act like a man in the face of a broken bone. Might keep whatever illusion of masculinity a steroid shot and a small dick will give you."

I stepped over his prone body and frowned at the keypad on the gate, deciding to completely ignore the men with the guns. I could hear the whispered conversation one of them was having with their superior over their hidden earpiece.

He wasn't happy, but they were going to let me in. They were just planning to make some sort of song and dance in order to scrape up some of the dignity Roid had scattered all over the ground.

As mentioned, this performance was mine and I did not like sharing the spotlight.

So I put my hand on the metal of the gate and gave a reasonable yank, expecting it to be at least reinforced with something supernaturals couldn't easily break.

When I easily ripped it off its hinges and held it in my hands, I realized it wasn't.

"Idiot humans," I muttered to myself, throwing the gate to the side where it noisily clattered on the concrete. Not before almost hitting one of the gunmen straight in the forehead, had he not ducked.

I grinned at him. "Nice reflexes, Skippy." I gave him a thumbs-up for kicks.

I turned to see Thorne shaking his head with an iron jaw, Silver gaping at me, and Duncan grinning.

Mad Scotsmen.

The most fun.

"Well, shall we?" I asked with impatience.

Thorne was the first to move, as always. When he moved in step with me, I gave him a sideways glance.

"You know, chivalry is not dead. You could open a door for me every now and then."

He gave me a look. "You mean rip a four-hundred-pound solid steel gate off its hinges for you."

I nodded while giving him my 'of course' look.

He grinned. "Next one, baby, I'll get."

"You better, or you're not getting lucky tonight."

"Oh I'm totally fuckin' getting lucky tonight, if we survive this," he muttered as the warehouse doors opened to our welcoming party.

One might've called it a small army.

"Oh, all of this for little old me?" I called to them. "I'm just so flattered. If I'd known it was going to be like this, I would've baked a pie, or at least brought a bottle of wine."

No one seemed to be very interested in the social graces of a vampire visiting a compound full of humans who were bred to kill her.

And Duncan was there. But he would've pissed off human, vampire, werewolf, witch or demon, so surely his reception was pretty much normal.

Then again, the same could've been said for me.

An older man stood out in front of the men in the slayer

commander outfits, looking like he should have been in Florida driving a convertible jeep and banging a woman half his age, not standing in front of armed GI Joes on steroids preparing to converse with a vampire, her prophesized mate who was technically meant to be on the other side of the standoff, his best friend, and a vampire assistant there for kicks.

Literal kicks.

I didn't miss the one he landed on Roid when he'd walked past him.

I was reasonably sure it caused moderate to severe internal bleeding. So fun.

The man had short hair that was slicked into something I wouldn't rightly call a quiff, but it was something in the same family. Less hair wax, perhaps. It was still jet-black in most places, the silver that cut through working in a George Clooney kind of way. The George Clooney theme continued with his weathered tanned skin that was somehow still fresh enough to not look tired and old, but wizened and mature.

He was wearing a linen button down, casual slacks and Chuck Taylors.

All around him men were wearing combat boots and Glocks. I was reasonably sure he wasn't carrying.

I stored that and saw past the easy demeanor he was trying to portray by all of these things alone. Everything in his persona was deliberate.

Meant to throw me off.

Still not my first rodeo.

I opened my mouth to say hello, but a firm hand on my wrist stopped me. "I've got this," Thorne muttered in my ear.

The rough command in his tone combined with the fact that he didn't give me sufficient time to argue meant he was successful when he stood slightly in front of me.

"Alexus," he greeted, nodding slightly in a gesture of respect. However, his jaw remained hard and the single word was clipped out in a way that told me the respect was grudging at best.

Alexus smiled in patronizing satisfaction at the small gesture, which of course made me hate him immediately.

If I hadn't already just on principle. Just because I was in love with one slayer didn't mean I automatically wanted to preserve the lives of the rest.

"Thorne," he greeted. "You've always been one of our best soldiers and yet you continue to surprise me by bringing in a vampire who is still a corpse, just not a dead one. Not yet anyway."

Yeah, I hated the guy.

"Easy," Thorne muttered to me, moving his hand back to squeeze mine as if he sensed that I was inches away from darting forward to snap his neck.

I glared at the back of his head but stayed put.

Alexus had watched the entire exchange with the shrewd eyes of a leader watching his enemy's moves and storing away every single one for future use.

I knew the look because I was doing the same.

I noted the gaps in his formation, the men who were shifting back and forth in unease, the one who kept flickering his glance to the roof that told me, if I had been a human, that's where the snipers were. But I wasn't a human, so I knew their heartbeats and could tell there were fifty-five souls in the compound.

"And she listens to you?" Alexus continued with wide eyes as he watched me rock back on my heels. "My, we have a lot to talk about, don't we? This conversation will be *interesting*."

Thorne waited a beat. "And this conversation is to be had

outside where I'm staring down the barrel of a gun?" he asked, voice even, calm, deadly.

Alexus didn't miss a beat. "You've been off the reservation for some time now, but even you know we don't let vampires run around without muzzling them. And we certainly don't invite them in."

"There's a first for everything," I added. "Like me not killing you for insulting me and, in turn, Thorne. Total first for me."

A small muscle ticked in his jaw, rippling the easy look he was trying so hard to maintain in order to surprise us when the callous warlord or leader or whatever he was came out.

"We have to take precautions. She is known for her body count, and we don't need any more throats ripped out. That's what they do. Vampires, in case you haven't forgotten, rip throats out in order to drink the blood of human beings."

I smiled at him, showing fang. "Well I don't rip out throats for sustenance. Too messy. It's merely for recreational purposes, if that helps."

He glared at me, then Thorne. "You're taking up with that? And letting it train our men?"

Obviously someone had been chatting if he knew about that.

"Considering she saved the entire New York faction, yeah, I let her fuckin' train them," Thorne snapped. "And considering she's the most beautiful fuckin' woman on this planet and I love her, yeah, I took up with her. We really goin' to talk about this here?"

"I will talk out here until I believe my men aren't at risk," he returned.

I rolled my eyes. "Dude, you're not at risk. We can't snack on you on account of the whole 'your blood kills us' thing. So you're not likely to get drained, and Thorne asked me a big favor in not killing you. For the greater good, apparently. The greater good being your continued survival and some information on the war that's brewing and has been going on while you've been having Mexican standoffs in the middle of a secret survival slayer compound parking lot." I paused, looking around. "Though, you could've just painted a big old sign on the roof saying 'All ye vampires come, the slayers live here.' Secrets are meant to be secrets, and you just blew your own cat of the bag." I shook my head. "I mean, dude, a warehouse in the middle of bumfuck nowhere with security that would likely only keep out a miscreant human or two. But a miscreant vampire?" I did a finger wave. "Miscreant vampire on the premises, with little to no effort."

"Isla," Thorne muttered, his mouth twitching.

I gave him an innocent look. "What? This is like our version of meeting the family, right? They're showing me who they are with semiautomatic weapons, and I'll show them who I am with sarcasm, fangs, a great witty repertoire, an even better ass, and some saucy dismemberment if they don't lower their fucking weapons from my boyfriend." The last part was uttered in much the same tone as the rest of my monologue, but I moved my slightly vacant and what some might call insane smile to Alexus. "Now how about we go talk about that truce."

"A prophecy?" Alexus repeated, leaning back in his seat with a blank look on his face, much like some businessman would when he was presented with some form of information he knew he was far too smart to believe. "You come here, risk everything we've built, everything we are, as well as breaking everything we stand for by sleeping with this creature instead of killing it, and you tell me that it's all dreamed up by the gods and communicated by a *witch*?" he surmised.

My hand flinched on Thorne's thigh. His covered mine.

"It's also written down in a very old book," I offered through clenched teeth. "And old books are like the Internet. If it's written, then it must be true."

"You've known me for centuries, Alexus. We might have our disagreements, but that doesn't mean you don't know what kind of man I am. What I would do for our society. That I would never risk it if I wasn't sure. There's a war coming. You've seen the hybrids. You lost three men to them yesterday alone."

"And we exterminated the vile abominations," he protested defensively.

"And how many were there? Two?" Duncan cut in. "You couldn't shoot more than that in a bucket. You sure as hell couldn't win a war against them. Though I'd be happy to see you try, since slayers on this earth are nothing but an annoyance, like lasses who won't bed ye until you marry them. I'll do it, marry the lasses or save the fuckin' slayers, because the end result is the same: I get fucked. Only one in the good way. But I'm getting paid for this, so all is not lost."

His eyes moved to the one woman in the room who wasn't me. He'd obviously clocked her the moment he walked in, because she had boobs and a vagina and was not hard to look at.

Yes, she was wearing the unflattering female version of the male outfit, but even the shapeless garb hinted at her slim figure and gentle curves. And her dirty blonde hair was slicked back into a tight bun, harshly showing her makeup-less face. Yet she had a soft sprinkling of freckles and sun-kissed skin to counteract the whole GI Jane look she had going, making her look slightly younger and softer.

But her violet-blue eyes that didn't belong to the childish and pretty face told me that she wasn't soft. That the world had done to her what it did to a lot of humans—fucked them over. And there were two options when the world did that. People might argue that point, but people were idiots.

You either gave up, let the world continue to fuck you while you coped with alcohol, drugs or just by letting the monotony of life become something that you accepted and didn't change until you died from an overdose or suicide or just a fucking boring heart.

Or you got even.

By doing something with your life to prove to the universe that it couldn't get you down. Working hard to fight back—not just with fists, but they helped—so you died from a heart attack brought on by the stress that came with fighting or with a knife in your heart or fangs at your neck.

Those were the two options. There were variations on the methods in which those options went, but there was one thing in common with them both.

Death.

You made a choice on how to live that ultimately was your choice on how to die.

With fire in your belly and fight in your heart, or with weakness in your soul and a tasteless nothing on your tongue.

She was a fire kind of girl.

So that, in addition to her freckles, her eyes and the fact that she had a vagina and breasts, gave Duncan his pause.

"I thought I might only get fucked one good way in that analogy. Wanna change that?" His eyes twinkled and the teasing and crassness of his statement combined with his rough accent and not-disagreeable physique would've made a lot of women melt.

But when you were the fire, had it inside you, you weren't likely to melt, even at a Scottish vampire with cheekbones to cut glass, muscles to rival even Thorne's and a twinkle in his eye that told you he'd give you the best orgasms of your life.

But then the fangs meant they might be the last ones you'd ever get.

She tilted her head as the man beside her stiffened more than the rest already had.

"You know what I want to change? More than anything?" she asked sweetly.

He folded his arms, leaning back so his chair balanced on two legs. "Your capacity for pleasure? 'Cause I can do that. And pain. But I promise you'll like it."

She gave him a look, shaking her head slowly and seductively. Then something whizzed through the air as her hand moved with impressive speed. The knife landed right beside Duncan's ear, the gentle hum of the enchanted blade vibrating in the air.

"What I what to change is the 'un' in 'undead,'" she said sweetly. "If you want to get fucked so bad, I'll feed you to the succubi in the dungeon. After I kill you, of course."

The resounding silence in the room was more like a roar, hard faces on everyone.

Well, not everyone. I was grinning.

I elbowed Thorne. "I like her," I stage-whispered.

Duncan gaped at her, and then he grinned too. Because he was a cocky asshole, he yanked the blade from the wall and ran his tongue along the cold, enchanted metal that would most likely be excruciating to touch, let alone lick.

"Well, we've decided to start the foreplay with pain. I approve, lassie," he growled.

She glared.

I continued to grin. "Seriously? Do you think she'd want to go for cocktails after this?" I asked Thorne. "Or do you think the whole me being a vampire thing might stop her from wanting to share a cosmo with me?"

Thorne's hand squeezed mine once more. "Let's make sure they don't try and kill you before drinks," he murmured. Then he looked to the table. "Such an attempt wouldn't be wise, considering not only would you start a fucking war with my faction, but I'd likely make it so this one was burning to the ground when I walked away from it, covered in your blood."

His fury and the cold certainty of the threat did things to me. Things that made me move my hand higher on his thigh. His hand was firm enough to stop me before I got to the goods.

He gave me a look, still tinged with the promise of murder—which, of course, only turned me on more.

"What? You can't do things like promise mass murder and then not expect me to get all hot for you," I told him innocently.

His eyes darkened slightly before he was back to business, focusing on the man at the head of the table gaping in disgust, rage and more than a little bit of fear.

Thorne scared him.

Not because his threat was real but because for whatever reason, the charade he was playing as some leader of some faction of slayers in the middle of nowhere was just that. Thorne was playing a part too, coming to him and pretending like he had the upper hand when Thorne had it all along. I didn't know the hierarchy of the slayer life, but I knew what a pissing contest looked like. And I knew what it looked like to win one, considering I won at… well, everything.

"You're betraying everything we stand for," he hissed.

Thorne eyed him. "No. We stand for the protection of the innocent and those who can't protect themselves. I'm making sure that I'm doing that."

"By making a deal with the Devil?"

"No, I'm not the Devil. Not even really related, just distant cousins," I cut in. "Though I am a *big* fan of his work."

Narrowed eyes around the table were the only response.

"Making a deal with the Devil would be making no deal at all," Thorne said calmly. "Would be to clutch to millennia-old prejudice in order to hold onto a distorted form of nobility you think you have. Which you don't. Not if being noble means being stupid. And stupidity can't be an excuse when you're hundreds of years old, which means that's malice. So no, I'm not making a deal with the Devil, or sleeping with one. If that's what you also want to insinuate." His hand flexed in mine. "But if you're going to continue with your stupidity, I might just be looking at someone doing his work for him."

I grinned wider at the pinched way Alexus's face went at Thorne's words.

My man was kicking ass.

"And just so you know, the council knows that, should I decide it to be so, I can make it so the war fought on the outside isn't what kills us all," Thorne continued, eyes narrowing on the man at the head of the table. "I can make one on the inside that does that."

He gave him a pointed look, though I didn't really understand why Alexus paled so much at it. Sure, Thorne did a great homicidal look, almost better than me—*almos*t being the operative word there—but he'd been doing that since we'd walked into this little party.

I was someone who didn't leave things unsaid or hinted at anything. I would rather threaten someone up front; it saved time and was just part of my persona.

Thorne obviously didn't roll that way because his words

were saying something to Alexus without actually coming out and saying it.

The rest of the table seemed to be as confused as I was—apart from Silver, who was sitting on Thorne's other side. He was grinning.

Well, that pissed me right off. Silver knew something I didn't. I would have to have words with Thorne. Serious words.

But the silence that descended after his vague threat was something that even I hesitated to fill. It was loaded with an energy that communicated the precipice of the entire rest of the night.

Whether it would end in blood and death, or whether the blood and death would come at a later date instead.

That's what all moments seemed to be these days and nights: a slight escape from the battle I had tasted since the moment Thorne's blood was on my tongue.

Because something didn't taste sweet without destruction to follow.

Alexus cracked his knuckles and held his jaw so tight it looked like his teeth could possibly shatter under the exertion of such a motion.

One could hope.

Instead, I was disappointed to see that he used his mouth for something else.

"This is not a truce. Nor is it permanent. This is only until this war is over. Then we fight our true enemy," Alexus gave me a long and pointed look as the hate in the room increased tenfold.

I may have only been able to sense Thorne's emotions, but that didn't mean I couldn't see the rage from the rest of the inhabitants of this meeting to understand they were not down with this decision at all.

I really hoped someone decided to be a bad little boy and try to kill me anyway, just so I could kill someone.

"Oh, our true enemy?" Thorne said, standing stiffly, hand at his belt and the other at my waist. The way he eyed the room before focusing on Alexus told me he sensed the same rage in the air.

Silver was poised for battle too.

Duncan still leaned leisurely on the wall, but his eyes glowed with something that told me he was also craving a fight.

We were vampires, after all.

"Our true enemy," Thorne continued, "is death. Not those who cheat it. And we would be rather hypocritical if that indeed was our purpose, to eliminate all those considered deathless." He squeezed my hip. "And this order, to ensure no one lays a finger on Isla, it's as permanent as death itself. Because that's the only thing that's gonna ensure I don't come after every single one of you and your families should you decide to come after what's mine. Even then, I won't let the grave stop me because I don't expect to let it hold me for long." He paused. "Not that Isla can't take care of herself. She'd likely kill whoever tried to come within five feet of her."

"Oh I'd let them come within five feet," I added. "I need a workout every now and then. And I like to make it last. Death, that is. It's permanent, after all." I paused. "For slayers, at least. And especially when I'm the one dealing it."

Thorne glanced to me, his eyes dark. "Those who make that decision will have to hope Isla is the one who kills you. Because she might be a vampire, but I'm a fucking man, and anyone who touches my woman or threatens her immortality is one who will never die. I'll make sure of that. You'll spend eternity in fuckin' hell between the underworld and earth."

And on that, he half dragged me out.

And I let him.

Because fuck, was that one hell of a parting note.

TWELVE

One Week Later

"UGH," I GROANED, OPENING THE DOOR.

I left it open as I twirled around to walk back into my living room and pour myself a drink. I sure as shit needed one. "Because the first thing I want to wake up to is the king of all vampires, AKA the one who tried to have me executed."

The door closed as Rick sauntered into the room. "You must get over that incident at some point. Plus, it has been clarified, many times, that I hadn't planned on executing you. Merely torturing you in front of a crowd before letting you get away with your undeath," he commented dryly.

I glanced at him over my shoulder. He was, like always, clean-shaven and wearing an immaculate suit, dusky gray this time with a crisp white shirt open at the collar, exposing his tanned and impressive neck. And he was somewhat making a joke.

I turned my attention back to my glass and the liquid I'd poured into it.

"Whatever," I dismissed. "I miss out on anything interesting—and by interesting, I mean any mass murders and such—since I've been napping?"

Things had been rather uneventful since we got back from Oklahoma, with truces—unprecedented as they were—on both sides giving us somewhat of a lull in the assassination attempts. They'd come, surely, but for now, it was the calm before the storm.

I didn't like that. I liked the storm. Which was why I was getting more and more frustrated at the lack of action in seeking out the witches. Apparently war was just a lot of waiting around and then high concentrations of drama and blood in short periods of time.

True, there was still drama and blood in this past week because I was... well, me.

I'd finally had to succumb to laevisomnus after Thorne got more than a little testy. And my slow reactions got my arm ripped out of its socket by a hybrid who'd gotten the best of me while we exterminated a nest of them.

I didn't really get what his problem was. It grew back.

But he'd been alarmed enough to demand Scott and Duncan take care of the rest, then dragged me and my newly growing arm back to my apartment and ordered me to "get some fucking sleep before I fuck you into unconsciousness."

Obviously, I'd let him fuck me into unconsciousness.

And then I'd woken to him sitting right next to my bed, hands resting on his chin, watching me.

"Dude, have you been watching me sleep for—"I snatched

my phone from the nightstand, glancing at the date. "—four days? If so, that's three days too many and takes it into creepy territory."

He'd moved then, from the chair to the bed, where he'd pinned me with his body and piercing stare. "Creepy is looking at the woman you love do her best corpse impression for four fucking days, three hours and eight minutes and having to remind yourself that she'll be coming back to you with some sarcastic bullshit in no time," he growled. "Knowin' that still didn't make shit better. So I'm going to have to fuck you into my skin so I can feel you in every inch of me."

Then he did just that. During which he'd given me a great breakfast of his blood.

I was supplementing with vodka, since he'd just left to go back to his place to make sure the truce was still holding steady and exert some authority.

He'd been loath to leave me and I'd been dreading it, which was why I'd insisted he go.

I had some work to do as well, which didn't include the war and the witches and the curse. I had a company to run too.

But then Rick had ruined that plan. I placed my bottle back in its place, turning to see him standing unnaturally close to me.

Like right up in my grill.

I frowned at him. "Ever heard of personal space?"

His eyes flickered over every inch of me. "You've found yourself in the middle of things you don't understand. In the middle of a war that has no place for you at the same time as it's the only place you belong." His voice was rough, not flat and emotionless as was his default.

I screwed up my nose in unease. "The only place I truly belong is the shoe department at Barneys," I countered.

His eye twitched. And his hand came up to push a red strand of hair from my face.

The gesture gave me pause.

It was tender.

Kings didn't do tender.

Neither did vampires.

And yet he was doing both.

"You need to leave this behind, Isla," he growled. "This death wish you have, throwing yourself into situations where the underworld beckons you."

I scowled at him. "You're the one who put me there in the first place," I hissed. "Remember? You stood in this very apartment and all but ordered me to be a part of this war."

His eyes went to stone. "And now I'm ordering you to take yourself from it."

I blinked at him in surprise. I couldn't even mask it. Of all the things Rick could order me to do, this was the most confusing.

And fucking irritating.

"Sorry, not your call," I told him.

"As your king, it's precisely my call."

Well, that was the wrong thing to say.

"You think you can control me?" I asked, my voice tight. "Because of a crown or a title or blood? No. Those things can't control me. I can't even control me. It's them." I tapped my head. "The demons, the remnants, the darkness—they're in charge. I just drive the bus while they tell me which way to go. Sometimes I'll go off-road when I'm feeling brave or bored, but most of the time the demons are doing the driving and I'm doing the steering. You'd do well to remember that since they're currently deciding whether to run you down."

"You won't run me down," he declared. "Won't destroy me.

Because part of you knows that what I can offer you is more than Thorne can. A crown. Power. And something more than the death that awaits you, that's written in this fucking prophecy," he seethed, his eyes alight with fury.

Again he caught me by surprise, his sudden unfurling of emotion and exposure of sentiments towards me that I thought were long lost.

I was wrong, apparently.

There's a first time for everything.

Luckily I recovered quickly.

"Sorry, but I can't date you, or even be your queen. I'm kind of fated to be with this other guy. Written in the stars. Or in blood. Fate of the world and all that. But if the entire human race didn't depend on that? Maybe. Or maybe not. Considering the whole *love* thing."

Something moved in his face, the furrowing of his brows and the intensity in his eyes slightly jarring, even for me.

"Didn't you say yourself, Isla, that you didn't like rules? A prophecy is a rule, the biggest of our kind. Most important. You'd think it'd be your biggest victory yet," he invited.

I raised my brow at him. "Is the leader of our race insinuating that I should break a rule that may or may not end the world in order for him to get laid? Dude, that's a lot for a man to get his end away."

He clutched my hips. "It's more than that and you know it. And you also know that prophecy is not a reason for what you are going to die for. Because that's what will happen. I can taste it."

I gave him an even look. "You know what *I* can taste? Apart from the sweet aftertaste of Thorne's blood that satisfied my hunger after he'd satisfied another kind of hunger." I ignored the sharp pain that came with the flexing of Rick's hands at my hips at this. "I taste hidden motives." I stepped from his hands, the struggle only slight but enough to give me pause. Not that I showed him. I made it look effortless and graceful because that was just how I rolled.

"No, I don't believe your feelings for me go to the deep part of you that breaks through all that honor and duty and kingmanship that you cling to like a baby clings to a security blanket. Yeah. You've got the hots for me—you're only inhuman, after all. But it's something that stems from whatever Thorne and you enjoy that is starting to get on my nerves." I folded my arms, the ultimate female battle stance that was even more dangerous than showing fang. "So I'm going to have to demand that you tell me."

A muscle in his jaw ticked. "I'm your fucking *king*. You don't demand shit of me. Not if you want to live."

I rolled my eyes. "Another death threat? The ink is barely dry on my pardon. A personal best for me, for sure. But victory doesn't taste as sweet with empty threats. Sure, I'll take it, but I know you're not going to kill me."

His eyes darkened. "I might not kill you, but that doesn't mean I won't do the same to someone else. I know you don't need to kill a vampire who loves a human in order to end their immortality. Merely prey on the mortal who is so much more susceptible to things like death and you've killed an immortal in a way that they're dead for eternity."

He'd barely spoken the words before I had him by the throat and slammed against the wall so hard the plaster cracked and my favorite painting went tumbling to the ground. "You see, that was just stupid," I whispered. "Threatening Thorne like that. Because you speak as if you have some knowledge on ending immortal's lives. Then you must know those immortals in question would likely do something to preserve their eternity. You know, basic survival and all that. So it baffles me, when you know how narcissistic I am and concerned with my remained survival—and, by proxy, Thorne's—that you'd so blatantly threaten me. Love makes people unhinged. I'm already unhinged, so I would have likely hurt you, king or not, if you threatened a favorite pair of shoes of mine. Now that you've threatened Thorne?"

I shook my head.

"I'll toast marshmallows on your corpse without fucking hesitation," I hissed, squeezing his throat so the pleasing crack of bones resounded in my ears. I also reveled in the explosion of blood vessels in those calm eyes, filling them with crimson.

Then I was staring at the roof, pressure on my own throat and a niggling pain in my back from shards of glass belonging to the coffee table Rick had just ruined by slamming me onto it. He towered above me, the crimson in his eyes already retreating with the speed of his healing, but there was still blood in them.

I lay there, mostly because his hand was at my throat and I couldn't exactly move, but I could've attempted it. I was just too interested in where he was going to take it, considering the king hadn't ever lost control like that in the short time I'd known him.

It was pretty fun seeing that side of him. You didn't really know someone well until you'd seen them homicidal.

"You break all my rules so consistently, Isla, and without reproach. You think you're untouchable," he whispered. "That because of my feelings for you, you'll survive this war."

"No," I choked. "I'll survive this war because I'm awesome."

Then I moved, pushing myself up so I could reach under the sofa where I'd idly taped an enchanted blade Sophie had made for me a week back, before she'd disappeared on some prophecy mission, and lifted it to Rick's throat.

His hand was still at mine, but it paused at the proximity of the fatal blade. His eyes didn't radiate much fear, if any.

Not because he didn't think I'd do it; he couldn't know that, considering *I* wasn't even sure. No, it was that same look he'd had when Sophie had turned on him in the woods. A resignation with death in a way that he wouldn't passively welcome it—a warrior would never do that—but in the way that a warrior knew death was inevitable for them. In a way that meant the warrior might spend their life fighting battles against death but recognized that death would always be the truest victor.

"I'll survive this war not because of feelings a man has for me, mortal or vampire," I informed him. "I'll survive because you two might be warriors intent on survival, but so am I. And I'm also a woman. We're great at double standards. So I'll make sure I'm taller, better, faster, stronger, to quote Kayne. Why not throw some Gloria Gaynor in there too? I will survive. I *must* survive. And that means Thorne will too. And that will be the last time you threaten him."

I lowered the blade.

"And now you'll tell me what the fuck is going on with you I've had more than enough of being in the dark. I know monsters are meant to reside there, but then no one would be able to marvel at the mastery of the winged liner I've perfected over the years. So in the light it must be. It's easier to see the blood there, anyway."

Rick towered over me, as I was still on my back on the coffee table. Technically he had the upper hand. If you were stupid enough to believe technicalities, that was. And for a moment, I thought he actually might be.

Stupid.

But of course you didn't live for a millennium and lord

yourself over a race of immortals if you were stupid.

Many mortal kings were stupid merely because those they ruled over were as stupid as their rulers. Not the case with vampires.

So this one extended a hand that wasn't exactly an olive branch but wasn't exactly a dagger either.

I took it.

Because I wasn't stupid either.

Brushing the glass from my skirt, I regarded him. "You going to spill it?"

"I can't say this without Thorne here," he said.

I frowned at him. "I thought you were the king of an immortal race. You spend a good amount of time telling me there's pretty much nothing you can't do, although I would like to see you fold a fitted sheet, just as a side note. But I thought you'd be more than willing to expose the secret, if that's what it is. Such a lovely way to undermine Thorne and give you a shot at whatever you've fantasized would be us."

His level gaze unnerved me. It would have turned me on too, if it weren't for the whole *love* thing. "I'm a man and a vampire. I don't need underhanded tactics to win me what I want. That's not how a man does things."

I rolled my eyes. "It's how a vampire does things," I stated. "And this particular one"—I pointed at my chest—"is rather an expert at underhanded tactics."

He stared at me. "You'll find out. He will tell you and I will. And I crave that moment because I know exactly what kind of vampire, and once you understand the depth of what this is and what's been hidden for you, prophecy won't stop your wrath. But I also know what kind of woman you are. I see it in your eyes. The love. It isn't prophecy.

So that's how I know that the wrath of the vampire will

never measure up to the love of a woman, no matter how much I wish it to the contrary."

The pause was loaded with that foreboding I'd been ignoring like I did the fact that velvet was trying to make a comeback.

Rick stepped back. "I am interested in watching the battle between the woman and the vampire nonetheless."

And on that parting note, he was gone.

"I'm not happy about this," Thorne grumbled as we walked through the halls of the king's mansion.

The king who had been at my home, not a handful of hours before, doing things like trying to seduce me, kill me, and then finally freak me the fuck out about secrets. Secrets I couldn't even demand to know since Sophie had come back from her little witchcation and requested this meeting, here of all places.

"I honestly feel like so many of our conversations are beginning with you either not being happy enough or you being very happy." I paused. "The very happy on account of they begin at some point in the night or early hours of the morning when I get bored of the fact that you have to sleep and wake you up in the most inventive of ways."

I enjoyed the way that, despite his insistence to stay dark and broody and all around pissed-off alpha badass mode, his eyes flickered with that depraved darkness I loved so much.

I wondered if that was with the memory of the certain wonderfully depraved act I'd committed that very night in order to up his spirits for the fact that we had to be in this very mansion where, not a few weeks ago, we'd been scheduled for execution in front of my family and peers.

It had lasted until we got inside, past the grim-faced guards posted at the door, at least.

He had to get with the program that that was the way vampires rolled. If everyone stopped going to places where they were almost executed, then they wouldn't be able to go anywhere, especially not the hottest parties.

Or maybe that was just me.

Not that this was exactly a hot party. But it was necessary.

"I'm not happy they canceled *Twin Peaks*," I retorted when his broody silence served as response to my words. "Or that we're in this war at all. But here we are, and we need a war council now that we're finally planning on fighting in a war. Because I was under the impression that's what you actually do. It was a good thing I stayed out of the last ones because I likely would have made them a lot worse, out of pure boredom. The movies make it look so much more bloody and cruel and devastating. Why is it that I never get to have that?"

Thorne stopped our walk to yank me to his body. "Because, Isla, you've had bloody, cruel, and devastating. That's what you're gonna have for eternity. Because that's what we are. The war outside is nothing to what's going on to between us. How about you enjoy fighting that war for a while?"

"A while?" I asked his eyes.

"Eternity," he promised.

I grinned at him. "If you can survive me that long."

Something moved in those eyes. "Babe, I can't survive you. Don't ever want to. You're the most exquisite end. And the war? Promise you'll fight that war for as long as our eternity."

It jarred me, his last statement. Never had we really questioned what we had. Never had Thorne even opened up the possibility that he considered less than eternity an issue.

He was so sure, the stubbornness of an alpha male who'd gotten what he wanted for as long as he had.

Sure, at the beginning we'd both fought it, being that we were natural enemies and all that jazz, and fighting before sex was pretty much the best kind of foreplay. And afterplay.

But after we 'went steady' and I wore his football jersey and class ring, there were no doubts that either of us would go anywhere—apart from the grave, obviously. Some wondered whether their significant other would go out for a pack of cigarettes and never come back because of the boredom humans inevitably got with the monotony of life. For immortals, it was more. It was wondering whether their significant other would be coming back from the werewolf hunting expedition.

Monotony of life may have been terminal for humans, but it might be the only thing that would save immortals.

Problem was, when you had eternity, monotony might just kill the soul.

You know, for those of us who had them. It just bored the utter shit out of me.

But there Thorne was, asking me to love him forever, like something in front of the double doors opening for us might push me to go out for that proverbial pack of cigarettes.

The doors opened but Thorne stopped me so my answer wouldn't be heard by the inhabitants of the room.

It amused me slightly because it was a total human gesture. The only way they couldn't hear my answer was if the conversation was going on in the car we'd come in. While still on the highway.

But I played along, meeting his eyes.

"I don't make a lot of promises," I told him. "Wait, I guess I do. Because a broken promise is the most fun a girl can have with her clothes on." I winked at him. He didn't wink back, so I continued, not wanting to get overly sappy when the vampires of the room could hear me exchange the hearts and flowers. It would totally damage my street cred and ruin all the badassery I'd accumulated.

"I can tell you that I'm a fighter before I'm a lover." I paused. "Or I'm a lover and a fighter. Because that's the only combination that ensures the most fun a girl can have with her clothes *off.*" I gave him another look. "So since you offer both of those things, a great battle for an eternity that supports my skills, I'll make that promise."

My words may have been flippant and a little sarcastic, but in that wretched and somehow beautiful language that lovers seemed to have in which they saw the words under the words, he saw.

That I was promising more than I ever had.

Because that was what you did when you were tangled up in that bloody and terminal illness people called love. You made stupid eternity promises, despite the sense of foreboding at the look in your lover's eyes.

Because the words under Thorne's wordless stare at my words and the intense kiss he pulled me in for were troubling. They made me think of a story that was much simpler than some wordy prophecy that wasn't going to win any Pulitzers.

Once upon a time, a slayer and a vampire fell in love.
There was blood.
And pain.
And destruction.
The end.

THIRTEEN

"So we're going to kick ass and take names and figure out how to win this war, get this spell off moi and then go for tacos?" I asked the room at large. I focused on Rick, who was sitting on his throne, one ankle crossed over his knee, doing a great Thorne impression with his darkened eyes and broody disposition, yet the blankness of his face and the lack of emotion beneath the darkness signaled a storm that I didn't even understand. And I totally got the ending to Lost. After Sophie spoiled it, of course.

Though, it could have been something to do with his visit. One I obviously hadn't told Thorne about because I wasn't an idiot.

"Well sorry, Your Highness, but you're not invited to the taco part of the equation. Too much heat. And it seems that you and the old ball and chain don't see eye to eye." I glanced to Scott, who had somehow found his way into another war council despite not being a warrior in any way, shape or form. "No offense," I said in a way that totally meant to offend.

He grinned at me. "But I'm invited to tacos, right? I love tacos."

I rolled my eyes at him. "Yes, Scott, if you manage to survive this fucking thing, which is doubtful, you can come to tacos. And pay, of course."

His eyes lit up. "Aces."

I seriously wondered whether he'd fight extra hard to hold onto his immortality purely for the fact that he'd finally snagged himself and invitation that didn't have to come with some borderline creepy stalking. I was sure he had some kind of tracking app on my phone. In fact, I knew he did.

"I'm more of a nacho man myself. And after a fight I'll need a good fuck. But I'll pop in for a taco," Duncan cut in.

I clapped my hands. "And I'll get the margarita jug!" I exclaimed. Then I frowned at my absentee witchy partner in crime and her newest pet. Well, I was happy the pet wasn't there, but she was the one who'd called us all together in the first place.

Being late was just plain rude. Which was one of the reasons why we got on so well.

Thorne and I were already an hour late.

As if I'd summoned her, the witch in question sauntered through the door. She looked great, as usual, wearing black hot pants that tied up at the front and were pretty much classed as underwear considering the amount of leg and ass cheek they showed. But then the leg was covered by thigh-high boots with laces up the front and a small heel, so it balanced.

Her simple black tank was tight and showed off her arms and shapely chest. Her neck boasted a good amount of silver and her hair was in its signature bird nest. While her eyes were framed with her signature gel liner that cut me with its perfection, it was the dark circles under them, the almost translucent quality to her pale skin and that slight emptiness behind her eyes that worried me.

"What did I miss?" she asked, clinging to nonchalance and perfecting the act.

Almost.

"Oh, obviously about a hundred memos that the 'I blew the entire cast of Metallica' look is out," I informed her happily, giving her outfit a pointed look. "And that you're paying for the first eight margarita jugs."

Her eyes lit up in that empty way. "Margaritas? Does that mean tacos after we get this over with?"

I grinned at her. "I love that your mind works like mine."

"Doesn't bode well for the rest of the world, considering its survival relies on the way a crazy vampire and an equally crazy and possibly possessed witch think," Duncan muttered.

Sophie and I simultaneously flipped him the bird.

"Now that everyone's here, could we possibly stop discussing fucking Mexican food and start discussing how we're going to combat a faction of immortals who are currently plotting to overthrow the entire fucking way of life that you two so fondly like to live and wreak havoc in?" a voice asked smoothly and calmly, wrapping over the profanity in the sentence with added inflection that gave it an almost physical quality in the air.

I glanced to Rick, who was now leaning forward slightly on his elbows, giving me an even look, but the storm was closer to the surface.

"Sure, if we must," I replied. "But don't pretend that sass"—I gestured to his face—"isn't because you're not invited for tacos. I didn't make the rules. I just break them."

His jaw ticked.

I smiled.

Thorne shook his head with a small, satisfied grin as he pointedly yanked me into his side, laying a kiss on my head, his eyes still swimming with that strange intensity.

"We need to talk through this shit about the fighting so we can go home and do the other thing that you said goes with fighting," he murmured in my ear.

My stomach fluttered.

"Sex, you mean?" I asked, not murmuring. There wasn't much point in murmuring, other than for the air of seduction. "Yes. That's a great motivator."

My own eyes darkened at the group at large.

"All right, is there a PowerPoint presentation on how we do this, or does someone just start speaking?" I paused, looking around the cavernous room. "Wait, why don't we have one of those maps on a table with little figurines representing everyone in the fight and their place in it, like in *Game of Thrones*? I think the Isla figurine would've been wonderful."

I pouted at the single computer in the middle of the rough semicircle we'd formed.

Rick pushed off his throne to strut over to the laptop, pressing a few buttons. The room darkened slightly so a square on the wall to the left of us illuminated like a movie screen.

On it were various pictures of decapitated bodies and flaming building appeared.

And more videos of wreckage and corpses—human, werewolf, vampire, and hybrid.

"Show and tell got a little more gory since I was in school," I commented. "No, wait. It's actually less gory considering at my school—you know, a few centuries ago—such contraptions didn't exist. Everyone brought in their own severed limbs."

"We've got the location of one of the witches. She's in the dungeon at Isla's childhood home in Russia," Sophie stated bluntly.

I frowned at her. "So they're not together? How did I miss that?"

She gave me a look. "They *were* contained in the place where they were bound, and the binding magic on their power still remains. But it seems they are somehow tied to all of this prophecy stuff, since they've been getting stronger with each of the events that have happened." She paused, her eyes going glassy. "With the fall of the immortals comes the rise of those once banished beyond the shadows."

"Here we go," I muttered.

The moments that followed were loaded with foreboding, but thankfully silent.

I let out a breath. "Thanks to whoever decided not to give you another prophecy or weird riddle for us to decipher. We've got quite enough, thank you very much."

She scowled at me.

"So the gist is, these witches are somehow connected to the hybrids? Not just because they're the ones who are needed to create them, but it seems they've got a definite stake in this war, since the more the hybrids and the movement in general gain traction, the more powers they have."

Sophie nodded, looking around the room. "Isla's right, for once."

"Isla's always right," I shot back, scowling.

She ignored me. "Because of their growth in strength, the strongest of them all are cloaked to me. After their separation, I could only follow one."

"To the motherland," I declared cheerfully. "That should be enough for you to issue me another pardon or whatever to go and kill my entire family on your behalf for treason, right?" I asked Rick.

His even features flickered slightly with my words. "It's not that simple."

I gritted my teeth. "Pretty sure it is that simple. Vampire law states that no Vein Line may be challenged by members within that Line or outside of it without a breaking of any of the ancient laws. If so, a vampire has the right to exact vengeance on the Vein Line in question as approved by the Sector. And if the Vein Line has direct ties to Ambrogio, such actions have to be sanctioned by the king himself." I crossed my arms. "Let's forget the fact that my family have spit in the face of that particular law throughout the years by trying to assassinate me, getting off on technicalities and the surety that I'm no rat and abhor authority more than I do plaid, so they knew I wouldn't go tattling to the king about their indiscretions." I pointed to Sophie. "Witchy has provided the due evidence of a little thing I'd like to call treason, plus the fact that Evgeni pretty much declared his allegiance to the cause that day he came over for a chat and to try to rip my heart from my chest." I paused, remembering the mess he made of my favorite sweater. "I'm still pissed about that sweater."

Then the thought of the rest of that day, the first time Thorne and I had kissed, turned my anger into something else for a hot second. "So I'm pretty sure you can sanction a mission to go blow them off the face of the earth and piss Hades off by making him have to deal with the nightmare that is my mother," I declared.

Rick kept my glare with his level gaze. "The Rominskitoffs are one of the oldest Vein Lines in our race."

I widened my eyes. "Really? Oh my gosh, I hadn't even realized. You've just blown my little mind. So?"

"So it's not easily that I can sanction such a mission to annihilate most of them, on the word of a witch and traitor, no less," he said.

I rolled my eyes. "I got that little piece of paper from you and Sweater Set that makes me the *ex* traitor now," I reminded him.

"That won't matter to a lot of vampires who your parents call friends."

"My parents don't have friends," I corrected. "Either vampires with whom they've committed depraved acts over the years and who likely consider themselves just as superior to the rest of those of the fanged persuasion, or other vampires who want to use them to further themselves in this society. And finally, the vampires who likely are afraid of my brothers' wrath if they even glance at them in the wrong direction considering Viktor disseminated an entire Vein Line for someone spilling blood on his jacket," I clarified. "Sadism, violence, and fear do not make friendships." I paused, glancing to Duncan, then Sophie. "Fuck, it totally does."

Rick walked around the room. "My position on the throne is being challenged by a lot of Vein Lines behind the scenes, and as this rebellion takes more of ours as causalities, powerful families watch what decisions I make. These families consider themselves untouchable because of their blood and position. And they're partly correct. If I officially sanction a removal of your family from the earth, then I disrupt the ideals of those vampires already tempted to throw themselves in with the traitors," Rick explained.

"So you're not going to give me my sanction?" I seethed. "Because of fucking *politics?* Isn't this meant to be war?"

He stopped his pacing. "Yes. And in war, politics are more important than ever. As are the battles you don't fight. Openly."

I grinned at the meaning behind his words. "Openly? So I get to do it?"

Rick gave me a look. "Without official sanction, until proof is obtained."

I grinned. "Sounds like permission to me. Plus it's better to ask for forgiveness than permission." I paused, then laughed. "Wait, I don't ask for forgiveness. Or permission."

The air turned, and waves of fury pulsed through me with such a ferocity that I was sure they originated within me. I was momentarily confused as to what I was pissed about until my gaze landed on Thorne, who was holding his body stiffer than he had already been throughout the earlier conversation, which was pretty darn stiff.

"You're tellin' Isla that she's gonna go and do your dirty work with all of the risk and accountability while you sit here on your fuckin' throne and get to win the popularity contest?" he seethed. "If this all goes wrong, *Isla* is the one who gets fucked here, not you."

I grinned at Thorne wickedly. "No, honey, if this all goes right, I get fucked. And even wrong is the best kind of right in the conversation of getting fucked."

Thorne barely glanced at me, his emotions taking on somewhat of a life of their own. Their taste was something deeper and more complex than the simple fury at Rick's decision.

No, tasting it, experiencing it through Thorne, I could tell Rick's decision was merely a catalyst, the straw that broke the camel's back to detonate whatever had been simmering between them since they'd come face-to-face. Since before that, obviously.

Since the beginning.

Rick's smooth, emotionless face turned into something that was a controlled version of fury as he focused his attention on Thorne. "It's not a popularity contest," he clipped. "It's survival. It's being a king. Not something you'd understand."

"*Your* survival," Thorne shot back, stepping forward, his fury rippling behind him like a cape. "Not Isla's. Since the beginning it's been about using her to get what you want. And you wanted her too. But you didn't get that shit. Even when you're a king, you don't get the queen. 'Cause that's what she is. She doesn't need a crown or a fucking mansion where she executes people to keep said crown." He stepped forward again. "She's a queen and she's fuckin' mine, not just because she chose but because the traditions and legends you love so fucking much are the things that make sure she is meant for *me*."

Something flickered in his eyes. Beyond the rage, of course. A grim sort of triumph. One I didn't exactly like because it communicated that I was some sort of prize to be won or lost or possessed in whatever fucked-up little game was going on here.

I was all for fucked-up little games, just not one where I was used as a pawn.

I opened my mouth, stepping forward to say something resembling that exact sentiment but with more profanities, when Rick bet me to it.

"Typical fucking human nature to focus on something as inconsequential as a woman in the face of the end of the world," Rick hissed.

His voice was no longer smooth, nor emotionless; it was warped and thick with rage, as was his attractive face.

I wasn't going to pretend it wasn't a little hot. Sophie's eyes met mine and she gave me a wicked little grin to tell me that she echoed my sentiment.

Thorne didn't step forward that time, but the way he held his body, coiled and poised to pounce, told me this was going to come to blows very soon.

I waited.

I wasn't going to step in the middle. I wanted them to fight it out more than I wanted a new Birkin.

"No, that's where you're wrong. She *is* the fuckin' world, and you know that. So you're trying your best to get her killed. And that's the surest way to ensure your reign ends how it began—in blood."

Rick's eyes blackened. "And you're forgetting yourself, human, if you think you can talk to a king that way. And if you think you can finally best me over a woman whose legs you've gotten between and who you've fucked so you think—"

Rick was cut off by Thorne lunging at him and landing an impressive punch right between his eyes.

I was kind of disappointed that he cut him off; I wanted to hear all about my bedroom prowess.

Rick may have suffered the first punch, but the unmistakable crunch of bone on bone signaled contact with Thorne's cheek.

I winced a tad at the pain in that one, only staying with my arms crossed because it wasn't a death blow and Thorne only stumbled slightly before spitting out a mouthful of blood—and maybe a couple of teeth—before he lunged at Rick once more.

They were a blur of grunts and thumps of flesh on flesh as they continued to battle out what seemed to be centuries of frustration.

I would've loved to think it was all because of me. That would've been great.

But alas, even I wasn't going to be that vain.

Sophie came to stand beside me, eyes on the fight.

"We should probably do something, you know, before someone loses an eye or something," she said over the grunts.

She gave a wide-eyed Scott a look. "Sorry."

He grinned at her, then shrugged.

I kept my eyes on the blur of motion. "Probably," I agreed.

Then we watched silently for a moment longer.

"I wish we had popcorn," I commented.

"And wine," Sophie added.

"Wine would be key. A nice pinot."

She tilted her head at me. "I'm into merlot at the moment."

I turned to look at her. "Branching out? I applaud it, but I'm just a little more loyal when it comes to wine."

She poked her tongue out at me.

Duncan's bored-looking eyes met mine. "Lassie, we'll likely have to fight a war with one less king or you'll have to find another slayer to fit this prophecy with if we let the boys be boys for much longer," he commented casually.

I glanced back to the fight.

Thorne was breathing heavily and half of his face was covered in blood. A swollen hand signified at least a broken finger or two, and I reasoned he had to have a couple of fractured ribs.

Rick circled him, covered in a similar amount of blood, or maybe a little more—maybe I was just blood biased. Though he healed quicker, he was still looking a little less put together than he had moments before, and his suit was history.

I felt a pang of sadness at the poor innocent suit before I sighed. "I guess you're right."

Both Duncan and Scott motioned to move forward.

I held my hand up. "Um, what do you think you're doing?"

Duncan eyed me. "They're not likely to stop on their own. We're going to have to help the process along."

I nodded. "Well, of course. They're all hopped up on testosterone, so they'll rip each other apart. But why are you so adamant that the two men in the room joining the testosterone-riddled fight will actually stop it?" I shook my head. "You'll likely only make things worse, since you fight like a man. We fight like girls, and that means we're better."

On that, I darted forward, yanking Thorne back by the neck and quickly moving myself between them.

"Now, now, boys. What would your mothers say of you?" I asked, making a tutting sound. "You're both being sent to bed without any supper at this rate."

Thorne's eyes were wild and full of a fury so deep even I couldn't understand it. He tried to struggle around me; luckily, he was injured and I was simply stronger, so the motion didn't work.

"Isla," he growled, sounding more animal than man. "Get out of the way."

I gave him a look. "Nope, shan't."

Movement behind me told me Rick had obviously gotten sick of the intermission in the main event, so he was intending to forcibly remove me. The stiffening of Thorne's body to attack told me that too.

I kept my back to him, the attack that Thorne never expected coming.

I grinned at Sophie, who had crossed her arms and was standing casually.

"Thanks, sister," I said.

She shrugged. "Anytime."

I turned to see Rick frozen in place. Actually frozen, obviously mid–attack stance. His foot was hovering and the beads of blood dropping from the cut on his forehead were suspended midair.

I reasoned that the little spell also stopped that gash from healing considering it was still open and angry.

"That's a nifty one, Soph," I commented. "I feel like we

could've used that in a lot of our other battles and saved a lot of pairs of shoes from getting ruined," I accused.

She shrugged again. "That would've made it too easy and a lot more boring."

I narrowed my eyes at her, wondering if she was telling the truth or if it was her newly found powers that offered her the ability to deep freeze a vampire king.

Unfortunately I didn't have the time to ask at that particular juncture, as Thorne was getting a little antsy if the taste of his secondhand rage pouring through me was anything to go by.

"Okay," I hissed, looking between the two of them. "Although I totally agree with solving any and all problems with violence, and I don't believe in such things as a proper time or place, unfortunately I'm going to have to contradict two of those core beliefs I hold dear." I paused, glancing at Rick's frozen body, smiling slightly at how awesome it was to see the king who valued control so highly to literally not be in control over a single thing in his body. Then I focused on Thorne. His heart, though even, was beating slightly faster, not with fear but with the rage that had all but consumed him in the most puzzling of ways.

"We've got other things to do, so you two need to sort this out. You've thrown punches, now call a truce. For as long as it takes us to sort this out. Then I'll gladly schedule a Pay-Per-View fight and pocket eighty percent of the profits. But for now, cool it."

Thorne's heavy breathing was the only response to my little request, though there was something in the air, in his feelings which were still washing through me and numbing my hands.

A tingle that picked at the little part of me that had been brewing, that itch that something between these two was more than nature.

That it was something that might change everything.

That it had something to do with Thorne's demeanor earlier and the promise I made before we walked in.

I didn't know why I was thinking of all of this, considering we only needed one creepy seer and that was Sophie. I sure as hell didn't want the job, but the surety of the feeling was there just the same.

I glanced to the witch in question, who was regarding the two men with a furrowed brow, her eyes seeing more than was in front of her.

"Okay, could you take the other two out for ice cream or to hunt that faction of hybrids that was troubling Lewis downtown?" I asked Sophie. "You could always get ice cream after. With me. When I sort these two." I jerked my head at Thorne and Rick. "And by ice cream I mean copious amounts of alcohol. For tomorrow I guess we go to war. And we party like sorority girls in Cabo on the eve of any war. Tradition and all that."

Sophie grinned. "It's a date." She gave Duncan and Scott a look. "Let's go kill some hybrids."

Duncan grinned. "Finally."

Scott looked a little more hesitating, his eyes on me.

I rolled mine. "Yes, run along. You don't have to be glued to my side for all eternity. I've already got one of those and he's causing me enough trouble."

I gave Thorne a pointed glare. His eyes were clearing slightly and his wounds were healed a little.

Scott moved to do what I said.

"Toodles," Sophie said cheerfully with a grin and finger wave that were comical when paired with the little goth rocker look she had.

I blew her a kiss with the free hand that wasn't holding Thorne in place.

When she turned her back and ushered the two vampires out the door rather like a soccer mom might to two rambunctious children, I called to her.

"Ah, Soph?"

She turned. "Yeah?"

I nodded to Rick. "Better unstick the king before he starts to rust or something."

"Oh shit, right," she muttered.

The air changed slightly, thinned out perhaps, and Rick's foot came down hard on the floor.

He blinked once, looking dazed for about a second before he got himself together enough to glare at Sophie's back.

"Oh, don't you dare focus any rage on the witch who most likely saved what remained of your suit," I snapped to him.

He moved his eyes to me. "This is not your matter to involve yourself in."

I narrowed my stare, letting Thorne go to cross my arms and stand between them.

I was reasonably confident they weren't going to lunge at each other immediately. If they did, I was confident in my abilities, even without Sophie's little freezing trick.

"I disagree, considering I was the thing you were hissing about before the fight began. Plus it affects my day. And anything that affects my day enough to fuck up my plans is going to get interfered with by me."

Rick moved his glare from me to Thorne. "This isn't about you, Isla. This is between us."

The words hung in the air with a feralness that didn't suit the regal king I had come to know, got annoyed with, and thought about shirtless from time to time.

The man I had come to know, got annoyed with, who consumed my heart and soul and I dreamed about and experienced more than shirtless as often as I could stared right back at him.

Their stare-down was more than I felt like handling. One could only weather so many macho men stare-downs without either suggesting a threesome or an explanation. The true Isla in me was very disappointed in the direction I went.

"Okay, I'm about as over this as I am about Miley Cyrus and Liam Hemsworth being so on-again/off-again," I announced.

Two heads snapped to me.

"Oh look, they noticed the beautiful, amazing and eloquent vampire in the room," I said sarcastically. "Yes, I'm speaking. And I do it much better than the both of you, but regretfully one or both of you will have to speak when I'm done." I narrowed my eyes. "That speech being the story of just how you two know each other and why you just can't seem to get along. I mean, I'm all about a jelly wrestling match. In fact, I'm happy to call my lube guy to get enough KY to fill an Olympic-sized swimming pool, but it seems we've got to work together in making sure the world doesn't end in blood and destruction. In order for that to happen, I really need you to either kiss and make up—and if we go for that option, you have to wait until I have a recording device—or figure out how to fight it out without actually killing each other."

I gave Rick a look.

"Because if you kill the man I love I'd have to kill you, and that would unwittingly be giving the revolution assholes exactly what they want. And I *hate* giving people what they want at the best of times. I'd much rather get what I want. And what *I* want, in addition to a tennis bracelet from Tiffany's and the newest Gucci bag, is for someone to finally explain your fucking deal," I demanded.

I sighed at the silence, then paced the room. "I'm going to start pulling teeth at some point," I warned.

Thorne gritted his teeth, the waves of emotion coming off him confusing.

The rage wasn't. The rage was familiar and expected. It was what lingered beneath that. Something like fear, but not the same taste from the times I'd been in danger—which was far too much lately, even for my liking. It was some other kind of fear, one I didn't understand.

"How do you two know each other, she asks for the very last time," I said, coming to a stop in front of Thorne and trying to ignore his fear as it gave birth to some of my own.

Thorne's eyes met mine with a hard resolve and something resembling apology in them.

"He's my brother," he gritted out.

Those three words bounced off the stone in the room and then hit me with enough force to wind me.

I stared at Thorne. Then Rick, who was holding himself still and giving me an even and blank look.

Then I waited. For one or both of them to yell "Psych!" and laugh about the epic joke they'd been playing.

No one said anything. And the three words chased away whatever silence tried to settle after them.

Thorne was watching me intently and didn't make any move to come to me, which unnerved me. At any point in our lives so far, whenever he sensed any kind of strong emotion from me, or just in general, he needed to touch me. Be near me.

But not now.

I looked around the room, inspecting the well-dusted corners.

"What are you looking for?" Thorne demanded.

I snapped my gaze back to him. "Not what, *who*," I corrected.

He frowned in response. "Who the fuck are you looking for?"

"Ashton Kutcher, of course," I snapped. "I'm thinking he must be making like a comeback show or something, considering the only explanation for what you just told me is that I'm being punked. He better get here soon because even being on TV hasn't calmed my temper enough not to get a lot of blood on a lot of the camera crew if they don't show soon."

Silence descended once more. Thorne was yet again giving me that look.

"Ashton isn't coming, is he?" I asked.

Thorne didn't even grin, just shook his head.

I stared at him, clenching my fists and trying not to go with my first instinct, which was to lunge at Thorne.

I focused on Rick. My rage was also with him, but the cut of the lie wasn't as painful when it came from someone you expected at least a little betrayal from. He was a king, and a vampire, after all.

And I didn't love him. Nor expect him to love me.

He might have considered himself somewhat infatuated with me and asked me to be his queen more than once, but the coldness of his heart rivaled mine.

And two cold beings couldn't love each other.

Demons couldn't love demons. They didn't have the capacity for it, needing the human part of the equation to change their chemistry and heat up whatever was left in their chest.

It was only then that I realized that true betrayal only came from people you loved.

And that it hurt.

A fuck of a lot.

"Explain," I commanded Rick, not looking at Thorne, and doing my best to block out every single fucking one of his emotions. My own were already shaking through me with such a force that I was surprised I didn't crack my fangs from my gums, considering they were extended.

Rick's face was blank as he held my eyes, something swimming in his that wasn't the rage that had all but disappeared in a rather unnerving second. "You are aware of the origin stories of both his race and ours?" he asked after a moment of regard.

My mind unwittingly went to that storybook Thorne's nitwit little sister had under her bed before it snapped back to the present moment.

I looked to the ceiling. "Please don't anyone else give me a fucking history lesson. I had enough blood shed over it the last time around." I moved my glare to Rick. "Yes, I know the fucking origin story. Greek gods, blah blah blah, human love, meddling of said gods, blah blah blah. I'm also aware of a little thing called biology. I know we stretch it a little when our species give birth to human children who eventually turn into vampires, who then die and then the female ones reawaken in order to further the race. Weird on Mother Nature's part. But she also made it possible for Donald Trump to exist, so we'll just roll with it." I paused, steeling myself to give me more strength needed to fight a werewolf before flickering my gaze at Thorne. "But he is *human*." I noted his heartbeat before thankfully moving my attention back to Rick. I couldn't unhear the heartbeat that was previously comforting and quickly becoming haunting, but I could control where my gaze went.

"You're a *vampire*, so forgive me for thinking you're spouting a load of fucking bullshit when you say a human slayer, birthed to kill vampires, shares blood with a vampire who just happens to be *king of all fucking vampires*. Doesn't really jive." I paused. "Plus Thorne's parents are both dead. Assassinated by vampires, which is the reason for your immense hatred of our damned species, isn't that correct?" I asked Thorne, keeping my voice as flippant as I could. Which was pretty darn flippant. "Or was that just a big giant lie? Because one of the two of you is telling big old porkers, and if one lie exists, then I'm sure as shit more exist."

His hands were tight at his sides, balled into fists. "They were my parents," he told me fiercely. "In every sense of the word, except biology."

I blinked at him. "Ah, honey, I think maybe you might not have passed the right science classes. Biology is pretty much the main thing that determines parentage."

His eyes never left mine, rage lingering in them. Unlike Rick, he didn't have the ability to turn off his emotions and present a façade like only a vampire could. When you burned hotter than an inferno, it couldn't just be snuffed out, and even when it was, embers remained. The embers of fury were there but something different moved, an intensity that was reserved for me alone.

"No, babe, you're wrong. They loved me, cared for me and taught me to be a man. That's pretty much everything a parent does. And they gave me the gift of not having to grow up with anyone who shared my blood."

"Your *vampire* blood. That's what you're trying to get me to believe, right?" I asked, a lot of disbelief in my tone and a scowl on my face.

Rick chose that moment to cut in. "You are aware of the fact that a mortal man was chosen to protect mankind from the race of vampires."

I rolled my eyes. "Yes, by a god. That's the story. I already got that story too." I gave Thorne a glare. "From my beloved, of course, but then again, he's also the one saying he's the brother of a vampire king, so who knows if what the fuck he says is true. If a*nything* he says is true."

Thorne flinched at my words, more so than he did with any of the hits Rick had landed on him, the insinuation that everything he had said to me was a lie causing more damage than the still-healing bones and cuts.

I hated that I could see that, feel that through our connection.

I hated that I even cared.

Rick either didn't see the reaction or didn't care. Most likely the latter because he carried on.

"Well, it forgets that the vampire was once a mortal man. And a different legend exists, a truer one not taught at Mortimeus because it will shatter every belief that vampires hold dear. A truth about the blood that belongs to the gods. The gods do not give gifts or curses lightly. For Ambrogio had a brother. One whom he quarreled with over the very woman Apollo cursed him for."

"She must've had a golden vagina," I muttered.

Rick ignored me.

"Ambrogio was a traveler, though Caius was his companion, as the legend chooses to leave out. And the fact that he was first to encounter Selene in the days before Ambrogio. Caius was more noble in his pursuit of Selene and loved her from afar, even when she chose the man he shared blood with."

Something flickered in his eyes that I chose to ignore at that moment. Something that tumbled the waves of Thorne's emotions.

"Caius was filled with agony when he watched Ambrogio love the woman he wanted more than life, then, when the curse was cast, watched that same woman die. He had moved on and created a family of his own, but he would forever love Selene." Rick paused. "True love is the only thing in this world that is truly deathless." Another pointed look. "So when Ambrogio, broken and now a complete vampire, came looking for blood to sustain him and murder to damn his soul so he didn't feel the pain of heartbreak, he found it in killing the village where he'd once shared a life with Selene until love had ruined it all. And it was his brother who sacrificed his life in order to save what remained of his family. Ambrogio drained his brother without hesitation. Or he tried to. Whatever remained inside him, left over from the woman he loved and killed for love, it stopped him from taking everything from his brother. He didn't kill him, but he didn't leave him for life either. He left him somewhere in between. Which was where Eleos found him. And she offered him the gift his sons would get."

He paused.

"The same version of the story Thorne no doubt told you, save a few details."

I glared at him. "A few fucking pivotal details," I hissed. "Still, you haven't filled me in on how you two are brothers from the same mother, or so I assume."

Rick's eyes swam with a sorrow that I didn't it have it in me to care about.

No, I couldn't give two shits about his sorrow right then. Or even Thorne's. That was the beauty of my own all-consuming rage; when you got really angry at someone you loved, it did the nifty little trick of hiding the truth of the hurt, for a time at least.

Band-Aid over a bullet wound and all that.

Rick saw my anger and continued with his voice even. "We do share the same mother. And father. Much like Ambrogio and Caius. For it was the curse of Eloes that she didn't inform

Caius that his future sons would have the gift, and so would the sons after them. But only because of the shared blood with Ambrogio in his veins. And when the Vein Lines of vampires were created, so were the Vein Lines of the Praseates. Of those two brothers to counteract one another. Only once in a millennium is a new king made. And his wife is killed, of course."

Rick's eyes flickered again as he spat the bitterness of the sentence onto the floor.

"It is lore of our kind accepted, the reason behind it known only to the royal family. But this law exists so that the queen cannot birth another which the gods designed. Another, stronger Praseates than the world has seen, with the strength of the two vampires but the humanity of the two mortals they used to be."

Another melancholy-filled pause, and I struggled to digest what Rick was saying while at the same time not being bowled over by Thorne's unrestrained emotions.

Rick carried on.

"But my mother was loved by my father. And he was a man who took little stock in legends, or maybe it was his love that told him that. So he sent her away, without the heart to kill her, yet with the heart of a king who knew he needed to obey some of the most sacred laws that included killing the queen after an heir was born.

"So my mother was kept in hiding. And she hid the fact that she was growing my brother in her belly from my father. Who may have not had the heart to kill her but would not have lacked the heart to kill the baby that would grow to be one of the strongest slayers to live on this earth." His eyes flickered to Thorne. Or in Thorne's general direction. I didn't follow them. I couldn't.

They came back to me.

"So my mother birthed Thorne and then in secret sent him away to a family where he would grow up and be forgotten about." He paused. "And he was. Until two hundred years ago, when my father found out and tortured and killed my mother when she didn't give up Thorne's location. The torture of her housemaid should have been his first decision, considering he didn't have to kill her in order to get the information. He did anyway. Then he ordered the assassination of Thorne's family. And Thorne himself, but he escaped unscathed. The first time, and the second, and the time after that. It has been an ongoing game for centuries, killing the line of those who gave Thorne shelter."

Rick paused, giving Thorne a sideways look that wasn't completely filled with hatred.

"I am of the knowledge that that's how he has come to acquire the small human in his care. Her parents were descendants of Thorne's adopted family."

My mind worked over that statement, remembering the night Thorne told me about his 'parents'' assassination when his sister was three years old. I had believed him without question because of the sheer amount of pain in his eyes as he'd recounted it.

You couldn't fake that.

Apparently you could fake the details.

It pissed me off that my sheer rage at this was somewhat undercut by the thought of Thorne having to reexperience the murder of his parents through the centuries as their ancestors continued to die.

There was a long silence.

"And how did you find out that you had a brother?" I asked, my voice more than a whisper.

Rick gave me an even look. "My father presented me with

the corpses of Thorne's parents as explanation. Along with my mother's, of course."

I restrained a flinch at the emptiness to his tone, knowing that one could only have that little feeling if their sorrow was too deep to show.

"And you don't have the heart, like your father, to kill the one who has the power to kill you?" I asked.

He gave me an even look. "No, I also lack what my father did," he answered. "But I also have love for the memory of my mother. And every time I get the chance to finish what my father started, I remember what my mother died for."

The sheer magnitude of Thorne's emotions rolled through me with enough force to take me off my feet.

If it weren't for my sheer stubborn need to not let either of these men see the weight of all of this on me.

No way would I show these two men how hard the betrayal of the truth was hitting me.

To the core.

I kept my eyes carefully on Rick. Because that was safe. Safer for whom, I didn't know.

Maybe Thorne so I didn't do anything I might regret, like kill him for betraying me.

Most likely me, as looking in the face of the man I didn't have the heart to kill, even in the face of the betrayal, might actually kill me.

And survival instinct, especially in the face of heartbreak, was pivotal.

So I kept myself together, on the outside at least, even gaze on Rick.

"Right," I murmured. I was going for pensive. Maybe flippant. Or uncaring. My voice shook only a little, but a little was too much so I steeled myself to make it stronger. To make me stronger. I wouldn't let a man, or a vampire, or a fucking age-old story that shook every known belief of our race weaken me. I wasn't just that kind of vampire. Or kind of woman. "See, I didn't know your mother. Or your father. But I'm thinking if I don't leave this very moment, I'll most likely piss off your mother's spirit and please your father's greatly by killing the both of you."

Then I turned on my heel and sped from the room as fast as my feet could take me.

Because even though I didn't run, it was against my nature as a vampire and a woman. I had to.

There were always two choices in situations like that—well three, if you counted killing them all as an option. Which I should have but couldn't because of that limp and broken organ in my chest. In situations of heartbreak, there was either run or fall apart.

And no fucking way was I going to fall apart.

I was going to run.

Regroup.

And then I was going to attack.

But for now, I had to run because of survival.

And then I had to run because I was a fucking vampire.

Because I was fucking me.

FOURTEEN

H E FOUND ME.

He always did.

But then again, I wasn't exactly hiding. I was drinking.

A lot.

And I was drunk.

Because Dante was making the drinks. He made good drinks. And because Dante must have seen the murder in my eyes, he didn't ask, only poured.

Then he left me to my silence. Which was what a bar in the middle of the day offered.

Thankfully.

Or maybe not so thankfully. I itched for something, *anything* to hurt.

"Have you got any friends to… you know?" I slurred,

getting an idea on making something hurt. Or making someone hurt. Because wasn't that what sociopaths did? They hurt people because the face of pain in someone else was at least something besides the emptiness of not feeling anything inside?

It was that kind of hollow feeling that drove people insane. Dante gave me a look. "To fuck?"

I snorted, having a little trouble staying upright on my stool, but I managed. I was impressed with myself, and Dante. Increased metabolism meant only a determined immortal and a talented bartender could get them this side of fucked-up.

Too bad I was already that side of fucked-up. But that's why humans drank, wasn't it? To cure part of their fucked-up selves by distracting it with fucking up another?

If it was, they had the right fucking idea. Drinking for fun was one thing. For survival was another, and I hadn't gotten it. Until now.

"To *kill*," I corrected. "I'm thinking I need to kill something. And you're the only being within a five-mile radius with enough evil to make it justifiable, but you're making the drinks and if I killed you, then I'd have no one to make the drinks and I need the drinks. See my dilemma?" I asked the demon.

I could've killed the many humans scattering about the place, going about their day. I yearned to, in fact, to kill the innocent and get the rush that came with doing so. It was another form of alcoholism, my old crutch from another life, another version of heartbreak. It tempted me, that switch I knew I could turn to distance myself from whatever humanity and hurt I was fostering, but something stopped me enough to keep my seat and continue to stare at the demon.

"So, I repeat my question. You got any friends?"

The demon in question grinned. "I've got friends," he said. I perked up.

"But none I want you to kill," he continued. "On account of them being *friends*."

I pouted. "Boring." I sang the word into my glass, looking down to see if there were any answers down there.

"Anyone *I* can kill?" Dante offered.

I glanced back up to the flames behind his eyes.

"Because I've been rather feeling like doing some killing of a certain slayer who seems to have rattled the woman who had half an arm dangling off and still found it in her to joke to me about someone's bad choice of shoes instead of drowning herself in booze in a shithole in the middle of the day," he continued, his voice thick. "And now you're wounded again, it seems. And I know your first instinct is to kill, but perhaps not the right person. I know from experience that killing the right person in order to get survival from that wound you're currently nursing is damn near impossible. So I'm offering to do it for you."

I twirled my glass between my thumb and forefinger, thinking his offer over. He was serious. Every immortal who offered to kill someone for you was never speaking in the figurative sense like those wretched humans were. Death was something rather serious when you could mostly escape, so when offered as a favor, or for a fee, it was not to be taken lightly.

There was no fee that Dante requested, which was rare. But then again, he'd be getting a nice juicy soul out of the deal.

Something in me, something carnal and not entirely simply mine, convulsed in a hot burst of agony of the damnation of Thorne's soul. Of the silence in his charred chest—if Dante was to make good on his offer—that would no doubt haunt me for the rest of my days.

"No," I said finally. "It's tempting, it really is. But if there's killing to be done, I'll do what I've always done and get the blood on my own hands. It's much easier to live with. Or be undead with. Or die with. Whatever."

Dante gave me a look, and beyond the flames I saw something almost rather human until it burned away.

"Yeah, blood still stains your hands, no matter who kills whom," he agreed. "Just try to remember your own blood can stain your hands just as easily, even if you're not the one to deal the killing blow. You just have to decide what you can live with. Or be undead with. Or die with."

His words hung in the air in such a way that even a drunk immortal saw the truth to them.

Which sucked, considering this particular immortal was drinking to escape from the truth.

The door opened and closed, and both Dante and I went on alert at the same time. Dante because he likely had some sort of witchy warning system on every time a mortal strutted through the door, and because he could sense a human soul a mile away.

Was his soul even human?

I sensed it because of that heartbeat that signaled my demise.

The air heated up. "Either this is the slayer I've heard you've got yourself, which means he's dead, or this is another slayer walking into my bar. In that case he's dead too," Dante seethed, forgetting the words he'd just uttered to the contrary. And the fact that he'd already met Thorne once.

Thorne's heartbeat didn't falter, and neither did his step.

I didn't look up from my glass. "Kill away. Save me the job," I muttered, waving my hand, forgetting the words I'd just muttered to the contrary.

For it was a selfish need to rid myself of the pain that came with Thorne's presence, the raw kind of agony that was nigh unbearable, even with the healthiest dose of booze that had me wanting the pain of the silence of a heart that beat inside my chest somehow too.

The steps continued but Dante's heat subsided. I glared up at him. "Aren't demons supposed to follow through with killing humans?" I snapped.

He eyed me. "So are vampires," he said. "But demons can sense souls. And his doesn't belong to me. Or even to him." He gave me a look, then melted into smoke as demons could do.

I'd cursed that ability more than a thousand times when cowardly demons used it to escape when they were losing a fight, and I cursed it once more.

Because now I had to make the choice. I had to choose between my nature—the one that urged me to rid myself of the pain with blood—and the heart that didn't beat but still somehow bled.

He stood there, inches away from me. I could tase his scent and his presence; my drunk self craved it, itched to forget about everything that wasn't the two of us.

But for once, I didn't listen to my drunk self. For once, I listened to the logical part of me. Or maybe it wasn't the logical part of me. Maybe it was the truest part of me. The vampire in me that he'd begun to banish.

But you can't escape nature.

So I welcomed her.

"Isla," he began.

I didn't let him finish, my hand around his neck and slamming him against the wall with a rough clatter.

I squeezed tight enough to constrict almost all of his airflow. He was getting just enough to breathe and prevent brain damage. Maybe. I wasn't the best judge after Dante's cocktails.

And Dante's cocktails, coupled with the agony in my chest,

meant I cared a little less too.

"No," I whispered. "You don't get to speak. It's a little late for that. For whatever bullshit you're going to spout. Because you've already done it. Lied, betrayed, and pretended to me."

I paused, my focus coming in such stark color it carved Thorne out of the very air around him, making him somehow separate from it. I kept his eyes, despite the pain it took to do so.

"I can lie, cheat, and steal with the rest of them. But the lies? I'll tell them to myself. The cheating? I'll cheat death. And I'll steal all the hearts of men who decide it's a good idea to betray me. And I don't mean that in that figurative romantic way. I mean it in the literal, 'I will rip your beating heart out of your chest cavity and show it to you' kind of way," I promised.

Then I let him go, mostly because I was getting thirsty. Definitely not because he was turning blue and his heartbeat had slowed.

I let him stumble to the floor, then turned to retrieve my drink from the bar. I sucked it dry before looking back to see he had managed to pull himself up, his eyes glued to me. I used the pull of the numbness of booze and sheer force of will to watch him straighten himself on unsteady feet with a detached stare.

"You haven't stolen my heart," he rasped. "'Cause I gave you that shit for free. Just like I'll give you my last fuckin' breath if that's what it takes to get you to listen."

I leaned over to tag the bottle I knew was enchanted to get a fully grown werewolf drunk. I swigged it, savoring the burn that took off a layer of skin at my throat. Twirling on my seat and cradling the bottle, I scowled at Thorne.

"That last breath, is that a promise? Because you only get to explain why and how you fucking betrayed me as long as you stop breathing after."

He eyed me. "I didn't betray you, Isla." His words were fierce, almost tangible, so sure that I almost believed him.

You know, if he wasn't completely full of shit.

I tilted my head. "Betrayal," I said slowly, enunciating, "is the breaking of a contract of trust or confidence which produces conflict in a relationship as a result of treachery or lies." My voice was robotic. "In other words, fucking everything up by not telling the vampire you claim to fucking love that you not only know the king she's been working for, but you're his *fucking brother* through some fucked-up mythical history that not only makes you older than you claim to be, but also a technical prince and a fuckbucket of epic fucking proportions," I screeched.

He stepped forward, looking like he was going to make a mistake and do something suicidal like try to touch me. I held up the bottle in a 'stop' gesture.

"I wouldn't. I'm drunk and absolutely *raging* mad. I'll likely forget I need you around for the purposes of your blood and kill you where you stand. Which is what I would've done without hesitation before now if that hadn't been the case," I hissed.

The lie was convincing enough outwardly, thanks to the rage and booze. Inwardly, I wasn't fooling anyone.

Thorne stopped. "You wouldn't have," he said surely, seeing beneath the words that any outsider would've likely believed.

But then he wasn't an outsider.

That was how this all became such a clusterfuck.

Oh, how I wished I'd killed him in that alleyway before he'd stolen whatever you could call my heart.

"Really? Because when someone who doesn't trust anyone, even herself, trusts a *human—a slayer*, in fact—who then turns out to be a bigger liar than Stephen Glass and Herodotus combined, she gets a little murdery. I don't suffer liars well. In fact, the last person who lied to me about the way my butt looked in a pair of jeans got his arms ripped off." I gave him a look. "Scott's arm grew back. Should we test just how many of your brother's healing qualities you possess?" I asked sweetly.

"I didn't tell you at first, Isla, because telling you would likely have been a death sentence. Because I didn't know if I could trust the beautiful vampire who spoke in nonsense and wisdom at the same time and took my fucking breath away at the same time as giving it back," he growled, running his hand through his hair in a gesture of frustration I knew well, considering I frustrated him often.

His eyes never left mine, nor did the hurt that came with that stare. And the anger. "I could barely trust my heart around you, and anything that would give me the potential of losing you?" He shook his head once. "No. I wouldn't do that. Then when I found out I had to trust you, considering you possessed whatever heart I have, there wasn't time."

I glared at him. "Here, time me," I ordered, not waiting for him to get out a stopwatch or a phone. He could count; he was hundreds of years old, after all. "'Isla, due to some fucked-up creation story that is a mix of gods, fairy tales and the plot to a fucking HBO show, I am the brother to the very same king of vampires who once asked you to be his queen and is now hiring you to investigate a war that may get you killed but will also give you the chance to kill the family intent on raping you for your spawn on the occasion of your Awakening,'" I blurted.

Then I glared at him. "You weren't timing," I accused. "But I'm guessing that was under a minute. And I even threw in some little gems of my own, you know, artistic license and all that. I think I improved the original that you and your brother performed not hours ago. I bet the reviews for mine will be glowing."

"He asked you to be his queen?" he seethed.

I gaped at him. "Of *course* that's all you got from that. So I'll tell you what I told him. I'm not in the market for a crown to be gained through marriage. I don't like the thought of something messing with my hair or my undeath like that. So no to the queenship. And being any sort of trophy for a vampire to own and possess and shine like a little toy. I'm something that can be fought for, sure, but I can't be won. Although it turns out I can be lost. And congratulations, sir. You may be one of a few freaky-deaky versions of slayer vampires, but you've got yourself the title of being the first man, vampire, slayer or whatever to have lost what can't be won and to have broken what I thought either didn't exist or was too broken to be smashed and warped any more than it was." I paused, holding his eyes and welcoming the hurt, from both him and myself. "Obviously, I was wrong."

I tossed the bottle on the ground, sending it smashing on the floor because it felt like the right thing to do for dramatic effect. Then I jumped to my feet, meeting his eyes. "And I swear to everything that is unholy, if you say another fucking word to me right now, I'll forget even my own survival in order to kill you where you stand," I promised. And at that point, if he had, I would have.

Why not sacrifice the only blood I could survive on? Considering I'd already sacrificed the heart I didn't even know I had to him.

He didn't speak.

And I turned on my heel and left him.

But not for good. Because I needed blood to survive.

And if there was any moment in history that I resented

that fact even more, it was right then when I stumbled out of a bar with an inebriated body and a broken heart, like countless humans before me.

It was only natural that the blows kept coming. That was how it worked, after all.

I smelled the blood before I saw him. Even if my diet was slightly altered to men I loved who in turn were lying pieces of shit, I still knew blood like I knew shoes.

And I still knew this blood.

"No," I whispered before the elevator doors had even opened.

And then I stepped out of the elevator, even though I didn't want to. I knew what was waiting for me at my front door.

But there was no other choice.

I may have made an exception earlier to run for survival when there was no other choice, but I wasn't going to make a habit out of it.

Not when there was still a difference between running for survival and running for cowardice. I was not a coward. Cowards were the people who knew how cruel and stark reality was and refused to look it in the face. Did everything humanly possible to avert their eyes, in fact.

Since I was inhuman, and not a coward, I did the opposite.

I stared at him.

For a long time, I thought.

It *felt* like a long time.

And immortals measured time differently; long was only relative for how long you were alive considering time on this planet was short for mortals.

When time was infinite, long was… long.

There was blood.

Obviously. There was always blood in death, whether you could see it or not. But there was blood this time.

Mainly because they wanted to send a message, and in a society of vampires, blood was the easiest and most logical way.

But there was also blood because I knew Lewis fought. Hard.

Even though he was past his prime when the strength of a mortal was at its most. Even though he was likely overworked, hadn't slept and taken by surprise.

He still fought.

Because I'd taught him what little there was to know about fighting an immortal who could snap your neck as easily as blink. I'd informed him of the odds, which didn't exist at all, when he'd requested I show him something.

"Don't need to kill them, Isla. I'm not a stupid man. I'm aware of when I'm bested. Cops have to be like that, husbands have to be like that. Guess all humans have to be like that to a point. Some are just too stupid to realize it. I'm not stupid, so I'm not gonna think that a couple of well-placed moves or bullets is gonna get me anywhere but dead if it comes to that. Just need to know that as a man, a husband, a father, a cop, and a human, I'm gonna leave this world with a bit of dignity, and hopefully at least the blood of the person who took me from that mingled with my own."

And he was right.

I could smell it. Smell didn't have a temperature; I was sure most scientists—human ones, at least—would argue that.

Smell was smell and touch was touch.

But vampires had it different than that. With heightened senses, everything melded into one another, as everything was connected in a way.

Human blood was warm, by characteristic and by smell. The heat of it gave something warming about the scent. It's aliveness. Vampire blood, on the other hand, was chilled like a displeasing cold glass of wine.

And it was on him.

I could smell the differences in temperatures, but unlike a wolf, I couldn't distinguish identity by blood.

Merely species.

Merely alive or dead.

You didn't need vampire smelling skills in order to know Lewis was dead.

Just eyes.

Ones that stared into his last glassy unseeing gaze that haunted me more than anything sightless eyes had ever done.

Maybe it was the eyes that gave me that most amount of pause. The scent of death in the air. The blood. The emptiness in his chest where the heartbeat I'd became accustomed to was.

Maybe it was all of it.

Or the humanity that was growing inside me like a tumor.

Whatever it was, I stood there staring at the body left for me, thinking about the widow created because of me, the fatherless children, the man who had deserved life—if any such individual existed. The pain of that almost doubled me over.

But then I wasn't human.

So I broke my gaze and moved. Purposefully, I stepped over his corpse with a thick throat and opened the door into my apartment. I put my handbag on the vintage side table that was purposed for that alone.

Hung my coat up.

Calmly walked to the bar.

Poured myself a drink.

Stared at it, sitting amongst the different bottles on the cart, sourced from Italy especially to go with the décor.

Well, the latest décor at least, after the last furniture got ruined. I was going to make sure this new lot lasted a little longer. There was enough destruction on the inside; I needed some part of me to have the illusion of something on the opposite side of destruction, even if it was a vintage coffee table and a twelve-thousand-dollar sofa.

I continued to stare at the drink, although it offered no answers, only memories.

"Prophecy, eh?" Lewis asked, leaning back, drinking the cheap spiced rum I'd stocked specially for him, despite the fact that it was offensive sitting beside a four-hundred-dollar bottle of whisky.

I sat on the sofa across from him, my classy drink in my hands. "Apparently that's the word on the street. Well, not on the street, considering I'm thinking prophecies are meant to be kept on the down low, but yeah. Witch said it. Book said it. Another witch said it. Apparently that's the trifecta for future predictions. Sounds legit. If you're certifiably fucking insane. Which of course, I am, yet I'm not even convinced despite the people around me being so. Which scares me more than pageant toddlers, that the people around me are even more insane than me, just better at hiding it until now."

Lewis sipped his drink and I cringed. "And you, an immortal being who can live forever on human blood, breaking the laws of physics as we are meant to understand them, who speaks of demons from hell, witches with the powers of the gods and men who turn into wolves, you can't believe in something as simple as love?"

I frowned at him. "Keep up, rookie. It's not love. It's prophecy."

"One and the same. Love always brings about a future that's

the beginning or the ending of someone's world. For mortals, it's usually two people. More if there're kids involved. Therefore, it's the beginning. And the end." His eyes twinkled in a way that made me know he was thinking of his brats. Their photos peppered his cluttered desk.

"But you're an immortal being in a world much different than mine, so it stands to reason that whatever love you feel, what you have, that's going to have a power that reflects its owner. World-changing, world-ending kind of stuff."

I gaped at him. He continued to drink his drink. "Wow," I said finally. "You're just as insane as the rest."

He grinned at me. "I'm thinking you need to figure out a way to get into the institution, considering worlds depend on it."

There was a pause. A long one. I'd spent the years reading a lot of different emotions on his face. Mostly when he was around me it was a mix of disapproval, anger, frustration, or a grim sort of amazement. Usually it was mingled with a healthy dose of impatience.

Apart from the instance of our first meeting, when he was obviously a little rattled, Lewis had never felt fear when I was around him.

Which was another reason I had a grudging respect for him.

It was one thing to fear the unknown, the monsters incorporeal and only imagined in the darkness. It was quite another to find out they actually existed. And were even worse because they existed not in the darkness but in the light.

It took a lot to see that and not feel fear. Stupidity, maybe. Bravery. But stupidity and bravery were kind of tangled up in each other; in order to be brave, one had to be stupid enough that whatever cause they were fighting for was worth dying for. And Lewis had that. It was the warrior look in his eyes. That welcoming of death if it came to that.

But no fear.

And as long as I'd known him I hadn't seen what was in his eyes right then. Not fear, but something akin to awkward nervousness.

He cleared his throat. "Know you've got a few years on me," he began.

I laughed. "A few centuries, grasshopper."

He didn't laugh. He rarely did. But I knew he was laughing on the inside. Of course he was. I was hilarious.

"Yes, well, despite that, it's human nature for me to respond to the fact that you're still young enough to be my daughter."

"I was old enough to be your mother when we first met. Or your girlfriend." I waggled my brows.

He frowned at me. "Human nature to respond to your looks and lack of any form of maturity to think of you as younger than me," he corrected. "Because I'm human and because you're likely to be the most irresponsible immortal being I've ever met, I've grown up as you haven't. Became a father. And I think watching my girl grow up made me realize I consider you another one of my children. One who could kill me as soon as look at me, and who swears and murders a lot more than my daughter, who hopefully will never dress like you. But I know I want her to have the spirit you've got. So for whatever it's worth, from a younger man who's got the years in maturity on you, I'm glad you're not dead. And I'll have to make sure that man of yours makes it stay that way, considering he's a lot more mortal than you and that means I'll have to forget my badge for a second to get a father's revenge."

I blinked at him. Once. Twice. "Well, you've got one thing in common with my biological father, at least. You both easily talk about homicide, though his talk is usually about me."

A muscle in Lewis's jaw ticked. "Well, likely that creature isn't going to say it and if he did it wouldn't mean much, but I will because it needs to be said. Proud of you, Isla. Despite the fact that you wouldn't know when to act your age, or any age, you are a good person, despite being a vampire. Despite doing everything you can to convince yourself to the contrary. So how about you fight in this war? And win it. Not just for the human race and because I want my daughter to have a future one day, but because I want both *of them to have a future."*

He stood, draining his drink.

And then he left.

And the next time I saw him was moments ago, his throat ripped open so brutally that his white shirt was crimson everywhere and the bones in his neck exposed.

As were the brutal bites on the rest of his body. Literally ripped apart by the hybrid vampires created for the war where I'd pissed off some key players.

And where my humanity had obviously became known if such a gesture was made. Of course, that meant I'd have to rip it from my body like the proverbial Band-Aid. Quick and painless.

Or full of pain. Whichever.

The smash of glass bottles shattering on my floor made me realize I'd overturned my bar cart.

Then I realized how comforting destruction felt. How wrong I was before to want something on the outside to contrast the chaos on the inside. So I kept going until everything in my apartment was in ruins.

Apt.

Now my outsides matched my insides.

With less blood.

The blood was splayed on the front of my door.

And on the inside of my chest.

I stared at the room, figuring the blood was covering the ruined sofa too, even if I couldn't see it.

And then I stood in the middle of the destruction, reveling in it.

One single crimson tear trailed down my cheek.

Then I ripped off the Band-Aid.

FIFTEEN

One Week Later

I'D BEEN A BUSY LITTLE VAMPIRE IN THE DAYS AFTER THE
'events,' as I liked to call them. And I didn't like to have to
call them anything because that would mean I'd have to
think about them, and thinking about them came with that
strange niggling in the bottom of my chest where my humanity
used to be.

Ain't nobody got time for that.

I'd gotten the intel on this human from Dante, who treated
me like a human might a dog they were unsure of, wondering
if it was going to bite them or not. Which was precisely how he
should've treated me.

I was feeling very bitey lately.

Which was rather inconvenient, considering the only person I could actually bite was the man who'd betrayed me. I'd

been avoiding him like open-toed sandals with pants.

And he'd been trying to find me. I knew that.

He'd turned up at the office a couple of times. I had a lot of fun watching my security escort him off the premises. But it was rather annoying having to pay their hospital bills when he broke their bones. Then again, it was satisfying pressing charges that ensured he got locked up in prison for twenty-four hours.

That was until some idiot bailed him out.

Then I had to go back to avoidance.

I would've gone straight to murder, as was my usual process when it came to betrayal, but obviously I couldn't murder the only blood bag who was keeping me undead.

So he stayed alive. For the time being.

And I stayed clinging to the old Isla who'd murdered her way through Europe. She may not have been happy, or good, or in touch with any form of reality, but she wasn't plagued with pain. In order to feel pain you had to feel in the first place.

I wasn't going to be doing that.

So I ignored the yearning and stubborn bleeding of that mangled thing in my chest.

I couldn't avoid him forever, though I did have forever up my sleeve. I was unfortunately rather peckish.

So after a couple more murders, I'd have to find the courage to meet him. It'd just take a couple of kills.

I was starting with this sniveling mess.

He had some connection to the faction of rebels who had been boasting about Lewis's murder. Planted, of course. There was a plan in place in order to trap me, I knew. They expected this reaction. We were vampires, after all. Vengeance was what we did best.

And although I may have been known for being borderline insane and unpredictable, if there was anything more predictable than taxes in life, it was vengeance.

But that was dependent on the humanity they were so very sure I possessed.

That would be their downfall, not mine.

I'd gotten the information about a certain human involved in Lewis's death the day after the funeral.

So I was feeling a little more homicidal and delicate after watching his widow sob at the side of the coffin that held her husband, as if she might clutch it forever to stop him from being buried in the ground and being dead forever.

The permanent kind of dead.

It wasn't that that rattled me, for this was new Isla. Such common displays of human grief bounced right off me.

No, it was his daughter, the one he'd once compared to me. She was the one who speared through whatever place inside me could still feel.

She wasn't sobbing or clutching her mother, mixing their tears like her siblings were.

She wasn't anything. She was just standing there, at the edge of the place where life and death met, staring. Empty. Dry eyes. Not a single sob. Just the quiet kind of sorrow that I recognized even from my spot across the street, away from the wretched mourners.

It was that sorrow that had me feeling a little touchier. Had me lose my cool and kick down the door to an unremarkable house in suburbia outside New York City and potentially kill a shrieking human woman wearing a house dress with curlers in her hair.

I was reasonably sure I only knocked her out.

Maybe.

It was her son I'd been focused on finding, and his heartbeat and smell weren't exactly hard to find in the small and extremely depressing house.

He didn't hear me burst in, as he was glued to a bright screen in the darkness he'd made himself since it was just after midday and had headphones covering his ears.

I hated when my entrance was fucked up, so I darted over to the curtains and ripped them down, bathing the cluttered and dirty room in harsh sunlight that made him blink a couple of times in confusion.

When that didn't have the desired effect, I yanked the headphones off rather roughly and hefted his computer across the room so it crashed against the wall covered with a Dracula movie poster.

I scowled at it before turning my scowl, and my fangs, to him. "Dude, *Dracula?* Could you be a little more fucking original?" I asked conversationally.

His eyes, which had dilated with the change in light and focus—and, finally, fear—widened in shock and then realization as they focused on my fangs.

"You can't be out," he hissed, his voice shaking. "It's daylight. Sunlight burns the skin of the monsters!" He shook a battered and dog-eared paperback at me that he'd snatched off his desk for whatever reason, as if doing so might bring about the truth of its words.

I rolled my eyes. "Wrong literature, dude. Get with your Ancient Greek mythology and mix it with some *Buffy*. Only because of her killer fashion sense, though, not because of any of the lore," I said, wandering around the room, picking up a wooden stake and tossing it between my hands. He actually had a wooden stake in his fucking room. They'd picked the right sucker, that was for sure. "The darkness is only comforting to those who like their bad deeds cloaked in shadow, or at least that's when all the juicy meat is at their most vulnerable.

Me? I like to see all the depraved and fucked-up shit I do."

I grinned, then plunged the wooden stake into my own heart.

It did smart a little, considering the sucker was reasonably sharp, but it was worth the pain to see every ounce of blood drain from the idiot's face.

I yanked it back out, screwing my nose up at the bitter scent of urine mixing with old Cheetos and fear as his bladder let go.

"Dude," I said, sauntering up to him and tossing the bloodied stake at his feet. "You honestly just made yourself the 'wet your pants guy.' Little bit of advice if you ever next find yourself in this situation: don't be that guy. He ain't ever going to lose his V-card." I glanced around the dirty room, plastered with art of the creepy variety and fan posters from stupid movies. Novels and old books covered every surface not littered with figurines still in their packages and crumpled energy drink cans that humans used to try to replace for sleep.

I'd done it once, out of curiosity. The thing was bitter and gross. Even extra energy wasn't worth that.

Then again, it wasn't what gave me energy. The serial killer I'd drained after that did.

My gaze snapped back to the sniveling mess I was loath to call a man with a raised brow. "Not that your chances were particularly good anyway. But hey, look at the bright side. If they made a darker, worse and less funny version of the *40-Year-Old Virgin* and were looking for someone uglier than Steve Carrel—no mean feat, of course, I mean that guy can act but I wouldn't bump uglies with him. Anyway, I'll tell the producers to look you up." I paused with a meaningful glint in my eyes. "You know, if you're still alive and all."

He was shaking so badly that his teeth kept clashing

together in a jarring and all around displeasing sound. "Why are y-you here? What d-do you want from me?" he cried.

I rolled my eyes. "More clichés, great. I'm here because a little bird, or a little demon, told me that a certain group of vampires have been getting fat and pathetic humans to do their dirty work." My eyes roved over him. "And it's just sad, really. Mostly because dirty work is the most fun, but also because humans do the job so poorly." I paused. "Though I guess he died in the end. Lewis, that is. The police officer you had a hand in murdering, just in case you forgot. So you did do your job, which I'm sure you'll be satisfied about. Unfortunately, the one successful thing you've done in your pathetic life might actually be what ends that pathetic life."

I grinned. "It almost certainly will be, in fact."

I sauntered up to him.

"So, now that we've established that, you can spill it as to who exactly told you to going into the precinct and lure the officer from his cluttered desk to where you got him murdered," I said calmly.

His eyes bulged and he held his hands up. "I didn't get him murdered," he squeaked. Like a mouse. Or a rat. "I promise I didn't murder him. I didn't even *touch* the dude."

I tilted my head, assessing him. "No, but you didn't need to, though. You knew his fate, did you not?"

Tears streamed down his acne-scarred cheeks. "No, I swear."

I sighed dramatically before leaning down to snap his thighbone in a smooth and satisfying move.

Although his all-encompassing howl was even better than the snapping bone.

I smiled through it until he quieted to hitching sobs. "Oh no, scream as much as you want," I invited. "I knocked out dear old Mom, so she'll be sleeping for a good while, and no one else is close enough to hear you. Even if they were, they couldn't help you." I paused. "But, dude, living with your *mom*? Going with all the clichés. Be original."

I stepped back, circling the room as he sobbed about his leg, then turned back around with crossed arms.

"Now, let's try this again now that you've understood the punishment for lying and the fact that I'm very good at telling when a man is lying." I paused, the flinch of pain that came with the untruth of that statement stabbing through me in an intensity that shocked me.

I swallowed it by stepping forward and placing my hands on either side of his chair so I could stare into his beady, pain-filled eyes.

"You knew they were going to kill him, didn't you? You just didn't care. Because you were likely promised to be something more than the cliché you are."

He was shaking so badly the chair was starting to vibrate. I hoped he wasn't going into shock. That was a much too easy way for him to die.

"I've got all day," I stated. "Mom might not, and once she wakes up, dazed but thinking she just had a nice nap, she'll come in here, try to hide her disappointment for having such a loser for a son and likely ask if you want a snack. Then I'll have to turn her into the snack, in front of you."

I was convincing even myself. Had I even been able to drink her blood without doing the whole *Exorcist* thing, I idly wondered if I'd actually do it. Kill a woman who was only guilty of indulging a fully grown man she happened to have given birth to.

"Okay, o-okay," he spluttered between his sobs. "They said they'd turn me. All I know about them is on that." He jerked his head to the laptop on his desk. "I just wanted to be like you. I wanted to be different. More. I'm sorry, I just wanted to be a vampire, immortal, extraordinary—"

I cut him off by snapping his neck. Quicker than I planned, but I was growing bored and impatient. "There's nothing more common than the desire to be extraordinary," I informed his corpse as I let it go. He collapsed unceremoniously to the floor.

I stared at his eyes, confronting me with their accusation in death.

I felt nothing.

Neither the vampire nor the woman in me.

I turned on my heel and left, snatching his laptop as I went.

I met Sophie for coffee after I killed the forty-year-old virgin. Though I thought he was closer to thirty.

She was best with technology, and I also wanted an update on where we were with killing the witches to hopefully free me from Thorne's connection.

I was convincing myself that when I stopped needing his blood to survive, that would happen.

Freedom.

Like I wasn't entombed in this shit forever.

Like there wasn't some prophecy that literally said everything to the contrary.

I was great at denial.

"Cream or sugar?" the young barista asked.

"Just a swig of O Neg," I deadpanned.

Sophie grinned.

The barista gave me a vacant look that he wore probably when someone told him a name he'd fuck up on a cup, like John.

"Excuse me?"

I glanced at Sophie and rolled my eyes. "It's only fun doing this when they're smart enough to get it. Insulting idiots is about as satisfying as draining crackheads." Then I turned back to the barista. "Just black," I rectified. "Like my heart."

He went off with a frown and Sophie turned to me. "Still mad at Thorne?" she gathered.

I put my finger to my chin. "Well, let me see. Am I still mad at the man whom I thought I loved, and almost died for, for lying to me before finally tell me he's the brother of the king of vampires and that his race of slayers is actually descended from vampires themselves and he's basically immortal?" I pretended to pause in thought. "Fuck yes, I'm still mad at him. And if I didn't need his blood to survive, I'd throw his delimbed body off the Empire State Building."

The barista came back with the coffees at the exact moment I said my last line. Of course he did; I'd perfectly timed it that way so I could enjoy his blanche and the slight shake to his hand when he passed me my coffee.

I grinned at him. "Thank you so much," I said sweetly. "You have a blessed day now."

We walked to a table and Sophie sat, opening the laptop I gave her. "You wouldn't throw him off the Empire State Building," she argued.

"You're right. I don't want to have to elbow tourists out of the way in order to get to the edge. I'll think of somewhere with less foot traffic while you brainstorm witchy ways to break this prophecy so I don't have to live on his blood and I can kill him. Since we seem to be on pause with the killing the witch thing." I sipped my coffee and glared at her. "Which does not please me, side note."

She gave me a look. "You're not going to kill him, even if

that was possible."

"Really? And why is that?"

"You love him."

"And?" I looked anywhere but the probing gaze of my best friend.

"You can't kill the people you love?"

My gaze snapped to her as I narrowed my brows. "Oh I beg to differ, since they can certainly do the same to you. And have you heard of fucking Shakespeare? The guy literally wrote plays that were kind of famous on people in love being the reason for each other's deaths. In fact, I think you can only kill people you love. Look it up. I bet that wretched emotion is the number one cause of death in the world. Even above slippery bathroom floors and no bathmats."

She didn't respond, obviously understanding my need not to continue this conversation. Instead she focused on the screen and I focused on watching idiotic humans go about their days from our window seat.

But as it always did, watching humans made me homicidal, so I watched Sophie tap at the keys of the laptop with impatience.

"Can't you just say 'accio information' and then get what we need off that thing?" I demanded, anxious to continue my little vengeance mission.

I was still peckish and it only got worse with passing moments. Which meant I was cranky.

Oh, and because I was in the midst of the most awkward breakup *ever*. There wasn't a clean break in this situation, thanks to the whole 'fated to be together' prophecy thing and the very fucking frustrating fact that I would, at some point, have to see his face, or at least the vein in his neck, which was unfortunately attached to his face.

And feel his emotions.

I could barely feel my own. Immortals didn't react to things quite like humans did. Lies, betrayal and death were all part of the status quo, obviously. But in a species where true attachments were rare, when they did happen, there was no such thing as a 'small lie' or an 'overreaction.'

Or maybe that was just me.

Or women in general.

Some women ate too much ice cream or drank too much wine and cried over romance movies. Not me. I planned executions of idiots in the rebellion trying to treat me like a woman while forgetting I was a vampire.

Hence them likely not expecting me to kill the human. I knew the mastermind of this wasn't stupid. I was learning that more and more. And that there wasn't likely one singular mastermind. Perhaps there was a leader of sorts, but in such rebellions there were likely to be a few different creatures who considered themselves leaders, and the truest one probably wasn't the one on the throne.

It was likely the one standing behind it, in the shadows.

That was the way most rulers ruled.

With Rick as the exception.

Though I wasn't talking to him either, king or not.

An asshole was still an asshole, regardless of blood or a crown.

Sophie scowled at me. "No, you can't work magic on technology. It's humankind's answer to magic, and we can only manipulate natural resources." She nodded to the laptop. "This is not natural."

I rolled my eyes. "I'm hearing too many excuses and not enough results."

She raised her brow at me. "This may not be natural but

you are, which means I can work my magic on you."

"You could try," I challenged.

I wasn't joking. Fighting was the best way to distract me, and with her new juice she'd make it interesting enough that I might just forget the huge gaping hole in my chest.

Or at least make a new one.

She shook her head. "Not worth it."

Then she went back to the computer, tapping away, her brows furrowed as she stared at the screen.

I tapped my fingernails on the wooden table, sipping my coffee.

An hour passed.

"You've been at it for long enough. What's the skinny?" I demanded.

She looked up. "It's been less than three minutes, Isla. The skinny is more or less the same."

I scowled. "Well if you don't get any information soon I might have to go look for a fight. Werewolves are always fun." I narrowed my eyes at the finger that paused for a split second on the keyboard. "You seem to have a connection to one who's stalking you, I could take care of my ADHD and your little dog problem with one stone. Or two fangs. What do we think?"

She didn't look up from the screen. "No, Isla."

I stared at her head. "You like him. You lurvveee him? Sophie and Wolfy, sitting in a tree…."

Her head snapped up. "I don't like him," she hissed. "I just don't want you to kill him."

Her eyes glowed, and there was a faint flicker of blue on her fingers that most humans would just consider to be a trick of the light.

But I knew by the way the air hummed that I'd woken something. Maybe I wasn't the only one with emotions close to the surface.

I held my hands up in surrender. "Don't zap me. The static would mess with my hair and I just got it done." I patted the top of my head protectively. "I won't kill him."

She stared at me another beat, trying to gauge my sincerity most likely. Whatever she found must have pleased her because her head went back down to the screen.

"But you do like him," I continued. "Because not wanting someone to get killed is the epitome of liking them. Especially between you and me. So what's the deal? I'm not liking the combination of your new powers and the howl at the moon part of this little nursery rhyme that everyone is taking as gospel. The ingredients add up to trouble. You and I may be great at almost all kinds of trouble, but this one? No. So you're going to have to tell me what's going on."

She snapped her head up again. "Done," she said, closing the lid on the laptop.

I frowned at her. "That timing is suspicious."

She narrowed her eyes at me, reaching for her coffee. Her hands still glowed slightly. "No, it's just right, in fact. I've got places to be and you've got another immortal to annihilate. The human you killed was good at hiding his online dealings in the deep web, and the immortal he was dealing with was better, but I'm the best."

She yanked out her phone, typed quickly and then tapped her finger on the screen. I heard mine vibrate in the depths of my bag.

"I sent you the location on his rerouted IP address, and I'll do a profile on him as soon as I get back to the office, just in case he's not home. He'll most likely lead you to the one you're looking for. I have no doubt in your powers of persuasion."

I grinned at her. "Neither do I."

Her eyes were sparkling, but then they turned a little too serious for my liking.

"I'm sorry about Lewis, Isla," she said quietly. "I know he meant something to you."

I straightened my spine. "He meant nothing to me," I lied. "He was human. Humans die. It came at a rather inopportune time, of course, but it was also rather opportune for me to get the leads I need to end this shit. Lewis wasn't exactly useful to me anymore anyway, considering his main purpose was procuring me free-range, cruelty-free snacks and now I don't need them."

The tone I'd adopted was so good I was even convincing myself.

Sophie raised a brow but didn't call me on it. Friends were good like that, seeing when you were lying to the world, and them, and most importantly yourself, and understanding the need to go along with that lie too.

"Speaking of snacks," she said. "Thorne's come around the office. Once, or about twelve times. He's been demanding I tell him where you are and alternately just hoping he'd run into you, I think."

I snorted. "He'll not want to be hoping to run into me. It doesn't bode well for his physical well-being."

"You need him alive," she pointed out.

I nodded. "Yes, *alive*. But that doesn't mean he has to be whole."

Again, Sophie didn't call me on that little lie.

She didn't let it go either.

"You have to forgive him."

I lifted my brow in warning. "Is that right? Because I don't think I do. He should've told me."

Sophie sipped from her mug. "Yes, and when do you think

he should've told you? The first time you met, when prophecy and everything more than that told him you were everything he needed to breathe while age-old instinct urged him that you were the only thing he needed to kill? Or any of your other encounters before you got together during which, if I remember correctly, you promised you'd kill him? Or how about when the death threats stopped?"

She paused, as I sipped from my own mug, pretending that the coffee was satisfying the aching burn in my throat. Pretending that the sheer need for blood, for Thorne's blood, for Thorne, wasn't driving me crazy. Or *crazier*.

Sophie, unaware of my internal struggle, put her cup down to continue the lecture.

"Oh wait, that's right. The death threats have yet to stop. Then there was that whole war of the worlds that you were fighting. The secrets you had to keep about your relationship in order to stop the entire warring community, both sides, from coming after you. Then you almost died, and he had to watch and feel what the world would be like if he lost you. Then he was supposed to tell you something that he most likely hasn't told anyone but those he trusts with his life? Because such knowledge could be the thing that kills him if left in the wrong hands. And merely giving you that information was all the more fatal to him when you already hold his heart in your hands. So when do you think, between all that, it would have been the ideal time for him to let you know that he's not just a mortal slayer but an immortal version of one who is related to the vampire king who may or may not be in love with you and has you fighting on his side in a war that may kill you all? Where you two just happened to be prophesized to bring about some kind of beginning or end along with four others." She tapped her fingers on the table, eyeing me. "When, Isla?"

I stared at her. Sipped my coffee. Glared at her. Wished I could do some magic. Then I picked up the fork on the table, idly weighed it between my thumb and finger, contemplated spearing her with it and then put it down.

"When? Well, there was that time when we were.... Oh wait, there was a time in *any* of those situations when he could have slotted that in there," I snapped. "The truth is something that can easily fit into every conversation, especially when it changes everything." I drained my coffee and stood up from the table.

Sophie stayed sitting. "No, that's when the truth doesn't fit anywhere," she muttered, her eyes faraway and yet close at the same time.

I wanted to play the counselor to my friend, I really did, but the pause I'd have to give her to talk about whatever truth lay behind her eyes meant mine might come out too. And this coffee shop, this whole fucking island wasn't big enough to contain that particular truth.

"Whatever. I'm going to kill some things. Are you going to come?"

If there was something that worked better than shoe shopping to avoid all of life's upsetting and rather inconvenient truths—to unintentionally quote Al Gore—it was killing things.

She stood, clearing her eyes. "I'd love to, but rain check? I've got to get us prepared for this fight with the witches and do some more research on them, and then I have a coven meeting."

I screwed up my nose. "Homework and meetings with crusty old witches? Boo, you whore."

She hefted her black studded bag onto her shoulder. "This homework might be the difference between life and death when we finally face these bitches. Do you still disapprove?"

I scowled at her. "Yes I do," I informed her snippily, crossing my arms. "I disapprove on principle."

It just happened to be that the lull in our plan to fight the war coincided with my vengeance mission and my little 'let's dodge Thorne so we don't kill him' game I had going on. Handy.

Sophie's eyes went from light and teasing to inquisitive. I didn't like the way she started to peer at me.

I self-consciously rubbed my upper lip for milk foam, even though I hadn't had anything milky. "What?" I snapped.

"When was the last time you fed, Isla?" she asked.

I folded my arms. "Who are you, my mother? Or her opposite and slightly less evil twin?"

"Isla," she warned. "You're going into an uncertain situation, could be attacked at any moment, and are about to go and kill more things. You need to feed."

"I'm on a diet. Low blood. It's all the rage. Keeps me young," I lied. "Plus, I'm so much more ruthless when I'm hangry that I even scare myself. It's *such* fun."

"Isla. Whatever is going on with Thorne, he is, for better or worse, what you need to survive."

"His *blood* is," I corrected. "The only other things I need to survive come in the form of television shows, a good torture every now and then and high-heeled shoes."

She gave me a disbelieving look. "Whatever you need to tell yourself to get through the night. But promise me you'll call him and grab a midnight snack after the latest killing."

I crossed my fingers over the area of my chest where my heart would be. "Hope to die," I promised. Or, more aptly, lied.

No way was I going to him for anything. Yeah, I needed his blood to survive, but I also needed my sanity. The little sliver I held onto, anyway.

She gave me another look that told me she saw right

through me. "Okay, well, at least call me, or Duncan or freaking Scott if this gets more complicated than one kill," she ordered.

I grinned. "Of course. I'll make it a party."

No way was I calling anyone. Plus, Duncan was taking it upon himself to fight some hybrids in Oklahoma. Coincidence? Me thinks not.

"Well kill him slowly for me, then," she requested, leaning in to kiss my cheek.

"Now *that* I can promise," I said cheerfully.

And then I darted out the door to kill things.

Like my humanity.

Like that love that seemed unable to die.

Like it might be the only part of me that was truly deathless.

SIXTEEN

THE INFO AND ADDRESS SOPHIE GAVE ME WERE GOOD. And happily enough, the demon was home.

And not expecting me.

Which was great.

Whatever the plan was, it was hopefully at the very least eschewed by the fact that I didn't leave the human alive.

Or maybe that was the plan, to have me circling the basement where I'd chained the demon to a chair. I had Sophie send me a quick picture of how to do a rudimentary Devil's trap—they didn't just exist on *Supernatural*, one thing the producers got right. I didn't have chalk so I'd had to use two tubes of my favorite lipstick, which was rather fucking inconvenient.

I brushed off my knees when I finished, tossing the empty tube to the side.

"You know, this was my last tube, and they discontinued

this color," I seethed. "So you just got yourself the Isla special. Being that I'll make you hurt in so many ways even your boss downstairs might learn a few things."

I glared at the demon who looked far too terrified. His daddy would be so disappointed. Not to mention he'd only managed to burn up my arms with his little fire trick.

They barely smarted, though the healing process was annoyingly slow considering the lack of blood in my system.

I could work around it.

It was actually rather calming and nice compared to the utter agony in my chest.

I circled him, cold and predatory. The look was freeing— welcome, in fact. Just like the killing of that human had been, letting myself out of the shackles I had been tricking myself were accessories for the past few centuries. Ones that had become tighter with Thorne in my life, tighter in a way that I thought was comforting when I was under whatever illusion had me thinking it was actually a forever kind of thing.

Nothing was forever.

Except death.

And I needed to have some fun in my life before death.

It was so damn boring doing this 'proper behavior for human society' thing.

Blah.

I embraced my true nature, smiling as I unearthed the enchanted knife that had been humming with magic in my purse. I welcomed the pain that came from holding it, shooting into my injured arms, renewing the fire within them.

The nifty thing about those enchanted blades was they worked on any supernatural creature. Kind of a blanket kill switch.

Handy.

I wondered why the slayers hadn't been more successful at disseminating our numbers. It only took a stab in the proper organ to end an immortal with this. How had they not gained more of an upper hand?

Oh, that's right. They were human.

Basically, at least.

Apart from one.

I didn't swallow the rage or sorrow that came with that little thought. I embraced it, welcomed and channeled it into the stare I was aiming at the demon in front of me.

"You know," I began, twirling the knife in my palm and puncturing the skin, just for fun. And to show my crazy. Most times I wore it like Prada, and anyone with an eye for it would see it. But sometimes I got tasteless and uncultured swine who didn't know Tom Ford from Target and sane from… well, me. So I had to educate them.

Oh, how I'd missed educating them.

It was worth the excruciating pain that came with the cut that was so much more than just a simple cut. No, the magic in the blade was designed to leak out once blood was spilled, rendering the immortal it punctured immobile with pain.

That was unless the immortal was me. Pain was my jam.

"Someone once told me not to bite off more than I could chew." I moved licked the blood off my palm, my eyes on the demon, who was now shaking.

Curious.

"You know what I told those people?"

I darted forward so my nails fastened around his neck, the pulsing of his artery vibrating my palm, the blood calling to me.

Not in a way that I wanted to wet my rather dry whistle, but I grinned in the face of his desperate fear nonetheless.

"I told them nothing," I whispered. "I bit them. And reminded them that I'm a fucking *vampire*, and I don't chew shit. But they got the message. You know, with their deaths."

I leaned forward, intending to rip his throat out. For fun rather than sustenance, of course, on account of the whole vomiting blood situation should I decide to swallow.

I bet that was one of the worst reactions a girl could have to swallowing.

Fuck, why didn't I have a pen and paper around, or at least a camera crew when I had thoughts like that, so I could look right at the camera and utter it before the kill shot.

"Please don't kill me," he blurted, his voice shaking.

Steam rose off the exposed skin covered in rudimentary and rather ugly ink, the little lipstick trap making it so the flames couldn't leave his body.

"Really, dude? A tribal tattoo? Please tell me you've got a wallet chain and GTL is your Sunday routine. After collecting souls for the week, of course" I said, pausing from my immediate plan.

It wasn't the bad tattoos that made me pause, though I would be removing them for him later because I was a kind vampire like that. No, it was the pleading and utter terror in his voice.

Yeah, some demons were cowards, and I would like to think I was pretty darn scary, but this was something else. This wasn't the fear of an immortal with a very real experience of the world and the knowledge of an immortality coming to an end.

That was very different to an ignorant human's fear, much like a little rabbit with its frantic eyes and heartbeat and not much coherent thought.

But this demon was behaving like... well, a human.

I squinted at him.

I wasn't hot on demon lore, considering they kept their shit tight, and also because I didn't really care where they came from, just that they poured great drinks, gave great orgasms and put up a good enough fight when I felt like killing something.

They were from the underworld, that was the one thing agreed upon. But the underworld was a tricky place. There was Hades, the original bad boy himself. Daddy to all demons and uncle to all vampires. It was certain that demons existed. Therefore the underworld existed, so therefore Hades existed.

Which, of course, gave credence to the whole prophecy thing.

And then there was the question of binary oppositions.

Because for the underworld to exist, didn't there have to be a kingdom in the sky for all the saints to go to?

No, but then again, was there honestly such a thing as saints in this world?

A scary thought, or a comforting one for me, at least. Because there only need be one place for all the souls on this earth, since they were all depraved.

It was only a matter of how depraved.

But that was getting away from the point.

Which was that people didn't know much about demons except that they came mostly in the same human shape, apart from ones from the deepest levels of the pit if you believed the lore.

They only *resembled* humans; they weren't *actually* human. Which was why I paused in the face of humanlike fear.

"I promise I'll tell you whatever you need to know. Just don't kill me. This isn't what I signed up for," he babbled, his voice increasing to a pitch that didn't match his bulging muscles and douchey disposition. Oh, and the fact that he was a fucking demon.

"What you signed up for?" I repeated. "Well, none of us sign up to be monsters, buddy, but we are. For better or worse. I personally like worse. That's *so* much more fun." I ran my eyes over the steaming and now writhing demon. It must not have been that fun, or comfortable, having fire burning through your body when it couldn't find release.

I wondered if it was like having ice freeze your veins in the place of the fire that had been there once before.

Nope. Couldn't go there.

My mind was a wandering fool today.

More so than every other day.

"Run, my pretties. Be free," I called out, gesturing with my hands.

The demon continued to shake with his fear and pain. "Who are you talking to?" His eyes darted around the empty room.

I tilted my head with a smile. "Oh, just the monsters I'm letting out to play." I tapped the side of my head. "Sometimes it's too depraved for even them up there."

Then I sauntered up to him, leaning on the handles of the chair, smiling seductively at him for a moment. I locked eyes with the fire and experienced the inferno that was his skin, singeing my arms slightly but yet somehow feeling like nothing more than a small flicker of dying embers.

I stared into the flames as I plunged the dagger into his thigh.

I left it there while he screamed, checking my manicure until he calmed down.

"I was going to talk to you!" he howled. "You didn't need to do that."

I looked up from my nails. "Oh I know, but I brought the

knife and all, and I had my heart set on at least a little torture for today." I shrugged. "Sucks to be you, dude."

"They didn't tell me it was going to be like this. Immortality means not dying, right? Well I feel like I'm going to die, just like I would as a human."

I nodded. "Well yes, you're not as dense as your haircut and tattoo communicate you to be, but…. Wait, you were human?"

He gaped at me. "What else would I be?"

I gaped back. "Um, the demon that you are?"

I wondered if there was such a thing as mentally challenged demons.

Even the Prince of Darkness might drop the odd one on its head every now and then.

"They came to me, those women. They were beautiful. One was like you, with the fangs." He nodded to my mouth.

"And the beauty, obviously," I added.

He swallowed. "The other was hot, like I'd totally take her home anytime, but there was something… off about it. Like the chicks who wear all that makeup and they're all good to look at for a while as long as you don't look too close and realize… you know?"

"That they're big old uggos who perfected the art of contour?" I finished for him.

He nodded distractedly. "Well, that's what she was. And then there was a man who was like you too, but he was a creepy dude. Cold, but empty. He'd kill me as soon as look at me."

I gave him a once-over. "Could you blame him? He'd probably be doing humankind a favor, which was most likely why he didn't do it. You know, since he's trying to annihilate humankind, or use them as cattle, depending on whose war song you listen to."

Steam continued to rise off the demon's pain-drenched

face. "Can you take that out?" he gritted out.

I nodded. "Yes, of course I can."

He waited. I didn't move.

"I can, but I'm not actually going to," I clarified.

He waited, perhaps for mercy, or kindness or for me to simply be impatient enough to speed the process along.

He was sorely mistaken if he was thinking such things could be found in a vampire.

But then such things couldn't be offered by humans either. They were only merciful when they wanted victory, kind when they wanted to be recognized, and patient when they wanted anything.

Depraved.

"We going to sit here all night? Because I'm not the one with the magical knife in my thigh, so it's going to be a *much* more comfortable wait for me." I held up my phone. "Plus, I've just discovered this little game called Candy Crush. It's wonderfully addicting."

"You're insane," he hissed, the fury in his voice finally resembling somewhat demonlike behavior.

I grinned. "Of course I am. But then again, crazy is relative. I consider that hairdo paired with those tattoos and that tank top to be the epitome of insanity." I shrugged. "Fire with fire is the cliché. But I despise clichés. I do enjoy the spirit of it, though. I just prefer crazy with crazy. And honey, my crazy is so much cooler than yours."

He eyed me again. "They just promised me eternal life," he relented. "I didn't know it would come to this."

I quirked my brow. "They promised you eternal life and you didn't think such a thing would come with pain and blood and a lot of fucking strings? My, my, you are a stupid one. This is, of course, considering I believe the demon who is telling me, or at least insinuating, that he was once human. Which is too much for even my crazy. Do I look new?" I paused. "Of course I do, because I'm immortal. But I'm not an idiot. I'm not concerned with the steaming holes you pop out of as fully formed, human-shaped monsters, mainly because the humans are also human-shaped monsters. But seriously? You know this will take so much longer if you cling to lies."

"I'm not lying, I swear. Until a year ago I was just working at a gym, trying to get my break in the fitness model industry and fighting with my girlfriend about whether or not the baby was mine. It wasn't," he added, as if I might care.

"Well, thankfully for that child," I muttered.

"And then someone came to the gym, asked me if I wanted more than what I had—proper strength, a better life. A forever life." He paused. "It's weird, you'd think I would've kicked a stranger out who said that, but he was just so convincing. I knew it couldn't be possible but I knew it was true. You know?"

I sighed. Sometimes ignorance and stupidity were endearing. That truth we were talking about earlier? The one that took up all the space? Well, it seemed to fit into empty minds every once in a while.

I sighed. "So you're expecting me to believe you were just turned for no reason, apart from to kill a human cop? And that if someone was choosing from the humans around here to make immortal, that someone would chose *you*?"

A poor choice.

He shrugged, crying out at the pain the motion gave him. I imagined he was feeling the effects of the magic like acid at that point.

Wondrous.

"I don't know, I just know that it wasn't a nice process, becoming this," he hissed.

I rolled my eyes. "No way? Turning a human into a demon was painful? Gosh, that's not a surprise at all. It's a little more invasive than a nose job, and those are meant to smart a little too, if those extreme makeover shows are anything to go by. But I couldn't care less about your poor little human body transitioning into a demon, despite it being impossible," I continued, leaning forward. "I'm more interested in the police officer you got killed and then some information on your superiors."

He blinked. "I tell you, you'll take the knife out?"

I grinned. "Sure."

He sucked in a breath as steam continued to rise. "I didn't kill any cop. I just drove the van," he said quickly. "Took him to where I've been taking people since they turned me into this." He glanced down at his steaming arms. "I took the people down there to him, and they never came back." He paused, eyes flickering with something—humanity, perhaps. "Some I kept for myself because that's what I need to do. He told me that, to live forever, I have to…."

"Kill?" I finished for him. "Of course you do. Immortality doesn't come for free."

He swallowed. "Yeah. But now I'm thinking it might not have been worth it."

I shook my head. "You think? Keep talking," I demanded, not wanting him to think that he could tell me all of his regrets, which I thought should have started with the tattoos and not letting witches turn him into a demon.

"So, after I knocked him out, I took the cop there. Didn't expect to bring him out, but I had my orders. Bring him out and put him outside some fancy apartment. That's it. That's all I did, I swear."

I smiled at him. "Oh, I believe you."

"So you'll take the knife out?"

"I'm a vampire of my word," I told him. Then I wrenched the blade from his thigh, inspecting the black- and red-tinged blood on the steel. "One more thing," I said, looking up at him. "The place you took him, you got an address?"

He nodded rapidly and rattled it off.

"And that's everything?" I clarified.

"I promise."

"Great," I replied.

I plunged the knife into his temple.

Then I decided it was time to eat.

Hopefully the killing had tarnished my soul enough to help me survive my next meal.

And maybe Thorne would too.

It was his heartbeat I heard before the roared "Isla" when I waltzed into his house.

I may have accidentally broken the door off the hinges while coming in. It was his fault for locking it, really. He was a slayer with immortal enemies; what the fuck would a locked door do anyway?

Plus, I liked being able to bring destruction upon his house. I hadn't ruled out burning it to the ground on my way out.

He burst forth from where he'd been sitting at the dining table sharpening knives, a couple of books scattered around him and an empty glass beside a half-full bottle of whisky.

At least it was the good stuff.

His eyes flared at the singed remains of my shirt and the slightly pink skin from the burns that were stubbornly slow in healing.

"What the fuck happened?" he demanded, eyes roving over me to determine whether there were any other parts suffering the similar fate.

His emotions were only a twinge in the air. I could barely taste the flavor of them, guessing it was because of the lack of his blood in my veins. I should have been thankful, but then why did the air feel so damn empty without knowing his emotions were attached to mine?

I kept my face even.

"Demon. Long story. One I don't want to tell you. We have that in common, not wanting to tell each other long stories. Mine doesn't really rival yours, considering it doesn't sever relationships and turn centuries of belief on its head. But it is a doozy. And has fire." I held up my arms. "And blood. But of course, all the good stories do."

I narrowed my eyes at the flickering intensity in his and steeled myself against the strong urge to let him do what his gaze was telling me he yearned to do—namely snatching me into his arms and likely ripping my clothes off before owning me right there.

I tingled between my legs at the thought.

I made a mental note to get laid after this.

But the thought of going to someone else, letting someone else into the body that I had given Thorne without realizing I'd taken it from myself, it roiled my stomach much the same way the idea of taking another's blood did.

But I wasn't going to die from the wrong penis.

It was the 'right' one that may kill me yet.

"I didn't come to chat. Or exchange soulful stares, as seems to be your preference," I continued. "I came for a snack. I've got a big battle coming up and I need to be at my best. You see, I didn't want to see you. Actually, I would have done literally anything, even worn plaid, if it meant I didn't have to see you. But it seems that a girl's gotta eat, so she's just gotta do things like face the asshole who broke her—" I cut myself off quickly before I could say the word 'heart' like some big idiotic girl from some Ryan Reynolds romcom. I watched that shit for shirtless Ryan, not for the women who made me cringe for our entire race in general.

"Trust," I finished, watching the way his eyes flared with something at the single word. "So here I am. Open a vein so I can get this over with and we might get through this with both of us surviving. If I kill you, I die too. And I'm rather attached to surviving."

His eyes didn't move from mine. Neither did his hands, which were fisted at his sides and shaking from what I knew was the pressure of wanting to touch me.

I knew it because mine were doing the same, yet my arms were crossed casually across my chest, and I did a good job at hiding the outwards rattling of my broken pieces.

Inside, it was almost as deafening as Thorne's heartbeat.

He stepped forward. An inch. Too much. I could taste his emotions and the depth of them. The blood running through his veins called to me just like those muscled arms, that musky scent and the promise that was more than blood.

And that was everything in the blood.

Life.

Death

"You die, Isla," he growled, "and I die. And the world, it seems. I'm not one to give two fucks about the world. It can burn in front of me as long as I've got you by my side. So no way am I going to let you die. Even if that means I have to do whatever I can to stop you from killing me."

I grinned at him. "You want me not to kill you? How about

you stop breathing?" I requested sweetly. "Or blowing out any of that hot air you call words and the dream that you seem to have that I'll *ever* be by your side again." I kept my smile because that was the battle armor I wore to the worst of the wars between my heart and soul. A woman to be feared was one who smiled while inside a battle raged. "But I love breaking dreams almost as much as I love breaking in new shoes."

Another inch, another rattle of my teeth at the proximity of his heartbeat, at the blood that called to me louder than Chanel, than anything ever before. That turned the burning in my throat into an inferno like the one that had been burning in the demon's eyes. The one I couldn't feel.

I thought it was because I was made of ice.

And perhaps I was.

Perhaps there was only one fire that could melt me.

And destroy me.

"You're my dream," he growled, his voice thick, eyes almost dark.

"Well that's where you made your mistake. I don't live in dreams. I'm undead in all your nightmares."

He stayed put. "You're not going to let me explain shit, are you? Apologize?"

I glared at him. "An apology is the weapon of a weak man, Thorne. Or of a devious asshole. Which one are you?"

He didn't answer.

The slight tilt of his head, baring his throat, was the only thing I needed. Or the last thing that shattered whatever self-control I'd been kidding myself I had. But it was the self-control of consciously not biting him straight away, torturing myself with his mere presence because, despite the lies I told him—and, more importantly, myself—it was his company and his words I craved almost as much as his blood.

But then my fangs sank into his neck like butter and the explosion of heat and ambrosia on my tongue made me forget about anything but blood.

And Thorne.

I registered the way his hands went around me, pulling me closer to him, imprinting his body on mine while I brought his lifeblood into my veins.

His hands tangled in my hair, tearing at it with force, not to stop me but to urge me on.

I also registered the movement of those hands to roughly knead my ass and then lift me.

A slave to instinct the second my fangs pierced his skin, I wrapped my legs around his waist as I continued to drink my fill of his blood.

Let it warm me up.

Let it melt me.

Let it destroy me.

For who wouldn't welcome destruction if it was like this? The world destroyed everything, after all; why not make my own destruction as beautiful and as ugly as it could be?

The hands that had been at my hair returned once more.

He grabbed a palmful, circled it around his wrist. And yanked.

Hard.

There was pain.

From the pressure at my neck, but mostly from the aching of my fangs being yanked away from the blood that found its home inside of me.

I hissed at his black eyes, not entirely human and not entirely vampire at that moment. Somehow I was both and yet neither.

I was one thing.

Thorne's.

Because he didn't flinch in the face of the danger and death I felt like promising him for yanking me from my meal. No, he welcomed it, his eyes electrifying and then slamming my mouth to his.

I didn't hesitate to return the kiss.

It wasn't kind. Nor gentle. Nor soulful.

Because that wasn't what real life was.

Or real death.

It was brutal, rough and most likely fatal.

His teeth sank into my lips and I cried out at the rush of blood that spilled into both of our mouths, burning us more, setting the house on fire.

Then my head was yanked back again and I unleashed my monster once more.

Only to see I was staring in the face of another one.

"This is it, Isla. Death. With you. It's a lifetime of death, and you're not fuckin' escaping that. You're deathless, but you're always gonna have death following you." The words of prophecy, repeated on his rough and garbled voice in the face of our current position, gave the words something they didn't have before. Something that made them settle somewhere they hadn't before.

"I'm always gonna be followin' you. At your side. Inside you. Fightin' with you. Fightin' for you. And that's eternity." His hand tightened as he threw me down on the bed, the legs creaking in protest at the force. I stayed there, chained by his words, his gaze.

Then it wasn't his gaze or words holding me down. It was him. His body covered mine, but not before he ripped my ruined clothes from my body in less than a blink.

I did the same to him, shredding his tee, raking my nails

over his corded skin and reveling in the smell of blood in the air.

He leaned forward and covered my exposed nipples with his mouth, roughly sucking and nipping at the sensitive flesh.

His hand at my hip bit painfully into the skin, intensifying the building of my climax.

His roughness made me feel gentle and strong at the same time.

Every inch of my body yearned for attention from him, but then my soul and my mind battled.

Hence me quickly moving so I was on top, the bedframe rattling on its hinges at the force I used to slam his body against the mattress.

He showed his teeth in a feral growl as I gained the upper hand, until he reached up to circle my neck, squeezing painfully at the same time he yanked me down to his mouth for a clash of the two.

My fangs brushed at his lips, cutting them in the ferocity, adding to the craziness of the kiss as I drank the droplets that came from him.

Then I detached, quickly moving a hand up to circle his wrists and stretch them over his head as the other worked at his belt.

He hissed out a rough breath as my fingers grazed his hard flesh. The waves of his arousal that poured into me through our newly reinforced connection sent me half wild with need.

"Isla," Thorne growled.

I snapped my gaze up to him through hooded eyes, flexing my grip on his wrists so the pressure worked at the bones almost to their breaking point. He didn't break eye contact with me, nor did he betray any amount of pain.

In fact, a fresh wave of desire flooded through me, and the

flesh at my palm twitched once with the movement.

My anger somehow found its voice at that moment.

"This isn't us. This isn't beauty. Nor is it forgiveness. This is nothing," I hissed, moving my body atop his, pinning him down while reveling in the control and my own wild need.

His eyes flared at my words, his initial response momentarily lost as I impaled myself on him, blinding both of us to anything but our connection as I began my frantic movements.

The sounds of Thorne's heavy breathing and the creaks of the bed and the brutal thump of our coupling poured into the empty air for an eternity, mingling with the roar of Thorne's heartbeat.

Then eternity ended and I lost purchase on Thorne's wrists. Our connection remained as he tumbled us through the air so I landed forcefully on my back, the feet on the bed collapsing at the same time as he surged into me in a brutal thrust.

"You're wrong," he growled, not stopping the assault of his thrusts, his eyes on mine. "Nothing between us? It's fucking everything. And it will be. For eternity."

And then there was eternity once more. Lost in each other without the words of whatever had haunted us and details that had ruined us.

But then even eternity ended.

As it often did.

I was thankful that I had superhuman speed at many points in my life. When I really needed to get across town before Barneys closed and traffic was a nightmare, for example. And after succumbing to the bloodlust and sinking my fangs into Thorne, succumbing to everything I was fighting against and letting him sink into me.

Yeah, it was helpful after lying in the remains of a bed we'd broken amidst feathers from pillows we'd ripped apart at some point. Lying in his arms, a moment of gentle in the brutal episode that had been our hate-making. I wouldn't call it the other thing.

Not to myself.

I wouldn't utter that word, even in my head. Words uttered in your head posed much more danger than the ones said out loud. I was of that opinion, anyway.

He had been running his hands through my hair, softly untangling the knots he'd created, his other hand clutching me to the expanse of his scarred chest that I'd come to know so well. For in it resided the beating heart that held whatever was left of me after all the years of being the soulless monster I was.

"Isla," he murmured.

It was the softness of his voice and touch that worked. Better than brutality or pain or ugliness, because all that was part of the status quo. The phrase 'kill them with kindness' existed for a reason. Mainly because kindness was the only thing that could really kill someone who'd only known cruelty.

Cruelty could be learned to weather against. Fight against.

Not the kindness and tenderness and the gentle touch of after-sex with the person whose heart beat with the power of the demon inside you.

It shocked me into movement.

I didn't think he was expecting it. In fact, I was sure of it, considering the gentle pressure on my shoulders didn't do anything to make me pause as I darted from the bed. I was a blur, even to his eyes, snatching some clothes I'd left in his closet in days of ignorance and shoving them on quickly.

Not quick enough, because even with the speed of an

immortal, buttoning a shirt with fake nails on was still a total bitch.

Even when I was trying to do it while walking, not running—because I didn't run, just walked with a purpose—to my car in order to get the fuck out of Dodge.

His palms found my wrists, stalling my motions.

I paused because the only way to continue my task would have been to dislocate his fingers.

I wasn't ruling it out.

"I would advise you to take your hands off me. Now. If you like them attached to your wrists, that is," I gritted out.

His eyes leveled on mine, possibly gauging my seriousness. "I've just been inside you, Isla, after five days and thirteen hours without that. You think I care about a couple of broken bones compared to what I get while I'm touching you?"

I blinked once at the words and the meaning and, worse, the truth behind them.

There was no room for the truth here.

Not when the rest of my mind was taken up by his lies.

I yanked my hands from his, the crack of bone resounding through the room.

I had to give it to him—he didn't flinch.

That sharp jolt of pain that ricocheted through whatever connection his blood had strengthened once again was enough to make me sink my fangs into my bottom lip.

He didn't even move his gaze from mine, just dropped his injured wrist—I decided against two at the last minute—to dangle at his side.

"When are you going to forgive me, baby?"

I glared at him for his soft tone. Then I glanced at a mirror and gave my own emerald eyes a death stare before focusing on him.

"When am I going to forgive you?" I repeated.

He nodded once. "You have to. Sometime."

I smiled. "I will," I agreed, and something sparked behind his eyes. "How about when the sun rises in the west and sets in the east, when the seas go dry and mountains blow in the wind like leaves," I said softly.

He blinked once. Twice. The intensity never left his eyes, but it made room for confusion.

I let out a frustrated noise. "Just when I thought I couldn't get any angrier at you," I hissed. "It's a *Game of Thrones* reference, Thorne. The fact that you don't know it makes you very close to losing a limb. You're already halfway there with a broken wrist."

I stared at his arms, trying to figure out which one would be better. Then I was pissed at myself for being unable to decide because they both belonged attached to his body.

So I moved my glare up to his eyes. "The reference, since you are so ignorant to the brilliance of George RR Martin, means never. Never fucking ever."

He stepped forward. "Never say never, babe."

"No, never say tweed. I can say never."

"Isla," Thorne began, stepping forward, his intention clear even after the breaking of bones and the warning in the air.

I silenced him with my glare. Oh, and the knife I fastened against his jugular. I liked to think the glare was pretty scary too.

I tilted my head and smiled at him. "Shh. The grown-ups are talking now." I pointed my bloodred fingernail between my breasts, leaving a trail of blood in my wake. "The grown-up being me."

"Isla," he tried again, the cords in his neck pulsing, the movement causing little beads of blood to rise where the knife punctured the skin.

My fangs elongated ever so slightly but I used the power of a woman scorned—yeah, they weren't lying about that. Who needs Ichor when you've got a woman's rage?—to send them back into my gums and forget the allure of the blood.

I tutted. "I wouldn't if I were you. Speak, that is. I'll likely give you the closest shave you've ever had in your life. And then in your death." I gave him another smile.

"You're not gonna kill me," he ground out, bringing more blood forth.

I stepped forward, my smile gone, rage taking over. The blade pressed harder and his nostrils flared as the pain got his attention. "Really?" I said. "Good to see you're so sure of that. Because I'm not. At all. You know what the price of betrayal is in my world, Thorne? Blood. And, more often than not, pain. With the grand finale being death. Cliché, I know, but clichés exist for a reason. They're memorable. And they work."

He continued to stare at me, unblinking and unyielding and unsettling.

In a way that dared me to do it. To end it all. In a way that he knew there had already been an ending, of my afterlife as I knew it, that day at the precinct.

He knew the silence in his chest was something that, even now, I wouldn't weather. Wouldn't fathom. Wouldn't endure, even if I didn't need his blood.

I needed the thing that pumped it around his body too.

And I hated that.

Hated him for loving me.

Hated me for making me love him.

People always talked about love and its power to create shit. Like it could build fucking skyscrapers. It couldn't. Not one thing could be built with love except perhaps false expectations. And box office profits.

Love created nothing. It destroyed everything. Handed someone the world and offered them the opportunity to crush it. And even if they didn't crush it, the power would still be there, hovering over the head of the owner of that world. It was the power itself, not the act of one or the other, that determined the destructive power of it all.

"Isla," he murmured again, the slight loosening of the blade at his throat making it more possible for him to form words without bleeding out on the spot. "I'm sorry about Lewis," he continued. His voice was even, sincere. Simple. "I'll kill them all, every single one for what they did to him. What it did to you," he promised.

His words were sure. Genuine. I could feel it, the distaste for the fact that I had to know loss. His anger at it all.

It was strong, his anger.

I remembered the girl at the coffin. Her dry eyes and empty shell and broken spirit.

And then I found my anger. It was stronger than his.

Much stronger.

Because that empty shell, that dispirited thing standing at the edge of a patch of ground that would eat the corpse of the one she loved, that was me. When Thorne's heart stopped beating.

And even though he was supposed to live forever thanks to the gem of his lineage that found us here, with my knife to his throat—or, if we wanted to get technical, his knife to his throat—it would always stop.

I would have to face the silence eventually. Unless I died first.

But the whole deathless prophecy didn't bode well for that idea.

"He's a human. Humans die," I said, repeating the earlier sentiment I'd shared with Sophie. "It was inevitable. Everything with a heartbeat is counting down the hours or minutes or years—or, in your case, centuries—until its demise. It will eventually stop. The clock. The heart. The life."

He saw more than even the witch who may or may not have had powers of telepathy. "You don't have to do that shit around me," he growled.

I glanced down to the knife. "Oh I know, but it's fun and it stops you from getting all handsy," I replied, deliberately mis-interpreting his meaning.

He didn't know when to quit. Maybe he thought he was too legit.

"No, you don't have to try so hard to be the monster you've convinced yourself you need to be in order to deal with your humanity. In fact, you don't need to be that monster at all. Or you can. But it's your choice. And I'll lie with the monster you choose to be or banish the monster you choose to abandon, Isla."

His words, plucked from my mind that hadn't even figured out a way to articulate that very dilemma, struck me dumb.

But they didn't mute me, because it would likely take someone ripping out my tongue for that to happen.

The knife pressed in once more, the slight stiffening of Thorne's body the only inkling that he registered it. The rest of his attention was on me, my eyes, my soul.

I steeled myself against it. "You're trying to banish some monster inside me?" I asked, my voice ice. "That's your prob-lem right there. Well, among a lot of others. Monsters can't be banished without creating another one in their place with the knight on his furry steed. How do you think the Devil became the Prince of Darkness? He was just a prince once, trying to fight monsters. Maybe slay a dragon for a princess. But I've got news for you: I don't need to slay a dragon. I'll fucking ride them. And I'm not a princess—I'm a queen." I lowered the knife. "And I'm sure that fucking epic placement of another *Game of Thrones* reference is lost on you, but nonetheless the sentiment is received. So stay the fuck away from me until I need your blood."

"Not happening. Ever."

I glared at him. "Never say never, Thorne," I hissed.

And then, thanking my inhuman speed once more, I left.

And that time I did run. Because I had dragons to slay. Most of which were my own.

SEVENTEEN

I DRAGGED THE SWORD ALONG BEHIND ME, THE SCREECHING of the metal on the concrete pleasing to me.

The ugliness of it suited the theme of the night. Of my now broken and warped soul.

The hybrids were either getting weaker or I was getting awesomer because I barely even broke a nail over the group that were supposed to be some sort of freak show guard dogs.

It was rather disappointing, actually, my lack of injuries and the lack of any real fight on their end.

I was itching for it.

Killing humans was like shooting fish in a barrel. Fun, of course, but you could only do it for so long.

You needed to throw in a little bit of action every now and then.

It was becoming apparent that the hybrids' strength

depended on the bloodline with which they were created. Which was both worrying and comforting. There was a much smaller concentration of powerful bloodlines because that was how aristocracy worked—a select few at the top and large amounts at the bottom.

The pool was smaller to choose from.

That was the comforting part.

It was usually the ignorant masses who listened to a party line like the one these rebels were spouting.

But apart from this bunch, the hybrids we had been encountering had only been getting stronger. Which meant more prominent Vein Lines were joining the ranks.

Which may or may not have coincided with the ruling Rick made about me. So if you wanted to get technical, it could partially be my fault.

Though people who grasped onto one singular reason, like me being in love with a slayer even though we'd been enemies for thousands of years and escaping the punishment of death that kings had been doling out for thousands of years, were likely looking for a reason to rebel anyway.

Maybe.

Even if they were, it might be pretty cool to be the girl who started a war. Or at the very least made it a lot more interesting.

I'd gone straight from Thorne's to the location the demon gave me.

It was in the sewers, which didn't bode well for my shoes, but the monster inside me liked the environment. The stench of blood and death and the darkness beckoned like a familiar friend, whispering my sins like sweet nothings, urging me to commit more.

I whistled "Arsonist's Lullaby," leisurely strutting through the dank dungeon like a vapid human might stroll through a park in the sunshine.

Sunshine might not be fatal as a lot of those insipid humans liked to believe, but this was where we belonged. In the darkness. Shadows.

Because all the darkest of deeds happened in the shadows.

I smiled as I reached the arch that opened into the wide room, open and high-ceilinged, water dripping at the apex of the roof echoing through the chamber.

"Well, howdy. How nice of you to invite me around for tea," I said, walking into the room, hefting the sword up so the grating stopped and the low click of my heels was the only thing echoing through the room.

The tomb.

Apt, as he was a dead man sitting there, rotting in the dark underground. We were all dead things, vampires, but this was something else. It was death personified in a vampire that was ageless in youth and yet ancient beyond the years of counting at the same time.

His hair was white. Pure stark white. It brushed at his shoulders, jagged and uneven, like he'd taken a dagger to it himself. But the strands glowed in the dark, stench-filled dungeon.

His face was strong and angular, sharp cheekbones giving him too many points in his skin to call him handsome, but he was ethereally beautiful, if you didn't mind the way the lack of vitamin D had turned his skin so white there was an almost bluish tinge to it. And it seemed powdery, like that old paper in ancient texts that, if handled wrong, might crumble into dust.

Though he was reasonably expansive in the muscle department, they were lean and more suited to a swimmer's body. They were there, though, under the moth-eaten black suit he wore with no shirt because he obviously wanted to show off his pale and sculpted chest while making a fashion statement.

It was his eyes that got me. A milky film over them from staring at nothing but the past.

What else did you do in a tomb if it wasn't stare at the past and let it ravage you?

For the present could ruin you, surely. And the future promised that same ruin. But it was the past, the permanency and unchanging quality of it that would wound and perhaps destroy you if looked at too closely.

Jonathan was a fleeting thought in my mind before he disappeared.

I found me after getting lost with the jarring beauty and power of the old vampire.

The very old powerful vampire.

I glanced at the blood on my sword. "Sorry for the damage to the décor with the sharp thing. Oh, and the many, *many* vampires I had to kill on my way in." I shrugged. "I'll replace them, I promise."

I rested the sword on my shoulder, wincing at the thought of the blood staining my jacket, but the gesture itself was badass. I could always buy a new jacket.

I was really turning dark side, sacrificing fashion for my new persona. What next, fighting a werewolf without even worrying about my manicure?

I shuddered at the thought.

"You want some advice, for free?" I paused. "Well, not for free. It's actually for the price of the forty or so hybrids and the handful of vampire guards you had posted to protect you from attack." I lifted the sword. "Oh, and I got this off someone, I forget who. But I like it, so I'll be taking that too. Hence the lie of saying it comes for free. It comes for a price. Blood. But that's the price of everything these days, and I promise I'm giving you a great deal." I focused on the unnerving eyes that hadn't moved, or even blinked, since the moment I arrived.

He was still. Statuesque in a way that vaguely had me wondering whether this vampire was just mad and sequestered down here in order to live in madness alone.

Not that one was really ever alone in madness. The voices would always keep you company.

But no, despite the living corpse routine, it was apparent that he was very much alive. The very air seemed to shrink to his will as it pulsed around him.

It would be a mistake to think him mad.

Mad eyes were never focused, never still. Not like these. Concentration, unfortunately, required at least a little sanity. And he had it, that unequivocal look that told me all of his attention was on me.

And he was dangerous.

In a way that sent prickles of discomfort down my spine and gave birth to something called fear.

The real kind.

It was right about then that I wished I'd stopped being so stubborn and actually called for backup.

Then again, I'd probably just add more bodies to the tomb.

Not that even Duncan would be a match for... whatever this was. Sophie's powers could work, but her words of not using her magic on unnatural things rang through my mind. Although he was a vampire, obviously, and I considered myself natural—as did Sophie, if her ability to use her magic on us was anything to go by—there was something more to him than mere vampirism.

So Sophie was out.

My mind flickered to Thorne. Not because I thought he might have something more than my vampire hitman friend and the witch with the powers of something more than anything 'normal' would have. No, because I wanted him there with me as I stared death in the face.

And perhaps welcomed it.

I blinked away the feelings. And that gaping kind of aloneness that I felt inside the tomb with this thing.

"Advice," I said, snapping my fingers. "You need new minions. Better minions. I'd recommend some great ones I know, except I don't really know that many, and the one I do know only has one eye. Although I'd give him to you in a heartbeat, you know, if I had one."

I waltzed around the cavernous room that stank of damp mold and off blood, the sword screeching along behind me.

"Also, he fights for the wrong side. Or the right. I forget which we are." I shrugged. "I'm not necessarily about 'sides' myself, but it is in my best interest to go with the one that isn't trying to kill me. Although, I guess technically the one I'm fighting for has tried to kill me in the past, so I'll amend that to the ones that have tried to kill me the most and really meant it." I stopped my journey around the room, careful to keep the space between me and… whatever he was wide. The dude freaked me out with the empty yet lucid stare.

"Anyway, the point is to get new minions and not rely on these horrid hybrids. They're not reliable. And rather too easy to kill, if you ask me."

I stopped talking, mainly because there was only so long I could go on—yes, even me—without having anyone speak back.

I was perfectly fine in an empty room talking to myself and letting my demons converse with each other. But it was the silence that came after my words that had me needing to shut up.

For about a second.

"Dude, do you speak, or do tricks or something?" I asked, resting on the sword casually. Or giving the illusion of doing so casually. I was ready and poised for an attack.

Because I could taste that in the air too, the violence. Not like a premonition or anything, just a violence that radiated off people, vampires, werewolves, demons, and witches alike. There were just some who hid it better than others.

The man in front of me wasn't trying to hide shit. Maybe because there was no one to hide from in a chamber on your own.

Again, silence. "It creeps me out, coming to kill someone and not even exchanging names first," I continued. "It's fine if you're sleeping with someone to not catch their name—in fact, it's preferred—but I think taking someone to their eternal sleep at least requires a first-name basis. I feel rather uncouth otherwise."

The vampire moved. And it was in such a way like those old dinosaur lizards moved, slowly and purposefully and super creepily. He moved so he could rest his elbows on his knees and lean forward slightly.

"You come into my resting place deigning to kill me?" he asked, his voice grating and almost painful to hear, the substance wrong somehow. Devoid of it all. Every single drop of whatever it meant to be human was drained from him.

I wondered if it was something I could hire someone to do for me.

"Your resting place?" I repeated, once again looking around the room that wasn't a room. It was a cave, in the bowels of an old decrepit apartment building in Manhattan that had stood empty for years despite its grandeur.

I knew why it was empty now. This man owned it all.

If not with money, then with the evil and wretched energy

of the room, turning it into something different than what it was.

"No, it's not very restful in here, if you ask me. Which of course you didn't, but I'm here, so I'll offer you an opinion anyway. You can't rest in a place that doesn't have a bed with Egyptian cotton sheets. Just not okay. And you don't even have a mini fridge or a TV."

The bones scattered around the place—human in nature, of course—were the only décor. "I know you're snacking on humans to survive, but you've got to *thrive*. And it's with the help of beers or wine that you'd do that."

"Are you quite done?" His voice echoed through the chamber, the simple words dragging out beyond anything I'd ever experienced.

"Done?" I repeated. "Oh, I'm never done."

His eyes followed my movements with the sword, as if he was expecting me to use it then and there.

"You are like her in many ways," he said finally, after yet another staring match.

"Like who?" I demanded. "I like to think I'm original, and if you're going to compare me to Amy Adams for like the three hundredth time, I'm not like her. She's like *me*."

"Her. Selene." The cold emptiness of his voice communicated no feeling, nothing. Perhaps the ghost of something or someone.

The name ricocheted through my mind and I realized something. Something that could not be true. That no way in anything would be true.

His eyes continued to rove over me, the milky film seeming to fall away as he looked the past and the present in the eye at the same time. "Yes, you are very much like her. Yet you come here to kill me. Interesting. Woman, a human one at that, she already did your job for you, a few thousand years ago."

He scrutinized me in such a way that I realized he wasn't seeing me, but the ghost a dead thing.

Beyond the dead thing that was already in front of him.

The power of such a stare did things to me. And not good things like Thorne's stare. No, the evilest of things. Things that made my skin crawl like insects were writhing underneath it.

"Okay, I'm really hoping you're actually batshit or at the very least talking about the singer that JLo played in a movie and you're just confused about the 'thousand year' part," I said, tightening my grip on the sword.

He didn't move. "You know who I am, child. Your blood responds to the call of its origin, after all. It's origin of death. And death has created spawn of depravity and evil and the wretchedness of this world that began with the wretchedness of love."

His words were flat and even and lifeless. Yet the bitterness of it all turned the air into something toxic that curled into those little crevices of doubt that I'd been fostering.

He clasped his hands together. "You know this. The end of things that come with this emotion. This *human* emotion. For it was humanity that birthed us, and it will be humanity that will end us."

I tilted my head. "If you are who you say you are—*big* if, by the way—I would argue that, according to the books and history, you're kind of wrong. The emotion was actually the beginning of something. Of our entire race, in fact."

He regarded me, and it was something akin to being stabbed with the enchanted blade in my belt. Or worse. An ancient thing was staring at me with eyes that had seen centuries pass like seconds and had seen destruction, Caused it. Birthed it, if you believed that.

And I did.

I believed that was what I was staring at.

No one could fake that. You could fake your tan, eyelashes, hair, and even orgasms, but you couldn't fake something like that. Never.

In the darkness is where I meet my creator. For it is in darkness that I was created.

I felt some kind of strong reaction once my body fully recognized I was standing in front of the creature responsible for my existence.

For Thorne's.

Then I had the gross kind of feeling that it made Thorne and me kind of like brother and sister if this was our technical daddy sitting in front of us. And that grossed me out.

"The beginning of the race of vampires, and then the Praseates, the binary opposition created out of the blood of my brother," he said. "Yes, this was the beginning. But every beginning is an end. Don't you know that more than most?" he asked as though he'd been some sort of spectator to the death I'd been living.

"No, I don't know that. All I know is that for some reason I found myself here chasing a lead. Chasing vengeance. And color me surprised that my trail of body parts brought me to the creator of all vampires. Or at least the first vampire himself. Sequestered in this dank cave among the rats and the shadows and filth beneath Manhattan. You'd think you'd be somewhere a little more... opulent."

His eyes flickered to his surroundings, as if he was only seeing them for the first time. "And where is it that I belong? Amongst the humans who I once was? The vampires my death created? That *her* death created? I think the shadows are the only place for a creature such as me. The sunlight was lost to me the moment I was cursed, despite it being given back to me, for what is walking in the sunlight if you've only your own shadow for company?"

I swallowed. "Peaceful?" I offered.

He laughed. The sound was ugly and harsh in his chest, like the muscles of his throat had forgotten how to do such a thing. "You do not believe in such a thing, child. There is no peace, even in death. If it does exist, it's in war. For the most blessed of peace is to be found amongst chaos and death. And chaos and death are the main characteristics of war."

I cocked my brow. "And that's why you're involved in this one? In the pursuit of peace?"

It took a long time for his answer to come. Or long for me. For him, maybe time moved differently. It must have been a fluid concept, down there in the shadows, where centuries passed like moments.

His eyes found mine and I struggled against everything inside me to keep his gaze.

"At the dawn of time, the humans were created to be the monsters they are. Natural monsters, capable of all depravity as vampires, in mind yet not in body. Just because they do not have fangs does not mean they cannot make people bleed, no?"

He sighed, trailing a long nail along the rock of his throne.

"We were created out of the depravity of that humankind yet given the fangs and the strength to do the things humans would not find the technology to do until later times. Until this world we live in now. We were born in the crack between light and dark, between life and death, between eternity and the end of all things. It is now that I wish for another end to this wretched life that has stretched on without change, without the darkness or even the true night. She is the moon, yet my night is never black enough for the moon to shine its light. So I feel the darkness in my soul, which is already in the underworld, damning me to be invisible to her for all time. And now we have another love which the world of these depraved humans relies on."

He stared at me, the moments moving like seconds, or years or minutes. I couldn't be sure; I was lost in this new version of time and space that had been created.

"Divine flesh, when severed, becomes immortal," he proclaimed, the words bouncing off the damp walls. "And divine not by the gods was cut. No, for the most divine of all flesh is a human heart, cursed with the most depraved of all emotions—love. It is that, the severing of my own flesh by the severing of her life, which turned me truly immortal."

He regarded me.

"Do you wish to submit, to sentence yourself to the darkness of that chasm? For the humans who deserve nothing less? For the fate of monsters is due to the monsters themselves. The reign of the night is needed for the preservation of death."

I stared at him. And continued to stare.

"You done?" I asked finally.

"Done?" he repeated.

I nodded. "Wrapped up the quick 'philosophy of vampires' seminar that you've decided to treat little old me to?" I took his silence as an affirmative. "Good, because I like where you went with that. All good stuff. Really valuable insights to both the human and inhuman condition," I praised, circling the room before I stopped, turning. "But you see, it's the attitude that you seem to have adopted that is startlingly like the very god who created or cursed you in the first place that I can't get right with. You watched empires rise and fall. The dawn of ages of the earth that were stained in blood. The horrors of humanity.

"Then, by logical conclusion—and it's a first for me,

coming to such a thing," I informed him with a smile, "you've also seen the triumphs of humankind. They're idiotic, for sure, with nothing much to offer about life that vampires couldn't observe. But then vampires only get to observe. Because in death we do not get to live as humans do. Or love as humans do, because we love as angels do and sin as devils do." I paused. "No, wait. Maybe we love as devils do and sin as angels do. That sounds more correct. One of them I heard somewhere and one of them I made up myself, but either way, it's the truth. The latter, anyway, because the sins of saints are so much more depraved than those of sinners."

I gave him a look.

"I don't really know where I was going with that," I admitted. "But I am curious as to why you haven't killed me if you're so intent on being involved in this war, for whatever reason. Don't get me wrong, I'm glad, but still curious. And also not stupid enough to think that I'm getting out of this undead," I added.

The stench of death inside the tomb was catching.

"You seek the witches?" he surmised instead of answering. I wondered whether his mind worked the same way mine did. To be that ancient, to have created an entire race through love and death, your mind must be unhinged in a pivotal way. After all, being mentally unhinged was the only way to survive with a broken heart.

"I do," I replied. "Among other things, like the end of this war. For selfish reasons, like a good day's sleep and a manicure that lasts more than one day." I frowned down at my nails. "If I wasn't involved, the war could rage around me for centuries and I wouldn't care much as long as it didn't affect my day."

He tilted his head. "So much effort put into the act of becoming the soulless creature Hades turned me into," he observed. "It is the very nature of our kind that the years do not touch us. Though it is not in our nature that we become those soulless creatures, but in our need to survive on the death of others. It is the very truth of immortality that urges a disconnection from the human part of ourselves in order to remain.

"So what has you part of this war, then? I imagine there's been more than a few of them that have passed you by, yet you decide to throw your lot in with the one that just happens to be the end of whatever you created."

"I didn't create it," he hissed, his voice losing that flat and disconnected quality and turning into something else. "That emotion ruined everything that created it. It was *her*," he spat. "She was my destruction. Lilith may have birthed you all, but Selene is the mother of all vampires. And now you are she."

I stared at him. "I'm not anyone but myself. Nor is my future anyone's but mine."

He sat atop his fashioned throne with his eyes on me.

Mine were on him.

I stared into the abyss and the abyss stared back at me.

"You are anyone's but yours. You are his. And the future is written. As it will be." He sighed, rising from the throne in an effortless gesture that was fluid and easy but somehow etched with all the effort in the world.

I held the sword and had been prepared for attack, but my body was not my own. I had no control over anything as he moved to me in a blur of motion, quick even to my eyes.

Up close he was even more terrifyingly beautiful. His eyes were not merely eyes; they were chasms, the irises almost completely white yet enshrouded with so much darkness it was a wonder the blackness didn't swallow me up.

His unlined skin was smooth, like marble, while somehow keeping that paperlike quality.

He stared at me in a way that told me it would be less than a flex of a muscle for him to end the existence he was responsible for creating.

Never would one feel so small as when presented with their creator.

Or so big when those eyes were focused on you.

"The child of the night wishes to walk in the light, fight in a war that is both hers alone and the world's at the same time." His voice was thick and heavy. "So be it. You will see where they are. Your fate will be death, in victory and in defeat."

And then the abyss didn't just stare at me. It swallowed me whole.

EIGHTEEN

"H ELLO. YES, ONLY ME," I CALLED INTO THE PHONE as I ascended the stairs onto the jet I'd just chartered. "Just checking in before I head out."

"Isla? Where the fuck are you?" Sophie hissed. "You've been missing for *three days*."

I screwed up my nose. I didn't realize that much time had passed underground. That was rather vexing. But whatever.

It had felt like seconds, and then I'd found myself up top in the smog-filled and dirty street without much memory of how I came to be there.

I had felt death encircling me, its touch still failing to release me. But I'd also known where I had to go next. I had the location drawn in my head, so I focused on that and not the fact that I had just met the origin for all life, and death.

If I focused on that too much, then I might just descend

fully into the ocean of crazy I was treading water in.

And I had shit to do.

"Around," I said vaguely, winking at the male flight attendant who was more than a little yummy.

"Is that Isla? Give me the fucking phone," a raspy voice demanded. Or more like roared. There was a slight struggle and swearing from both Sophie and Thorne.

I was interested to see who would win and whether Sophie would do something fun like give him a pig's tail or something.

"Isla, are you okay?" Thorne's raspy voice filled the phone and my skin tingled at the sound of it. I welcomed it at the same time I yearned for him in the flesh to chase away that death I'd come so close to. That I'd welcomed inside me.

I smiled at the human who handed me a glass of champagne. "A man who knows a way to my heart," I told him, taking the glass. "You and I are going to get along great."

"Isla," Thorne hissed. "Who the fuck are you talking to? And answer the goddamn question. Are you okay? And where are you?"

I sipped the drink. "That's actually three questions, so I'll just pick my favorite one. Which will most likely be your least favorite one. Isn't it great when things work out that way? I was talking to…." I looked up. "What's your name?" I asked the young human.

"Brent, ma'am," he replied.

I screwed up my nose. "First, don't call me ma'am. It makes me feel horribly old, and I'm not even at half a millennium yet, I'm still youthful and fun. Secondly, Brent? Dude, that's *not* a good name."

The young human's face contorted in puzzlement before he gave a mischievous grin. "Well then, Isla, what would you like my name to be?"

I was thinking of options, but the man on the other side of the phone obviously didn't appreciate it.

"Isla," he snapped.

I rolled my eyes.

"Rain check, Derek," I said with a wink.

"You disappear for three days and now you're talking to some man—"

"I can talk to whatever man I want," I cut in.

"Sure. As long as you don't mind me killing him," Thorne bit back.

I grinned. "You wouldn't. He's human. And I know how much killing humans goes against your nature."

"What goes against my nature is you disappearing to do God knows what and then sounding like you're getting on a fucking plane. It feels most natural to be killing the man who sounds a fuck of a lot like he's flirting with you. Human or not."

I rolled my eyes. "Whatever."

"You tell me where you are this fucking instant."

"Sorry, Dad, they don't allow phones in operation during takeoff. The plane might blow up or something, and that would just fuck up my day. It was all going so well. I'm going witch hunting. Hopefully that means on the way back I'll snack on Brent without the vomiting blood thing and I'll never have to rely on you for survival again. Toodles."

I hung up before he could spout more profanities that were most likely filled with "fuck," growling, "Isla," "mine," "I alpha," "protect," "control," etc.

I settled back into my plush leather seat and sipped my wine as the plane hurtled into the air towards the other side of the world that apparently housed a thousand-year-old witch who was in control of my life.

And death.

Or maybe I was escaping from the human-slayer-vampire thing that was in control of my life.

And maybe that's what the result would be. My death.

I frowned around the cave in distaste. It was dimly lit with a flickering torch hanging suspended midair. Obviously enchanted, but you'd think they'd use their magic for a little more than a fire. I mean, even the cavemen managed that. For witches who were meant to be big and bad and scary, you think they'd be able to jazz up a cave that stank and where filth scattered the floor, both animal and human. The stench of it was beyond pure human excrement, something danker and darker and just all around bad.

It was the unnatural kind of scent of enduring life when death was waiting. Had been waiting for too long. It was similar to the cave I'd just left in New York, though the smell was more rancid in here.

There wasn't a question of the soulless creature I'd encountered in the sewers. It was more of a benevolent evil. This was another beast entirely.

I circled the woman in the dim light, thankful at least I didn't get to see her properly, even with my eyesight.

"Seriously?" I asked, glancing around the cave. "You couldn't put up a painting, maybe a rug, some throw pillows. A scented candle, or twelve?" I asked.

I tilted my head at the witch who was standing in the middle of the room, just staring, not even really registering me waltzing into her abode without so much as a knock. It was unnerving, that empty stare that was full of pure malice and pure evil.

I'd landed in Albania a few hours before, and after procuring myself a vehicle—okay, stealing, but rentals were such a bitch to organize—I'd driven to the place up in the winding and unyielding landscape that seemed like civilization and time itself had forgotten.

I hadn't needed a map.

No, the imprint Ambrogio had left on my mind gave me the directions, so I hadn't even hesitated pulling off the road and onto a dirt track that led up to a cave overlooking the tumultuous ocean.

The sky had gone from clear to gray and stormy between my journey from the car to the cave itself.

Like nature had known what was coming and what was in store for me, so it decided to set the best backdrop for it.

I wasn't exactly scared for the meeting.

I didn't get scared.

I was rather excited. She wasn't even meant to be the most powerful of them all, and I got to do this by myself. I was so sick of having to drag the Scooby Gang around with me, especially the one with the thundering heartbeat.

The one thing that had dampened my mood was the fact that the muddied trail in the cave had ruined my boots.

Yes, I most likely should not have worn the brand-new thigh-high Choos with laces all the way up to the top of my thigh, but I had wanted to look all badass warrior princess and give off a 'save the world' vibe.

You couldn't save the world in flats.

That was just crazy talk.

I had given a curious glance to the whimpering and dirty human in the corner, her wide eyes focusing on me as her heartbeat pumped like a hummingbird, the scent of death lingering around her from the injuries she'd sustained.

Her black hair tumbled down her back, matted with blood and grime, meaning she'd been staying at casa shithole for a while. The ripped and filthy bloodstained nightgown she was wearing told me she would not be giving them a good review on Trip Advisor.

If she survived, that was.

Which was doubtful.

I moved my eyes back to the witch in the middle of the room, still doing that still and standing thing that was rather fucking unnerving.

The human was going to die.

They did that.

No point in bothering myself with that can of worms.

My eyebrow raised as I scanned her still form, not betraying the unease at the depth of her stare, not unlike the one I'd been subjected to by the origin of all vampires.

And the stench of the magic in the cave was almost enough to choke on.

Luckily I didn't have to breathe.

"So you're one of the ones who have been causing all this trouble for me." I drew my gaze up, then down. "Do many people tell you you're shorter in person? Oh no, wait, my bad. You probably haven't been seeing many people considering the whole 'locked up for eternity' thing. Is that a touchy subject, me bringing it up?" I asked apologetically.

I idly wondered how the human got there if she had indeed been trapped like the general state of the place betrayed.

But then I had other things to worry about at that present. And since the other two sisters had been set free, maybe they could bring her things. I'd have asked for a better wardrobe selection and an iPad.

I expected the wall of magic that hit me with the pain of

a thousand knives. Was hoping for it, actually, but that didn't make experiencing it any more fun. It was a lot less fun, if I was honest.

I had planned on staying upright but must have underestimated the amount of pain this bitch could unleash. Either I didn't remember her sister's wrath properly or this one was a hell of a lot more powerful.

I had a feeling it was the latter, which didn't make me super happy.

She did have the fashion sense of her sister, which didn't make me super happy either.

"Could just one villain dress like Cersei in *Game of Thrones*, for the love of God. One?" I asked through the pain as the beautiful yet terribly dressed woman approached.

She must have been told that it was all about the long black dresses, covered in lace and far too Morticia Addams for my liking. Only one person could rock that look.

Morticia Addams.

A lance of pain echoed through the bones in my face as her long, clawed hand fastened on my chin, the nails puncturing the skin and drawing blood.

"You disgusting excuse for a creature," she hissed. "You dare come into our home with your arrogance and your stupidity? You will pay for that with your death, and that will give us our freedom." Her eyes blackened. "And I will get vengeance for the sister of mine that you took from this world. It is all the more pity that she cannot exact it herself when we snatch her back from the grave. For we have done so before and so we shall do it again."

It was then it flickered, whatever glamour she was projecting to make her skin iridescent and flawless and her golden hair trail down her back in shiny curls.

In its place were gray, scraggly knots, crawling with things that looked alive. Her skin was marked with sores and wrinkles, drooping with age and evil and most likely whatever curse put them there in the first place.

I made a mental note to look up the person who did that and send them a fruit basket or something.

Her words registered through the pain and the image of her hideous face. "You know, I could recommend a great night cream for those wrinkles. Botox works too," I said through gritted teeth. "Though, I would have thought if you were going to go full ham and break all the laws of nature, dealing in the death magic that got you locked up here in the first place, you'd at least make sure it was worth your while, you know, for the complexion. Seems a waste otherwise."

More pain.

A lot of it.

"He said you'd be like this," she whispered. "Warned us that the prophesized one was not great like the original ones of our kind. Like Malena. Though he expects a *queen* out of you."

She pushed me back with a flick of her wrist and a fresh wave of unnatural power. She circled me, the skirts of her dress trailing along the dirty ground.

"He said a queen like you is what he wants. But he doesn't know prophecy. Of course, he knows what we need him to know. What he needs to know in order to bring you here to us. To give us what *we* need."

I idly wondered about the man she was speaking of. Rick came to mind, what with his continued insistences that I become his queen. Though it didn't make a lot of sense that he'd go to all of this trouble to fight a rebellion if he was behind it.

Then again, stranger things had happened.

And it was a lot more logical than whoever the faceless

leader of this coup d'état was being the second man who wanted me to be his queen.

I mean, I was queen material in that I'd rock the shit out of a crown and would look good on a throne, but that was about it.

Plus, the only way I'd look good on a throne was if it was mine and mine alone.

I was like Joey from *Friends*. I didn't share food. Or thrones.

Not that I even wanted a throne. They seemed far more trouble than they were worth.

You could still wear a crown as an accessory instead of a responsibility. And it looked so much better.

A fresh wave of pain as my spine lifted and snapped brutally at the unnatural angle.

I didn't make a sound.

The snapping of my spine was nothing, really. No big.

It was the dirty and cold magic flowing through my veins and chasing out whatever residual warmth Thorne's blood had given me that was uncomfortable to say the least.

Dying was uncomfortable.

I'd been doing it far too often for my liking. And these witch bitches were too responsible for it for my liking as well.

"But he has this hope that I can break you." She paused. "Which I can. It's laughable how easy such a feat is. And then when I break you, I could chip off whatever humanity you have inside you that attached to your core like coral on a reef. The process would be painful for you, to say the least.

"I'll give you an example, just so you can see the mercy I'll grant you with a death slightly less painful. Though not completely, considering the revenge needed for the loss of my sister." Her mask slipped once more as her fury overtook her need for glamour.

Then I didn't see anything because she started.

Maybe I did cry out that time.

Or maybe it was something inside my soul that screamed that shrill and haunting scream that echoes through the edges of the cave and polluted the air,

It was familiar, that scream.

Until I realized where it came from. The years became nothing but moments as her scream came into stark reality and my soul recognized it in a way I hadn't before. It was the same as the human woman's my brothers had murdered. Not before they took away everything she had inside her with their depraved acts.

I used to think that such a thing wasn't possible for vampires. Maybe because I believed we had no soul to be ripped out from us, or mostly because, despite my penchant for sympathizing with them, I did believe we were better than them.

Not in all ways.

Not even in a lot.

And our betterness characterized by our lack of souls making us less vulnerable was arguable at best.

Yes, I had thought that her soulless scream was not likely something an immortal could reproduce because of the sheer strength it would take for a creature to find that in an immortal. And I didn't think such creatures existed.

But the witch's clawed hand reached into my deepest core with ease and began the process of ripping off whatever had grown there, whatever had been put there by Thorne.

It was the most excruciating feeling of my life.

Then it stopped and I sagged onto the floor in an unceremonious heap of blessed relief.

She waited with a smugness I could taste in the air, along with the rancid stench of death, for me to yank myself up with every inch of will I had.

But I did it.

She let me too. In a way that bullies let people get up purely so they could knock them down again. With that sick sort of sadism that didn't have a greater purpose.

I always thought torturing something or someone in itself wasn't the mark of a truly rotten soul, not if it was for a reason.

Information, revenge, foreplay.

A prevailing goal for inflicting the pain.

No, the mark of that rotten soul was when the torture was for nothing more than sport. Like that child with the ant and the magnifying glass. Doing it because the process of hurting someone rather than the result that came from it was what excited them.

And I could see the light in her eyes from the brokenness she was creating.

"You see," she said, grinning and circling me. "I can do it. Take it away from you. Take it all away in pain and suffering until there is nothing left but the cold shell. The perfect cold shell in which he planned to make a queen."

I could sense the truth to her words. The part of me she'd been working on, chipping away from, felt empty, cold. In a way that was reminiscent of the murderous vampire I'd been after Jonathan. When human life, death and happiness, and unhappiness, meant nothing. But it was deeper than that too. It was the same kind of coldness that might have me turning into the child with the magnifying glass. And questioning if I'd been that child all along without realizing it.

"It's not that I can't do it," she continued. I idly wondered where the rest of the crew was and if they had tried to find me, then idly wondered if I cared.

"It's that I will need your blood—mixed with *his* blood,

of course—to get me out of here. But it's through you that his blood must be spilled. It must be the one who was fated to drain the mate, just like in the beginning, that will bring about the end."

Her smiling eyes had everything clicking.

I knew what she was talking about, the legend of the origin story coming to mind.

So he drained the blood from his one true love, sending her to the heavens to become somewhat of a goddess in eternal life.

Not quite living, not quite dead.

Deathless.

I glared at her. "You need a brain check more than you need a cut, style and color if you think that's gonna happen, bitch," I hissed. The prospect of having the emptiness inside of Thorne's chest be permanent and because of me filled me with enough dread to push past whatever residual pain remained from her dark magic.

Whether she had been expecting the strike or not, I didn't know. She was taunting me surely, but she also thought herself to be the best evil witch since sliced Medusa, so the pride that cometh before the fall was that much sweeter.

My punch hit her squarely in the chest with a crunch of bone not as loud as I would've liked but still satisfying, sending her across the cave to hit the wall.

The human, who I'd all but forgotten in the whole torture process, let out a little whimper and scuttled back against the wall.

I glanced at her. "Chill, girl, I got this."

I grinned at the thump of her body against the unyielding stone and the release of the fist of magic that had remained.

My punch had cut through that too, but it was powered by the strong desire to have Thorne's vibrating heart a constant state around me, even when it wasn't physically around me. It took her magic for me to realize I could still hear it. Whatever connection we had through blood, the distance of it didn't matter; I knew he was still walking around, possibly stomping around and swearing at that point, but still alive, his heart still beating.

And that's what gave me strength, in addition to the fact that I was already strong.

I may have tricked myself into thinking I hated him, but I hadn't realized that real love—the ugly, brutal and forever kind—well, it was hate too.

I walked over to her, confidently despite the huge effort it took to make the steps. She'd weakened me beyond my comprehension, and the fire at the back of my throat crying out for blood was sudden and intense.

But I ignored it.

"You see, it's okay for me to threaten Thorne with death and dismemberment because he really pissed me off, and he deserves a little bit of that and maybe some roughhousing. From *me*." I bent down and encircled her neck to lift her by it. The wave of discomfort that came with the contact of her icy skin almost had me dropping her on instinct. But I endured, even though my entire body rebelled at having such an unnatural and rotten creature in my hands.

That was saying a lot since I'd handled a lot of unnatural and rotten creatures in my time, myself included.

But this was beyond anything. I could taste the blackness of her soul, like tar, the deeds she'd committed to get the control over the underworld as she had, more than even a vampire could comprehend. Evil, depraved acts that marked her soul forever.

Deals with the Devil were common. A lot more common

than people thought. And the deals were usually dependent on the soul that was offered. Hades liked a nice juicy black soul like I enjoyed a full-bodied red and a tenderloin. But it was the purest of souls that were most valuable to him.

This blackened, mangled, and hideous thing wouldn't have even been accepted by the Lord of the Underworld himself.

Which was precisely how she remained as she was for as long as she had. She'd made her own deal, turned herself into the devil in order to escape the clutches of the one who should have welcomed her into his fiery embrace centuries before.

I steeled myself, clutching onto my fury and determination. "See, you don't threaten a girl's man. I'm thinking a few hundred years in a cave will make you forget the etiquette of such things, so I'll remind you. I would love to do it in a drawn-out manner that would fit the lifetimes worth of crimes you've committed, including to fashion and general taste levels everywhere. But I've got things to do, more witches to kill, and touching you is making me really, really need to be doused with industrial cleaner, or at least take a bath in Chanel No 5," I told her, squeezing harder and preparing to rip her head off.

"I wouldn't even like to imagine where someone like you goes after this. But please say hey to the reaper for me," I requested happily.

Then I ripped her head off.

I stumbled back only slightly with the force leaving her touch gave me. Then I regarded the headless corpse. It had taken a lot to lead up to this, and everyone had turned it into such a big thing, built it up. It felt somewhat anticlimactic. Like Christmas. All the fanfare and preparation and it was over in the blink of an eye.

Or the ripping of a head.

"Ding, dong, the witch is dead," I chanted in the empty cave.

Then the cave wasn't empty, the vibrating and familiarity of a comforting heartbeat echoing through the walls and my body.

"Isla!" Thorne's rough voice demanded as arms clutched me to spin me around.

His eyes, saturated with worry, ran over me. Once, twice, then settled at my eyes. They didn't hold the relief I thought they would considering he hadn't encountered any bleeding wounds or limbless stumps.

All in all, a win.

"That was much easier than I thought," I told him, ignoring the sense of foreboding that the fear and concern in his eyes gave me. Plus the fact that he shouldn't actually be there, since I was aware of how he'd know this location and be able to get there in such a short amount of time "They made it sound so damn hard at the start. Like these were some super big deals, Chuck Norris of the witch world. I'm not going to say I'm disappointed, but I'll just say it's anticlimactic," I told him, watching as Rick, Duncan, Scott, and Sophie came in.

The gang's all here, then.

I made a mental note to ask them how they got there, and how they did it so quickly.

"There's fashionably late to the party and then just missing the party," I informed them. "You guys kind of suck with the riding in to save the day thing, which is fine because I can save myself."

I moved my eyes to the human who may or may not have been going into cardiac arrest at the corner of the cave. "Oh, and I can save a human too. But I don't know, she might already be dead. Whatever." I shrugged.

Rick's eyes fastened on the heap in the corner at the same time Sophie strode over to her, kneeling and muttering some such curse or spell that sent the scent of sweet magic cutting through the dank bitterness of the cave.

Something moved in his eyes, something that added to the scents in the cave. Something I was more than a little familiar with.

I gave Thorne a look. "Oooh, looks like your big bro has found a little human to gaze at. Isn't that sweet? Maybe you can be the best man at his wedding?"

He didn't even glance in that direction, his eyes fastened on mine. "Isla," he demanded urgently.

"You have this thing of saying my name in that gruff tone like it actually means something more than the title of the most beautiful vampire on the planet. No matter how much you say it, it's not going to change the fact that this beautiful vampire is pissed the hell off at you and—"

And then nothing. Because without warning, midsentence, and midrant at Thorne, I was gone.

Like *gone*.

Anticlimactic indeed.

NINETEEN

I WIPED MY MOUTH WITH THE SLEEVE OF MY CASHMERE sweater, leaning back from Thorne's neck as I did so. I tried to lean out of his embrace entirely, but that didn't exactly work out.

I scowled at him and tried to shake off the sheer weight of the emotions that were either his or mine—I couldn't tell anymore. "I need to stop waking up to my ex-boyfriend's throat," I said, looking around the cabin of the small jet, which had been comfortably roomy on the ride over but now, with three vampires—well, two and a half—a witch, a human slayer, a half-dead human from the cave and a fully dead human formerly known as Brent, it was a tight squeeze.

Thorne's arms flexed around me as I once again tried to move from them. My body was still disturbingly weak from the little tangle I'd had with Morticia, so it wasn't in the position to put up much of a fight.

Which, of course, pissed me right off.

"Stay still, Isla," Thorne commanded. "And I'm not your ex anything."

"I beg to differ," I hissed. "And I don't do well with still. I know some vampires prefer it, but my general disposition, ADHD and the flying monkeys up here"—I tapped my head—"totally make the concept impossible."

He didn't move, but I did manage to take myself from the reclining position on the sofa in the small plane, to sitting upright, tucked into Thorne's side.

I hated the warmth of his body and the fact that my chill seemed to fit into the places where he burned just hot enough not to make me melt.

I hated how it felt like home.

Because monsters didn't have homes. Even the darkness was a temporary respite because of that damn sun that kept on rising.

"How is it that you all rode in here so quickly after I called you? And knew where to go?" I asked, deciding to forgo my struggle until I was strong enough to break some bones again. Thorne's wrist had healed annoyingly quickly.

"Quickly?" Duncan answered for me. "Lass, you were AWOL for nigh on three days after Thorne broke Sophie's phone and half the furniture in her office," he said, his face blank.

Sophie's was not. "I'm still considering a curse for punishment," she hissed at him.

"I vote for pig's tail," I suggested. "Oooh, or Pinocchio nose, on account of all the lies," I added.

Thorne stiffened and his emotions rolled through me, thanks to our strengthened connection.

I ignored it.

"And we knew where you were since I know which jet company you use, and then my spell worked at tracking you instead of the witch in question," Sophie explained. "We knew you were still undead, despite the radio silence, thanks to him." She nodded to the man holding me.

I gaped at him. "How did you know?"

His gaze was level on mine. "'Cause my heart was still beating," he said simply.

I frowned. "Don't give me that lovers bullshit," I ordered, hating the warmth it had given me. "Truth."

He yanked me to him. "That is the truth. Ever since that day where you were dancing with Hades, my heart doesn't beat for just me. It pumps blood for me and for you. Can't explain it any better." His eyes narrowed. "But you can explain how the fuck you keep going missing and turning up almost dead."

I scowled at him. "A 'thank you, Isla, for getting rid of two-thirds of our witch problem' would suffice," I snapped.

I puzzled on the lost days. Time must have moved differently like it had in the dank tomb with the first vampire.

"Oh, that reminds me," I said, glaring at Thorne. "I met Ambrogio a few days ago. Swell guy. Talked a little too much for my liking, though. And his security system was seriously lacking. I think he's batshit crazy, but then that's why I kind of liked him and didn't kill him, even though I'm almost certain he's not on our side in this whole thing. That and he's the father of our race." I looked to Thorne. "And yours, if we think about it hard enough, which I did. Then it really began to creep me out, and not in a good way, so I stopped." I returned my attention to the group. "Anyhoo.... I don't remember where I was going with this. I guess that's all you needed to be caught up on. Met the dude, was in some weird kind of stasis situation since I didn't come up from his tomb for three days, and then jumped on a plane, killed a witch, picked up a stray human and then promptly passed out. But I think I deserved a small cat-nap considering I feel like I'm the one who's done all the work lately while you slackers seem to come in at the last minute and try to take credit for all my glory."

The silence that had crept into my small pause blanketed the roar of the engine and the heartbeat of the man beside me.

I wiped my lip. "What? Do I have blood on my face or something?"

Rick was the first to gain his thoughts. "You met Ambrogio, the one legend says is the first vampire?" he clarified, voice even, the first time he'd spoken since we'd gotten on the plane. Most of his energy was spent on staring at the human.

I nodded. "The very one."

"And he is the one who informed you of the witch's where-abouts?" he continued.

Another nod. "Affirmative. Among other things."

Thorne, who had been stone beside me, flexed his body so it squeezed my own. "Other things?" he repeated. "What the fuck else kind of other things?"

I gave him a sideways glance. "Just things," I hedged, not too keen on giving him, or anyone, the specifics. "The best san-gria recipes, why he doesn't consider himself much of a people or vampire person. Some anti-aging tips," I snapped.

My eyes returned to the group at large.

"Now that I've let you know how I got to where I was going, I think it's time to swap your own. You didn't run into Lilith or anything, did you? Because that would be freaky-deaky. Plus, I hear she's downstairs with the big guy, so I'm guessing no one took a trip to visit Daddy Hades?" I searched the small little group that had unintentionally become my posse.

The Scottish rogue vampire hitman who was a loose cannon, as loyal as a hitman and a vampire could be; a witch with some serious personality disorders; a half breed, with now only half of his eyesight and a soft heart that somehow hadn't been hardened by the world; and then the king of all vampires who just happened to be my ex-slayer boyfriend/prophesized mate's long-lost brother.

Yeah, not a complicated powder keg ready to blow at any minute or anything.

Then I focused on the human.

Someone must have found her some clothes and a hairbrush and bar of soap while I was sleeping because she looked a little less like she'd lived in a cave than she did while she… actually lived in a cave.

Her inky black hair was tumbling around her face, still slightly damp from the shower she'd obviously had. She used it like a curtain to hide the small and pale features of her face. It was scratched up, and one of her eyes was purplish and swollen, contrasting her almost transparent skin. She was swamped in an oversized tee shirt that she had yanked over her knees and down to her ankles as she sat in the corner, hugged into a ball with her hands around her knees. Her heartbeat was thundering at a thousand beats per second, although I didn't exactly blame her.

"And what about that one?" I nodded to the human. "Sophie must have healed the mortal wounds, but she might just give herself a heart attack. What did you guys do?" I glanced to the corpse at the floor. "Apart from murder Brent." I gave Duncan a pointed look.

He shrugged. "I was hungry and he was the only one there considering we need one human to fly the plane and the other is off-limits, apparently." He scowled at Rick.

The unflappable king stiffened unperceptively, but for him that was a big reaction.

Interesting.

"She was a prisoner of our enemy. And a prisoner of our enemy is either an ally or an asset," Rick clipped, his voice even but his eyes flickering as he fastened on the little rabbit in the corner who didn't seem to be in the room at all.

She had that empty look about her that I knew far too well. That soulless look that I had caught a glimpse of inside myself as the witch had weaseled her way into the deepest parts of me.

I flinched even now at the memory.

The uber-protective male at my side obviously registered it, as he flexed his arms around me.

"I'm fine," I hissed before he could demand a write-up of my blood work or something equally insane.

He stiffened.

"So, has anyone tried talking to the little thing?" I asked, going back to ignoring him.

"Of course we've fucking tried that," Duncan cut in, his voice a boom that made the girl in question jump.

So she was in the room enough to register the sharp twang of a Scotsman who had likely just drained a human in front of her.

"Yes, I'm sure you were about as gentle as a giant doing keyhole surgery," I muttered.

I glanced to Sophie. "What about you? No wait, actually you'd be about as sensitive as I would be. We need someone with less balls and more vagina—in the figurative sense, of course." I focused on someone who fit the description a little more.

Scott didn't even seem offended; he just looked glad to be there. Which of course he was. I would reason he'd be glad if this plane exploded in a fiery ball of destruction so long as he was invited.

"She's not talking to anyone," Scott said, glancing to the side with a compassion that only those with either soft hearts or soft minds could create.

I was neither soft of mind nor heart. But the thought did bring something to my attention. "Is she like…?" I twisted my finger around my temple in the universal 'crazy' gesture.

"She's been through a lot. For a human, anyway. Their minds are so much weaker and smaller, so sometimes they have to shut down instead of deal with the things that attempt to destroy them," Sophie said softly, her eyes faraway, looking at the girl but seeing something else.

Or someone else.

I didn't have time for that right now.

"Or she's batshit," I corrected. "Luckily I am too. Do you know what the definition of insanity is?" I asked the entire cabin. Only Scott answered because only he would answer a rhetorical question.

"It's doing the same thing over and over again and expecting a different result."

I rolled my eyes. "No, that's the description of trying to master winged eyeliner. The definition of insanity is the thought that sanity exists."

My focus turned to the human and not Sophie's grinning face.

I smiled at her. "You've just got to find the crazy in you to match the crazy in them. It's okay, sweetie. We're all mad here," I continued, thinking there could not be a more perfect time to be quoting the Cheshire cat.

Duncan glared at me. "Speak for yourself. I'm not mad."

"Not true," I protested, giving the human at his feet a

pointed glance. "But I was speaking for *myselves*. All of them. The voices like it when I'm honest."

He barked out a grunt that was somewhere between a chuckle and a growl.

Even Sophie smirked. Scott, because he was soft of heart, and of head, was full-on grinning.

Three people were not. Rick, not hugely surprising since his default was Vin Diesel. Happy, sad, pissed off, excited—all the very same.

Thorne, not another huge surprise considering the amount of emotions rolling off him, none of them particularly jolly.

But neither did the girl. I guessed even my hilarity couldn't make a little human spill the beans after getting trapped in a cave with a crazy witch for an indeterminate amount of time, most likely being tortured before getting saved by a vampire and her merry band of monsters.

"Well, that's a bust. Should we kill her?" I asked.

Thorne, interestingly, wasn't the one to be all outraged at the suggestion like he always seemed to be about killing humans for no reason. In fact, he didn't even move.

Rick did, abruptly standing and moving in a blur so he was between me and the girl. "You try that and we have problems, Isla," he said smoothly.

Now Thorne was getting a reaction at Rick threatening me. Or just because he obviously still wasn't playing nice with his brother, even though the immortal human slayer vampire thing was out of the bag.

"Like we don't already have problems," I muttered.

Rick continued to glare.

"Okay, fine, we won't kill the human," I huffed. "No need for the dramatics. It was just a suggestion."

"Not one you need to be having. Ever," he commanded.

And because I recognized that furious insanity in his eyes, I conceded.

And then decided that yes, we were all mad here.

Hopefully insanity would be our saving grace, not our downfall.

I reasoned it was sixty forty.

"It's a bad idea," Thorne growled at Duncan, his eyes roving over me and flaring at my outfit. The desire in them and the hardening of his jaw as I strutted in added to the immense female sense of satisfaction that came with looking hot and rubbing it in a well-deserving asshole's face. He swallowed visibly before continuing. "A bad idea. Reckless, borderline suicidal and almost certainly not going to work."

It was somewhat of another planning session in my apartment in the days after killing witch number two. And if we felt like counting, I'd killed witch number one as well. I was going for the trifecta; then I could say I single-handedly saved the world. But then again, I didn't think I wanted to be infamous for that.

Luckily the witches weren't going to be the be-all and end-all of the war, considering there was the question of their oh-so-fearless leader, the hybrids already created, and their continued attacks on supernaturals throughout the globe.

I wasn't overly worried about the rest for now. I was more concerned with getting witch three out of the way, who just so happened to be visiting with my family. Such a visit just so happened to constitute treason; therefore, I'd get to kill them all while we were picking her up.

Apparently this was the witch queen of them all and likely

wouldn't be easy to kill. Or perhaps we couldn't kill her at all. Sophie had been away doing research and gaining her eye of newt for a spell to bind her powers. We would take her to go and have a little chat with her before throwing her in some pit and swallowing the key.

So much to do. So much time.

Eternity.

Though eternity seemed rather a lot shorter after all these brushes with death I seemed to be having.

I sank down beside Duncan, snatching his whisky. "I'm in," I said immediately.

Three sets of male eyes settled on me. Well, two; the third and most electric had already been glued to me.

Duncan's flickered with annoyance at my whisky grabbing, but a small grin tickled the corner of his jaw at my words. Rick's were impassive and blank, which had become their default after everything that had come out in the crown room.

Well, apart from when he looked at the little sparrow who was staying in the guest bedroom in this very apartment. It seemed she was rather attached to me, since she'd damn near lost her shit when Rick tried to demand she come to the palace with him.

She'd actually hidden behind me.

Me.

Like she thought I'd protect her or something.

She was definitely crazy.

But I conceded, mostly because it gave me a good excuse to continue ignoring Thorne, though it was hard since he kept hanging about the place.

And then Rick too.

It was like they didn't have lives as king of the vampire race during a possible uprising in the community and the head of the slayer faction struggling to keep up.

"You aren't aware of what plan we're referring to," Rick cut in smoothly.

The kingly brother, ever the diplomat.

I drained Duncan's whisky. "I don't need to be aware. I'm bored. It includes recklessness, a small possibility of success, large possibility of death. Add some Prada and a full-bodied pinot and it's my kind of party. Plus I want to test just how far this 'deathless' thing will take me."

"Of course you fuckin' do," Thorne seethed. "You're not doin' it."

Then there was the not-so-kingly brother, who was a slave to his baser urges. With the technicality of humanity and all that.

And the one I was fated to be with, apparently.

Pity that fate was a fickle bitch. Though I was fickler and bitchier.

I totally planned to outmaneuver that bitch. A woman scorned and all that.

I tilted my head at him. "I'm sorry, I think you have yourself confused with someone with any fucking right to make that call. You know, someone who isn't a spineless liar who deserves to be chained to the bottom of an ocean with a scuba mask and endless oxygen and just the pressure of the water and the small hope a shark might come along to tear him to shreds rather than live in that empty silence for the end of eternity," I hissed.

"Well detailed. Like it," Duncan put in with approval.

I grinned at him. "Thanks, though it's only option one. I have twelve more."

"Thirteen," he observed, obviously understanding the lovely irony of doing things in odd numbers, with thirteen being the most beautiful of them all.

"Exactly. And of course, they'll be carried out on Friday."

Duncan barked out a stiff laugh.

No one else was laughing. But then again, the sense of humor we had was only reserved for a special—read: awesome—breed.

Thorne burst out of his seat, darting across the distance to clutch my arm in a grip that caused my bones to crack slightly and dragged me out of the room.

I let him, only because I was not hot on ruining another set of furniture in my living room, and also because—and I'd never admit it out loud—he was strong enough to pull off such an act.

I was sucking down on his blood; he should have been anemic and weak, not all flushed with anger and stronger than he'd been before. Or maybe he'd always been that strong, and he had just been playing his part as a weak human to me in order to continue the farce.

Whatever it was, he managed to yank me into my room, shoving me so I tottered slightly into the area at the end of my bed which boasted great views of Park Avenue. Too bad he wouldn't see them from the ground. Which was where I planned on him landing.

"Can you fly?" I asked calmly once he'd slammed the door shut and rounded on me.

His eyes were black and darkened, his fists clenched tightly at his sides and jaw held tight. Ticking off all the little boxes for Thorne fury. Unfortunately, his jaw was also sprinkled with a liberal dusting of black stubble and his hair was artfully wild, brushing against the nape of his neck and framing his face in its inky curtain, making him look like the Devil himself.

Or at least his hot brother.

Oh no, wait, he was the hot brother of the king of all vampires. Who was nothing to sneeze at either.

But back to Thorne.

The muscles I swore had gotten bigger threatened to pulse out of the fitted black shirt which was trying to do the job of keeping them contained. As was the faded pair of jeans that encased his powerful thighs.

"What?" he clipped through gritted teeth.

I snapped my head back up to the swirling eyes.

"Your little slayer human vampire thing you've got going on," I said, waving my hand at the package that contained the man who was destined to kill me, yet also destined to be my 'mate,' whose heart beat in my own chest and who had lied and betrayed me. "Does flying come with the laundry list of qualities?"

His eye twitched and he shook his head in a curt no.

I grinned. "Excellent."

"You're not going to throw me out the window, Isla," he said blandly, crossing his arms.

I frowned at my response to the simple gesture, hating how much it turned me on. "Are you a mind reader too?" I snapped.

He regarded me. "No, I just know you."

"Well, that makes one of us. Since I have no fucking clue who you are," I hissed.

"You're clinging to this excuse. You've been doin' it for too fuckin' long, and I'm not doing it any longer," he growled.

I glared at him. "Do what, Thorne? Play the alpha male who broods more than he breathes? Good, I was worried about your lung capacity." I paused. "No, wait, I wasn't. As soon as Sophie finds a way to break this spell shit so I don't need you to survive, you can brood as much as you like. And breathe as little as you like. If at all. That's my preference."

His grip tightened and he yanked me closer so our bodies pressed together, showing me what I'd forgotten. That ice and fire could mix and create something colder than the arctic and hotter than Hades. And made you want to burn and freeze at the same time.

"No. See, that's what you're doing. Clinging to this denial that it's the blood, *my* blood, that you need to survive. That without that need you can do it without me. But I know your secret, Isla. This excuse came at a pivotal time for you. When you could cling to it to escape and distance yourself from me. From this. Because you pride yourself on being so fucking strong that you can't handle the thought of something making you weak. Of us making you more than what you are at the same time as making you less than what you were. Because what we have, babe, even without prophecies or blood or fucking immortality, it's immortal in itself. It's otherworldly, and it's got the power to burn through our fuckin' souls if we let it." His grip tightened. "I'm not gonna fuckin' let it. Not gonna let your soul burn. I'll gladly sacrifice mine to the inferno before that shit happens."

I gave him an even gaze. His words hit their mark but my self-defense mechanism—sarcasm and snark, in other words— helped me. "Sorry, babe. Too late on the soul front, considering mine's already burning in the pit. Has been since… well, since the beginning of my undeath. It's kind of part and package with immortality. The bloodsucking thing and then the sacrifice of the soul."

He stared at me. "No, Isla. Your soul hasn't been sacrificed to the Devil. Your soul is *mine*, whether you like it or not. No refunds, no returns and sure as fuck no running. And you tell me to breathe as little as I like? That's on you, babe. You're the thing that keeps my lungs sustained, not fuckin' oxygen. And I know it's not my blood keeping you sustained. Known it since I saw you in that station. My whole life has been a battle. Told you you were my greatest and bloodiest yet. And I'll go to war with a smile on my face, if it's fighting the war that gets me to where I need to be—by your side. Not winnin' you like a trophy or a prize because you're not to be won, or owned, or saved. You're to be weathered, fought, and fuckin' loved more than a simple human being could ever do. And I'm not simple. This sure as fuck isn't simple, but that fact is. The fact that you're never gonna push me away."

"It's not pushing someone away when they've betrayed you, Thorne," I hissed. "That's called logic."

He lifted a brow. "Since when have you and logic even been on the same planet?"

I glared at him. "Since my destruction came in the form of a slayer who brought me to the edge and then hurled me off with lies and secrets," I snapped. "Because you told me to trust you, and then you kept things from me."

"And you're not keepin' shit from me?"

I pursed my lips. "A girl doesn't tell a man the secrets she holds. That's just common sense. And my secrets aren't the pivotal truth to my identity and haven't ripped through everything we've fucking had or ever would have." I paused. "Plus, my secrets? My truth? It's darkness," I admitted.

He didn't even blink. "If it's in the darkness that this is going to take you, then that's where I'll go."

I stared at him. "You don't even know the demons that lurk in this darkness, the depravity."

He stared back, unwavering. "I don't need to. Only thing I need to know is that's where you're going to be."

He was saying all the right things. All the ones that settled into whatever parts of me were left to accommodate him while my brain—either the logical part or the crazy part, I couldn't decide—urged me to forget. Maybe not forgive just yet, but at least forget long enough to lose myself in him once more.

But the other part, the logical or crazy part that remained, steered me towards the storm.

So I pushed myself from his grasp, trying to find some distance.

"You don't know what you feel for me. You know what you *think* you feel, tangled up in danger and forbidden love and war and strife and fucking prophecy. Take all that away and what do you have, Thorne?"

He didn't seem to like the distance I'd just created. He surged forward, not just so his hands cupped my chin and my body pressed into his, but so his soul met mine through the connection we shared, through the blood he made spill as he pressed his thumb into my mouth and pierced his skin with my fang.

"What's left when we strip all that away, when we take away everything on the outside that you think makes this somehow more. Or somehow less. But it's wrong. Because without everything on the outside, we're the truth. We're *everything.*"

His hand left my mouth and moved to circle mine in his large palm, giving the illusion that my small and pale fingers were delicate and precious and hadn't known death. Hadn't dealt death and evil.

He took them and didn't take all that away, accepting it all without words instead.

Then he laid that death-filled hand on his life-filled chest, where his heart vibrated.

His eyes met mine. "It's through my life that I almost lost you. From the origin of it all. I'll regret that, that lie for as long as I live. But I won't regret what I am. Or what you are. Because my heart is thousands of years old, and my thousand-year-old heart knows things. Just like yours does. And the outside stuff is white fucking noise compared to that shit. What we know, what we are."

His words were said with such conviction, such love, that I was helpless against them. Me. A vampire. Arguably one of the strongest and most brilliant of our kind, laid to waste by mere words.

It was the mistake of idiots, dreamers, and lovers who thought love itself was a cure to reality, sent from God to temper the burn of mortality. The Devil's greatest trick wasn't convincing the world he didn't exist. No, it was to make humans think that God sent love from the heavens to save them when he sent it from the underworld to damn them.

And there I was, damned.

Not because I was a vampire or a murderer.

Because I sinned as an angel did and loved as a demon might.

TWENTY

I EYED THE HOUSE, PERCHED ON TOP OF THE HILL LIKE SOME kind of nefarious idol. Despite my familiarity with it and my lack of fear towards it, I did, for a second, get a snapshot of what the locals of the town below saw every day. Cowered and bowed to every moment of their existence.

The menacing presence of the house itself, seemingly alive with the sheer coldness, even when nestled in the Russian summer with snow surrounding it. The darkness from the blackest midnight couldn't reproduce the aura of the house.

Evil, if such a concept existed, would live there.

"Home, sweet home," I said, holding my arm out to the stone fortress that was too harsh and ugly to be called a castle.

Though my mother would like to think of it as so, and the humans in the town below her servants.

Though they were, to an extent. The town had been around

for centuries, for as long as I'd been undead. And for that time, the locals had always known. From whispered legends passed over campfires, and now with the background noise of television sets, were the stories of the Upyr and the ones who resided in and lorded over their town.

The watchful eye of the Rominskitoff clan meant the townspeople were probably the least likely in all of Russia to get killed by a vampire. Drank from? Maybe. Tortured? Also a big maybe when my brothers were in town. But killed? No.

My father had made some kind of blood vow with the original settlers of the town. A homicidal, sadistic, sociopathic vampire he may be, but he always kept his word.

He'd even given me a pony I'd asked for as a child. Of course, Viktor slit its throat in front of me a day later.

Father knew or expected such a thing would happen. Yet he got the pony. Because he was a man of his word. And a homicidal, sadistic, sociopathic vampire.

"I don't like it," Thorne muttered against the crisp bite of the Russian summer.

He was bundled up in his leather jacket, thin yet warm wool underneath. Not burdened with too many layers, since it was hard to fight in a cozy wool sweater.

I tried to imagine it. "You don't own any wool sweaters, do you?"

He glared at me, which was becoming the norm considering he spent the entire flight muttering curses and setting his iron stare on me—and, on occasion, Duncan, when he decided to poke the bear. Because doing that in a pressurized metal box flying thirty thousand feet in the air was a good idea.

Then he'd decided talking to me was somehow a better idea. "You could get hurt," he rumbled.

In an uncharacteristic gesture, I moved my hand to cover

his thigh and squeeze it. "I could, and I most likely will," I agreed.

His jaw ticked, but I continued.

"But I'm fucking awesome and tough and pretty well versed in surviving torture. I learned how to withstand it before I was even turned, and then multiple times after, so I'll still be able to kick ass and take names even with a limb hanging off." I paused. "Well, apart from my head hanging off, for obvious reasons, and I don't think that's classified as a limb. I wonder what they actually call—"

"Isla," Thorne growled, obviously deciding to cut me off before I went too far.

I always went too far. That place beyond whatever line decency stopped at? Yeah, that's where I hung out. And all the other cool kids too.

His hand covered mine. "What are you fuckin' talking about you withstood torture *before* you were turned?" he demanded.

I blinked, distracted for a moment at the way his thumb rubbed at the top of my hand absently, then following the movement to the pulse point in his wrist. The gentle vibration gave me pause for a second before I snapped my head up to him.

"Yeah. Of course. It's like the vampire version of the SATs," I explained.

There was a pause. A long one.

"As a teenager, one as breakable as a human, you were made to withstand torture in order to graduate from high school?" he seethed.

I gave him a look. "Dude, it was four hundred years ago. Pipe the alpha rage down. You can't change the past. And I wouldn't want to. I aced that fucking class. Because, as mentioned earlier, I'm awesome."

My eyes went to Duncan's form, gazing out the window in a troubling melancholy that disturbed me just the slightest with its intensity.

Duncan was never intense. Well, he was, but not in any kind of serious way.

This was serious in a way that even the death of his entire family three hundred years before hadn't been.

Not for me to worry about at this juncture.

We had enough to worry about. Sophie and her wolf were on another plane, or perhaps a train by now. They'd be meeting Thorne and Duncan at the back entrance to my old home while I came in the front.

I was the main distraction, followed by Duncan and Thorne. Hopefully, in all the chaos, Sophie and the wolf—whom I'd not been happy to hear was part of the plan—would snatch Malena with some nifty little spell and drag her back to the continental US where Rick could put her in his little gallery and perhaps gain an advantage in the war.

That was with all things going well.

If all things didn't go well, we all died.

Cheerful, really.

At least Thorne and I had reconciled, thoroughly, before our impending deaths.

"I even beat a certain Scotsman's record," I taunted Duncan, putting my attention on him and not me welcoming the grave for what felt like the hundredth time that week.

His melancholy snapped away like a rubber band, the mask of easiness that I thought was his natural state fitting quickly onto his features.

"Fuckin' cheated," he muttered.

"I won fair and square. Just because the little human

Duncan couldn't handle a little dismemberment. Boohoo, someone get you a fucking tampon," I shot.

He flashed his fangs at me in response.

I rolled my eyes, then grinned at Thorne, who was glowering.

"Dismemberment?" he repeated.

I waved my hand. "Oh, only a little. There was a witch on scene to fix it good as new." I turned the hand in question around in the light. "See, flawless as ever."

He frowned at the hand. "Jesus, Isla."

I quirked my brow. "Pretty sure he wasn't a classmate. At least not in my year."

He yanked me so I straddled him, his eyes swimming as emotions rolled off him in waves so palpable I had the completely irrational thought that they might bowl me over if he wasn't pressing me to his body.

Which was ridiculous, of course.

"This isn't a joke, Isla," he growled. "Life. Death. You being in any proximity to it or in pain."

"That's precisely what it all is," I replied. "Life. Death. A big fucking cosmic joke that we have to find the humor in, however dark it is. Otherwise, it'll eat us alive. And now that I'm all deathless and shit, I'm not a fan of it eating me alive. I eat people alive, not the other way around. And you can't take it seriously either," I ordered.

His hands tightened around me. "You don't have a say in that shit, Isla. Because you might not take your life, or your death, seriously, but I sure as fuck do. Considering it's mine too. So I'll take it as seriously as anything I ever have in my years on this planet."

Duncan made a gagging sound. With a flick of Thorne's wrist, a knife went hurtling through the air. He didn't take his eyes off me.

Duncan let out a string of curses. "Why do people keep throwing fecking knives at me?" he hissed.

"Because you keep existing to piss them off," I hissed back.

"Oh, it's not like I'm here, risking undeath and limb or anything, for you assholes."

I rolled my eyes. "Yeah, right. You're doing it for a paycheck and a good time. Plus that slayer chick wouldn't bone you and you've got to get your rocks off somehow. What better way than killing an entire Vein Line?"

Duncan's silence signified my victory.

Thorne's eyes had still been on me.

"We'll be fine," I told him. "We have to be. I've got us reservations at Eleven Madison Park on Wednesday. The foie gras is said to be to die for, so let's wait for that before we perish in this war, okay?" I asked him sweetly.

He yanked me into his embrace, kissing away my words, and maybe his doubts.

But not death.

It was with us, both when we landed and the entire journey through the stark and lifeless landscape of Russia, to the town I used to call home.

Or Hell. Just a little colder than the original.

With worse inhabitants.

Hence Thorne thinking me being used as bait was a "bad idea."

"It's the only idea we have," I told him and his angry eyes. "And the best one."

"Seconded," Duncan said from beside me, regarding the house casually. Just another Sunday for him, I guessed.

"You're not going in alone," Thorne said, the chill from his words wafting from his mouth in visible puffs.

I frowned at his words and then inwardly frowned at my concern for Thorne and the fact that he was cold.

That wasn't my problem. He was a grown-ass man, and I was toasty below room temperature, like always, so what did I care?

"We've gone over this. I have to go in alone," I told him. "Sorry, honey, but the 'meet the parents' stage of this relationship doesn't involve me taking you for dinner while my father gently gives you shit about not being good enough for his daughter. For one thing, there's no way in fuck my father would be gentle when he ripped your limbs off. Plus, they would've only thought you were good enough for me if you'd actually gone through with the initial plan and killed me like you'd intended to at the beginning. And there will be dinner—you. Hence the need for you to slip around the back and help witchy and wolfy—who I hate. Have I mentioned that? So, if an unfortunate accident befalls him while you're battling for your lives, I wouldn't be crying too much. Or at all. I might be dancing on his grave. You know, if I'm not inside my own. Which I won't be. Because I'll be saving your asses," I said to both Thorne and Duncan.

Thorne hardened his jaw, so much so I was worried it might crack under the force of such a gesture on icy skin. "I can take care of myself," he gritted. "And you," he added on an afterthought.

I grinned at him. "Of course you can," I reassured him, but my tone came off patronizing, as was my default. He didn't exactly look reassured, but I continued. "And I can't believe I'm saying it, but less drama at this juncture is preferable. We might still have the element of surprise since we arrived on an unregistered jet and the weather makes it impossible for them to catch your scent." I regarded the desolate tomb that held the undead remains of my family.

One I hoped, after tonight, would entomb the very dead remains of my family.

"So let's just make it look like I'm here for tea and a catch-up with the psychopaths while you and Duncan do your part with Sophie and her mangy mutt who are likely already waiting around back. Okay? Good. Great. Catch you on the flip-side, motherfuckers."

I turned around to face the music and hopefully end my parents once and for all.

I purposefully didn't say goodbye to Thorne or acknowledge that this might be the last time I was seeing him alive.

Because that simply wasn't an option.

I shrugged off the stiff and uncomfortable sense of foreboding that came with putting my finger on the button which was inside the mouth of an intricately carved depiction of Hades taking up a good portion of the stone beside the wooden double doors.

One had to literally venture into the mouth of the Devil in order to gain entry to this house.

My family.

One thing I got from them—subtlety was not in the Rominskitoff DNA.

Then again, neither was mercy, compassion, the ability to love, and apparently taste as my mother opened the door.

Wearing head to toe green velvet.

Velvet.

"Karl Lagerfeld thankfully declared this trend over, Mother," I said by greeting, waving my hand up and down at the tight-fitting dress that molded to every inch of her ageless and beautiful body. Her hair, the same red as mine, was chopped harshly to brush her angular cheekbones, helping to give the impression that every inch of her was hard, sharp, able to draw blood. Not just her fangs.

Her ivory face pinched slightly. "Isla," she said, her accented voice filled with distaste. Then again, that was ever present whenever she talked to me. "What a surprise."

I smiled. "Well, I missed the last four hundred or so Christmases, so I thought I'd pop in for a chat. Maybe share a glass of blood. I would've brought a willing young virgin to share, but Viktor and Evgeni must've seen to making sure there are none left of age." I paused. "Oh, you mean you're surprised to see me undead, not just at your doorstep presenting you with the stark truth of just how bad your fashion choices are. Right. Yes. You exposed me to the king and then got yourself a seat to my execution, which I bet was as coveted as the runway seat at a Celine show. That's probably why you're surprised, is it not?"

Her face remained impassive, but something moved in her eyes. Rage, perhaps. She looked like she wanted to unleash it. I was very tempted to poke at her once more to finally see such a thing happen. In all the centuries I'd had the displeasure of knowing my mother, never once had I witnessed her raise her voice. Or even contort her facial features into a scowl.

The most she did was a slight raise of her brow and perhaps a lip curl of distaste. Otherwise, it was the mask that she had perfected to give the world a show of a beautiful, ageless, red-haired woman with ice white skin, eyes like emeralds, lips like Snow White herself and the body of a pinup girl.

It was only right before you died that you saw Medusa underneath.

Which I guess boded well for me when she stepped back, opening the door fully.

"Come in. We are not uncouth enough to discuss such matters on a *doorstep*." She spat the last word as if we were sitting in the gutter sharing sips from a glass bottle in a paper bag.

"Why, thank you for the kind welcome, Mother, especially after you tried to have me executed. Why wouldn't I want to come into the childhood home in which you tortured me, and I will likely be outnumbered by the entire family that shares my blood and will want nothing more than to spill it over the marble floor that's warmer than your heart?" I asked with a smile.

The heels of my boots resounded on that marble floor, echoing through the cavernous room that opened to the house of horrors I used to call home.

It may have been centuries old with stone-walled interiors, but it wasn't exactly cliché vampire trappings with burning torches mounted on the walls for light.

Since electricity was invented, it filled the room via a huge crystal chandelier handing from the high ceiling. The space itself was stark and unwelcoming, a grand staircase which spanned a balcony and spanned off to one set of stairs on each side. Why have one set when you could have two?

Upstairs were bedrooms, drawing rooms, libraries, and other various well-decorated spaces those of status and decorum boasted in a centuries-old structure.

And then there was the downstairs. The spanning dungeon that stretched completely underneath the structure itself. It was part of the original design. As it should've been, I guessed, since my father was the architect.

And what does a newlywed young vampire aristocrat of a noble Vein Line want when building the house for the family he planned on furthering the race with?

Family room? Where the children can play, break each other's arms, use human limbs as chew toys?

Of course.

Kitchen, where more humans were hung upside down and drained in crystal jugs so fresh blood could be served to all of those at the baby shower?

Definitely.

And a dungeon in which you can imprison your enemies, your friends who turned into enemies, humans for torture and your fifteen-year-old daughter who tried to set the aforementioned humans free once.

Necessity.

Even though there were stacks of stone underneath us, I could hear them. The faltering heartbeats that were weak but racing with fear at the same time.

The perfumed air, done so by one of the many terrified human servants, couldn't disguise the metallic twang of blood, nor the bitter stench of death.

Then again, death was Mother's perfume of choice.

She walked into the middle of the sprawling space before turning on me. "Where is this conversation to take place, Isla? What have you come to do?"

I tilted my head. "Well, since I'm on your turf, you choose. We could always go to the sitting room for tea. I always liked the view of the town and the unyielding and depressing sprawling landscape you lord your terror over. Or we could do the cigar room if we wanted to indulge in some of the harder stuff. You know, I love the many bound books and smell of rich mahogany." My *Anchorman* reference went straight over her head, as expected. I idly wished Sophie was there to appreciate it, or at least to zap my mother so she gained three hundred pounds and split out of that criminal dress.

She was there, of course, just not within hearing distance for excellently placed movie references. And it wouldn't be half as funny when I told her later.

"Or," I continued, "we could skip all the formalities and go straight to the dungeon where you could finish what you oh-so-gracefully started. You know, my execution?" I said sweetly. "I know you dislike me, Mother, but that was rather intense, even for the woman who arguably was the reason for the Cold War because of a slight at a party."

Her mouth twitched. "You were sleeping with a slayer, Isla," she hissed. "An unforgiveable crime to the Vein Line. You've always been a disgrace, but that was treason. You were beyond redemption at that point."

I eyed her. "Or maybe I was *redeemed*. And that's the fucking point."

She laughed, the sound cold and cruel and welcomed by the cold, cruel house. "You are a vampire, Isla. That will never change. Whatever this childish hope is that you are somehow able to be anything else than that is the reason I had to take such measures to shock you back to yourself."

I gaped at her. "So getting me executed was your way of teaching your wayward daughter a lesson? Some parents just cut their children off financially, perhaps ground them. Or maybe just disown me and let me live my own undeath."

She blinked at me with a look so full of malice it surely would have stabbed me with something akin to hurt if I had any shred of affection for the reptile who birthed me.

Luckily I wasn't plagued with that.

Hadn't been since she killed my husband and every friend I'd ever had and presented me with their corpses.

Or since before then.

Since birth.

"That is not an option," she hissed. "And execution was never going to happen." She waved her hand. "That king—though such a title being given to him is blasphemous—is infatuated with you. I witnessed that at the Feast. I knew even treason would not push him to do the duty that the gods themselves put upon him," she bit out. "His humanity is almost as good as yours. So I knew he would at the most kill the human, and he didn't even do that." Her curled lip turned into a grin that brought my blood down in temperature precisely to the same as her heart. "But that was all the better, considering it exemplified his incompetence for the right people and helped our cause. Immensely."

I blinked at her. "Cause? You're admitting that you're part of this idiotic thing Father has headed to reinforce your idiotic belief that you're better than humans and you'll rule the earth with bad fashion choices and sadistic pleasures?" I asked.

She gave me a look that was distinctly maternal, perhaps the only one I'd ever had in the entire stretch of my existence. One that looked at a small child with impatience at its stupidity. I knew mothers did that, despite their insistence to the contrary; I'd witnessed enough of humankind to know they did. Children were so frustrating after all. No wonder people shook them.

Mother shook me.

And broke me.

Bled me.

So this was the shaking mother look.

"Don't act dense, Isla," she snapped, wandering over to a shaking maid in the corner who could've been a statue holding a silver platter had it not been for her accelerated heartbeat that was pursued by terror.

The maid's eyes bulged slightly at my mother's approach, but she mustn't have been new, for she didn't flinch as Mother snatched a goblet of blood from the tray.

From the maid's grey pallor and lack of flush skin, I guessed it was her own.

Charming, making the terrified help drain themselves and actually serve their own blood on a fucking silver platter.

"You may do your best to act like a superficial and insipid idiot at every turn, but I know even you have something akin to a brain," she continued, wandering around the room, inspecting it for specks of dust. I knew she was hoping she could find it, if only to beat a maid or two. She turned, sipping demurely. "I also know that you've been investigating like some little character in a horrid human fiction book. Not for your race, or even the king whose reign is running short. No doubt serving your own agenda, as you always have."

I gaped at her. "You're accusing me of having my own agenda?" I argued. "Yes, I forgot, you did just get back from your mission in Uganda building wells for children and your extensive work for humankind. I do know how hard you work to make sure this world isn't too overpopulated and the soil is well fertilized with bodies. That's how you grow such vibrant roses in the middle of Russia."

My eyes went to the table in the middle of the room, the ostentatious vase that was always filled with countless bunches of bloodred roses.

Never dead. Always vibrant.

Always.

Through the centuries, that vase of bloodred roses greeted any prisoner, visitor or guest to the Rominskitoff household.

Roses were, after all, the sigil for the house. The beautiful symbol of blood with thorns that were only visible after you got too close.

"Yes, Isla, continue to spout your nonsense," Mother said blandly. "But your purpose was to end up right here, getting the information you so wished to get so you could run back to your precious king in order to get a sanction to finally grant your revenge. Our death." Her shrewd eyes inspected me. "That's all you've wished for since that day that human of yours was taken care of, isn't it?"

I narrowed my own eyes at her, hatred flowing through my veins with white-hot intensity. "'Taken care of'? The moment you massacred my husband and every other single person I'd come into contact with and liked in my short existence in the sunshine of life before I plunged into the eternal night of un-death? Yes, that may have been what tipped the scale of me purely wanting to escape from you for a lifetime of torture and abuse to actually wanting to exterminate you. Or maybe it was the centuries of assassination attempts, of children's bodies at my doorsteps, of my meathead brothers coming to rip out my heart or ruin valuable sofas. Or perhaps it was the threat of having me raped and impregnated, then killing me after steal-ing my unborn child." I paused, my eyes flickering down her body "Or it could be the dress. Pick one."

She observed me. "It baffles me to see how you came from such noble blood to sully it so with your... humanity," she spat. "Never have I been more disappointed to have created such a *thing*."

"Never have I been so disappointed to be your creation. But I think I've improved greatly on the original model," I hissed. "Now come, Mother, let's stop with the niceties and you tell me Father's evil plan, as I'm sure you're itching to do before you lock me up and torture me."

She laughed again. "Oh, you think your father is the mas-termind of such a complex and brilliant revolution?" she asked incredulously. "His concerns have always been too much with uniting the family instead of the race. Perhaps that is where you got your weakness from, as he's the reason his golden daughter has managed to escape her deserved fate for the centuries he's allowed you to run around like a common street vampire."

I blinked. Father had allowed me to survive? Was him watching and condoning my torture since age five considered compassionate or me being his golden girl? My mind snapped back to the party at Thorne's the night of the explosion, my father saving me from what would or would not have been a death blow.

"No, your father buries his head as he always has. It is not with him that the brains of the revolution were built. And it will not be him who helps leads the races into the new era where the rightful creatures will take their rightful places."

I crossed my arms, wishing I'd brought a tape recorder or something. This was a lot of propaganda to try to remember. "If you tell me it was one of my idiot brothers, I'll fall off my Choos," I commented dryly. "They likely couldn't lead a blood-hound to one of their murder scenes, let alone a whole faction of psychopathic supernatural creatures."

Mother's eyes narrowed once more. "Your brothers are loyal soldiers to the cause," she snapped. "But no, they are not leaders."

Something in her eyes gave me pause. "So you consider yourself to be the queen?" I asked, then laughed. "You have the grand plan of wearing tasteless gowns, a tacky piece of head-wear and sitting on a throne made from the bones of children you've slain? Yeah, and they told me I was delusional when I wanted to persuade the government to make short skirts on obese people illegal."

In a flash, Mother was across the room, her manicured hands at my throat, crushing my windpipe.

It happened, or I allowed it to happen, merely because I wasn't expecting it.

Mother may have thrived on violence, but only when she was a spectator and instigator.

Her eyes glowed with fury and bloodlust. "You must learn, Isla, to shut that mouth before I give in to my baser instincts and rip that tongue out," she murmured, squeezing so the bones in my throat popped and cracked, the sound echoing in my brain.

It hurt, surely, but I was more than a little satisfied that I'd rattled her enough to react in such a manner.

She let go, stepping back to straighten her dress and hold out her glass to be refilled.

The time it took for the maid to scuttle about and refill the glass was the time it took for me to heal my windpipe and glare at my mother.

She made use of my silence.

"I will have the position I deserve at the top tier of this new world order," she informed me. "For it is what my blood entitles me to. But I leave the leading up to those who have the, shall we say, knack for it." She paused, and through the slightly uncomfortable pain of my bones knitting back together, something moved in her eyes, a deep and sick sense of satisfaction that filled me with that same foreboding that had simmered within me since the beginning of this entire train wreck.

Her eyes flickered to the staircase and she grinned.

"Boys, come and say hello to your sister."

"Great," I rasped, my voice scratching with the effort it took to form words.

Evgeni and Viktor sped down to stand beside Mother, both glaring at me. No, that wasn't right. Evgeni was glaring, but Viktor was grinning in the way that I knew would be followed by some sort of pain.

"Oh, it's sadist one and sadist two," I greeted. "How nice I get to see both of you assholes before I kill you."

Viktor laughed. "As insane as always, sister."

"Coming from you, an insane person who is also a socio-path, that's an immense compliment. Killed any babies lately? Or managed to find any females from half-decent Vein Lines to forgo reason and class and marry you?" My gaze darted between my meathead brothers. "Why don't you just marry each other? I'm sure you'd satisfy each other sexually, and then the world would be saved from the utter horror of having any of your offspring walk the earth."

Viktor struck first. He was always the hothead.

Luckily I was prepared and broke the arm that he'd intended to plunge into my chest.

The cracking sound echoed through the foyer, much like my windpipe had earlier. I grinned at him. "The fist through the heart again, brother?" I asked, shaking my head. "So predictable."

I then used my strength to snap it almost off. I would've been successful if he hadn't taken advantage of his new position to kick out at my legs and break my femur.

I gritted my teeth against collapsing on the ground but unfortunately let his arm go. Then he was free to backhand me with enough force to send me flying into the stone wall and crashing into a painting before we both tumbled less than gracefully onto a sideboard, crushing that on the way down.

"Viktor, darling, try not to damage the furniture," Mother requested, sounding vaguely irritated at the loss of her tasteless décor.

Not her two children engaged in a death match. No, this had happened many times before, though I guessed this time death was actually on the table.

Not mine.

Not again.

I pushed myself up, shoving my rib back into my body, grinning through the blood in my mouth and showing fang. "In my opinion, Mother, I'm improving the décor," I informed her.

I didn't get to say anything more because Viktor, like the raging bull he was, charged at me. I was prepared, gripping the shard of table I'd procured and shoving it through his neck. It slowed him down enough so that I could get traction to detach the entire thing from his body.

The ripping of flesh and bone was even more musical than Lady Gaga to my ears, and I was a total Little Monster.

As was the strangled scream that came from my mother's throat as she watched Viktor's head tumble on top of her Persian rug.

Though I didn't exactly know if the scream of fear was due to the rug or watching the daughter she hated decapitate the son she didn't quite hate.

She wasn't capable of love. She was quite likely to love the rug more.

Of course, then she found her decorum, because it wasn't seemly to scream over a bloodstained rug or a beheaded son.

The following silence was something as beautiful as the sound of the ending of Viktor's undeath.

"Look at it this way, you don't have to worry about a way to cut the apron strings. He was still living at home and he was six hundred years old, for Hades's sake. I saved you millions," I commented.

It was at that point that Mother gave Evgeni his command. Which was what I needed, though Evgeni was slightly less brutish and dumb than Viktor. He didn't charge immediately and his fights were more practiced, purposeful, nuanced. He circled me while I willed my internal bleeding and cracked skull and cheekbone to sort themselves out. I could fight with the pain, ignore it even, but I knew Evgeni had catalogued every single one of my injuries and would try to use them to his advantage.

"Not good choices got you here, sister," he warned softly.

"The only bad choice I've ever made was shoulder pads in the eighties," I hissed. "Killing my loving brother was even better than investing in two new Prada bags after it became apparent they were only doing a limited release."

He surged forward, a quick jab to my just-healing cheekbone, shattering it once more and then darting away before I could snatch his arm and yank it from the socket.

His eyes glowed as he grinned at me. "I'll make your death slow, sister," he promised. "Long enough to last to your Awakening. And then you'll wish I killed you."

Erotic and sadistic promise lurked between his words.

Yuck.

I may have loved *Game of Thrones*, but that didn't mean I wanted to get all Lannister up in here.

I was more of a Jon Snow type of girl. Namely because of his resemblance to my Thorne. Though Thorne had more muscles and was even hotter than Snow.

I sighed at the revulsion Evgeni brought forward. "Family. Can't live with them, can't kill them." I paused. "Oh wait, you can kill them. Thank God."

I jerked forward, much more gracefully than Evgeni, and stole Viktor's move—he wouldn't mind, being dead and all—plunging my fist through his chest and ripping out his cold and unbeating heart.

The bulging of his eyes and wet groan of pain were indeed beautiful. Better than Lady Gaga and Hozier combined.

Though, that would be a great single.

I held the organ between us with a grin, then dropped it at our feet at the same time Evgeni crumpled to the ground.

I turned to face my mother, same sadistic grin in place. It widened when her horrified expression met mine.

I glanced to where she was staring, the not quite fully dead Evgeni. "I'll finish him later. First, I would really love to finish you, and that fucking dress," I said with a smile.

Fear contorted Mother's features for a moment. But only a moment. Then something akin to smug satisfaction replaced it.

Right about the time I heard the thumping of a heartbeat and a roared "Isla."

Then a body barreled into me and sent me hurtling into the stone wall once more.

I reacted quickly to the snapping hybrid going for my jugular, ripping its head off. "You interrupted my vengeance speech," I hissed at it.

Then I jumped up to see the crowd of them that had entered the room, Duncan and Thorne fighting them off.

It looked like the distraction was working. And I was mighty glad they were still alive.

I darted over to the closest hybrid, snatching it out of the air before it got close to Thorne, who had too many bleeding wounds already.

His eyes locked with mine as I snapped its neck while he stabbed another hybrid, his gaze flickering over my injuries. "You okay?" he yelled in concern.

I punched a passing vampire. "Oh yes, peachy."

My eyes went to the twitching corpse of Evgeni.

I glanced to Duncan, who was now closest.

"Duncan, could you be a dear and finish killing my

brother?" I asked sweetly.

He grinned a bloody smile. "It would be my honor."

It was amidst the noisiness and bloodiness of battle that some sort of silence came hurtling in.

Thorne's thundering heartbeat was still there, as was the fresh scent of his blood.

But I'd just kicked a corpse of a hybrid from my feet, preparing to take on the next one and then hopefully my mother when a cultured and accented voice spoke.

"Stop, Mon Ange."

I froze. Literally froze in the middle of the room. The vampire hurtling for my throat was only stopped by the very accurate throwing of a knife which embedded itself in its skull.

It must have been the last thing Duncan did before he was overwhelmed by the newcomers who accompanied the owner of that voice.

"Isla!" Thorne roared.

It was his voice, the rough desperation in it, that swam through the fog created from those previous words, which were remnants of a long-dead life. From a long-dead man.

My gaze settled on Thorne—or more accurately, the vampire holding a blade to his neck.

He didn't seem overly concerned about that. Nor the variety of injuries that sent the delicious and sweet scent of his blood through the bitter air.

No, his horrified gaze was focused on me, for some reason.

Yes, I'd had more than a few injuries myself, and my shoulder had unfortunately been dislocated, but otherwise I was quite fine.

As fine as someone could've been when some idiot vampire held a knife to the throat of the man she loved. I forgot the voice for a moment, everything else fading into nothingness but the bloodlust for the man who would not die in front of me.

My heels rolled back in preparation to rip the head off the current vampire threatening Thorne and the considerable number of vampires that stood between me and him.

Not that that mattered.

But then it did matter when the voice spoke again.

"I wouldn't bother with the human, Mon Ange, though I do know you have a weakness for them."

Again, I was frozen. Well, my thoughts of before were frozen, the voice and words working a strange magic over me.

Thorne's panicked and horrified face left my vision as I turned in slow motion,

Then I traveled. Without moving, I hurtled through time and space—four hundred and sixty years, to be exact.

Yet the sun was not shining. My heart was not beating in my chest and my ribs were not constricted with my corset pressing into me. I couldn't hear the laughter of children or mutterings of French or taste the champagne and strawberries in the crisp garden air.

Yet there he was, escaping the sunshine and the garden and the sweet smells of humanity to walk through the unfeeling stone, through the stench of death, carrying it with him in his ice-cold form.

In the unbeating heart in his chest.

In those crystal blue eyes that no longer held anything.

Yet they held everything.

They held the reminder of the girl who died that day.

Although they didn't *hold* her. They clutched her in a brutal grip, then squeezed until she shattered and broke viciously.

And then cold, immortal hands encircled my neck,

squeezing in a caress that cracked a small bone only just healed.

I searched his eyes, unable to look away from the man I thought I'd buried yet at the same time carried with me for going on half a millennium.

The human man I'd thought I'd loved.

Who I thought I'd killed.

"Surprised, wife?" he asked gently, thumb moving over the area of my neck where he'd snapped a small bone so hard it had popped from the skin.

He pushed it back in just as a rough growl, a bellow, sounded through the chamber.

I didn't glance that way because my molecules had seemed to still at the presentation of a living corpse. I was familiar with living corpses—I was one, after all—but I didn't expect that of my human husband, whom I'd witnessed my mother murder, to be presented to me with cruelty in his gaze and fangs in his gums.

"Yes, I expect you are surprised," he continued, his French accent still prevailing but dampened some by the years of speaking English. Of walking on this earth.

Undead.

While I'd carried his human ghost around in my mangled heart.

"You were a beautiful human, but you make a rather stunning immortal," he mused, eyes running over my face. As did his hand. The other stayed gripping my neck and keeping me in place with the firm promise of ripping it from my body should I move.

I couldn't move. Even without the hand.

The hand from my face trailed down the center of my chest, ripping the already torn blouse to expose my breasts to his hungry and cold eyes.

Another bellow, somewhere beyond this moment, that had to be a hallucination of some kind.

But the icy grip of reality taunted me that all of this was in fact happening.

His fingers traced over the ridges of the area where my heart had once beat for him.

Where it had broken for him.

"Yes, my wife is such a beautiful immortal. Much more than I'd imagined. And once we rectify the situation of your humanity and those attached to it, she will be utterly radiant." His eyes flickered to the side, where the thundering heartbeat and waves of fury and fear had been hurling from.

"But first, I'm sure you're wondering how I'm standing here in front of you, aren't you?" He gave me a conspiratorial smile. "Well, I wish I could apologize for the treachery, but the problem is, I'm just not sorry. Not at all. I got to spend the last days of my human life fucking my little wife into oblivion while knowing the promise of immortality awaited me. And such an immortal life that was beyond what my bloodline could offer me."

He paused, his fingers trailing between the ridges of my breasts. His eyes followed them for a moment before they met mine once more. "You see, I'm not born into a line that boasts a connection to the Ichor of the creator himself. No, I was much more of a 'street' vampire, as your mother would call it. That was until I was offered an opportunity to ascend the station my blood had given me, and all I had to do was play the part of a vulnerable human and make you fall in love with me. And I played my part very well. I even found myself growing quite fond of you. I have followed you with interest throughout the centuries. I would have come to claim what was rightly mine, but I was rather busy building a revolution. You see, I have the unique gift of being unremarkable. For it is the remarkable vampires who can't live in the shadows they were born to. I thrive in the shadows, alongside the many who weren't born remarkable and don't have blood to make those shadows into grandeur with false light."

His eyes flickered to the sparkling chandelier above us. "So I was recruiting the darkness dwellers within a race already banished to the darkness by humans and myths and the fear of being unmasked. And not just vampires. I'm charismatic, you see. It's only the elite vampires who consider themselves above mixing with different species. It's with me that the idea came to unite us all under a common purpose. To bring us all to the light, of course. Then watch the fucking world of humans burn."

His accent on the harsh words was like a blade to the soul I'd created around his death.

"So there you have it, Mon Ange. The knowledge that my human murder was merely an inhuman death and a birth into my immortality and position at the throne, which I consider mine not through blood or divine right but through the darkness. Navigating it, becoming the lord of it and those who reside in it." His eyes flickered to my mother.

"Not bad for a street vampire, if I do say so myself. Though I will need a queen. And I already have you. I do already *own* you," he mused. "Once I exterminate anything that tries to challenge that, of course. And who has sullied that which I own with its human paws."

The rage and violent promise of his words did something to the frozen molecules of my body, trapped somewhere between the past and the present.

Perhaps it was the words. Or the threat. Or sense

returning, however little I had, finally clutching me in its grasp, firmer than the cold hands at my neck.

Or it was the emotions of the one I'd loved, truly loved more than this creature in front of me. The ocean of feelings crashing against the harsh rocks of my psyche, breaking through suddenly and brutally.

I didn't move because, despite my rage combined with Thorne's, he did have me vulnerable. I knew a death grip when I felt one.

Jonathan had one on my neck.

But Thorne had one on my heart. And his death would crush it. I was going to crush Jonathan either way.

"I'm not yours," I hissed through his grip at my neck. "I never was. And the only thing I'll be to you is the vampire who kills you."

He regarded me and my words. "There's the bloodlust I need in a queen," he murmured. "Though unfortunately, you're wrong. I'll be the one to do the killing. I will admit you're good at it, but I'm better. And I'll make sure to be the vampire who kills everyone you care about and then kills whatever humanity lurks within that package I own before I claim it. For now, I'll have to be the vampire who kills *you*. Because I'll do you a mercy to make sure you don't have to witness the death of your love. It'd be just cruel to make you witness that twice in an eternity."

The truth and meaning to his words had me moving, despite the possibility of death if I did so. I was willing to brave that possibility instead of the certainty of it if he was able to carry out the threat I knew wasn't empty.

So I moved.

And the threat was carried out, the soundtrack a brutal ripping sound that combined with a sharp and intense lance of pain followed by nothing.

No, not nothing. A wave of sorrow so deep it rivaled any form of pain I'd ever experienced.

And then nothing.

The blessed and cursed nothing of the dead.

TWENTY-ONE

"**S**HE SHOULDN'T TAKE THAT LONG TO HEAL," A FRANTIC voice growled.

"Nay, she shouldn't," a thicker, less frantic voice agreed. "She needs blood."

The voices were far above me, like I was at the bottom of a well and two men were looking down at me discussing my fate.

"Well get out of the fucking way so I can give her more," the voice growled.

The familiar voice. The alive one.

Thorne.

His thundering heartbeat traveled the depth of whatever underground well I was trapped in, encircling me in the reality that came with it. That heart that was sending blood around his body.

It was then I noticed the burning at the back of my throat,

uncomfortable and growing in intensity with every beat of his heart. Thirst. My body craved blood to chase away the grave that still beckoned me. I could taste it, the bitter twang of death.

"You've given her enough. Much more and you'll be dead-er than she is without the *un*dead part of the equation. And then she'll wake up and kill me for letting her drain you."

"Get out of my way," the voice seethed. "I'll give her every fuckin' drop if need be."

"This would be a great time for the witch of the hour to work some fuckin' hocus pocus," Duncan muttered.

The air swirled with magic, even through the fog I was currently in. "Kind of busy trying to contain a witch queen and her powers so she doesn't kill us all," Sophie's voice gritted out painfully.

"I thought women were meant to be able to multitask," Duncan accused.

Not the smartest thing he could have said.

Liquid, warm and enticing, snaked between my lips.

"Isla." Thorne's voice was thick. "Drink. Come back to me. Now," he ordered.

At first I couldn't find enough strength to do more than let it trickle down my throat.

But it was blood. It was still life. So with great strength, I detached my hand from his and reached to cradle the head of the man whose neck was attached to my mouth.

Tasting him was where I realized I'd only been drinking with my fangs and filling on the surface. His blood showed me what drinking from the soul was like, the dark, twisted soul inside of me, and what it was to fill that creature up. It was the realization that those wretched human clichés about love were correct and he did complete me.

But not just to make the better me. He completed the

monster within me.

And that wasn't what I feared, the monster within me. No, I welcomed her, that beautiful, ugly thing that treated death as a tax write-off and torture as a way of life.

I feared that once I looked at it in the mirror, I'd realize I wasn't a monster after all. Merely a broken girl from centuries past with fangs, a new hairdo, and a murderous disposition.

A monster on the surface and yet a human to the core.

Thorne's blood revealing the lack of monstrosity within me might just be what killed me.

Because being a monster was easy. Fun even.

But being human? It wasn't that. It wasn't fun or easy. It was pain and suffering and death and destruction.

And love.

Which is just another word for destruction.

"There we go," Duncan murmured, relief apparent.

I managed to flutter my eyes open to see a blurry muscled figure standing in front of me with his arms crossed. He wasn't wearing a shirt, and blood mingled with the auburn hair on his chest, trailing down his muscled midsection.

My eyes yearned for someone else, though. Someone with inky black hair. It was mussed with dried blood, framing his bruised and battered face. His jacket was off, and from the scent of it, on me. The dirty fabric of his tee clung to the ridges of his muscles and he was coated with blood like Duncan. Unlike Duncan, he had wounds to match it. Mostly they seemed merely surface scratches Apart from the nasty gash at his neck, covered haphazardly with stained white gauze. Even with his blood in my mouth, I craved to taste the wound. It was only his eyes burning into me that stopped me, gave my animal inside the restraint it needed.

"What happened?" I asked, my voice thick and rough as I

used my newly healed vocal cords.

Thorne stood, seeming loath to do so, his hand on his neck, jaw twitching as if he urged to move. "Your *husband* broke your neck," he explained. "And you crumpled to the floor with a certainty of death. Stayed like that, even through the battle that had all of his soldiers eating grave dirt. While he and your mother ran like cowards." He paused, his eyes alight with the fury that was burning through me. "You stayed dead. Through that. And through us transporting you to the airstrip. And takeoff, not to mention two hours of flying."

One word cut through the rest with the utter betrayal wrapped up in it.

Husband.

"That was real?" I asked, my voice less than a whisper. "Jonathan was real?"

Thorne nodded once, stiffly. "Real enough to snap your neck," he clipped.

Duncan stepped forward, kicking the body of the copilot away distractedly, Duncan had obviously needed a pick-me-up too.

I noted the man's faint heartbeat with relief.

Duncan leaned forward, clutching my chin, his eyes softer than I'd ever seen them. "Wish I could kill your mammy for that one," he growled. "She scampered off in the chaos after the neck breaking." He paused, searching my face with something akin to sympathy. Which I loathed. "You never knew?"

I gave him a hard and chilled look, maybe trying to seep some of the ice out of my veins. "That my family hired a vampire to pose as a human and have me fall in love with him when I was a naïve child, only to kill him in front of me in order to turn me into the vampire they'd always tried to make me be?" I asked coldly. "No. No I didn't."

I didn't glance to Thorne, though I didn't miss the way he flinched at my words, or the bitter edge to his emotions. "They're dead, then, at least? My wretched family. Not including my mother."

Duncan shook his head once, face stormy. "We got the two brothers, at least. Not your father. He wasn't there."

I remembered my mother's words against my father. "I don't expect he was," I mused, them glanced to them. "I don't think he's involved. In fact, I think we might have an ally in him."

Duncan let out a disbelieving snort.

I leveled my gaze at him and recounted my mother's words.

"Just because he's not bothered to start a revolution doesn't mean he's anything to you," Duncan said, not unkindly.

"I know," I snapped, sitting up and rubbing my neck.

It didn't hurt, though I felt the icy handprint from Jonathan's touch still. I craved Thorne's fire to take it away, but he stayed away, his eyes glued to me.

I couldn't stand his gaze so I flickered my own to a tight-faced Sophie, who was staring at a woman being held by the wolf.

I screwed my nose up. "Oh, the wolf survived. Yay," I muttered.

Sophie glared at me. "Glad to see you're not dead, Isla," she hissed. Small beads of perspiration dotted her brow.

I focused on the reason for that, and the dank and stifling quality to the air that was polluted with dark ugliness.

She was beautiful, that one. Otherworldly so. Different than the others, whose ugliness flickered like a television screen on the fritz. Her picture was much clearer, the truth buried much deeper.

I'd expected her to have harsh black hair and darkly

beautiful features, but she was the opposite. Her hair was so golden it was almost white, tumbling down her back in shiny curls that looked well shampooed and cared for. Her face was pale and delicate with small features, apart from large brown eyes.

That's where it got me.

Never trust a blonde with brown eyes.

But the rest of her stayed with the sweet, innocent image, her small and petite body encased in a simple white dress with long sleeves

You couldn't hide it, though, the rotten magic seeping from her very soul, even more mangled than mine and Duncan's combined.

"So this is Malena," I mused. "All the trouble for her." I focused on her dark brown gaze. "I will say, I'm not your biggest fan. At all. Maybe in another life, where you didn't curse me and create gross and annoying abominations of my race, we could've been friends." I paused. "No, even then, I could forgive all that, but not that you were having sleepovers with my mother. We're just going to have to kill you," I said apologetically.

Her eyes narrowed slightly and the air in the cabin pulsed.

Sophie glared at me. "Try not to rile the witch with enough power to grind us all to dust," she gritted out.

I held up my hands. "Sorry, I was under the impression you had it handled."

"I do," she hissed.

I gave her a look. "If you had it handled, then you would have allowed for some gentle riling," I shot back.

A warning glare.

"Fine, I won't talk to her," I conceded.

So then I was faced with looking into the quicksilver eyes that had been on me since the moment my fangs had been in him. Since the last time I saw him before my husband broke my neck.

"So we got the witch, killed half of my family and hopefully put a dent in the war. Must mean we're done, right?"

His gaze didn't flicker. "No. It means we've only just started." He said the words with grim certainty.

I sighed. "Yeah, I was afraid of that.

The slam of my apartment door had an ominous echo to it.

I went straight for my bar, tired—no, exhausted—from the hours passed. They'd felt like years, like I'd lived the past five centuries of my existence crammed into thirty-six hours. Killing my family, facing the fact that the entire existence I'd created, the entire persona I'd created, was based on artifice. Did that make *me* artifice? I glanced down at my pale hand, half expecting it to flicker with transparency, signifying the end to this pretend undead life I'd created.

Thorne's fury crept up behind me, lurking, slithering like a snake, rearing to strike.

I turned, bracing myself for it. For the explosion of everything that had been simmering for the entire plane ride that he'd been mute, sitting beside me, stoic and letting me wade through the pit of snakes that had become my psyche.

I'd seen a lot to have an idea of how to predict what people would most likely do in most situations. What I didn't expect him to do was cross the yawning expanse of a couple of feet and clutch my face between his hands, capturing me in his gaze for a split second before his mouth plastered on mine, sending my whisky glass tumbling to the ground as it took everything I had just to hold on.

He didn't speak the entire time he explored, worshipped and equally punished every single inch of my body, loving me, hating me and saying everything that would need a century to be said.

We didn't need them, words. Actions spoke louder and all that.

But for two hours, I didn't feel incorporeal or unsure about who I was. It didn't matter who I was.

For I was Thorne's.

And I was alive.

"Why didn't you tell me?" His gruff voice cut through the silence of the loneliest hour. Or that's what 3 a.m. was meant to be. For someone who'd spent five lifetimes pretending she wasn't lonely, I'd never felt less alone than during the time when the city that never slept seemed to doze.

I glanced up at him from my perusal of his chest. Every inch of it was corded muscle, ripples and ridges I knew as well as my own body. I knew all of his scars, the ones that knotted his tanned flesh, marred it and became the part of him I loved. The warrior.

I stroked his face, which had been swollen and almost purple mere hours before.

I searched those eyes, feeling an overwhelming urge to escape the conversation, to escape my own head. Problem was, I could run from real life demons, but I couldn't outrun the ones residing in my soul, hiding in the shadows.

His eyes offered a promise that I wouldn't face them alone. And for once, I didn't want to.

He didn't say anything, just waited. Funny, I was the one

with eternity but he had more patience than me, acting as if every second wasn't sand in the hourglass of his death.

Maybe it was only me who noticed that.

"You've seen, met and battled to the death with my family. You know they're perhaps the reason *you* exist. Their vile existence the reason for history painting us as the villain." I paused. "And I, of course, am the reason pop culture adopted us as sex symbols, though they butchered most of the folklore. Not that it was accurate anyway."

My eyes left his. I wasn't ready to tell all of this with that connection. I already itched for distance while still craving the intimacy.

"Now it's all a fucking shambles since all of that was built on a lie. Jonathan was a lie. My existence, if that's what the past five hundred years was, was a lie."

Thorne clutched my chin, titanium fire in his eyes. "No, don't you let him take that," he growled. "He will die a thousand times over for what he's done. I'll make sure of that. But he will not take you with him. It was a lie, what he did to you, but you, this, what sits before me is the starkest truth I've experienced in my years on this earth. Complicated to say the least. Magnificent. Frustrating enough to make me want to claw my hair out, but not a lie," he said softly.

I blinked at him. "You say things like that with such conviction that I may just believe," I warned.

He pushed the hair from my face. "Good," he murmured.

I searched his face and felt the emotions in him that I was even struggling to contain.

"It is a terrible kind of beauty, what we have, the kind that hurts to look at and hurts even more to feel. Because I hate to quote Led Zeppelin, but I can't fucking quit you. I know they didn't add the 'fucking,' but it was needed for emphasis and I'm taking artistic liberties. It doesn't bode well for me or for eternity, the inability to let you go."

His arms tightened around. "It might not bode well for eternity, but it bodes well for me. Can't quit you any sooner than I'd quit my heart from beating," he rumbled.

"We've still got a lot to get through," I whispered. "A war to fight. An ex-husband to make sure is really, really dead, and a witch-werewolf romance to kill," I listed.

His mouth twitched. "Oh, and defeat the faction of evil creatures set to try and take over the world and enslave humankind?" he asked dryly.

His wording made me go up on my elbow to meet his eyes.

"You think this war is a battle against evil?" I asked. "I really hope not, because I fear that insanity is worse than mine. There's no such thing as a battle against evil. You should know this. Because evil lives forever, deathless, not in the souls of those people and creatures who are depraved and wicked to the core. No, the truest of evil exists in the hearts of people who try to convince the world and themselves that they're good. Inside the very humanity we're trying so fucking hard to save.

"So you're saying we shouldn't even try to save them?"

I glared at him. "No, Buffy, that's not what I'm saying. I'm just letting you know that we're not fighting for a cause. We're not fighting against evil—we're fighting *for* it. And the sooner you realize that, the easier we'll be rid of that self-righteousness that will be fatal to us all. And I'm rather attached to my existence, and my evil, wretched heart. It's dark and bitter, but at least it's pure. After all, what's purer than evil?"

He moved forward to clutch my face. "If evil is your heart, your soul, then I'm evil too, baby. And no fuckin' way is it wretched. Even if it is, your wretched heart is mine forever. And my wretched heart is yours."

At that very moment, as if his words had willed it so, the low thump of his heart somehow became a deafening roar in my ears, vibrating my entire body with its force.

I scowled at the interruption of the moment. Then again, it had been getting far too much like a Nicholas Sparks novel for my liking.

I may have been in love, but that didn't mean I had to hurl myself off the cliff and land in the soft clouds of hearts and rainbows. Give me storms and hurricanes any day.

Nonetheless, I was glad for the interruption, but not the nature of it. His heartbeat, which had always been so calming to me even in the midst of the hatred-filled fighting of the past few weeks, was now uncomfortable in its force, seeming like it was chattering my teeth.

"What could I have possibly done between the space of a few words to anger you again?" Thorne asked dryly, noting my scowl and irritation.

I glanced up at him. "Your heart. It's so fucking loud."

He laughed, the sound vibrating his throat. "Sorry, babe. I will try to rectify this in the future. We can't all have that stillness you boast."

As if to make his point, or maybe for some foreplay, he laid his callused palm on my chest.

The teasing look immediately left his face, and his emotions poured through me with panic and dread.

Because that resounding roar of a heartbeat was not coming from his chest.

It was coming from mine.

EPILOGUE

E NDINGS ALWAYS WRAP EVERYTHING UP SO NEATLY, DON'T they?

Except there's no such thing as ending when immortals are involved. It's at the end of the beginning, perhaps, that things are starting to make the most sense. Fall into place. For at the edge of the destruction of this world is where reason and peace lie. If reason or peace could reside anywhere, it would be there.

Eros watched the two of the fated from her perch in the space between mortals and humans, between dark and light and good and evil. She watched and was both saddened and gladdened by the fact that her prophecy was indeed coming to fruition. The first of the three would define the fate of the world and the fate of the three themselves.

Yet they were not finished with heartbreak, or blood, or despair.

This was an ending, after all.
It had only just started.
They had seen blood. But they had seen nothing yet.
"For the blood will run," she whispered against the wind.
And then, like the wind, she was gone.

"And Eros, the fairest of all immortals, arose,
who frees us all from our sorrows but ruins our hearts' good
sense,
breaking the wisest intention of gods and mortals alike."

THE END...
OR
THE BEGINNING

ACKNOWLEDGEMENTS

Once again, the special people in my life had to brave the crazy that descended when I lost myself in this book. I became somewhat of a vampire myself, sleep a long forgotten friend with Isla in my head. I would never have been able to come out somewhat human or sane, for that matter, if it wasn't for these people.

Mum. You've always been my biggest cheerleader, my best friend and my sometimes therapist. If it wasn't for you, I wouldn't know the magic of reading and I wouldn't be able to write a word. Thank you for telling me I could be anything I wanted to be. I'd never be who I am today if it wasn't for you.

My **Dad.** You're not here with us but you're the reason why I can shoot a gun, ride a motorbike, shop like a champ, and believe in myself. I miss you every day.

Amo Jones. You continue to show me how lucky I am to have found someone who my crazy can play with. I know I would have gone off the deep end already if it wasn't for you. Harley and Ivy forever.

Andrea and **Caro**. You two ladies are so very special and your generosity and support is amazing. I'm so lucky I have you.

This book wouldn't be what it is without my wonderful team of betas. These special ladies helped to make this book what it is. **Ginny, Amy, Sarah**, and… you are wonderful.

Carl (with a silent L). I can conjure up vampires easily enough but I couldn't have ever dreamed of having someone like you in my life. Real life with you is so much better than dreams. I'll go on any adventure with you.

Harriet, Polly and Emma. My girls. The ones who talk me down when I'm getting crazy, or bring a bottle of wine and get crazy with me. True friendships are rare in this world, but I've got it with you ladies.

And to **you, the reader**. Thank you. Thank you for reading my books. Thank you for taking a chance on something different from me. Thanks for every e-mail, comment, and review you give me. I treasure each and every one.

ABOUT THE AUTHOR

ANNE MALCOM has been an avid reader since before she can remember, her mother responsible for her love of reading. It started with magical journeys into the world of Hogwarts and Middle Earth, then as she grew up her reading tastes grew with her. Her love of reading doesn't discriminate, she reads across many genres, although classics like Little Women and Gone with the Wind will hold special places in her heart. She also can't get enough romance, especially when some possessive alpha males throw their weight around.

One day, in a reading slump, Cade and Gwen's story came to her and started taking up space in her head until she put their story into words. Now that she has started, it doesn't look like she's going to stop anytime soon, with many more characters demanding their story be told as well.

Raised in small town New Zealand, Anne had a truly special childhood, growing up in one of the most beautiful countries in the world. She has backpacked across Europe, ridden camels in the Sahara and eaten her way through Italy, loving every moment. For now, she's back at home in New Zealand and quite happy. But who knows when the travel bug will bite her again.

OTHER BOOKS

The Vein Chronicles
Fatal Harmony, Book One

The Sons of Templar
Making the Cut
Firestorm
Outside the Lines
Out of the Ashes
Beyond the Horizon
Dauntless

Unquiet Mind
Echoes of Silence
Skeletons of Us

Greenstone Security
Still Waters

Made in the USA
Middletown, DE
02 November 2017